THE **FORTUNES** OF **TEXAS**

SHIPMENT 1

Healing Dr. Fortune by Judy Duarte
Mendoza's Return by Susan Crosby
Fortune's Just Desserts by Marie Ferrarella
Fortune's Secret Baby by Christyne Butler
Fortune Found by Victoria Pade
Fortune's Cinderella by Karen Templeton

SHIPMENT 2

Fortune's Valentine Bride by Marie Ferrarella
Mendoza's Miracle by Judy Duarte
Fortune's Hero by Susan Crosby
Fortune's Unexpected Groom by Nancy Robards Thompson
Fortune's Perfect Match by Allison Leigh
Her New Year's Fortune by Allison Leigh

SHIPMENT 3

A Date with Fortune by Susan Crosby
A Small Fortune by Marie Ferrarella
Marry Me, Mendoza! by Judy Duarte
Expecting Fortune's Heir by Cindy Kirk
A Change of Fortune by Crystal Green
Happy New Year, Baby Fortune! by Leanne Banks
A Sweetheart for Jude Fortune by Cindy Kirk

SHIPMENT 4

Lassoed by Fortune by Marie Ferrarella
A House Full of Fortunes! by Judy Duarte
Falling for Fortune by Nancy Robards Thompson
Fortune's Prince by Allison Leigh
A Royal Fortune by Judy Duarte
Fortune's Little Heartbreaker by Cindy Kirk

THE **FORTUNES** OF **TEXAS**

MENDOZA'S RETURN

———— ⚒ ————

USA TODAY BESTSELLING AUTHOR

Susan Crosby

⟨H⟩ **HARLEQUIN**® THE FORTUNES OF TEXAS
™

Special thanks and acknowledgment to
Susan Crosby for her contribution to the
Fortunes of Texas: Lost...and Found continuity.

Recycling programs
for this product may
not exist in your area.

ISBN-13: 978-1-335-68035-8

Mendoza's Return

Copyright © 2011 by Harlequin Books S.A.

This edition published by arrangement with Harlequin Books S.A.

For questions and comments about the quality of this book, please contact us at CustomerService@Harlequin.com.

® and TM are trademarks of Harlequin Enterprises Limited or its corporate affiliates. Trademarks indicated with ® are registered in the United States Patent and Trademark Office, the Canadian Intellectual Property Office and in other countries.

Printed in U.S.A.

www.Harlequin.com

USA TODAY bestselling author **Susan Crosby** believes in the value of setting goals, but also in the magic of making wishes, which often do come true—as long as she works hard enough. Along life's journey she's done a lot of the usual things—married, had children, attended college a little later than the average coed and earned a BA in English. Then she dived off the deep end into a full-time writing career, a wish come true.

Susan enjoys writing about people who take a chance on love, sometimes against all odds. She loves warm, strong heroes and good-hearted, self-reliant heroines, and she will always believe in happily-ever-after.

For the Broderick family—Sean, Kelly, Chase, Cameron and Jorie—everyday heroes. You're an inspiration.

Chapter 1

Melina Lawrence looked over her shoulder and winked at her sister Angie, the most effervescent bride Melina had ever seen.

"Don't trip!" Angie mouthed just as the wedding planner signaled to maid of honor Melina to begin her walk down the aisle.

Melina smiled, both at her sister's teasing caution and the beauty of the moment. The church was full. Happy faces greeted her with each step. Then about halfway down the aisle she spotted someone who didn't belong in the crowd—Raphael Mendoza. Rafe Mendoza. Rafe, the love of her life—in high school, anyway, and a little beyond. Homecoming king to her homecoming queen. They were voted most likely to wed....

But they hadn't.

He came sharply into focus, the guests around him blurring into a muted montage of color. Why was he here? He lived in Michigan, fifteen hundred miles from Red Rock, Texas, where he was born and raised. Where they'd gone to high school together.

Don't trip. The muscles of Melina's cheeks ached as she tried to maintain her smile. All of her senses overloaded so fast it was dizzying. He gave her the slightest of nods as she moved past him, her pulse pounding in her ears so loudly she couldn't hear the music.

Don't trip. Her legs kept moving but felt numb.

When she could see clearly again, she noticed the expressions on the faces of old friends—sympathy, but also people's blatant curiosity of a gossip-worthy event.

Angie must have invited him to the wedding but hadn't bothered to tell Melina he was coming. Then again, her sister still believed in fairy tales and happy endings. She'd never given up on Rafe and Melina finding their way back to each other. Angie had adored Rafe as the big brother she'd never had. Adored him so much, she'd gone into an extended and dramatic period of mourning for him ten years ago, after Melina and Rafe broke up when Angie was only twelve....

It was the look on her mother's face—full of understanding and maybe even a little annoyance—that drew Melina back into the moment. She managed genuine smiles for her mother and Gramps, seated next to her, then noted the panic in her about-to-be brother-in-law's eyes. She smiled consolingly at the very sweet Tommy Buchanan, then took her position alongside seven bridesmaids. The guests rose for the bride's shining moment, Angie's gaze locked with Tommy's all the way down the aisle.

The music faded out, then the family's longtime minister asked, "Who gives this woman to be married to this man?"

Jefferson Lawrence eyed his daughter, seeming to ponder the question, until she whispered loudly, "Daddy!"

He chuckled but dutifully said, "Her mother and I." He lifted Angie's veil a bit, kissed her, then presented her to Tommy and took a seat next to his teary-eyed wife of thirty-two years.

Melina went through the motions. She passed the groom's ring to the minister without fumbling, then handed back Angie's white-tulip bouquet after the celebratory kiss, during which Tommy bent her over to much laughter and applause. Then Melina slipped her hand into the crook of the best man's arm and followed the newlyweds up the aisle, leading a parade of bridesmaids decked out in lemon-colored chiffon gowns escorted by ushers trying not to trip over the voluminous dresses.

Because everyone was standing, Rafe was blocked from Melina's view until she was a few feet away. For years, she'd anticipated running into him again. He wasn't supposed to look this good, this sexy. This tempting.

And he'd come alone.

And everyone there knew their history, used to have bets on how it would turn out. *Now* what would happen? Melina feared she'd be back in the spotlight again, with Rafe an unwilling focus as well.

The guests departed for the reception at the nearby Blue Sage Inn, then a lot of picture-taking ensued before white limos carried the bridal party to the reception. The festivities were well under way with music, appetizers and an open bar.

Because the early March day had crept into the low eighties, many guests had wandered into the courtyard from the main room, but Melina spotted Rafe instantly. He was crouched down, talking to Gramps, who looked so different without his usual Stetson and Wranglers, wearing a tux instead, his horse long ago replaced by a cane, and for today, a motorized wheelchair.

"You're awfully jumpy," Angie said to Melina as the wedding party sat down at the head table. "Aren't you having a good time?"

Melina kept her tone neutral, not an easy task when all around her people were looking from Melina to Rafe and back again. "You invited Rafe."

Her sister's lips compressed. "It's my wedding. I get to invite who I want."

"I hadn't realized you were still friends."

"We've stayed in touch." She clinked her water glass to Tommy's, kissed him then looked at Melina again. "Now that he's moved home, I thought he'd like a chance to reconnect with old friends."

Shock jolted Melina. "Moved home? To Red Rock?" Her breath felt trapped in her throat.

"A few weeks ago. He bought the old Dillon house, but his office is in San Antonio." She smiled. "He looks good, doesn't he?"

Yes, he looks good. He was a man now, not a boy, and it showed in every inch of him, from his stylish hair to his sharper facial features to his powerful body, fitted into a perfectly tailored dark gray suit.

"He's aged really well, don't you think?" Angie asked.

"Aged?" Melina replied, stunned. "We were born the same year, you know. Twenty-nine isn't exactly over the hill."

Their younger sister, Stephanie, leaned past Melina and said, "It is when you're a single woman." She elbowed Melina. "I know you're famous for your patience, Mellie, but sometimes it's better just to grab hold, you know, not keep waiting for the perfect man. And I do have to agree with Ang. I mean, just look at Rafe. He's like a dark prince stepped out of a grown-up fairy tale."

"That's quite a label, Steph," Melina said, although agreeing about his physical perfection. His perfect height. His thick, black hair, those deep, brown, smoldering eyes that could coax out all her secrets…

"But he's a lawyer, not a prince, and life isn't a fairy tale. Except for Angie's," she added, lifting her glass, putting on a smile, not wanting to take away even the tiniest bit of her pleasure. "To your happily-ever-after beginning."

After dinner, the official toasts were made and the cake cut, then the dancing began.

Rafe still hadn't left. He danced several times, but never twice with the same woman, and he never approached Melina. She partnered with the best man, Tommy's twin brother, Jay, then with several ushers, and eventually her father, who was having a great time in the role of father of the bride. It was the kind of arena in which the boisterous cattle broker shined.

"You fixin' to say hello to your former fiancé?" her father asked as they danced, his disapproving tone apparent.

Melina stopped short of rolling her eyes. He never pulled punches. "I wasn't planning on it, but I won't be rude, either."

"Best you don't go opening up those wounds, girl."

"I don't intend to."

"Then maybe you should stop giving him the eye, so he doesn't think otherwise."

She wasn't aware she'd been giving him the eye. In fact, she'd been trying not to, since everyone in the room seemed to be holding their breath for something to happen between them, some kind of contact. Any kind of contact. Almost everyone knew what their plans had been. They'd wanted to buy the old Crockett building on south Main, open their law practice downstairs and create an apartment upstairs, at least until the second baby came—with two more to follow. The building was still there, but the plans had gone up in smoke years ago. It had finally stopped hurting to drive past it.

"A lot of water has flowed under the bridge since we broke up, Dad," she said, putting the past in its place.

"Since *he* broke up. I remember how long the tears lasted."

She remembered, too, almost as if it were yesterday. Total heartbreak was hard to forget. "I was nineteen. I can handle things better now." Or could she? She'd only imagined coming face-to-face with him before. The truth was entirely different. He still made her heart pound—which could also be all the pent-up anger she'd held for years.

"You haven't been serious about a boy since Rafe."

"I've had my share of fun, Dad, believe me." She had, too, but she'd kept her relationships light and short-term on purpose. She didn't ever want to grieve over a man like that again. Her pride had taken an enormous beating. Once was enough. People should learn from their mistakes. And she'd definitely learned. "Who needs serious, anyway, Dad?"

"That's my girl. The only thing I take seriously is your mother, and that's worked just fine for me." He whirled her around. Always the best dancer on the floor, he guided her through a series of steps practiced and memorized through the years. Her mood lightened. She stopped wondering what Rafe was thinking and why he was hanging around at a wedding reception, which didn't seem like something he would do, given a choice.

Then suddenly he was gone, having disappeared during The Chicken Dance. Smart man, she thought. If she could've slipped out, she would have, too, especially since she wore a dress that required holding it off the floor so that she wouldn't trip and yet still somehow flap her arms. She was pleased and relieved that Rafe wasn't watching. Knowing he'd gone left her free to be silly instead of sophisticated like him, big-time attorney that he was.

She tried to picture him acting like a chicken in his power suit and tie and his pristine white shirt, an image she couldn't conjure up. She wondered if his hair ever looked less than perfect.

A long, long time ago, things like that had mattered little to him.

And a long, long time ago, *she* had mattered a lot.

* * *

Rafe leaned against a tree, hiding out with a few other guests who'd made a quick exodus upon realizing what song was starting up. He and the others grinned conspiratorially at their narrow escape but otherwise waited in silence, not wanting to call attention to themselves and be dragged back in.

From where he stood, Rafe could see the entire room in all its festive glory. The bridesmaids were especially easy to spot. If their gowns had been white, they would've resembled melting marshmallows, like Angie.

She seemed so young. Last year at his mother's funeral she'd looked somber, her clothes dark and sedate, as expected for the occasion. Now she looked like a starlet at a Hollywood premiere, all bright and sparkly. She was twenty-two years old and married.

Rafe's glance slid to Melina as she danced, stumbling a little, the best man catching her before she fell. If all had gone according to Rafe and Melina's plan, they also would've been married right after college graduation. They would have traveled a little before starting law school. Down the road they'd planned to open their own practice—together. Later, when the time was right, they would've started a family. It was all mapped out.

Their plan had been set into motion when they were fourteen. He had lived in Red Rock all his life, but the Lawrence family had come to town when Melina was a freshman. Rafe fell in love with her the first time he'd laid eyes on her. For him, that was it. He'd never strayed. The Mendoza men were known for their passion—about life, work and their women—and Melina had loved him hard and completely in return.

Rafe had never doubted that love. At least not until she'd made choices without talking to him. His passion hadn't died, it had shifted—away from her, from them, and into his career instead.

It seemed like a lifetime ago. *Was* a lifetime ago. He'd followed the plan, finding more success than he'd dreamed possible, thanks to some lucky breaks, good timing and a few smart, risky choices. Melina had made a one-eighty turn in another career direction. He wondered if she had regrets about that, if she'd reacted emotionally instead of logically then couldn't—or stubbornly, wouldn't—go back.

The gimmicky dance ended. Rafe watched Melina fan herself, her cheeks flushed, her blond hair tumbling free around her shoulders, the swell of her breasts glistening. She was even more beautiful now as a woman than—

She headed straight toward him, across

the room, then through the exit to the court-yard. The air had cooled, night settling in. She stopped, closed her eyes, breathed deeply. Rafe inched farther into the shadows, away from the soft glow of thousands of tiny decorative lights that turned the space into a kind of fairyland.

He didn't know what to say to her. Words usually came easily to him, but he had no idea how to start a conversation with the woman he'd once loved, the one who'd hurt him more than he'd ever thought anyone could.

He'd intended to leave the reception before now, to get away from the possibility of making small talk with her. He didn't know why he hadn't taken off, especially since he knew only a handful of people beyond the Lawrence family, who didn't seem to care much about talking to him, anyway.

He'd been debating going to see Melina ever since he moved back, had even checked out her Facebook page, knowing he needed answers after all these years so that he could find that "closure" that people talked about, needing it in order to move on with his life. Especially now that he intended to make Red Rock his home again.

Melina opened her eyes then, keying in on

him as if she'd known all along he'd been watching her.

"I thought you'd left," she said, hesitance in her voice and body language.

Was this it? His opportunity to get answers? "I wasn't interested in flapping my wings," he said, keeping the conversation going.

She half smiled. "I wasn't so lucky."

They stood about ten feet apart. "How are you, Melina?"

"I'm doing very well, thanks. And you?" Polite, cool words.

"No complaints." He took a few steps toward her. "Thanks for the card you sent after my mom died. It meant a lot."

Her expression changed in an instant to one of sympathy. "I'm sorry I couldn't be at her funeral. I was on a cruise, my first vacation in years, and I didn't hear about her passing until I got home and the funeral was over."

"I know. I understood."

"I admired her so much." She reached out as if to touch him, then let her hand drop. "I felt so bad that I hadn't stayed in touch. But I couldn't, you know? I just couldn't."

He understood that, too. He wouldn't have stayed in touch with Angie except that she hadn't let him go. She'd written and called now and then, always hopeful there would be a reconciliation, but Rafe had cut off all other communication with the Lawrence family.

"Tommy seems like a good match for Angie," he said, changing the subject, but also leading up to the issue—that he and Melina had been a good match once, too.

"I agree. She needs a Prince Charming like him. He's big on romantic gestures. It was his choice to have the reception here instead of at the church. He wanted her to feel like a princess."

"I was surprised to see how much this part of town has improved," he said. "The only eyesore left is the old Crockett building. I'm surprised it hasn't been razed by now."

Melina went silent for a few seconds then eyed the reception hall. "I should get back." Her entire mood changed, her expression, her posture, everything.

"You might want to wait a few more minutes," he said, spotting a conga line forming.

She looked tempted but said, "I have responsibilities as maid of honor."

Her comment took Rafe back in time—not in a good way. "And we all know how seriously you take your responsibilities."

Her blue eyes turned icy. "And my commitments. I suffer no guilt from what I did, from the choice I made. My grandparents needed me. I acted honorably. Can you say the same?" She gathered her skirt with both hands and swept past him, leaving a trail of unfamiliar perfume and righteous indignation in her wake.

What the hell did that mean? How had he acted dishonorably? *She'd* dropped the ball, not him.

Rafe swiped a hand down his face. He should've trusted his instincts and stayed away. Or at the least left after congratulating the happy couple. This wasn't the time or place for a serious dissection of a painful time in his and Melina's past.

The desire to satisfy his curiosity about her had overruled his usual caution and common sense, dredging up memories that should've been buried long ago—for both of them. He'd thought his were expunged. He'd assumed hers were.

As a lawyer he should've known better than to assume anything. Ever.

Chapter 2

Sunday passed in a blur for Melina. First came a wedding breakfast with just the Lawrence and Buchanan families, then Melina and Jay, Tommy's brother and the best man, drove the newlyweds to the San Antonio airport for their flight to Hawaii.

They all stood at the curb of the departure area, unloading luggage and saying goodbye.

"I saw you and Rafe talking," Angie said into Melina's ear as they hugged. "Are you going to see him again?"

"Red Rock is a small town."

"That's not what I meant."

Melina smiled, not giving her sister an answer—maybe because Melina didn't know the answer herself.

"I told him about Elliot," Angie said, her voice overly casual.

"Angie! Why would you do that? He's our patient. You can't—"

"I didn't give Rafe specifics. He knows you're an occupational therapist, and he gets the whole privacy thing. I didn't tell him Elliot's name or the names of any other pertinent people involved. I asked hypothetical questions because he's a lawyer, and I thought he could help."

Hope battled irritation at her sister for overstepping her position as Melina's administrative assistant. "What did he say?"

"That it's not his field of expertise."

Melina felt her jaw drop. "That's it? He had no opinion as a human being? As a former ballplayer? As a former little boy with big dreams?" Her voice rose with each question so that Tommy and his brother Jay turned and stared.

"I'm only telling you what happened, Melina. Geez, calm down. I didn't ask him for his opinion or advice *except* as a lawyer. Don't get mad at him. Again."

She'd been over being mad at him—or so she thought until she'd seen him yesterday.

Then a tidal wave of emotion had swamped her. She wasn't drowning now, but she sure was being beaten up by the waves.

"Anyway, you didn't let me finish. He said if you want to talk to him about it, you should call him."

"When did this happen?"

"As he was telling me goodbye at the wedding. He said he'd been thinking about it."

Could she get him involved? Melina wondered. Given their history, could she ask it of him?

"And don't be mad at me, either, okay?" Angie said, grabbing Melina's hands. "I wouldn't be able to enjoy my honeymoon if I knew you were upset with me." She batted her eyes playfully.

Melina laughed. "Right. Like that's going to happen."

She grinned. "I told Steph not to change one thing in the office while I'm gone. I'm the one who's been working for you for four years, but I know our little sister. She'll think she has a better way to organize things."

"I won't let her. I promise."

"The plane will leave without us, Mrs. Buchanan," Tommy said. "And I'm anxious to get lei'd, you know." He winked and pretended to drop a lei around her neck, Angie's laughter joining his to make music together. With a last hug goodbye for everyone, they ran into the terminal without a look back.

Tears stung Melina's eyes as she watched them, madly in love and happy to show the world.

"How about we go somewhere for lunch?" Jay asked as they headed out the airport.

"No, thanks. I'm still full from breakfast."

"How 'bout we go to your place and have ourselves a little fun?"

Tommy's twin was twenty-two years old. He'd been coming on to Melina since they'd first been paired up for wedding events. "No, thanks."

He eyed her. "You know, I've been hearing for a long time how the best man hooks up with the maid of honor at these things. You're real pretty, Melina. I think I'm okay looking myself. So, why not go for it? Your age doesn't matter to me, if that's what you're worrying about."

She couldn't help but laugh. "Well, I'm honored, Jay, truly I am. But the answer's the same." Between his comments and Stephanie's at the wedding, Melina felt ancient. "It's sweet of you to ask, though."

"No harm in it," he said, appeased.

They didn't have much to say after that. He

dropped her off at her townhouse, and she was grateful to plop onto her sofa and close her eyes, relishing the peace and quiet now that her duties were over. But soon the pull began—the memories of days gone by, the should'ves and could'ves.

She dragged out two cartons from the back of her storage closet, untouched for years. She had thrown away a lot of the things Rafe had given her—a stuffed armadillo, dried corsages and a half-used bottle of perfume she couldn't bear to wear again—but she hadn't been able to part with the yearbooks and scrapbooks.

Or the gold locket he'd given her after they'd made love for the first time.

Melina ignored the tiny jewel box lodged in the corner of the carton until after she'd skimmed through the books, afraid to take a deeper look. Almost every personal note in her yearbooks was a comment on her and Rafe as a couple and their future together. She'd almost forgotten how much like *one* they'd been. Their mutual plan to become lawyers working for the greater good had been shattered before the end of their freshman year at the University of Michigan in Ann Arbor.

Michigan had been a long way from home

for a couple of born-and-raised Texans, but they'd had each other—until her Grandma Rose had a stroke and Melina's world had spun on its axis....

All her life Melina had adored her grandma. Being clear up in Michigan while Rose had been hospitalized had been hard, but when Rose had been sent home barely able to walk or talk, it had been excruciating for Melina. She couldn't focus on college when her beloved Rose was struggling, so when the Christmas break came, Melina used the weeks to help her grandparents, then made the decision not to return to Ann Arbor for the time being.

Rafe hadn't understood. Melina stood her ground. And their relationship began to unravel slowly, steadily. While Melina was immersed in caring for her grandmother and comforting her suddenly vulnerable grandfather, Rafe was experiencing the new freedom of college. She'd gone the opposite direction, locking herself into the role of caregiver, giving up her freedom, not regretting it at all.

Except that she'd resented Rafe's freedom, even though it had been her choice to help her grandparents.

And then came the letter from him, ending the relationship, securing her new role in life. She hadn't known how to fix it, so she hadn't tried....

She blinked away the memory. Finally she pushed up the lid of the small gray velvet box. The locket inside didn't contain photographs but was inscribed with the words, "We've only just begun."

He'd given it to her in such a tender way, made her close her eyes and lift up her hair. She'd felt the brush of his fingertips against her neck, then his lips. Finally a kiss on her mouth, so soft, so loving, she'd cried. She'd buried the indelible moment deep, had built an impenetrable wall around it—until she'd seen him, looking handsome and successful and so very sexy.

Melina snapped the lid shut, and with it, the memories. She tossed the box into the carton and stacked the rest of the items inside. Then right before she shoved the cartons into the closet, she pulled out their senior yearbook and tucked it under her arm.

The only way she could move forward was to look back first.

The next morning Melina looked up Rafe's business address on the internet, mapped directions, then made the drive to downtown San Antonio. His office was on the fifth floor of a building overlooking the River Walk. She had to identify herself to the lobby security personnel and get permission from Rafe's office before she was allowed up the elevator, so the element of surprise was gone by the time she reached his office, a richly appointed, incredibly quiet space of dark woods and leather.

One of the things they'd promised each other all those years ago when they'd made the mutual decision to become lawyers was that their office wouldn't be luxurious, that they wouldn't have more than they needed to do the job. The building they'd picked out changed hands frequently, with long periods of vacancy between. As Rafe had noted at the reception, these days it looked ready for demolition.

It had hurt when he'd said that so easily about their one-time dream house.

Rafe's attractive and curious assistant escorted Melina into Rafe's office as soon as she arrived. He got up from his desk and came around it.

"Thank you, Vonda," he said as she closed the door on her way out. "This is a surprise."

Melina rarely got flustered, but being alone with him in his office, this tangible symbol of his success, stabbed at her. The last thing she needed was to be defensive or cool—or let her ego or pride get in the way. A little boy depended on her doing the right thing, saying the right thing.

And yet frustration built inside her, a growing need to yell at him, to say what she hadn't been allowed to all those years ago when he'd broken up with her—by letter. She'd made so many speeches to him in her head through the years.

"Very nice," she said, tamping down her emotions, moving around him to look out his window. She loved the River Walk, always had, no matter how many tourists roamed the area. His view was pretty but obstructed slightly by hotels and other tourist attractions.

"What can I do for you, Melina?" he asked, having come up behind her.

She moved away, not turning around to look at him until she could no longer feel the heat from his body, imagined or otherwise, radiating into her space. "Angie said you were willing to talk to me about a new patient my partner and I just took on."

Rafe indicated a leather sofa. "I don't know that my answer will be any different," he said as they sat at opposite ends. "But I thought I should know more."

"He's a ten-year-old boy named Elliot Anderson, and he has Asperger's syndrome."

"You'll need to educate me about Asperger's."

"It's a form of autism spectrum disorder. They're smart kids, and they can totally focus on something they have an interest in, but they have difficulties socially. They don't tend to make eye contact and don't know how to interpret expressions to understand how someone feels. It makes it hard for them to be part of a team, any kind of team, especially because they can be very direct."

"Okay."

The intensity of his unswerving eye contact made her stomach flutter. She wished he'd sat at his desk instead. "Elliot wants to play baseball," she said. "His father has worked with him on hitting for several years. Apparently he's exceptional."

"And he's come up against resistance from the coaches, Angie said."

"One coach, not all of them. And 'resistance' is putting it mildly in this case. The Andersons moved to town after registration was closed for this season, but the league could make an exception if they wanted to, given that the family hadn't moved in yet. Elliot and his parents showed up at a practice, hoping to talk one of the coaches into taking him on, but it didn't go well."

"In what way?"

"The coach was pushing the players hard, berating them, even ridiculing them. Elliot, who only knows how to comment honestly on what he observes, told the coach he was mean."

"Kids—and parents—often think a coach is mean," Rafe said. "Did he know about Elliot's condition?"

"Not at that point, and if Elliot had left it at that, maybe it wouldn't have mattered, but he added that the coach was fat. Elliot doesn't distinguish between a compliment and an insult. He was stating what he saw was a fact."

"What happened?"

"His father intervened. He explained privately about Elliot's condition, and then told the coach how the only way Elliot can learn about team play is by being on a team. There aren't any special-needs teams in town, only in San Antonio, and Elliot probably doesn't belong on that kind of team, anyway." She paused. "I'm gathering that Angie didn't tell you who the coach is."

"No, but I'm going to guess it's Beau Bandero."

"Yes."

Rafe got off the couch and moved to the window, looking out as she had earlier. "He built that sports complex with his own money. He owns it."

"He's the king, all right."

"Which means he sets his own rules. And he's a bitter man. Always has been, even in the days we played together. But after his injury knocked him out of the majors, he probably got worse." Rafe faced her. "So, what did Beau do next?"

Melina clenched her fists in her lap. "He let Elliot get up to bat, then he hit him with the first pitch."

"Intentionally?" He looked at her in shock.

"Who knows? Another coach happened to catch it on video, but it's impossible to know the truth. People with Asperger's often don't feel pain to the same degree that others do. Elliot just stood there waiting for another pitch, like he does when his dad pitches to him. Beau chewed him out for not running to first, called him too stupid to play. Elliot told him he didn't know that rule because no one had hit him before."

"And that wasn't good enough for Beau, I guess."

"He told Elliot it was too late to join the team this year. He'd missed four practices already, and he needed more practice than the average kid."

"The schoolyard bully grown older but unchanged."

"Elliot's probably been called stupid before, and weird, and all sorts of other names," Melina said. "He's probably been bullied by kids his own age who don't understand why he's different. But for an adult to do it? Consciously? That's criminal."

Rafe leaned against the window jamb, his arms folded. He couldn't remember being angrier at Beau—and there'd been plenty of anger in high school, even fistfights. The competition between them had been fierce, producing a natural enmity. "What's your job in all this, Melina? How did you get involved?"

"Occupational therapists are experts in the social, emotional and physiological effects of illness and disease. We plot a different course of treatment for each patient, depending on their needs." She crossed her legs and relaxed against the sofa. "I help stroke victims so that they can get back to living their lives. Children with autism need self-help skills. In Elliot's case, my partner and I hit a dead end with attorneys being able to help, especially given the narrow time frame." Her voice grew stronger, more insistent. "Elliot can't afford to miss the practices, Rafe, and the season starts in a few weeks. He may be a great batter, but he needs to learn about teamwork."

Silence deadened the air for a few long seconds as he weighed her words. He'd hoped she'd come to him to open up a discussion between *them,* to settle things, that maybe she was feeling the same as he was—still trapped in the past and all that never got said between them. But obviously she'd come to see Rafe the lawyer, not Rafe the man.

"You want to pursue legal action against Beau?" he asked.

"We don't see an alternative."

"And you want me to handle it." Not a question but a statement of fact. She wouldn't have come to see him except that she was fighting for this little boy and didn't have anyone else to turn to. It was the second time since he'd moved back to Texas that he'd been sought for skills outside his specialty.

"Please," she said.

"Mel, I haven't done anything but corporate work since I finished law school. The Americans with Disabilities Act is way outside my expertise. I'm not even sure this is an ADA case."

"You always were a quick study."

He almost laughed. The idea was ludicrous. And yet here she sat all calm and business-like, except for the fire in her eyes, as if daring him. Like in the old days...

She stood, her eyes gone dull. "Never mind. Apparently you prefer making more money for already rich tycoons than helping one little boy with an almost impossible dream." She glanced pointedly at a glass case on the wall filled with baseball trophies from his days as a player, T-ball through college. Nothing she said could speak more loudly to him than that one look.

She walked to the door, grabbed the handle.

"I'll do it," he said. "Or at least, I'll see if I can do anything. I need to research a few things first. But maybe even more important, Melina? You need to consider that my getting involved could work against what you're looking for. You know my history with Beau."

"If I had other options, I would use them."

He reached behind her and opened the door to the waiting room. "Vonda, how does my schedule look for tomorrow?"

"You're free after two o'clock."

Rafe looked at Melina. "I'd like to meet the Andersons. Do you think they could come in tomorrow at two?"

"I'm sure they'll move heaven and earth to

be here. I'll call you if they can't, but I don't think that's likely. Should Elliot come, too?"

"Yes. I need to see him for myself."

"They don't have much money," she said quietly.

"Okay."

"Thank you. Listen, I've got a ton of material on Asperger's. I could drop off a couple of books at your house. Leave them on your porch sometime today, if you want," she said as they headed to the entry door.

"That'd be good."

"Angie said you bought the old Dillon house."

"It needs work, but my dad and brothers are helping when they can." They stepped into an empty, quiet hallway, the door shutting behind them.

"I didn't think you'd ever move back," she said.

"Me, either." He didn't elaborate on his reasons. "So, Beau's gotten fat, huh?" he asked.

Her brows went up at the change of subject, then she nodded. "Beer belly."

"Drowning his sorrows."

"You're probably right. I'll see you tomorrow, Rafe," she said, then left, the unfamiliar perfume he'd smelled on her at the wedding trailing enticingly in her wake.

Rafe returned to his office and closed the door. He couldn't read her. If she hadn't needed someone to plead Elliot's case, would she have contacted him?

Probably not.

He opened his desk drawer and pulled out a small box. He'd always kept it in a place where he could look at it frequently, reminding him how tenuous love could be, but he hadn't looked inside for a while. He did so now, revealing a small, pretty promise ring he'd given Melina their first Christmas at college, only to have it mailed back to him some months later, a one-word note included. The tangible, devastating memory of a promise broken.

He didn't owe her anything, even if she was still the one he'd never gotten out of his system, and still the sexiest woman he'd ever met. But he could do this. He would try to help young Elliot but also wipe the slate clean with Melina.

He would be able to get rid of the ring, get it out of sight and out of mind.

Then he would finally be free to move on.

Chapter 3

Rafe pulled into his garage a little after seven o'clock that evening. He saw the living room lights were on even before he spotted his father's pickup. He was probably sanding woodwork, a tedious process on the way to restoring the hundred-year-old house in a neighborhood where the homes were old but well maintained. Rafe had recently furnished one of his four bedrooms for his father, who'd become a fixture, not always spending the night, but staying often enough to warrant a bed of his own. Luis Mendoza had seemed to age ten years since losing his wife, Rafe's mother, to pneumonia a year ago.

Rafe unlocked the back door and stepped into a dark kitchen, turning on lights as he went.

"Hey, Dad, I'm home!" he called out above the sound of sandpaper scraping wood.

"In the living room!"

There was no evidence that his father had eaten—no dishes, no jumbled-up McDonald's bag in the trash. Rafe passed through the dining room and on into the living room. "How's it going?"

"Almost ready to stain." From where he was kneeling he arched his back, stretching and groaning.

That's how I'll look in thirty years, Rafe thought, although the same could be true of his three brothers, as well. Their mother's DNA showed up in other ways—drive, work ethic, sociability and deep love of family, but that could also be said of their father, too. Rafe missed his mom more than he could say, so he could only imagine the depth of his father's loss.

Rafe had expected to have the kind of marriage his parents had—with Melina. He still grieved the loss of that dream, and the children who hadn't come.

Rafe laid his suit jacket over the back of his leather sofa then crouched next to his father and rubbed his back. "How long have you been at it?"

"Couple hours." He angled away from Rafe's touch and gestured to the entryway table. "Melina stopped by, left you some books and a DVD."

"She said she would." Rafe checked out the materials. The DVD was marked "Elliot Anderson." He took the disc out of the case and headed to his television. "I haven't eaten yet, have you?"

"Nope." Luis stood. When he turned sideways he almost disappeared. He'd probably lost thirty pounds, twenty of which he couldn't afford to lose. "Is that the way the wind's blowing these days? Melina Lawrence again?"

"It's a business thing. I might be helping her out with something."

"She was gone for your mother's funeral, but she came to see me as soon as she got back." He brushed wood dust from his shirt. "I don't understand why she hasn't gotten married yet. She's about the best catch in Red Rock, that's for sure. Doesn't know how beautiful she is. Loves people. Smile that lights up the world."

Rafe hadn't seen much of that famous smile since he'd returned, but he remembered it, as well as the slow, sexy one she'd perfected, the one he'd likened to her crooking a come-hither finger at him.

"I'm surprised you're even talking to her, though, son. You suffered a lot."

"Everyone moves on, Dad. You seem to be okay around her."

"For me, sure. But not for you. I don't want to see you hurt again."

"I'm okay. But thanks for the support."

He slid the DVD into the player then hit the start button. The quality wasn't bad, but the camera was a pretty good distance away.

"That Beau Bandero?" his father asked, coming up beside Rafe.

"In the flesh."

"A lot of flesh, too. Heard he's been drinking a lot. It shows— *Did he just hit that kid?*"

Rafe didn't answer, wanting to hear the exchange between Beau and Elliot, which happened just as Melina had described. "What do you think, Dad? Intentional?"

"Don't know. Play it again."

They both watched intently, then watched it again. One more time. "I can't tell," Rafe said.

"Beau's got his problems, but I don't think hitting a kid with a ball is something he'd do."

Rafe eyed his father curiously. "You've always championed Beau."

Luis shrugged and moved away, picking up his sanding tools. "I know what he had to put up with at home. Mr. Bandero was hard on him. Working at his ranch, I saw it all the time."

"Well, Beau's lucky that people aren't willing to drive their kids to San Antonio to play ball. Some parents will put up with a lot to have their kid trained by a former big leaguer." Rafe turned off the DVD without ejecting it, figuring he'd watch it a few more times later. "I'm going to heat up some left-over pizza. Sit down, Dad. Put your feet up for a while. You don't need to work all day at the ranch then exhaust yourself here."

"It's the only way I can sleep," his father said softly, dropping onto the sofa, his shoulders slumped.

Rafe closed his eyes in gratitude. *Finally.* Finally, he wasn't hiding his pain.

"I miss your mother so much. The nights are too quiet, and the mornings too empty." He made an effort to smile. "Been thinking about getting a dog."

Rafe sat next to him. "Why don't you just move in with me? You know there's plenty of room."

"I need to be at the ranch. Mr. Bandero's been very patient with me, but everyone seems to think that because it's been a year, it's time. That I should be recovered."

"Not everyone understands that recovery is individual, Dad." Although Rafe had also been hoping that by now his father would be emerging from mourning.

"That's what Melina said, too. She also said I should tell you how I'm feeling." He shrugged. "Figured you knew, actually."

"It's hard to miss the signs. You've lost too much weight."

"Your mom was the ranch cook, and a good one. I can't bear to sit down at the table to eat someone else's cooking, son."

"I get that. Which is why I think you should live with me. We'll take care of each other."

"Wouldn't that cramp your style with the women?"

"I'm as celibate as you."

"That won't last for long." He put his hands on his knees and shoved himself up. "I think I'll skip dinner and head back to the ranch. Thanks for listening."

"Nope. Dinner first, then you can leave."

Luis crossed his arms. "You're a pushy kid."

"Yeah? Who taught me to be that?"

"Your mother."

Rafe laughed, slung an arm over his father's shoulders and headed to the kitchen, the only completely remodeled room in the house. He lingered over pizza and beer with his dad, getting him to open up more, trying to figure out if there was a way to help his father then deciding he was already doing it. He'd made the right decision, moving back to Red Rock, being there for his dad, which mattered even more than Rafe had thought.

After his father drove away, Rafe watched the video again. He sat on the sofa and opened one of the books Melina had dropped off, but he couldn't focus on it, and he'd already researched a lot himself.

Seeing Beau on video brought back memories Rafe had put aside. He didn't want to think about them now, either, didn't want the memories to affect what he did regarding Elliot. Rafe and Beau had been baseball rivals since they were kids, the intensity fierce and unrelenting, but Rafe needed to ignore that for now. Would Beau do the same?

Restless, Rafe took off for a walk. Although Red Rock had grown substantially since he was a child, it was still a small town, easy to negotiate on foot. He came to Red, the restaurant owned by his aunt and uncle. The classy eatery was closed on Monday, so Rafe didn't stop. A little farther down the street he came across Melina's office, a small, rustic storefront with a shingle that read simply Red Rock Occupational Therapy Group, Melina Lawrence and Quanah Ruiz, AOTA-Certified Therapists, Specializing in Stroke Rehabilitation and Autism Spectrum Disorders.

The blinds were shut, but Rafe had glanced inside once before and knew it had a small lobby where Angie worked as administrative assistant, and a doorway leading to whatever other office space was in the back.

By asking around a little, he learned that Melina lived around the corner in a twelve-unit townhouse complex, her two-bedroom end unit purchased less than a year ago. What he didn't know was her phone number.

He'd been headed to her place when he'd left his house. He just hadn't admitted it to himself.

Rafe used his cell phone to call Information, but she wasn't listed. He tucked his phone back in his pocket then kept walking until he was in front of her building. Lights were still on downstairs, but he really couldn't just drop in on her.

Or could he?

It was nine-thirty. Was that too late? He hesitated a little longer, then decided to go home. He had questions for her and had planned to catch her at her office the next day before the meeting with the Andersons. It was better to just stick with the plan.

Rafe took about ten steps, stopped, then turned around and made his way into the courtyard of her complex, ignoring the chastising voice in his head. Steam rose from a narrow, rectangular, lighted pool. Someone was swimming laps, but it couldn't be Melina, because she had a paralyzing fear of the water after a childhood experience.

He moved around the courtyard as unobtrusively as possible, spotted the door to her unit then hesitated again. He had no idea how she would react to his just dropping in, yet for a reason he couldn't articulate, he wanted to know.

"Rafe?"

He spun around. Melina was resting her arms on the pool's edge, staring at him.

"What are you doing here?" she asked.

"You're swimming," he said in amazement, moving closer. "You never even liked bathtubs."

"Hand me my towel, would you?" she asked, pointing to one on a chair nearby. She swam to the steps and climbed out, her bright blue one-piece suit clinging like a second skin, her breasts firm, her nipples hard, her wet skin shiny.

He'd almost forgotten how perfectly built she was, not lithe and athletic but curvy and lush. They hadn't slept together all that many times, at least not overnight, but he'd loved being able to wrap himself around her in bed and touch her whenever he wanted. The few times they'd been able to afford a motel room, it'd seemed as if they'd made love more times than there were hours in the night. Otherwise, their dorm rooms had allowed for only quick get-togethers, pleasurable but not as satisfying.

Now, standing in front of her, Rafe opened her towel and draped it around her. He was more than a little tempted to pull her against him and rub her through the towel to dry her off.

"What are you doing here?" she asked again, not moving away but wariness settling in her eyes.

"I was out for a walk."

Still she didn't try to put space between them, as if frozen in place. He took it as a sign, inching closer, memories of her consuming him. His gaze dropped to her parted lips, her breath coming softly, quickly. He bent toward her....

Melina spun away from him. "Let's go inside," she said, pulling her towel tightly around her, then pressing the button for the electric pool cover.

Her body ached for him even as she called herself every kind of idiot. She'd almost kissed him, almost forgotten why they weren't together. If she hadn't come to her senses— She didn't even want to think about it.

Melina was trembling as she walked to her house, cold from the night air, but she'd also pushed herself hard in the pool. Seeing Rafe this morning had set her on edge all day. Caught between the past and present, she'd barely been able to focus on anything. Even Big John had called her on it—and if a sixty-two-year-old cantankerous stroke recovery patient noticed, it was a sure thing that everyone else she'd worked with today would've seen a different Melina.

"I'll be right back," she said to Rafe once they were inside her living room, then she hurried up the stairs to her bedroom, stripped off her suit and grabbed her jeans and a sweatshirt.

In a hurry, she knocked her robe off the hook in the closet. Her gaze landed on the framed letter that had hung under her robe. The letter he'd sent all those years ago. She'd

finally stopped noticing it—until just this moment. Now it seemed to have its own spotlight.

She didn't have to read it to know what it
said, as it was burned in her memory. She'd
framed and hung it to remind her of what
could happen if she let someone hold her
heart, as he had done.

She closed her eyes for a few seconds. He
hadn't even called her. After all those years,
all that love, and he hadn't even felt that he
owed her a phone call ending their relationship.

It all came back to her in one stab-in-the-
heart moment—all the pain, all the loneli-
ness, all the anger. And now she had to go
downstairs and face him as if nothing was
wrong.

It's been ten years, she reminded herself.
*You're not the same person. He isn't, either.
Let it go. Just let it go.*

She towel-dried her hair, stared in the mirror for a few seconds, then padded downstairs. He was thumbing through the yearbook
she'd left on the coffee table.

"It seems so long ago." Rafe straightened,
no discernible emotion on his face, even
though she remembered that the book had

been open to the homecoming photos, when they were crowned king and queen.

"A lot of life has happened since then, that's for sure," she said casually. "Would you like something to drink?"

"I'm okay, thanks."

She went into the kitchen, separated from the living room by an open bar counter. She poured herself a glass of water, more to keep distance between them than because of any real thirst.

"When'd you learn to swim?" he asked, leaning against the countertop.

"A couple of years ago. I'd watched so many people conquer fears in order to recover from debilitating diseases or injuries that I decided it was hypocritical of me not to defeat my own." Of course, she'd also advised a lot of her patients to forgive those people responsible for causing them pain and yet she had never forgiven Rafe—which was also hypocritical. The framed letter was proof of that. "It took me over a year of lessons twice a week."

"Good for you. So, the nightmares stopped, too?"

"For the most part. I can still see my cousin drowning, but now I see myself diving in and saving her instead of standing by helplessly."

"You were five years old when it happened, Melina."

"I know." And the impact of the experience had changed her life for years. She'd never spent a hot summer day in the river as a teenager. Never even splashed in a kiddie pool as a child.

Melina set down her water glass. "Why are you here?"

He didn't answer right away, as if gauging her mood. She knew how to keep her expression blank, even though she wanted him to leave. She didn't want to picture him in her house—or to give in to temptation again. Because no matter how much pain still lingered, she couldn't escape the attraction that was still there, powerful and tempting. She'd wanted to kiss him by the pool. Turning away had been close to impossible.

"I had a few questions before we meet with the Andersons tomorrow," he said. "I would've called but I didn't have your number."

"Yet you know where I live."

"Some information is easier to obtain than others. I'm guessing you don't have a land-line, that you use only your cell? Anyway, can you find out when the team is practicing again? And is there a way you could get me a team roster, as well?"

"I'll put my spies to work on it." She crossed her arms. "Anything else?"

A few beats passed. "If this is making you uncomfortable, I can call you tomorrow at your office."

She looked at the counter for a moment. She could so easily slip back into the part of their relationship that had worked so well— talking. At least until the very end. Until then they'd talked all the time, about anything and everything. She'd missed that so much, even the occasional argument.

"It's just weird, Rafe. I haven't seen you in all these years, and then…" She gestured toward the pool and their almost-kiss. "We need to keep it just business between us. So, do you have more questions?"

He slid his hands into his pockets, signaling something, but she wasn't sure what.

"In your professional opinion, *should* we be fighting for Elliot to play ball? Will he be able to do okay at it?"

"His having Asperger's won't prevent ultimate success, but it will take him longer to learn and he needs more intensive, individual work, which his father has been giving him."

"For batting, you said. But what about the other skills, like catching and fielding?"

"I honestly don't know. I only know that he can't learn to be part of a team without *being* on a team. It's the socialization process that's hard. But, most important, Elliot wants to be part of it. He's enamored with the idea of playing ball. He says over and over that he wants to be with *them,* meaning the other kids." Needing to do something, she set her glass in the sink. "That drive, that need, can take him far. He just requires more help than the average kid to get there. And perhaps success might be measured a little differently than with other children, but doesn't he deserve that chance?"

"Are you sure you didn't go to law school, after all?" he asked.

She didn't appreciate the reminder, but she didn't call him on it. "I hope that means I've swayed you, because he needs an impartial advocate."

"I'll let you know tomorrow after I've met him and his parents, and dug around a little more."

When she didn't respond, he glanced at her kitchen clock. "I'd better get going. If you can get that info and fax or email it to me before we meet, I'd appreciate it."

She nodded, then followed him to the front door, noting how he'd taken one last glance at the yearbook, in the same way she had with his trophy case in his office. He was holding back, just as she was, she realized. There were things that needed saying, and at some point they would have to be said.

But first things first. Elliot was more important than long-buried emotions. It wasn't like her to hold so much inside, but it was necessary this time.

She held the front door open as Rafe stepped outside. One safety light stayed spotlighted on the pool all night, even though a decorative metal fence prevented anyone from accidentally falling in.

"Did you get the material I left with your dad?" she asked.

"I've already watched the DVD several times. I wish it was more definitive." He turned to face her. She was unable to read his expression. "Good night, Melina."

Her throat closed. The way her porch light spilled onto him took her back to all the times they'd kissed good-night by her front door. She hadn't known disappointment then—or loss. She'd come to hate him since then for that.

And yet she wanted to haul him upstairs and make love with him.

She'd heard it said that there was a fine line between love and hate. Walking that tightrope between those two emotions was too risky, especially without a net.

"Good night," she said, then shut the door, burdened with doubt that she could work with him, but knowing she had no choice.

For Elliot's sake she had to put her personal feelings aside for now.

For *her* sake she needed to lock those feelings away forever.

Chapter 4

Melina had just finished making the introductions the next day at Rafe's office when Elliot Anderson, who'd taken a seat on the sofa between his parents, hopped back up and rushed to the glass case on Rafe's wall. "Wow! Look at all the trophies, Dad. They're awesome!"

Steve Anderson sent a look of amusement to Rafe then followed his son, coming up behind him. He was a smaller version of his father, both sporting matching crew cuts.

Rafe joined them, grateful for the icebreaker of the trophies. "I see you're an Alex Rodriguez fan, Elliot. That's a cool jersey you've got on."

"A-Rod, yeah. Number thirteen. First-round pick of the 1993 draft. He never went to college. The Seattle Mariners signed him. Then the Texas Rangers. My dad took me to see him play but I was too little to remember. I got pictures, though. The New York Yankees got him now. His batting average is—"

"Not now, Elliot," his father said. "We're here to talk to Mr. Mendoza."

"I know. We looked him up on Google." Energy and excitement burst from him. "Rafe Mendoza was a pitcher for Red Rock High School. His senior year his ERA was 2.28. His batting average was .432. He got forty-six RBIs and six home runs. He struck out 205 and walked forty-two. He went to college at the University of Michigan on a baseball scholarship. His ERA was—"

"Elliot, *this* is Rafe Mendoza."

"I know, Dad. He had 362 at bats, and—"

"Would you like to hold one of the trophies, Elliot?" Rafe asked. Melina had told him that the best way stop a running commentary was to redirect him.

"Yes!" He bounced up and down. "Can I choose which one? I want that one," he said, indicating the very large MVP trophy from Rafe's senior year at Michigan.

"How about one you can hold in your lap

instead?" Rafe asked, pulling down a smaller but fancier trophy, one with brass pennants and other game paraphernalia replicas.

"Okay!"

"Go sit next to Mom," Steve Anderson said.

Elliot ran to the couch, leaped into the air, turning at the same time, and plopped, grinning. He accepted the trophy and began to examine every inch of it.

Rafe moved his chair in front of his desk, removing the barrier that sometimes stifled conversation. "I hear you're a good baseball player yourself, Elliot."

"My batting average is .754. That's higher than Rafe Mendoza. My dad is teaching me how to pitch."

"Do you like to pitch?"

"Yes, yes, yes. But I like to hit more. My batting average is .754."

"Can you catch fly balls?"

"Sometimes." He seemed to be studying something in particular on the trophy. "I have to wear sunglasses. I like to wear sunglasses. I like to wear uniforms, too, like the other kids. I want to be on the team."

"What's your favorite thing about baseball?"

"I want to be with the kids." He stopped examining the trophy and looked at the prize case again. "I want pictures like that on my wall to look at all the time."

There were several team photos in the case—Rafe's high school and college teams, all-star games, too. He understood Elliot's desire to be part of something that united people in a common effort, one that brought acceptance and camaraderie. Until Rafe had moved back to Red Rock, he'd been part of some business teams in Ann Arbor, as corporate counsel. Going solo was taking some getting used to.

Rafe asked a few more questions, received enthusiastic and hopeful answers, then he wanted to speak to the parents without Elliot present. Melina offered to wait in the lobby with him, but his mother took him, instead, saying that her husband could speak for both of them.

"I've watched the video of Beau pitching to Elliot and hitting him," Rafe said to Steve Anderson. "Did you have a better angle? Do you think it was intentional?"

"I don't know. He didn't throw really hard, but Elliot had a sore spot on his hip because of it."

"How did Beau react after he'd hit Elliot? I heard what Beau said, but the video was being filmed from too far away for me to see his expression."

"I was too busy trying to keep my wife from charging him to notice." Steve Anderson smiled grimly. "She was seeing red."

Unexpected protective instincts rose up in Rafe, too. Elliot deserved better. "What can you tell me as his parent about him joining the team? I need to know what my argument is."

"Elliot learns from experience, not what people say, but by trial and error—not by being shown, but doing, again and again."

"How does he deal with mistakes? Will it make him put the brakes on, or will he be able to just keep going? Everyone goofs, and it's important to just keep on playing. Can he do that or does he freeze?"

"I can't give you just one answer," Steve said. "He gets frustrated by different kinds of things. Those are lessons for him. We talk about it and try to work it out."

Rafe looked at Melina. "In your opinion, could the experience hurt him in any way?"

"He's behind, but he's bursting with determination. This is his passion. He'll work harder than most, I'm sure. It'll be really good for him socially to be part of a team. Fitting in is important to him."

"Honestly, Mr. Mendoza," Steve said. "I don't think Bandero is going to give an inch. And since he owns the place, he's free to do whatever he wants. I don't want Elliot to be a topic of discussion around town, especially since we've just moved here and haven't even made friends yet. On the other hand, I want him to have a shot at doing what other kids do. There have been enough success stories to give us all hope."

"I've known Beau since my own T-ball days, Mr. Anderson, and maybe you're right about him not budging, but there are other coaches and other teams. Let me see what I can do. Plan on going to the practice tonight, but just sit in the stands and watch."

"We can't do that. Beau has a no-parents rule. Only players and coaches are allowed at the practices."

Rafe didn't comment on the unusual rule. "I'll call you after I've talked to Beau." He stood. "That's some boy you've got, Mr. Anderson."

"Steve. Thanks." He hesitated. "Can we work out a payment plan with you?"

"This one's on me, one ballplayer to another," Rafe said. "It'll be my pleasure."

"Thank you," he said, his voice gruff.

They all walked to the door together. When

Rafe opened it, he saw Elliot standing at his assistant's desk. Vonda was giving him her complete attention.

"Beau Bandero," Elliot said. "Third baseman for Red Rock High School. Batting average .620 in his senior year. Hit ten home runs, got forty-six RBIs, on-base percentage was .716. Got drafted by the Houston Astros. Didn't go to college, just like A-Rod. Called up to the majors in his second year. Played in the majors seven years until—"

"Son." Steve interrupted him with a look of apology to Vonda. "It's time to go."

Rafe shook hands with Steve's wife, Debbie, then he approached Elliot. From behind his back he pulled out a baseball and handed it to the boy. "This one's not to play with, okay? This one is to keep indoors. See this autograph? He was my favorite player when I was your age." Rafe remembered the moment he'd had it signed, too, as if it were yesterday. "He was done playing ball, but he was still my hero."

"Cal Ripken! Wow! It's Cal Ripken, Dad. The Iron Man. He played 2,632 games straight, and 3,001 games altogether. He had 11,551 at bats and 3,184 hits. In 2001 his salary was $6,300,000. In 2001 A-Rod's salary was twenty-two million. In 2001, Manny Ramirez made—"

Steve took him by the shoulders and turned him toward the door. "Time to go, Stat Man. Say goodbye."

"Goodbye," Elliot said, but Rafe could hear him rattling off more statistics as they went down the hall.

Rafe invited Melina back into his office. They stood just inside his closed door. "What a great kid."

"He is. I'm fortunate enough to meet a lot of great kids." She cocked her head. "That was very nice of you to give him your Ripken ball. I know how much it means to you."

"It'll be in good hands."

She cupped his arm. "Thank you for doing this."

Her touch made his breath go shallow. He didn't like it. Didn't want it. It complicated everything.

"I'm looking forward to it," he said. "I think I've needed a change from my routine. Kind of nice to get excited about a case again."

She gave him a look that seemed to remind him that his goal years ago *had* been to help those who couldn't afford good help. To fight city hall and win.

But "I'll be waiting to hear the results" was all she said.

* * *

On foot, Rafe studied the sports complex as he sought out Beau a couple of hours later. It was new, only two years old, Beau having built it as a tribute to himself, using money from a huge signing bonus he'd received from the Astros six months before he sustained a career-ending injury. The complex held four ball fields, with a snack bar and restrooms in the middle of the hub. All four fields were filled with boys and girls teams practicing.

Rafe spotted Beau and headed his way. After spending time on the phone with parents and coaches, Rafe had arrived ten minutes before practice started, but the boys were already limbering up. He'd learned that Beau coached and handled the day-to-day running of the complex. Apparently he micromanaged every detail, from choosing the snack bar food to chalking the lines to payroll, never giving anyone the chance to work independently or prove his or her capability.

To the question Rafe had asked most of the parents he'd called—"Why do you put up with him?"—came the most repeated answer, "There's no place else." One woman on speakerphone with her husband had added, "We all hold our breaths when the lists come out, hoping for a coach other than Beau for our kids."

But her husband said, "He teaches the skills. *Demands* the skill level be high. More than any other coach, frankly. He's just got a big mouth and no tact."

"He's made my baby cry several times," his wife said.

"Which won't kill him, honey."

So, the parents were divided, mostly by gender, and the coaches Rafe talked to were guarded, although one said he'd offered to take Elliot. Beau had turned him down.

Beau sent his team on a run around the field then stood waiting for Rafe to join him.

"It's been a long time," Rafe said, extending his hand to Beau, who shook it reluctantly, as if expecting to find a gag buzzer in Rafe's palm. "How are you?"

"Can't complain," Beau said. "Heard you were back."

"Yeah. It feels good."

"How's Melina? I haven't seen her in ages. We don't run in the same circles, you know."

Rafe managed not to grit his teeth. Their breakup had been big news, but that was ten years ago. Just by moving home, Rafe had stirred the gossip fires anew. "She seems to be fine."

Beau resettled his cap on his thinning brown hair. His eyes were hidden by sunglasses. "Something I can do for you?"

"I'd like to talk to you about Elliot Anderson."

Beau's mouth tightened. "What about him?"

"I want you to give him a chance to play."

"Oh, *you* want me to? Why should I?"

"Because he loves the game. He'll try harder than most of the other kids. Because every kid deserves a chance to shine."

"Personally, Rafe, I don't like shiny kids. I like 'em covered with dirt from sliding into second or falling down as they catch a foul ball. That kid, Elliot, doesn't know one thing about playing ball."

"He hits .754."

"That so? Well, maybe if we had a designated hitter position, I could use him, but all these kids gotta play positions. All these boys have been playing ball for years, and they still got a lot to learn. He doesn't even know to run to first when he's hit."

"About that…"

"Nope. That issue is dead. I didn't hit the boy on purpose. I'd never hit a kid on purpose. You leave that alone, lawyer." He dragged out the last word like an obscenity.

"Coach Wagner is willing to take Elliot."

"I know that. No. Is that clear enough for you? N. O. Rules are rules. Just like the army, we depend on rules. This is these boys' training ground for life. Life isn't fair, you know, Rafe? It just isn't. And this isn't about one kid but a team's worth of others who wouldn't get my full attention—*or* a teammate with the skills to help them win. I've got kids who come from San Antonio. You think it's because I coddle them? 'Course not. They come because I get results. I'm not a namby-pamby, soothe-their-fragile-little-egos kind of coach, and my teams win. Parents and kids like to win."

Rafe respected that—to a point. He tried a different tack. "You're saying you don't have faith in your ability to teach Elliot? To turn him into a winner?"

"Good one, Rafe. Good lawyering kind of language. Point is, I don't have time to work with him." Beau's grin came slow and self-satisfied. "You just can't stand that I got to go to the show and you didn't. You're lookin' for glory through this kid since you didn't get it in the big leagues yourself."

Rafe dug for patience. "What've you got to lose, Beau? Let the kid practice with the team."

Beau rubbed his chin, looking thoughtful.

After a good thirty seconds, he said, "Maybe I could, Rafe. Maybe I could. If you're willing to follow my rules." He leaned close. "I'm guessing you aren't gonna like them much."

Chapter 5

Melina stopped herself from drumming her fingers on her conference room table then smiled apologetically at Elliot's parents seated across from her. Elliot sat at a play table, pushing sand into piles with a small plastic bulldozer. Rafe had called a half hour ago and asked if everyone could meet at Melina's office. The Andersons didn't know why Rafe had asked for the meeting, either.

"Have you and Rafe known each other a long time?" Debbie Anderson asked.

"All through high school, although I hadn't seen him the past ten years. He lived out of state."

"I gather he and Beau have a history."

"They played ball together for years and were always one and two statistically at the end of each season. Who came out on top changed from year to year. It created a pretty solid rivalry."

"More than that, I think. But rivalry certainly can spur someone to work even harder." She glanced at her son. "All my life, whatever I've wanted to do, I've been able to. If I worked hard enough and dedicated myself, I succeeded. But no one ever put a roadblock in my way, either. I've always been given the chance—the right—to try."

"Me, too," Melina said, her gaze on Elliot, as well. "Excuse me. I want to get him one of our new sand toys."

Melina walked into the lobby just as Rafe came through the front door. Her pulse picked up in anticipation.

"Are the Andersons waiting?" he whispered.

"They're in the conference room."

He pulled her to the side and said quietly, "Beau will let him play."

"That's great—"

"With conditions."

The way he said it alerted her. She wasn't going to like the conditions. "What does he want?"

"Elliot has to have his own coach."

"I don't think Steve will object to taking on that role."

"No parents allowed, even under special circumstances. So, I offered. I think Beau knew I would."

A hot lump formed in her throat. "That's very generous of you, Rafe."

"There's more. He's worried about Elliot losing focus and being unable to get it back. He wants you there, too, or the deal is off."

She stared at him. She couldn't do that. It would be too hard being there all the time, watching Rafe, trying to remember why she shouldn't be attracted to him anymore.

Focus on the letter. Remember how he ended your relationship.

"Look, I know it'll be hard, Melina. But Beau is allowing Elliot to play and—"

"He's on the team?" Steve asked from the open doorway. "Mr. Bandero said yes?"

Debbie raced up beside him, hope and excitement in her eyes.

Melina had no choice. She had to put Elliot first—no matter how much it cost her personally. "Game on," she said, smiling, heading toward the conference room. Steve looked as excited as a kid himself.

"Elliot!" Debbie called out. "Coach Bandero says you can play on his team."

Elliot went motionless. "I can win a trophy?"

"There are some conditions," Rafe said, including everyone in his glance. "You have to have your own coach to help you at every practice."

"That's no problem," Steve said. "I—"

"No parents, remember?" Rafe interrupted smoothly. "I volunteered."

"Why would you—" Steve stopped whatever he was going to say. "Thank you."

"You're welcome."

Debbie Anderson looked worried. "I think one of us needs to be there," she said. "In case—" She looked at Melina.

In case he has a meltdown. In case he loses focus and can't get it back. In case, in case.

"Part of the plan," Rafe said, "is for Melina to be there, too. For the 'in cases.' Would that work for you?" he asked the parents.

"It's too much to ask," Steve said. "Both of you? How can we let you do that? Your time is too valuable."

"I'd love to help," Melina said. "It would be so much fun."

"There you have it," Rafe said. "Piece of cake."

"Where?" Elliot asked, looking around. "I like cake."

"It's a saying," his father said. "It means it was easy."

"Oh. I wish we had cake."

"We'll stop by the store and get some, buddy. Now I think we should get going so that everyone can enjoy their evening."

Goodbyes were said, including high fives with Elliot, then only Melina and Rafe were left.

"What'd you do, anyway, sell your soul?" she asked.

Rafe half smiled. "Are you free for dinner? I'd like to talk things over with you, get your input."

Melina's internal debate didn't last long. If they were going to work as a team to help Elliot succeed, they needed to establish détente.

"I'm free," she said. "But not at Red, okay? Not the family hangout."

"We'd have to leave town if you're looking for a place where no one would be wondering about us, don't you think? Maybe I could pick up some takeout and we could eat here."

The decision made, Rafe left. Melina raked the sand table, dusted off the toys and returned them to their cubbies. She straightened chairs, checked her schedule for the next day and generally fretted, then finally allowed herself to sit down and really think about the motive behind Beau's offer. She wondered if he knew what he was doing by forcing Rafe and her to work together. If he'd done it on purpose.

Maybe.

Probably.

It wasn't any secret around town that their relationship had ended badly. For years people had been anxiously awaiting a show when Melina and Rafe saw each other again, but that had died off. Too many years had passed.

But it might as well have happened yesterday, now that Rafe was living in Red Rock again. People had long memories when gossip was involved.

They needed to be careful not to add fuel to the rumor fires that would flare now—and the bigger problem for her of keeping her own fires under control.

She wasn't sure there was an extinguisher large enough to handle that.

Rafe made his way up the street to Red, the restaurant owned by his Uncle José and Aunt Maria Mendoza, and managed by his younger-by-two-years brother, Marcos. Their older brother, Javier, lived in town and showed up now and then to hang out with them, but their younger brother, Miguel, lived in New York City and rarely came home. They had a half-sister from their father's first marriage, Isabella Mendoza Fortune, a surprise but welcome recent addition to the family. Rafe liked that his family had expanded with the addition of Isabella, especially now that his mother had passed away.

The atmosphere at Red, a converted hacienda and historical treasure, appealed to Rafe. The interior and the courtyard were classy and colorful, filled with antiques dating back to the mid-nineteenth century, when Texas had become a state. Paintings depicting the battles between Texans and Mexicans to free the republic from Santa Ana's rule hung on dark wood walls, visually soothing and stimulating at the same time.

As was the exquisitely prepared food, the tempting, spicy scents drifting through the air as Rafe entered, making his mouth water. Even without the family connection, it would be his favorite restaurant in town.

"Hola, mi hermano," Marcos said, spotting him, giving him a big hug. "It's good to see you out of your suit and tie and looking like a Texan again. Did you leave your Stetson in the car?" he teased.

"Actually, I did. I found a couple of my old ones in the attic at Dad's when I went looking for my old trophies."

"Don't tell me you put up a wall of fame in your house."

"Nope. At my office." He grinned. "Surprisingly, people are generally impressed by such things, even if brothers aren't."

"Brothers are more honest."

Rafe laughed.

"You here for dinner?" Marcos asked.

"Takeout. You know what Dad and I like. Give me enough for leftovers, too, please. And a couple pieces of your Mexican chocolate cake." Rafe would take the leftovers home to his father when he and Melina were done.

Marcos had already started toward the kitchen. He stopped and turned around. "Two pieces?"

Rafe held up two fingers.

Marcos cocked his head. "You have a date."

"How did you come to that conclusion?" Rafe started to cross his arms, then realized how defensive it would look.

"Huh. You didn't say no. Interesting. So. Not just a date, but someone you want to keep private, even from your favorite brother." He narrowed his eyes thoughtfully. "I'll add taquitos and guacamole to your order. I happen to know your date has a healthy appetite."

"And you know this how?"

Marcos shrugged. "Small town. Big grapevine. Apparently you were seen talking with Melina at Angie's wedding."

"So? It would've been rude to ignore her. That doesn't make her my date."

"You're still not denying it." Marcos moseyed closer to Rafe. "Have you seen her since then?"

"On business, yes."

"So, a little while ago when you went to her office? Was that business?"

"Have you got surveillance cameras all over town?" Rafe asked, exasperated.

"Better. A constant flow of customers, most of whom know our family and Melina's. Everyone loves a good speculation, myself included." Marcos gave Rafe a good, long stare. "Dad loves chocolate cake. Melina orders it when she comes here. You don't eat dessert. Easy conclusion. Give me something harder to figure out." He took off for the kitchen.

"Good evenin'. Welcome to Red," said a pretty young woman with long brown hair. She stepped into the lobby. "We'll be able to seat you in just a moment. Unless you'd like to go to the bar?"

"Neither, thanks. I've got a takeout order coming." He extended his hand toward her. "I'm Rafe. Marcos's brother."

Her brown eyes took on some sparkle. Her handshake was firm and direct. "Oh! You're the one who's come home again. I'm Wendy Fortune."

"Fortune?"

"I know, I know. The Fortunes are famous in Red Rock. I'm from the Atlanta branch. Actually, I was exiled here." She glanced past Rafe. "But that's a long, boring story," she said. "Here's Marcos now. It was nice to meet you."

"Thanks. You, too."

"About ten minutes for your order," Marcos told his brother.

Rafe waited until Wendy was out of sight then said, "She's cute."

"Spoiled. Youngest of six kids and been indulged all her life."

Rafe heard something in Marcos's voice that he couldn't identify. "It sounds like you didn't want to hire her, so why did you?"

"I didn't have a say. Plus she's connected to our half-sister through marriage, you know." He shrugged. "She's learning. It's not an easy job."

"Well, she's attractive. That'll help."

"I guess."

Rafe grinned. "You guess? I saw you watching her walk away—and you weren't looking at her feet, *hermano*." He held up both hands in surrender while his brother pretended to throw a punch. "Dad finally told me he's having a hard time coping."

Marcos shifted gears just as easily. "He actually admitted it? Good."

The brothers talked until the order was ready, then Rafe made his way back to Melina's office. Through the open door to the conference room he saw Melina laughing with a tall man whose straight black hair was as long as hers. He spotted Rafe then whispered something to her.

Melina whirled around. "Rafe! That was fast."

Did she looked embarrassed? Flustered? Excited? He couldn't tell for sure. He only knew he felt pinpricks of jealousy stab him everywhere.

"This is my partner," she said. "Quanah Ruiz. Everyone calls him Q."

Partner? Oh, *business* partner. Q reached for one of the bags of food and set it on the table, then shook Rafe's hand.

"Rafe Mendoza," he said.

"I guessed as much. Melina was just telling me the great news about Elliot. Well done."

"Thanks. There's plenty here for three if you want to join us. Chicken enchiladas, chile rellenos and Spanish rice. Taquitos and guac. Mexican chocolate cake," he added, looking at Melina, who made a sound close to a whimper.

"From Red?"

"Of course. Q?"

Rafe wasn't sure whether he wanted the buffer or not, but was surprisingly pleased when Q said he had other plans.

Melina started opening up the foil containers the moment Q left. She'd rounded up paper plates, plastic silverware and a couple of Cokes.

"I don't think I've ever heard the name Quanah," he said.

"It's Comanche—his mother's side. You can see it in his cheekbones, I think. For all his imposing height and that long hair, kids respond to him instantly. He tends to work mostly with the children, and I take on most of the adults, but sometimes a child takes a shine to me instead, or an adult to Q, so then we adapt. It keeps us both fresh that way, too."

They sat down and started serving themselves and each other. "I noticed your grandfather is in a wheelchair," Rafe said.

"He doesn't use it all the time, just when he'd be on his feet for long periods. He needs hip replacement but won't do the surgery. He says he's too old."

"Is he?"

"He's eighty-six and in pretty good shape, actually. He's just stubborn. And I don't think he has the desire. He says he'd rather join Grandma Rose in heaven."

The mention of Rose's name stopped the conversation cold.

"Thanks for giving my dad advice last night," he said, changing the subject. "He finally talked to me about Mom."

"I'm so glad. Your parents weren't just married, they worked together. That's a double loss and a constant sorrow. The last time I saw him was a couple of months ago, and he didn't look well to me, but he seemed better last night. I'm guessing it's because of you."

"Thank you for saying that." He picked up a taquito and scooped some guacamole onto it. "I saw him wasting away, too. It about killed me."

"Well, he seems to have a purpose now, which always helps."

"I invited him to move in with me, but he hasn't agreed."

"Give him time." She took her first bite of food. "Oh, man. Best. Chile. Relleno. Ever."

He caught glimpses of her as they ate without carrying on much conversation. He'd forgotten how much he liked just watching her, how gracefully she moved, how her blond hair fell over her shoulders, leaving a curl over her breast. She wore her Wranglers like a second skin, and her deep turquoise shirt turned her eyes the same color.

For several years he'd been mingling in circles where the women wore a lot of black, whether dressed casual or elegant—edgy, sometimes fascinating women who were smart about business and capable of creating software to change the world.

Melina seemed mostly interested in changing the life of one boy.

As his father had noted, she didn't even know how beautiful she was, how wholesomely sexy.

"Are you okay?" she asked, looking uncomfortable at his long silence.

"Sorry. Just enjoying the food." *And the view.* "Marcos says hi, by the way." Rafe opened a foil packet containing one slice of cake and slid it toward her. "Don't look at me like that. I didn't tell him. Apparently we are the subject of speculation from having talked at the wedding and, as of tonight, from someone seeing me come here. Marcos guessed that we were having dinner together."

"I shouldn't be surprised. As much as Red Rock has grown, it's still a small town."

"Particularly when your families have been here for so long."

"Which can be both good and bad." She took a bite of cake, closed her eyes and savored it. "So," she said after a long exhale of satisfaction. "Give me the details about what happened with Beau, please."

"Bandero rule number one—I'm to be Elliot's coach at every practice and game."

"Every one? That's a big commitment."

"Rules are rules, as Beau says. Rule number two is that the same applies to you."

She sat back, looking perplexed. "I understand about being there for the practices, but why do I have to attend all the games? By then parents can be in the stands."

"But not in the dugout."

"What?" She was stunned. "I'm supposed to sit in no-woman's land?"

"Amazing, huh?" Rafe had been just as surprised as Melina. "Rule number three— toughest one—if Beau doesn't think Elliot is ready when the season opens, he will have to leave the team."

"No." Shaking her head, she put her fork down. "Rafe, that would be worse than denying him from the beginning. To work with him and get his hopes up then destroy them? No way. Absolutely not."

"There's no choice, Mel. And I plan on having Elliot ready to play, even if we have to practice every day. I've got enough family to get some scrimmage games going, give him some team experience. And Elliot also needs to learn how to work with a coach, not just his father. It'll be good for him in the long run."

She sat back and stared at him for a while, then a small smile spread across her face. "You're looking forward to it."

"I— Yeah. I am. I used to get into some pickup games with friends in Ann Arbor, but as I worked longer and longer hours, I stopped making the time. I've missed it."

"I can see why. It was a big part of your life for a long time." Melina started wrapping up the leftovers while Rafe gathered the trash. "What do you think Beau's motives are in setting the rules?" she asked.

"It's a power play."

She considered that. "Okay, I get that by him making *you* get involved. But *me?*"

He didn't look at her. "Either he's playing matchmaker or he's planning on it creating friction between us—for his entertainment. Which do you think?"

"The latter."

"Me, too. Let's not give him that satisfaction." He caught her gaze, held it. "Do you think we can manage that?"

"I don't *want* to be at odds with you, Rafe. But we have a history, and it's not going to be easy."

"Especially since the attraction is still there." Might as well put that on the table, he thought.

She hesitated then nodded. "Being attracted isn't the issue. It's what we do about it."

He knew what he'd like to do about it. For the first time since they'd met, they had their own homes, which offered privacy, a place where they could spend a whole night together, where it was comfortable and clean, where they wouldn't have to check out by 10:00 a.m. They could shower together in the morning, linger over breakfast wearing only robes, easily disposed of.

The silence escalated between them. He wondered if her thoughts were headed down the same path as his.

"I need to get going," she said abruptly,

reaching for her jacket and backpack. "Thank you for dinner. And for everything else you've done."

He followed her to the front door, waited while she locked it behind them. "I'll get a copy of Elliot's practice schedule to you, so you can plan. I know you weren't even consulted on this, and it's probably going to be a hassle."

She shook her head adamantly. "I'm happy to do it. Seeing the way his face lit up when you told him he could play. He's— Shoot. There's my dad. He's pulling up. Maybe you should take off while you can."

"I'm not a coward, Melina," Rafe said quietly.

Big, brash Jefferson Lawrence got out of his truck and swaggered over. "Daughter."

"Hey, Dad."

"Evening, sir. How are you?" Rafe asked offering his hand.

"Good, thanks. Real good." He faced Melina then. "Your mother sent me to track you down. She's been calling for a while."

"I had the phone off," Melina said, which wasn't entirely true. She'd had it on vibrate and had ignored it. "We were in an important meeting."

"She wanted you to come for dinner."

"I've eaten, thanks." She glanced at the bag of leftovers Rafe carried.

Jefferson eyed it as well. "Then come keep us company, Mellie. We'll catch up. Your sister's coming, and your grandfather is going to be there."

"Steph's working for me, remember? I see her every day. And I'll see Gramps tomorrow morning, Dad. Every Wednesday morning, as always. We go for a drive."

"Does he drive or do you?"

"He does. That's part of my job. To evaluate driving skills and see if someone should resume or continue. You know that."

"I'm surprised you haven't been in an accident."

He didn't know how many close calls there'd been in the past four years with various patients. Nor would she tell him. "You know why I'm riding with Gramps. He's doing okay. I'll probably turn him loose soon."

Her father cursed a blue streak, making Rafe laugh.

"Yes, it's funny until you have to live with it," Jefferson said.

"I hope my father lives long enough for that to be a problem, sir."

Jefferson looked into the distance for a few seconds then nodded. "Well, we've both lost our mothers, haven't we? Not in any hurry for our dads to go." His voice was raspy with emotion.

"No, sir."

He cleared his throat. "So, you coming home, girl? Your mother misses you."

Which was code for "your father misses you" or "your father wants you to get the hell away from Rafe Mendoza."

"Sorry, Dad. I can't," she said. "I'll check with her on coming over another night."

"You got your car?"

She smiled. "It's a five-minute walk home."

"Hop in. I'll drive you."

She figured he'd thought Rafe was going to take her. "I want to walk, but thanks. See you later."

He aimed a "so long" toward her and got into his truck as she and Rafe watched. He pulled out slowly. She could see him looking at his rearview mirror.

"You know he was stalling, waiting for me to give up and leave," Rafe said.

There was a lot she could say to that. Her parents had watched their daughter's heart break. Parents weren't very forgiving of such things. "My dad has never been subtle."

Rafe laughed. "Yeah. But he does what a father should. He loves and protects you. My dad's always been a good role model for me, but so was yours."

The words hung between them.

"Can I walk you home?" Rafe asked.

She was tempted. Over the past few days she'd been drawn back into his world, a world so unlike what they'd expected to have together. How very differently their lives had turned out—as a couple and individually.

He'd changed, was more self-assured and confident. He'd handled the situation with Beau without rancor, even though they didn't like each other at all. It took a persuasive man to do that with someone as stubborn as Beau.

"If you hadn't come along, Rafe," she said finally, "I'm sure I would've picked a fight with Beau, which wouldn't have accomplished anything. I probably would've threatened him with a lawsuit, too."

"Which also wouldn't have accomplished anything, since he hasn't done anything illegal. Yet."

"Yet?"

"Let's take it a day at a time, Mel. Let's try to work together as a unit, not let Beau goad us into losing our tempers."

"I can't even picture you losing your temper anymore." It was true. The Rafe from years ago, yes. He'd been passionate and emotional. This Rafe was smooth and controlled.

"I'm not as calm or patient as you might think. I've just learned how to channel my energy differently." He leaned a little closer, his voice softer, quieter, but somehow more intense. "I'm a man with normal needs, Melina. Normal wants. Even I lose patience when I'm denied for too long. Don't you remember that about me?"

She remembered. She'd loved when he'd let loose of his control, making her feel desired and cherished. He'd had a single-mindedness about him when making love that she hadn't appreciated then, not knowing any different. Now she knew.

However, he was being patient now, just standing and watching her, waiting for her to speak. Instead she went up on tiptoe and kissed him. After the barest surprised pause he kissed her back, feeling familiar and yet new in rediscovery, the taste of him tinder to the dry kindling of need stored inside her.

Can you go home again? she wondered, pulling back, touching her fingers to her lips, then briefly to his, seeing hunger in his dark eyes.

She felt the hunger, too, the need she was

afraid to show. But deep inside, her heart spoke to his again. If only his would answer.

"Yes, I remember that about you," she said softly, then she turned and walked away, knowing he was watching her, wanting him, and knowing she couldn't take that chance again. She'd grieved for him before. A second time would be even harder, maybe even impossible to survive.

Chapter 6

Years of practice kept Melina from slamming her foot against the floorboard while her grandfather was driving down Sycamore Avenue the next morning. He was scheduled to renew his driver's license in two weeks—if she gave the go-ahead.

"Next week, I want to drive my truck, not your dinky car," he said.

"I think that's a good idea, except how do you propose to do that since you can't get into the driver's seat without a stepladder? And then what do you do with it?"

"I'll figure out something. I'm eighty-six, missy, not a hundred and six. I still have a working brain. And I live by myself just fine."

"You know they can make you take a road test if they think it's necessary."

"So you've said. More than once."

"Because you seem to forget."

"I don't forget anything."

He wasn't an easy person most days, but he was more belligerent than usual today. Although she'd spent a lot of time at her grandparents' house as a teenager, she hadn't really gotten to know him well until the year she spent living with him and Grandma Rose after her stroke, caring for her. The year that had forever changed Melina's life.

The year she'd decided not to go back to Michigan but become an occupational therapist.

The year she'd lost Rafe because of her decisions. Although maybe it would have happened anyway.

"Seen Rafe lately?" her grandfather asked.

"Yes. He's been helping me with some issues regarding one of my kids." She scanned the street looking for potential hazards. "Thank you for talking to him at Angie's wedding, by the way. I think Mom and Dad ignored him."

He snorted. "I was a captive audience, wasn't I, stuck in the wheelchair for the day, as I was. Couldn't avoid him."

"You were more comfortable in the chair, and you know it. How come you're so ornery today?"

She grabbed the dashboard as he made a left turn in front of an oncoming car, the driver honking several times.

"Guess I should've waited a bit longer," he muttered.

"No 'guess' about it. What's going on?"

He didn't answer right away, then finally said, "Got up on the wrong side of the bed. My empty bed."

Ah. "Do you ever think about dating?" She tossed the idea out casually, although she'd given it a lot of thought. "You'd be prime real estate in the senior market."

He sort of laughed. "Real estate, huh?"

"All it would take is a little renovation, and you'd be good as new."

"You don't miss a chance, do you? I'm too old for surgery, and too old for dating folderol. I've had my share of casseroles delivered since your grandma died. None of them held a candle to her tamale pie."

His voice shook enough that Melina took her eyes off the road to study him. He was wearing his usual Western gear but looked fragile. "You're lonely."

"Hell, yes, I'm lonely. Any fool who says

otherwise in the same circumstances is lying. She was the fresh air I breathed for fifty-two years. It's been like inhaling smog since she died. It hurts." He gave her a quick glance. "No more talk about dating, okay? I'm not *that* lonely."

"Okay." She patted his shoulder. "I could use your help with something."

He sat up a little straighter. "Shoot."

"Pull over in front of Howard's, would you?"

"You planning on taking up some kind of sport?" he asked, parallel parking the car easily.

"Maybe."

He laughed. "That'll be the day. You almost flunked P. E. a few times."

"It wasn't from lack of skill but lack of interest," she said with a sniff.

He grinned. She was glad to have changed his mood. And she really could use his help.

After all, an experienced captain could make all the difference when someone was about to sail into uncharted waters.

Rafe had just arrived at the ballpark that afternoon and was making his way to the dugout to leave his backpack when his cell phone rang. He didn't see Melina and Elliot yet, but he was early. With time to kill, he answered the phone. "Rafe Mendoza."

"Rafe, it's Ross Fortune."

"Hey! It's been a long time, Ross. Since Isabella and J.R.'s wedding. How's the private investigation business?"

"Booming. Which says a lot, doesn't it?"

Rafe laughed. "Yeah. What's up?"

"My cousin Jeremy said he talked to you about this baby-on-the-doorstep business. He said you advised him to go to the police and report the found baby."

"That was my advice, yes. Did he?"

"The short version—he and Kirsten did, plus they got engaged, plus they were given temporary custody of baby Anthony. Lots of questions here, Rafe, and things are getting complicated. No one seems to be who they say they are. In the meantime, I'm out of ideas about how to search for the birth parents. I can't believe the baby was left without even a note."

Rafe saw a woman kicking up dust as she jogged across the diamond, a kid beside her. Rafe squinted, focused…

Even expecting her, he had to stare for several seconds before he realized it was Melina. He'd never seen her like this—wearing a baseball cap with her hair threaded out the back in a ponytail that swung as she moved. She also wore sunglasses, a Rangers jersey, black pants and shoes. Not cleats, he didn't think, but something athletic looking. And the jersey didn't hide the sway of her breasts as she jogged, either. He remembered how they felt in his hands, heavy and firm, and the texture of her nipples when he ran his tongue around—

"So, what do you think?" Ross asked in a way that sounded as if it hadn't been the first time.

Rafe tipped the phone back up to his mouth. "About what?"

There was a long pause, then, "What we've been talking about since you answered the phone—do you have any ideas where to look for answers about who baby Anthony is and where he comes from?"

"Not off the top of my head. As I told Jeremy, this isn't exactly my area of expertise. But if you and Jeremy would like to meet with me for dinner and do some brainstorming, I could do that. Regardless, I'd like to catch up with you."

"Sure. I'll tell you, Jeremy could use some answers. Between opening a new private practice here in town, the baby and his father's disappearance, he's got a lot on his mind."

"How long has William been gone?"

"Three months. Most of us have given up hope, but not Jeremy. He's sure William's alive." Ross sighed. "Well, give me a call after you've talked to him. Anything you can say or do to help will be greatly appreciated, Rafe."

"I will. Bye." Rafe ended the call and cradled the phone while he continued to stare at Melina as she neared, having slowed as she'd gotten closer, her cheeks flushed, her lips parted as she breathed a little harder than usual.

She wore a glove—an unscarred, brand-new baseball glove she was working a ball inside of, forming a pocket.

Peripherally he was aware of Elliot walking beside her, but he couldn't take his eyes off her. Last night after she'd kissed him, it had taken him more than a few seconds to gather his thoughts and make his way to his car. The kiss had been delicate yet hungry, soft and yet intense, triggering needs and wants he'd hoped to keep tamped down.

No such luck.

He'd driven home to an empty house and sat in a darkened living room, trying to figure out how he would be able to spend concentrated time with her when one small kiss could destroy his equilibrium so completely.

"Hi, Rafe Mendoza!" Elliot said as they reached him.

"Hey, sport. Are you ready to play?"

"Yes, sir. I am."

Rafe looked at Melina. Her cap brim and sunglasses did a good job of hiding her expression. "You look official," he said, wanting to tug on her ponytail. "Are you, um, planning to...play?"

"I thought I would help rather than just sit on the bench waiting for a 'what if' to happen."

"So, not only have you learned to swim, you've also learned to play baseball?"

"How difficult can it be at this level?" She kept throwing the ball hard into her glove.

She was adorable. Rafe was sure he'd never used that word in his life before, but nothing else described her at the moment. Innocence and enthusiasm danced across her face.

"Can we go play now?" Elliot asked.

Several kids were already out on the field tossing balls back and forth. Beau and three other men, probably his assistant coaches, strode up. "I'll catch up with you. Start the boys off. Pair them up for tosses," Beau said to one of the coaches, all of them looking like high school students. He glanced at Elliot. "Well, what're you waiting for? Go get with your team."

Elliot's eyes opened wide. He looked at Rafe.

"I'll be there in a minute, sport. You can do this. They're just tossing the ball back and forth. You've done that, right?"

"Right." He took off slowly, looking back frequently. Melina wanted to hug him and tell him everything would be okay.

Beau eyed her. "Interesting getup, Melina."

"Thanks. I thought I should dress the part."

"And what part might that be?"

"Assistant-assistant coach."

His laugh started low then grew to a guffaw. "Good one."

Her back stiffened. "I'm not kidding. I want to help."

"I have strict standards, you know? People bring their kids from miles away to train here. Somehow I don't think you'll inspire confidence."

She crossed her arms. "Well, first of all, since no parents are allowed at the practices, how would they know? Second, how do *you* know I wouldn't inspire confidence? Inspiring is something I'm really good at."

"Your lack of athletic skill was legendary in high school. Have you improved?"

"Why don't you just let her help?" Rafe interrupted. "What's the harm?"

Melina bristled. "I can handle this, thank you."

Rafe gave her a good, long look. "You got it," he said, then loped away, heading toward Elliot.

Beau glanced from Melina to Rafe and back again, a speculative twinkle in his eyes. She swallowed her irritation and thanked him for allowing Elliot to play. "I know you didn't have to. I think you'll be pleasantly surprised how quickly he grasps the rules."

"I've done a little studying on my own about his situation, Melina, and while you may be right about him grasping the rules, learning the skills isn't going to be an overnight thing."

"None of these boys learned overnight. Nor were they expected to."

"You're right. Their parents started them in T-ball when they turned four, then kept moving them up the ranks every year. They worked hard to get here."

"And you have a reputation to maintain."

"Damn straight."

They reached an impasse. She swallowed

her pride. "Rafe said you want me in the dug-out?"

"During the games. For practice you can sit wherever you want." He started walking backward. "I always admired you, Melina. You've got spunk. But here? In this place? I'm the boss."

"Got it."

He joined his team.

Disappointed, Melina made her way to the dugout to twiddle her thumbs. She kept working the glove the way her grandfather showed her as she watched Rafe and Elliot. Rafe didn't leave his side. She couldn't hear everything he said, nor could she see Elliot's expression, but his body language conveyed when he was nervous or pleased, tentative or excited. The other boys weren't talking to him, but they were also busy every second doing a drill of some kind or another, and Elliot wouldn't strike up a conversation with them. They needed to do the talking first.

Then batting practice started and everyone seemed to be holding their breath as Beau threw the first pitch. Elliot smacked ball after ball. Finally after a long string of hits, Beau said, "See that, boys? *That's* hitting. You could learn a thing or two from Elliot. He keeps his eyes on the ball."

"That's an expression," Elliot said. "It means I watch it real close. My batting average is .754," he added, which probably didn't endear him to his teammates, who didn't understand that he wasn't bragging but just being honest.

"Well, you're batting a thousand today," Beau said.

By the time practice was over, Melina was bored and hungry. She wanted to help. She wanted to play. She even admitted to herself that she wanted to be good at it, not have Beau laugh or Rafe patronize her.

"Good practice, sport," Rafe said as they all walked to the parking lot, where Elliot's parents would pick him up.

"I didn't catch any fly balls," he said, kicking at the dirt.

"You will. It just takes practice. Tomorrow night we'll work on that and on picking up grounders, okay?"

He nodded glumly.

"It was fun watching you hit," Melina said.

"That's easy."

"I'm a grown-up, and I can't do that."

"You're a girl."

Rafe laughed.

"Girls can hit balls, too, Elliot," Melina said, giving Rafe the eye so that he stifled his laughter. "We should watch one of the girls' games someday."

"There's only guys in the major leagues."

"Maybe it's time to change that," she said. "There are professional basketball leagues for women. And golf."

"Not football. It's hard. People get hurt a lot." He spotted his parents getting out of their car and took off running to them. "I hit a thousand!"

"I'm sorry for interfering with Beau," Rafe said to Melina as they followed Elliot more slowly. "He was being a jerk."

"What's new?"

"He's more of a jerk now than when we were in high school," Rafe said. "*Then* he was just relentless to get to the majors. *Now* he's fallen off the pedestal of success. It's a long fall, and a painful one."

They met up with Elliot and his parents and talked about how the practice went. "I told Elliot we'd work on fly balls and grounders tomorrow. We can't practice here, of course, but I'll figure out a place."

"Just let us know, and we'll be there," Steve Anderson said.

Elliot had climbed into the car and was buckling his seat belt. Rafe said quietly, "I think we need to keep it just him and me.

He's responding well to my coaching. Would you mind?"

"Will you be there?" Steve asked Melina. "Please don't take this the wrong way, Rafe, but I don't know you yet. Today everything was out in public. Elliot's—"

"I'll be there," Melina said, interrupting, understanding a father's hesitation. She looked at Rafe. "We could use my parents' yard. It's plenty big."

A few beats passed. "Works for me," he said.

Melina heard reluctance in his voice, but the words were enough to satisfy a protective father.

"I'll email you the address," she said to Steve. "Or I can pick him up. You and Debbie talk it over and let me know. Maybe you two would like to go out to dinner or something. Have a date night. Elliot could eat dinner with us at my mom and dad's house after practice. My mom would be beyond thrilled to have him."

"Thank you, Melina. I'll let you know. He doesn't take to new people and situations easily, as you know," Steve said, then leaned close. "I think he's already a little more animated, don't you?"

"I do."

"He put on a hitting clinic," Rafe said, then cupped Steve's shoulder. "You've done a great job teaching him."

"Thanks." The word came out as if causing him pain.

Melina and Rafe watched the family drive off then headed for her car. People were coming and going all around them, the parking lot a hive of activity.

"Want to practice with us tomorrow?" Rafe asked Melina after she unlocked her door.

"You mean you would deign to allow me to play, a mere girl?"

"I don't know about deigning, but I'd let you." His eyes sparkled. "Someone needs to run down the balls."

"Very funny. Would you like to stay for dinner after?" She hoped that sounded casual enough. If she was going to form a new kind of friendship with him, she needed to seem unaffected by him, even when he was smiling at her in that way that made her heart smile back.

"Maybe you'd better check with your parents first, Mel. I'm *persona non grata* with them, aren't I?"

"I can't see them saying no."

"Then, yes, thanks." He started to turn

away. "Will Elliot be able to be independent someday? Live on his own?"

"He should. Many people with Asperger's have good and productive lives. You can't even imagine how much playing baseball is going to help him. It's a microcosm of the big world he'll face."

"Is there anything I should be doing differently with him?"

"Maybe talk to him when the opportunities come up about not hurting someone's feelings by what he says, not just once but every time something happens. Repetition is critical." She cocked her head. "You seem to be enjoying yourself."

"I've missed the game." He looked toward the fields. "You came to every one of my games. I could hear your voice over everyone else's."

"Are you calling me a loudmouth?"

"If the human megaphone fits…"

She gave him a playful sock on the shoulder, then they both laughed, something that hadn't happened since they'd met up again. It gave her hope that a friendship was in their future.

"Hey, Rafe! I heard you were back." A leggy redhead wearing skintight jeans and a low-cut, body-hugging T-shirt strode toward them, swiveling her hips as she walked. "Hello, Melina."

"June." Although she was dressed provocatively, June Adams was one half of the couple who'd been voted the second mostly likely to wed their senior year, and had. She and Wade had been married more than ten years and had two kids.

June gave Rafe a hug, flattening herself against him. He set his hands at her waist and eased her back. Melina frowned at the intimacy.

"How're you, June?" Rafe asked.

"Well, I'm doing fine, honey. Just fine. What're you doing dressed in your playing clothes?"

"Helping to coach one of the teams. What's new?" Rafe asked, giving her his full attention when she touched his arm, letting her hand slide down to his.

At the sexy gesture, Melina felt jealousy rise inside her. She wondered how her husband would feel if he was there to see June flirt so blatantly.

"I'm doing an article for the weekly on the start of baseball season. How 'bout I combine a couple of stories and write about you coming home *and* your return to baseball."

"Beau's your man. This is all his."

June maneuvered herself a little closer, putting herself between him and Melina.

"He was the story last year. This year we need a fresh angle."

Melina knew a story couldn't be written about Rafe's return to local baseball without including Elliot, and that would have to be cleared with his parents. She shook her head at Rafe.

"Not interested, thanks, June," he said. "Good to see you. Bye, Melina." He headed for his car.

June turned toward Melina. "Well, don't you look precious in your baseball cap."

Melina ignored the catty tone, unusual for June. While they'd never been really close, they'd always been friendly with each other. "How's Wade?" she asked.

June examined her fingernails then looked toward the horizon. "We split up."

"Oh, June. I'm so sorry. I hadn't heard." So much for the busy grapevine, Melina thought.

"You're the first person I've told, except for my parents. It just happened. I can't even say it was something in particular that ended it, but that it's been coming for a while. We just grew apart. I know it's a cliché, but it's the truth."

"Doesn't make it any easier."

"No. But I'll recover. The kids haven't fully grasped it yet. They're so little, you know? Anyway, I'm looking for a better job, so if you hear of anything, let me know, okay?"

"Sure." Melina hugged her. June leaned in for a second then pushed away and left, not looking back.

A bright light clicked on in Melina's brain as she watched June walk away, not with the swagger of earlier, but slowly, more carefully, as if afraid she would stumble. Melina saw a new truth then, not just clearly but in full-spectrum color—she and Rafe never would've found the happiness they'd expected because, in the end, they'd wanted different things. They'd been right for each other as teenagers, with teenage dreams and idealism, but they were adults now, settled in jobs they were passionate about, jobs that were so different from their original intent.

What if they'd gone ahead with their plans? Would they have been doomed to failure as time passed?

She had little doubt that their desire for each other wouldn't have changed, because that had been a constant. But a long-lasting relationship needed much more than great sex to survive.

They could've ended up like June and

Wade, hurting, but also distressed for their children.

Melina headed to her car, trying to think ahead and how she would get through these next few weeks—months, really, since she had to attend the games, too, and sit in the dugout. Maybe being forced to work together would help her and Rafe become friends again so they wouldn't be uncomfortable when they ran into each other around town. Maybe they could start over, create something wholly different from the people they'd *become,* not who they'd been.

The true test would probably come when she saw him with another woman. Just that glimpse of him hugging June had fired up Melina. When he started dating someone and being together in public, that would be the true test.

She hoped it didn't happen before she was ready.

Chapter 7

"You dropped more balls than I did," Elliot said seriously, factually, to Melina as they walked toward her parents' back door the next day after practice.

She shrugged and smiled. "I'm just learning. We did okay, though, didn't we, coach?"

"You did very well." Rafe could see Melina's mother, Patsy, through the kitchen window. She'd been watching and cooking for the past forty-five minutes. Melina's father wasn't home yet, but her grandfather was perched on the back porch and had been coaching from the sidelines, directing his comments at Melina.

"Let me see that mitt," Gramps said to her

as she climbed the stairs. "Did you cinch it up with a belt last night like I told you?"

"Yes, sir, I did."

"Leave it with me for now. I'll work it a little more. You get a better pocket in it, you'll catch the ball more."

Rafe noticed that Elliot didn't look at her grandfather. Because of his gruffness? His age? His unfamiliarity? Not for the first time, Rafe wondered what it would be like to be in Elliot's head and see the world the way he did. He'd been excited about Rafe's trophies, and it had given them a connection they might not otherwise have had, but Rafe had to remember to be direct and specific with him. Elliot was more relaxed with Melina, but she wasn't new to him.

Rafe watched her toss her mitt and a ball to her grandfather then grip his shoulder and smile at him, getting a tender look in return. She'd always been like that—kind and caring, a toucher. She would've been a good lawyer, too, one who would've given her all for every client, every time. And she would've charged a sliding scale based on ability to pay, and done a lot of pro bono. At least, that had been her plan.

He considered his own achievements. He'd made a staggering amount of money for the few years he'd been in practice, but it hadn't come strictly from his profession. Mostly he'd let himself take huge risks by accepting a percentage in the businesses he represented instead of only a fee. Sometimes he lost, but mostly he won, selling his shares high, garnering great profits. It had given him a solid reputation in his field as well as the freedom to come back to Red Rock at a time when his father needed him.

Rafe followed Melina and Elliot into the house. She pointed out the bathroom to the boy, gave her mother a kiss on the cheek, then washed her hands at the kitchen sink.

"Thanks for having me, Patsy," Rafe said. "It smells great."

"Every once in a while you just have to have homemade fried chicken, I think," she said. "I invited your dad to join us."

Rafe couldn't hide his surprise. "Did he say yes?"

"He did. I've invited him several times since your mother died, but he's refused until now."

"He seems to be coming out of deep mourning finally," Rafe said.

"I think he's trying to, for your sake," Patsy said, lifting the last piece of chicken out of the cast-iron skillet, adding it to a platterful she was keeping warm in the oven. "You came home at the right time."

"Thanks." Rafe had always liked Patsy Lawrence, a feeling he knew used to be mutual. She was being polite but cautious with him now. Melina got her coloring from blonde and blue-eyed Patsy, although Patsy was willow slender, and her personality befitted the stereotype of a librarian, calm and knowledgeable.

"What can I do, Mom?" Melina asked.

"You can set the dining room table, please. Use the dark green tablecloth."

"I'll help. Let me wash up first," Rafe said, doing so, then going unerringly to the cabinet to get plates and glasses. He grabbed silverware from the drawer then went up beside Patsy.

"If my being here makes you uncomfortable, I won't come back again. I know Melina offered your house and yard without consulting you."

She smiled a little. "I admit it's strange after all these years, but...bygones, you know?"

Elliot came back and stood just inside the doorway, looking unsure.

"My daughter told me you love baseball," Patsy said. "I work at the library, and I saw a book there I thought you might like to read. It's on the kitchen table over there. Have you read it before?"

Elliot shook his head. He sat down to read. Rafe's hands full, he looked over Elliot's shoulder, seeing the book was baseball by the numbers—statistics of players and teams since the game began.

"Rafe Mendoza won't be in there," he said to the boy, smiling.

"You were good enough to play in the big leagues," Elliot said, not looking up from the book.

Elliot's comment struck a nerve that had laid dormant for years—until he'd gone to the field to speak to Beau the first time.

"Maybe. I had other plans," he said to Elliot, sensing Patsy's interest in their conversation.

He carried the place settings into the dining room, where Melina was folding napkins. As he set down the plates, déjà vu struck him. How many times had they done this, exactly this way? Too many to count. She'd been a constant visitor at his house, too.

"June and Wade Adams are separated," she said, looking up, connecting with his gaze. "She told me after you left. It came as a complete surprise to me. They always seemed fine whenever I saw them together."

"Remember their wedding?" Rafe said. He and Melina had gone together, just a few weeks after high school graduation. At the reception, they'd danced and dreamed out loud about their own future wedding. He'd never officially asked her to marry him, but he'd given her the promise ring, which meant he was promising to ask. He'd wanted to set a scene for that official proposal, something beautiful and memorable. If she wasn't going to be surprised by the question, she should be surprised at how he asked.

He remembered being happy that day, at Wade and June's wedding. His and Melina's lives were about to broaden immeasurably by going away to college and being independent. After dancing for a couple of hours, they'd driven to a hidden place by the river and made love, battling mosquitoes and laughing. Cherishing...

Then they'd sprawled, naked and satisfied, looking at each other, enjoying the sight. He hadn't dated anyone as curvy or as blonde as Melina since then—on purpose. No one who might remind him of her.

He wondered if she remembered that night in the same way. Then he saw her expression turn serious and her breath go shallow. She remembered, he decided, just as clearly as he, just as erotically. Her nipples were pressed against her snug T-shirt, then got visibly harder. So did he. And she noticed.

He moved around the table so that he could talk to her without being overheard. Barely any space separated them. "Why'd you kiss me the other night?" he asked.

"I couldn't help myself."

"What are we going to do about it?"

"It?"

He knew she couldn't be that obtuse. "You know, Melina. The attraction that never dies."

"It wasn't part of the plan I was formulating to only be friends with you," she said, moving a little closer, looking at his mouth. "Maybe it should be."

"Look who I found wandering outside," Melina's father bellowed from the kitchen, the back door hinges squeaking. "Can I get you a beer, Luis?"

Rafe's father's much softer voice didn't carry into the dining room, where Rafe and Melina jumped apart, caught like teenagers by their parents, and busied themselves setting the table so that by the time her father burst into the dining room, they no longer looked guilty.

"Hey, Dad," Melina said, going to give him a hug.

"How's my girl?" He patted her shoulder as she backed away. "Rafe."

"Sir." They shook hands, Rafe noting the suspicion in her father's eyes, the hesitance, but most of all the protectiveness.

His own father followed, a beer in hand. After greetings were exchanged, all the men wandered out to the back porch, taking Gramps a beer, as well.

Relief came over Melina once the door shut behind them. She wasn't sure what to expect putting that group of men together, but no fireworks so far.

She sat in a chair across from Elliot, who seemed comfortable being there, not fidgeting to leave. His parents had gone out for a rare dinner alone. Melina had hoped they wouldn't have to leave early and pick him up.

"Is Steph coming over, too?" she asked her mother.

"She's interviewing potential roommates now that Angie has moved in with Tommy. I think she's got three lined up for tonight. Would you grab the potato salad from the refrigerator, please? The rolls should be warmed enough, too. Green beans need to be put into a serving bowl."

Melina kept busy with the tasks but wondered if her mom wanted to ask questions and yet not be intrusive into her oldest daughter's life. After the food was taken care of, Melina rested an arm across her mother's shoulder and said, "We're doing this for Elliot."

Her mother smiled. "Are you?"

Melina nodded. "I figure by the time this is over, Rafe and I will be good friends, and I'll be glad about that."

"Your father's not happy about it at all."

"And you, Mom?"

"I see the hunger between you, Melina. I don't want you to suffer again."

The meal started awkwardly then smoothed out as time passed and conversation came more easily. Elliot kept his head down and ate well, including a big slice of pecan pie.

"Thank you for dinner, Patsy," Rafe's father said. "I haven't had chicken like that since…" He let the sentence drift off.

She laid her hand on the back of his. "It's Elena's recipe. She taught me how to fix it. I think of her all the time, but especially when I'm cooking certain dishes. She was the best cook I ever knew."

He nodded, looking down and swallowing hard, which brought tears to Melina's eyes.

"I miss her, too, Luis," Patsy said.

The whole table went quiet until Gramps said, "Did I tell you all that Melina thinks I should be dating?"

The conversation got lively again. Melina caught Rafe's gaze and smiled. It was such a familiar moment, all that laughter around the dining room table, although she felt the loss of her grandmother and Rafe's mother starkly.

The Andersons came to pick up Elliot, and the exodus began. Gramps yawned dramatically as his clue to Melina he wanted to go home. She couldn't manage a second alone with Rafe, but watched him go then drove her grandfather to his house.

After that she needed a swim. The day had been more cloudy than sunny, so the solar cover hadn't warmed the pool as much as it did on clear days.

Pent-up desire drove her lap after lap until finally she had to stop. She leaned her forehead against the side of the pool to catch her breath before she climbed out.

"Need a towel?"

The familiar voice didn't really surprise her. She'd been torn between wanting him to show up and wishing he would stay away.

She lifted her head. He was crouched, waiting for her, her towel held loosely in his hands, his eyes searching, questioning.

"Yes," she said in answer to everything and anything.

Then she climbed out of the pool and into his arms.

Chapter 8

Melina had just barely shut her living room door when she found herself up against it, her hands locked with his, arms pressed to the painted wood. The towel dropped to the floor. Her bathing suit didn't create a barrier but friction instead, exciting and welcome, as he moved his body along hers.

"I'll only ask once," he said touching his forehead to hers, his face taut with desire. "Are you okay with this?"

She nodded, then his mouth was on hers, attacking at first, then slowing, lingering, indulging. Savoring. His fingers tightened and released around hers, again and again, mimicking what was to come. He let go, freeing his hands to touch her, to slide his palms down her back and over her rear, cupping her, bringing her even closer as he dragged his mouth down her neck. Her wet hair dripped onto him and the floor. The scent of chlorine made her wish for a shower, but she didn't want to wait that long. Couldn't wait. This moment had been building, day by day. She needed him here and now.

Melina curved her fingers into his flesh as he sank slowly, exhaling hot air through her suit as he made a meandering trail down her welcoming body, stopping to nibble here and there, to run his hands along her breasts, her abdomen and beyond. She arched as his mouth settled between her legs, his fiery breath arousing, his teeth finding just the right places with just the right pressure. Then he rose, bringing along her towel to rub her hair, drawing audible breaths, deep and shaky.

She took him by the hand and led him upstairs and into her bedroom, wishing she knew what to say, wanting words from him, as well. And yet, what would they say?

He moved past her, flipped on two bedside lights, grabbed hold of her bedding and pulled it down, leaving only the bottom sheet. When he faced her he seemed like an entirely different person from her memories of him—a fully adult male instead of a young man, one who had life experience now. Other sexual experiences. She wondered—

"Take off your suit," he said, low and harsh, standing two feet from her.

She hesitated only long enough for the order to reach her brain, then peeled it off and tossed it toward her bathroom, where it landed with a splat.

Then he stripped, all the while watching her, revealing his perfectly toned body slowly, enticingly. She wanted to feel him inside her right now....

"I'm on the pill," she said, reaching toward him, needing to touch, to feel, to taste. He would be familiar and yet new. The memory of this night would replace others from so long ago. Was that a good thing? She would know soon.

She started at his chest, teasing him with light touches, exploring the planes of his body, going lower and lower, until he sucked in an audible breath. She wrapped her hand around his bold heat, swirled a fingertip around and around, glorying in the sounds he made.

"Keep it up and I won't be of much use to you," he said through clenched teeth.

"Oh, I fully intend to keep it up."

His laugh was filled with frustration and arousal. He let her explore for a little longer, then he took charge, moving her onto the bed, landing on top of her, maneuvering his legs between hers to nestle heat to heat, capturing her mouth with his in a deep, hot kiss that shut out the world, encasing them in their own erotic cocoon. She wrapped her legs around him, felt the hard heat of him press against her, pressure building inside her from the contact alone....

Rafe felt her arch and clench, heard her breathless sounds, squeezed his eyes shut when her fingernails dug into him and she moved rhythmically, powerfully. The moment she started to slow, he slid down her, took a hard nipple in his mouth and cherished it, then the other, arousing her again, ready to explode himself. His hands moved over her warm flesh, his mouth tasted her skin until he threaded his fingers through the soft curls between her legs—and then let his mouth go exploring.

He didn't have to wait for a response. She cupped his head, grabbed his hair, angled her hips higher. She was vocal and bold in her pleasure, then demanding as she pulled him up until he buried himself inside her, feeling her envelop him and tighten, finding paradise and satisfaction and a need for much, much more.

After a couple of minutes, Melina reached for the sheet to drag over them. Rafe had dropped onto his back, breathing hard, his arm across his eyes.

While she waited for him to say something, she looked around. Her bedroom was simple, the bed itself decorated with a white matelasse coverlet, a sage green dust ruffle and a few contrasting pillows—which had been tossed onto the floor in the heat of passion. Her pine furniture was bought at a yard sale and refinished. The real color came from family photos on the dresser and some of her mother's stunning art on the walls, single flowers in deep, rich tones, their bold colors at odds with her mother's calm, soothing personality.

What are you thinking? she asked Rafe silently. Maybe he'd fallen asleep. Or maybe he was avoiding talking to her. For all the heat between them, it had also been comfortable. No awkwardness of a first time, even though he had some moves that were new to her. Did he want to spend the night? Continue the relationship after this?

Or would this be it?

Finally he stirred, letting his arm fall away from his face. He opened his eyes and met her gaze, his expression serious. "We haven't lost our touch," he said.

Which told her nothing. "No."

He watched her a while longer. "Do you want me to go?"

Her stomach clenched. Her throat burned, tears threatening. He didn't even want to hold her for a while? "It's up to you, Rafe."

In truth she didn't know if she wanted him to go or stay. What could they talk about? To only discuss casual topics like Elliot or Beau or their families would dilute the intensity of their lovemaking, driven by a desire left unresolved for too long.

And yet, she felt good, too. He'd wanted her as much as she'd wanted him. Time and distance had only strengthened their physical compatibility.

She'd spent years keeping her relationships short and simple. If she could do that with Rafe, would it run its course by the end of baseball season, so that they could go their separate ways, the past buried, the future brighter for both of them?

"I'd be lying if I said I didn't want more." Rafe rolled to his side, facing her. "But I don't want to overstay my welcome."

"Your decision."

"No, it isn't. Yes or no, Melina? Go or stay?"

She decided she didn't want him to stay, that she didn't want to talk or hang out watching television or whatever other possibilities there were, since it was several hours until bedtime.

"If you leave, is that it for us?" she asked.

"Meaning what? You want to keep me as your stud?"

"Something like that." Her heart pounded so loud she thought surely he would hear it. She'd intended to be friends with him, not lovers, but maybe answering the attraction would help seal their future relationship. "I'm not seeing anyone right now," she said.

"Nor am I." He tucked her hair—her still-damp, totally messed-up hair—behind her ear then rubbed her lobe. "I'm game. So. How does this work?"

"We meet every so often for sex, but we won't spend the night." She didn't know why, but sleeping with him seemed more intimate than having sex with him.

"Well, now, that's a fascinating proposition, Mel. I'm to be your boy toy when the need arises, but that's all? We won't have dinner together or watch a movie? Sex only, no strings attached?"

She wanted strings. She wanted nights in his arms and waking up to watch the sunrise and a kiss goodbye in the morning. She *didn't* want her parents finding out and the reproachful looks that would follow, or the pity when it ended. Because it *would* end—she had no doubt about that.

"Yes, that's exactly what I want," she said, sure of her decision finally.

"And either of us can end it when we see fit, no recriminations, no blame? A no-fault affair, as it were?"

"We're adults. We can choose what kind of relationship we want." But even as she said the words, she knew it wasn't true. She was already falling in love with him again. If she'd ever stopped loving him.

He didn't speak for at least thirty seconds. Feeling almost sick to her stomach, she waited and waited.

"Okay," he said at last.

She wanted to weep. It was what she'd wanted to hear, and yet it wasn't enough.

"Have you been happy, Rafe?" she asked.

"Yes."

"Life is what you expected?" she asked, wanting more of an answer.

"More than I expected."

"Yet you moved back here…"

"I've made a whole lot of money, and that's not going to stop because I live here now. I have a certain skill that people pay well for, and an above-average tolerance for risk.

I won't apologize for what I've achieved. It feels good."

"Do you ever wish you'd taken a shot at the big leagues?"

"Now and then."

They climbed out of bed. He took her hand and pulled her toward the bathroom.

They didn't have much to say after that, just let their shower-wet kisses and soapy hands do all the talking. By the time he left an hour later, her body ached contentedly and her heart discontentedly. She'd entered into an arrangement that could lead either to a purging of past blame and hurt or a whole new level of agony.

Either way, she had to give it a shot, once and for all. Her peace of mind depended on it.

Rafe hadn't been home for two minutes when someone knocked on his front door.

Melina's father stood in the doorway. Rafe didn't invite him in, nor did he address the man. He'd always called Melina's mother Patsy, but he had never called her father Jefferson—or even Mr. Lawrence. Just *Sir*.

"I want you to leave my daughter alone. And before you say anything—I know you've been at her place for the past two hours."

"You also know we're working together on Elliot Anderson's situation."

Jefferson's gaze pierced him. His hands fisted. "My girl went through hell after you walked away. She's been steady on her feet for a while now. She doesn't need tripping up by you again."

Rafe clamped his mouth against the words that threatened to spill. *He'd* walked away? Like hell he had. The fact that Jefferson didn't know the truth made Rafe wonder if everyone thought the same—that Rafe had ended the relationship, when it wasn't true at all. He'd *acknowledged* the end, but *that* was it.

All Rafe said to her father, however, was, "Message received, sir."

The vague response obviously didn't please Jefferson. "You know, son, I did some checking on you. You were a real ladies man in Ann Arbor, weren't you? Cut a wide swath."

"So?" He'd had no reason not to. To his knowledge he hadn't broken any hearts.

"Melina's a good girl. She deserves to find a man to marry and bear his children. She won't do that if you keep stringing her along."

Rafe almost laughed. If only Jefferson knew the deal Melina had just presented Rafe with. Who was stringing whom along? Rafe did, on the other hand, understand a father's love.

"As I said, sir. Message received." It was all he could promise, after all. It was Melina's choice as much as his.

"I'll be keeping an eye on you," Jefferson said, then he stalked silently down the front path to his big pickup truck and rumbled away.

Rafe shut the door but didn't move. He shouldn't feel guilty, but he did. He'd done nothing wrong, yet apparently he was the bad guy in the breakup scenario. If that were the case, why had Melina let him back into her life? *He* was the one who should be leery.

After all, she was the one who'd broken his heart.

Chapter 9

Red hadn't yet hit its Friday-night stride when Rafe met up with Ross Fortune and orthopedic surgeon Jeremy Fortune for an early dinner. Marcos had given them a corner booth, announcing that Wendy Fortune would be their server, then winking at Rafe as he did so, as if to say, "You'll see what an experienced server she is."

"Howdy cousins," she said, eyeing the two Fortune men thoughtfully. "You all look like nachos and beer fans. A pitcher of light, and a big plate of extra-peppers nachos coming up."

The men had looked at each other and smiled. "Summed us up pretty well, I think," Rafe said, getting nods in return.

"I hear congratulations are in order," Rafe said to Jeremy. "Seems you've gotten yourself engaged since we last spoke in my office a couple weeks ago."

"Thanks. I'm feeling pretty lucky these days. Maybe you'd like to come to dinner one night and meet Kirsten? Are you seeing anyone these days, Rafe? Someone you'd like to bring along?"

"I'd like to meet your fiancée, and no, I'm not seeing anyone."

"That's not what the word on the internet is," Ross said.

"Huh?" was all Rafe could manage.

"You and Melina Lawrence have been linked."

"On the *internet?*"

"June's 'Around Town' column for the newspaper. It's on the paper's website as a daily column before it hits the stands in print." The often-gruff, dark-haired P.I. seemed to be enjoying himself at Rafe's expense.

Rafe stopped talking as Wendy set down a pitcher and three frosty glasses.

"Nachos'll be up in a minute," she said, walking away with purpose, hips twitching, which slowed the men's conversation for a few seconds.

"It's a rumor," Rafe finally said to Ross,

"based on nothing more than Melina's and my proximity on a couple of occasions. Purely speculation."

"Speak of the devil," Ross said as Marcos led Melina, her sister Stephanie and Q into the dining room, seating them in direct view of the men, although not within hearing distance.

Stephanie waved but didn't shout out a greeting the way her sister Angie would have. Still, it was enough for Melina to notice. She followed Stephanie's gaze then tentatively lifted a hand. Was she blushing? It was hard to tell from this distance, but Rafe thought her cheeks had gone rosy. Was she remembering the night before, especially what had happened in the shower? Or was she a little embarrassed, perhaps? Maybe she'd read June's rumors online and was being teased by her companions, just as he was.

"Is that the famous Melina?" Jeremy asked. "I haven't met her."

"The blonde is Melina," Rafe said. "The redhead is her sister Stephanie. The alpha male goes by Q. He's Melina's business partner." Rafe looked at Jeremy, changing the subject. "Still no word on your father?"

"Nothing," Jeremy said, shaking his head. "He's been missing for three months now, but

I can't shake the feeling that he's out there somewhere."

Rafe exchanged a glance with Ross. "He could very well be right," Ross said. "William's car was found, but not his body. He was supposed to get married the day he disappeared, and there was no reason for him to run away. I haven't turned up anything."

"And the police have given up," Jeremy added, frustration in his voice. "And now there's this baby, who mysteriously appears the same day that my father goes missing—at the same church, no less. We can't find any connection to the two events, but it's an odd coincidence, don't you think?"

"Here's your nachos, gentlemen," Wendy said. She was bright and perky without being obnoxious. "Y'all ready to order? Or do you want to hold off awhile?"

Rafe couldn't figure why Marcos thought Wendy wasn't a good waitress. So far, she was great, letting them enjoy their drinks and appetizer before ordering dinner, if that was their choice. She was cute, friendly without being over-the-top. The job suited her well.

The three men ordered their meals then returned to their discussion. Baby Anthony's fate was up in the air, except that Jeremy and Kirsten were prepared to give him up to the child's natural parents, if and when they were found.

"We thought Kirsten's brother, Max, was the baby's father, because that was what this girl, Courtney, told him," Jeremy said. "But that was apparently a lie. Then Courtney changed her story and said that a guy named Charlie is the baby's father, not Max, and that Charlie is bad news. So, Kirsten and I are acting as court-appointed guardians for the moment, because another big revelation followed—Courtney admitted she's not the mother. And then she gave Max the medallion the baby was wearing—"

"What medallion?" Ross interrupted, just as Rafe was going to ask for replay of the complicated story. "What are you talking about?"

"Baby Anthony apparently had on a small gold medallion when he was found in the car seat at the church. Or so the story goes."

"This is the first I'm hearing about it," Ross said.

"Because Courtney just turned it over, but she's also lied so much that no one knew—or knows—what to believe. Is she just trying to confuse everyone? Is she playing a game? If so, why?"

"Where is the medallion?" Ross asked.

"At home."

"I need to see it."

"It's just a trinket, Ross, but I can call Kirsten and have her bring it by. She and the baby are meeting a friend of Kirsten's shortly since I wasn't going to be home for dinner."

"If it's not too much trouble. Or I can go home with you after dinner."

"Not at all. I'll have her text me when she gets here so she doesn't have to get Anthony out of the car." He pulled out his phone.

Rafe had been half listening, his thoughts drifting elsewhere, like to last night in Melina's bed...and shower.

"I'd say June's 'Around Town' rumors are fact," Ross said, leaning close. "Or you want them to be true, at least."

"We have a past."

"A legendary one." Ross stood. "I'll be back in a minute."

Rafe winced. He wondered if Melina was hearing the same rumors and taking a lot of teasing. He pulled out his phone and sent a text message to her: "Free later?"

He watched her pick up her phone and look at it, then over at him. She could've nodded or shaken her head but instead texted back an answer: "Not free, but reasonable."

He smiled at her, then wrote, "Eight? Your place?"

"Don't be late," she wrote back.

"Kirsten's on her way," Jeremy said. "I'm going out front to wait for her. Don't eat all the nachos."

Which left Rafe alone at the table. He made his way across the dining room to say hello.

"We're celebrating my last day at the office," Stephanie said. "Angie will be back to work on Monday."

"We're celebrating a *successful* week," Q added. "Stephanie filled in admirably."

"And I didn't reorganize the file cabinets or anything." She grinned. "I did change Angie's desk around a little, just to mess with her."

"You wouldn't be a good sister otherwise," Rafe said.

"Have you been abandoned?" Melina asked.

"No. They'll be back. I just wanted to say hi." He started to walk away, then turned back. "Apparently we are the subject of public gossip," he said to Melina.

"You are the hundredth person to tell me that—or thereabouts."

He couldn't read her expression. Did it bother her? "I'd contact June and demand a retraction, except I think it might add fuel to the fire."

"It'll die on its own without that fuel," Melina said casually.

"Or not," Stephanie said with a smirk. Her eyes sparkled as she sipped her margarita.

Rafe excused himself, happy to get away from the curiosity in Stephanie's eyes as Ross and Jeremy returned to the booth.

Wendy brought their dinners just as they all took their seats. "Anything else I can get you?" she asked.

"We're good," Rafe said.

As soon as she left the dining room, the three men traded plates. She hadn't gotten one right. They all smiled and shrugged. So, she got their orders mixed up. She'd still get a great tip, Rafe thought. What she lacked in skill, she more than made up for in amiability.

Jeremy passed a plastic baggie to Ross. Inside was a small gold medallion on a chain. Ross stared at it, then set down his fork, opened the bag and dumped the item into his palm. The chain was delicate but the medallion itself looked like an old coin of some sort.

"Something wrong?" Rafe asked when Ross remained silent.

"I don't know. There's something about it. It's ringing a bell, but I don't know why. Obviously it has significance if it came with the baby. Can I hold on to this, Jeremy? I need to research it, if I can."

"Kirsten and I have tried, believe me, and came up empty. Have at it, Ross. I take it you didn't come up with any clues from the baby's car seat?"

He shook his head. "The brand is sold in every Walmart in the country."

"May I see the necklace?" Rafe asked.

Ross set it in Rafe's palm. "Did you have it appraised?" he asked Jeremy. "Is it gold? If it's a trinket it may be hard to track down its origins, but if it's gold..."

He passed it back to Ross, who frowned thoughtfully at it, then dropped it back into the baggie then into his pocket.

"No, we didn't have it appraised," Jeremy said. "We tried to find a match on the internet, but that's all. We haven't had possession of it for very long."

"I know some dealers," Ross said, picking up his fork. "The image is really resonating with me, though, so maybe it won't be that hard to track down. I must've seen it at some point."

The men spoke of other things then, including how much Red Rock had changed since they were kids. Although Ross was forty-two and Jeremy thirty-seven, Rafe had heard about them all his life—all the Fortunes, actually. They were like royalty in this area. Rafe felt on an equal footing with them, all of them professional and successful.

Marcos came up to ask how their meal was, and then the all-important question about how their service was. Gentlemen to the end, none of them mentioned Wendy's error. Rafe figured she'd get it worked out on her own when less polite customers pointed out her mistakes.

Ross and Jeremy took off after dinner. Q left, as well, leaving Melina and Stephanie alone. Rafe stood, figuring he'd join them, but another young woman came along and slid into the booth with them. Stephanie introduced her to Melina, then they called Wendy over and ordered something.

Rafe was at a loss. He couldn't go to Melina's house for another hour. He didn't want to go home. Just then Marcos came back to the table, their father behind him.

"I know you've already eaten," Luis said. "But maybe you have time to keep me company while I have dinner?"

"Of course, Dad. I've got about an hour before I meet someone. Plenty of time."

His father had just gotten settled when Beau Bandero showed up—with June Adams.

Rafe didn't think there were two people in town he wanted to see less. He knew, however, he needed to be polite to both of them.

"Evening, June. Beau," Rafe said as Marcos started to walk past Rafe's table.

"Where're you putting us?" Beau asked Marcos, who gestured toward a corner booth. "Okay, we'll seat ourselves in a minute. Mr. Mendoza, how're you?" he said to Rafe's father.

Rafe saw an entirely different Beau at that moment, respectful and genuinely happy to see Luis, shaking his hand and smiling, engaging him in conversation.

Rafe glanced at June. "I was sorry to hear about you and Wade."

She shrugged. "Been coming awhile."

"Still, it's hard. Especially on the kids." Rafe shot Beau a look, but he seemed immersed in his conversation. "You going out with him?"

Her brows lifted high. "I'm interviewing him, as you suggested. He offered to buy dinner. I don't turn down free dinners. Money's a little scarce these days."

"So it won't show up in your column, I guess. Who's in charge of writing speculation about *you,* June?"

She cocked her head. "You mad about that, Rafe?"

"I'm part of a dying breed, I think, of people who believe in an expectation of having a certain amount of privacy in our lives. And truth."

"I write what I see. If I don't see it myself, I verify what information I'm given."

"You ready?" Beau asked June, who nodded a goodbye then preceded him to their booth.

Rafe's back was to them, which was just as well. He eyed Melina, saw her watching them.

Something to talk about later.

"You and Beau get all caught up?" Rafe asked his father, not doing a good job of hiding his irritation. Beau had always admired Luis, had come to him for advice when Beau and Rafe were teenagers. Rafe had always felt it was a betrayal of some kind that his father had counseled Rafe's rival.

Taquitos and guacamole had been delivered to the table without Rafe seeing it happen. Even though he wasn't hungry, he snatched one up, dipped it in the guac, took a bite as his father sat back and eyed his son casually.

"Yes, thank you. We did. And you have no reason to be jealous."

"Jealous? I'm not—" He clamped his mouth shut. "Yes, I am. You always seemed so much more patient with him than me."

"I was responsible for how *you* turned out, son. Beau needed a strong male influence. He found it in me. Being ranch foreman, I was usually around."

"His father is about the strongest man out there."

"Hard's a better word for him. And he was too hard on Beau. Don't you remember at your games how he'd chew Beau out from the stands? Embarrass him?"

After a moment, Rafe nodded. "Do you think that's why he has the no-parents-allowed rule at practices?"

"No question. He'd probably ban them from the games, too, if he could." Luis took a sip of beer then set his glass down carefully. "It's probably difficult for you to see this, since you were going to succeed whether you decided to try for the big leagues or become a lawyer—but Beau only had one chance. The only thing he was good at was baseball. Mr. Bandero finally showed some pride in his son when the Astros signed Beau. Then he got injured, ending his career. And now you're rubbing your success in his face just by coming back here—not because you're doing anything in particular, but because that's who *he* is. He doesn't feel worthy. His father never inspired that in him. Just the opposite, in fact. Beau has to succeed now or else."

Rafe considered the long-winded argument. His father didn't often speak so emotionally, so it obviously meant a lot to him that Rafe understand Beau's situation. "He was never an easy guy to be around, Dad, but I can see that he has to put out winners now in order to prove he isn't washed up at twenty-nine. But surely you know that I don't kick a man while he's down."

His father patted his arm.

"How are you doing?" Rafe asked, changing the subject. "Except for dinner at Melina's last night, you've made yourself scarce."

"I guess she was right when she said I needed to tell you how I was feeling. I've been sleeping better in my own bed." He dipped a taquito into the guac and examined it as he said casually, "I accepted Patsy's invitation last night because I was wondering if something was going on between you and Melina, even though you've said it's just business. You avoided looking at each other so much, I decided there *is* something going on."

Rafe almost laughed. Apparently, they

couldn't look at each other, and they couldn't *not* look at each other. Both led to suspicion.

"No response?" Luis asked in surprise.

"I don't know what to say." Rafe glanced at Melina, who was laughing with her sister and the other woman. "We've both grown up and changed. We are making a point of getting along so that Elliot can have a shot at playing ball on a team. Melina and I probably would've avoided each other, if not for that. I'm glad we got forced to work together. Everything is okay." And in less than an hour, they would be in bed together proving just how okay they were.

Rafe left his father at the restaurant ten minutes before eight. Melina had taken off a half hour earlier after stopping by Beau and June's table then Rafe and his father's to say goodbye.

Rafe knew he had to move his car from the restaurant parking lot or June might have another news item to leak, but he didn't want to leave it in the guest parking spaces for Melina's building, either. In the end he parked on a side street and walked to her townhouse.

When she opened her door, she greeted him wearing a floor-length, lacy black negligee showing off her tempting cleavage. Red-painted toenails peeped out from below the frilly hem.

She didn't look shy or hesitant or restrained, and he found her confidence incredibly sexy.

But a couple of hours later as he walked back to his car, he found himself feeling dissatisfied, a feeling that carried over whenever they got together during the next week. During their brief time together each evening, they talked less and less, making love passionately, but in silence, and with little laughter.

When they were done, he would leave her bed, dress in the dark and let himself out into the cold, dreary night, finding less contentment each time, and yet, oddly, wanting her more, wishing she would talk to him the way she used to, wishing they could have breakfast together to start their days.

Since his return to town, he'd seen endless patience in her—with other people. With him, she never relaxed, never let him linger, never let him just hold her tucked close to him.

It didn't bode well for when baseball season ended.

Chapter 10

"You've lost weight," Angie commented when Melina arrived at work on a Tuesday afternoon over a week later.

"No, I haven't," Melina said, picking up her message slips from the corner of Angie's desk.

Angie stared coolly at her sister.

"Okay, maybe a couple of pounds," Melina conceded, although she knew it was closer to five, maybe more. "I've been busy. Between seeing patients and helping with Elliot's practice almost every evening, I'm always on the go."

"And you forget to eat?"

"I eat. Sporadically. Anyway, I could stand to lose a few pounds."

"You look great, Mellie, especially since you started swimming. This is about Rafe, isn't it?"

Melina pretended to read her messages but was really counting to ten. "Why would it be about Rafe?"

"Women lose weight either *for* a man or because of one. Or for her wedding," she added, holding her arms out, showing off her wedding-perfect figure, fifteen pounds lighter than when she got engaged. With her honeymoon tan not having faded yet, she was a knockout, but Melina thought it was Angie's inner happiness showing through.

"I'm just busy," Melina said firmly, then headed into her office, shutting her door, ending the discussion. Of course it was about Rafe. Keeping him close while also keeping him at a distance was taking its toll on her. She wanted to curl up in bed with him after they made love, to talk about things she didn't usually share with anyone, but he'd made it clear he was there only for the sex.

Every time he came over, the scenario was the same—they made love with wild abandon, their hands and bodies and mouths in constant motion, giving and taking as if it were the last time. They would shower after and arouse each other to the point of no return, then go to bed again and make love much more slowly and tenderly.

Then he would stretch out on his back with his eyes closed for a minute. After that he would roll out of bed, get dressed, give her a short, soft kiss and leave.

He showed up every night at the same time, left at the same time. The two hours in between were exciting, and yet...

And yet she was restless. He seemed fine with the arrangement, didn't seem to want to take it beyond what it already was.

Melina sat at her desk and stared at a painting of an endless field of bluebonnets her mother had painted as an office-warming gift.

You're the one who set the parameters, she reminded herself. But he was a hot-blooded man with a mind and will of his own, and if he wanted to change the rules, he could, or at least try.

In fact, she would welcome it, because she'd spent enough time with him both in bed and at the ballpark to have taken that dangerous, irresponsible step of falling in love with him again, especially after watching him with Elliot day after day.

Rafe had endless patience with the boy. There had been no need for Melina's presence, because Rafe knew how to divert Elliot when he got frustrated and settle him down to focus on practicing again. Elliot expected perfection of himself. Rafe let him know it would never be possible.

There were only nine more days until the first official game. Eight days until the final team practice, when Beau said he would decide if Elliot would go or stay. Melina didn't know who would be more upset if Beau wouldn't keep him—Elliot or Rafe. Or what the end result would be.

Would Rafe have a legal avenue to pursue for Elliot? And what kind of life lesson would it be for Elliot if he'd tried his hardest and been denied the opportunity to play? He hadn't been told of the possibility of not playing with the team. Maybe he should be warned.

Melina shoved her hair back from her face and blew out a breath. She couldn't think about it right now. She'd worked with four patients today and needed to enter notes into their files. She opened Big John's first. He'd had a stroke three months ago and had a staff of therapists—physical, speech and occupational. She'd retaught him how to make scrambled eggs today and bowled with him using a Wii. He was only sixty-two and wanted to drive his truck again, to get back to work at his job as an electrician. He was working hard toward that goal but was ornery as all get-out.

Melina had also worked that day with Elliot and a girl named Cindi in their classrooms at school. And then there was sweet Deenie, who was eighty, had no family nearby and was trying to live alone after hip replacement. Her daily, uncomplaining perseverance usually brought Melina to tears. She'd rearranged furniture and cabinet contents so that Deenie could maneuver easily around her tiny house, but everything was a struggle for her, with only slight improvement day by day. Melina checked in on her more often than she was scheduled for or paid to, because she worried about the frail woman.

A knock on Melina's office door startled her. Angie stuck her head inside. "I'm heading home. And Rafe's here to see you." She waggled her eyebrows and grinned.

"See you tomorrow, Ang. Please tell him to come in." She looked at her watch, surprised to see it was only twenty minutes until practice started. She backed up her data then shut off her computer as Rafe walked in, leaving the door open.

Melina didn't get up to greet him. She didn't know the etiquette in this situation. They were secret lovers. Did that mean they should hug hello as friends might? No, she decided, even though they were alone in the office.

"Hey," she said as he stood just inside the doorway. "Have a seat."

"I just need a minute. I wanted to let you know that I can't come over tonight. Wasn't sure if we would have a moment alone at practice to tell you."

She waited for him to say why, but he didn't. "Okay. Thanks for letting me know."

He hesitated a moment longer then turned away. "See you at practice."

Melina didn't move until she heard the front door close. He could have sent her a text message telling her, but he'd chosen to come in person. Why? He also could've chosen to tell her why he wouldn't be coming, but he hadn't done that either. Why not?

This was Tuesday, an unusual day for a date, if that was what he was up to—and the reason he wasn't giving.

By the time she reached the ballpark, she

was thoroughly annoyed. She was good enough to sleep with but not to confide in or be open with?

Are you open with him? her conscience asked, chiding her.

Well, no. Not completely.

So, whose fault is that?

Okay, okay, okay. She got it. By trying to keep herself from getting involved emotionally, she'd created an environment where her emotions were tested all the time. Oh, for the simple days of high school and pure, uncomplicated love.

When she got to the field, she waved at Elliot then sat in the dugout and watched the sky darken. The air smelled of impending rain, although it wasn't forecast until the overnight hours.

Melina spotted June Adams's sexy stride from across the field. The black tote she carried was too bulky to be a purse, so Melina guessed it was a camera bag and that June was here in an official capacity for the newspaper.

She popped into the dugout. "Hey, Melina. Mind if I leave my bag here while I take a few shots of the kids?"

One of Elliot's quirks was that he didn't like his picture taken, but Melina didn't want to explain that to June, who might see Elliot as newsworthy. He wanted to fit in, not stand out.

"June," Melina said, "I'm going to ask a favor of you—that you take pictures on any other diamond." It wouldn't matter if the camera was aimed at the other kids on his team, Elliot would react to it, believing it was on him, although, contradicting all that, he really wanted a team photo, craved that. When it was his choice and he was prepared for the photograph, he was okay with it.

June frowned. "I want to shoot Beau's team. The article's about him."

"He coaches another set of kids right after this one."

"I can't hang around that long. I've got kids to get home to and feed." She slipped her camera strap over her head. "What's the big deal? Beau said I could come today."

Melina fired a look at Beau, who looked back—or maybe he was looking at June. Melina had prepared him for Elliot's behaviors, how sometimes he calmed his own anxiety by rocking his body rhythmically, that he often needed to line things up in a row—his baseball gear, for example—but the photo taking hadn't occurred to her.

She could ask Elliot, but it would interrupt practice to do so, and they weren't wearing uniforms yet because the season hadn't started, so she thought he might object, even if asked. So far he hadn't had any outbursts in front of his teammates, and Melina hoped it would stay that way, for his sake. Acceptance was something he was looking forward to, part of being on a team. It was as much a goal for him as learning to play.

"Could you hold off for just a minute, please," Melina said to June, then jogged over to where Rafe stood next to Elliot, who was taking grounders from one of the coaches. She explained the situation.

"I'll talk to June," he said. "Stay with Elliot."

"Where's he going?" Elliot asked right away, not even seeing the ball coming at him so that it scooted past.

"To talk to the lady in the dugout for a second. He'll be back. Just go ahead and play, Elliot. Everything's fine."

"I need him. I don't know how to do this."

She heard anxiety building in his voice, fear in his eyes. "I'll be right here, I promise."

"I need Rafe Mendoza."

Normally Melina would've taken him aside and talked to him, but she was trying not to make a big deal in front of his teammates. As a matter of course, he got enough teasing at school. He'd learned to deal with that, but his teammates were different. He wanted their acceptance. "He'll be right back. Coach Greg is waiting on you, Elliot. Keep practicing."

Melina knew Elliot and Rafe had gotten close in the past couple of weeks, but the depth of Elliot's dependency startled her. She walked over to stand right next to him. "I'm here with you, and Rafe just has to talk to the lady for a minute." She didn't want to pull Elliot off the field, but she could see he was determined not to be apart from Rafe.

"How about if we walk over there to-gether?" she said to him quietly. "Slowly, okay? Don't run. I bet he'll be on his way back before we get there."

Melina felt people starting to stare, includ-ing Beau. The kids had a vague understand-ing that Elliot was new to playing baseball and needed more help, and since their goal was to win, they'd accepted Rafe being his personal coach. But to pull Elliot out of prac-tice was another thing altogether.

She pleaded silently with Beau, who or-dered the kids to give him their attention. Some did, some continued to watch Elliot, noting how he'd started running. Thunder rolled in the distance. He called Rafe's name.

Rafe came out to meet him, shifting his glance to Melina momentarily. "Hey, sport. What's going on?"

"I need you."

"I'm here." He turned to June. "Are we okay?"

She nodded.

Just then the skies opened up and rain came down hard.

"Everyone in the dugout," Beau shouted.

Because they were only a few feet away, Rafe, Elliot, Melina and June ducked inside the covered structure first. Melina watched the other kids eye Elliot, but he didn't look at them in return, so he didn't see the curiosity and, from a few of the kids, the ridicule in their expressions. One mouthed "Baby" to another, who smirked.

She decided to talk to Elliot's parents. Explaining the situation to his teammates might help. Then again, she wouldn't blame his parents if they decided against it, since he would feel even more different. At this age, it was tough to make that kind of call.

Beau talked skills as the rain poured down noisily. Elliot sat on the bench and rocked. Eventually his actions slowed and he seemed to be paying attention again. Melina and his parents had been working with him on apologizing, on understanding the importance of doing so, but he hadn't grasped the concept routinely. But out of the blue he said, "I'm sorry for walking off."

To Beau's credit, he didn't push Elliot to say why. "Thank you, Elliot. We accept your apology, don't we, boys?"

Everyone nodded or shifted or made some kind of sound. Melina tried to thank Beau with her eyes, but his hardened, as if to say, "This isn't the end of this."

They all stayed in the dugout listening to Beau's lecture until practice time ended, then they raced to the parking lot to catch their rides home. Melina decided to call the Andersons later rather than try to talk to them in the rain. She wondered if Elliot would be quieter than usual, making them wonder what had happened.

Rafe and Melina hunched under an eave, waiting for traffic to thin before they went to their cars.

"You probably don't know it, but that was a big step for Elliot, apologizing like that, without anyone telling him to," she said to Rafe.

A few beats passed. "I told him to. I whispered it in his ear. I shouldn't have?"

"Oh." The wind went out of her sails for a moment. "No, it's okay. I was just excited because— Well, it's good that you reinforced that behavior. Thanks."

"What was going on with him?"

"He panicked when you walked away. I'm a little worried about the level of attachment he has with you, Rafe. What happens if you can't make it for a practice or game sometime? Maybe I need to be more involved so that he would adapt to having me work with him, just in case."

"I'll talk to Beau about it."

"What'd you say to June, anyway?"

"I appealed to the mom in her. She won't take pictures or do any kind of story without talking to the Andersons." He looked at the sky. "Looks like it's not going to let up. I should get going."

He'd barely looked at her, and kept himself more than a foot away. Worst of all, he seemed in a hurry to get away.

"Why aren't you coming to my place tonight?" she asked, unable not to.

He finally focused on her. "I have a meeting with Ross Fortune. Will you miss me?"

"Yes."

He closed his eyes for a few seconds. When he opened them, his expression was entirely different. She saw tenderness and a building desire, his eyes darkening by the second. "That's what I've been waiting to hear," he said, his voice low.

"Did you think it doesn't matter to me whether I see you?"

"We never talk, Mel. We have sex—great sex—but that's it. I don't know how you feel about anything."

"I thought it was what you wanted."

"I thought it was what *you* wanted." He inched a little closer. "Maybe now that we're a couple of weeks into this relationship, we need to go over the ground rules, make some changes. Can I come by after my meeting?"

Relief raced through her, stealing her breath, weakening her knees. She'd been afraid he was starting to let her down gently. Her heart stopped pounding against her chest like a bass drum in a parade. "Yes."

"How about we do something really different tonight?" he asked, a mischievous smile forming. "How about we just talk?"

She smiled back. "We can try."

He laughed, then they ran to their cars as rain pelted them. Between the soaking in the rain and the late hour, by the time she drove back to her house, she was starved. But not just for food.

She wanted something more. Much, much more. And she didn't think talking was going to satisfy that hunger.

Chapter 11

Rafe got home in time to change clothes and towel-dry his hair, Melina on his mind the whole time. Their relationship was about to undergo a change, one he wasn't sure either of them was prepared for. To spend time talking meant letting each other in. They'd both been hesitating about doing that. He knew fear drove him, but is that what drove her, too? That the past would catch up with them, and they'd have to deal with it instead of ignore it?

And would he get to stay overnight now, to sleep with her? It'd been a long time since he'd held her all night. The last time he'd done that they'd been committed to each other, with plans to marry and have children. Now they both seemed determined to avoid such commitments.

His doorbell rang. Ross was right on time. They pulled up a couple of bar stools at the kitchen counter, but before they opened the lid on the pepperoni pizza Ross had brought, he set the baggie holding the gold medallion on the counter next to Rafe. Then he added a second one.

Rafe looked them both over. "Duplicates?"

Ross nodded. "I knew it looked familiar. Bear with me here, because this is going to sound totally off the wall, but I woke up from a dream this morning, one in which Ryan Fortune appeared to me. Do you remember him?"

"Vaguely. He died a few years ago, right?"

"Of a brain tumor. His widow is Lily, who, as you know, was to marry William Fortune the day he disappeared."

"I'm following you so far."

"I know it had to be a dream, but I swear I saw Ryan's spirit at the foot of my bed, Rafe. He told me he hoped the medallion would help to reunite baby Anthony and his father— as if I knew who his father was. And that very second, I was sure where I'd seen that medallion. I had to hunt for it, but I finally found it with some family papers. My sister and brothers and I got these as Christmas gifts from our mother thirty-two years ago. I was ten years old."

"Are they more than trinkets, after all?" Rafe asked, intrigued.

"They're rare and expensive. At the time my mother told us a crazy story about their history that none of us believed, knowing her penchant for telling tales." He pushed up the lid of the pizza box. "I did what you suggested and had the medallion appraised. It's worth a small fortune. Because I had no choice, I called my mother, whom I rarely speak to, and asked where she got them, because I know she wouldn't have had enough money to buy them herself. After some prodding she told me that William Fortune had given them to her. Since he's gone missing, or possibly worse, I can't verify that story, but there's no reason not to believe her."

"So, your sister and brothers also have matching medallions?"

Ross nodded, then pulled a slice of pizza from the box. "I talked to my sister. She still has hers. I contacted my brother Flint, who's been living in upstate New York. He said he lost track of his medallion, but that he'd be on a plane down here within the next week.

As for my brother Cooper, he's pretty much a nomad. When he checks in with one of us, we'll tell him what's going on. Who knows? Maybe Ryan Fortune's spirit will visit him and tell him to call home."

Rafe snagged a slice of pizza and let the story run through his head for a minute while he ate. "So, either Flint or Cooper must be the father? It's too much of a coincidence otherwise. Although it's odd that the baby was left without a note saying so."

"There's a lot that doesn't make sense. Yet. At least we can run DNA tests with Flint. Maybe Coop pawned his along the way—or something. But, as you say, it would be too coincidental for it to turn up in Red Rock around an abandoned baby's neck."

"To put it mildly. What does Jeremy say? Are he and Kirsten getting too attached to give up the baby when the time comes?"

"There's always that danger, but they seem committed to finding the parents. And you know, we keep talking about the father but forget we don't know the mother, either, now that Courtney has admitted she's not. What a mess." He looked bemused. "This is one of the most complicated cases I've ever worked on as a P.I., and it might turn out that the kid's my nephew."

The men finished up the pizza then Ross took off. Rafe decided to stop by Jeremy's place to see the baby for himself since he had time before heading to Melina's. Jeremy was performing a late, emergency surgery, Kirsten said, inviting him in. In the background, the baby cried.

"I'd given up walking him and put him in the swing, but that hasn't made him any happier. He's gotten a little spoiled because Jeremy walks him a lot." She looked askance at Rafe. "You wouldn't be interested in trying, would you? I fixed myself a bowl of soup, and it's getting cold."

For as much as he liked kids, Rafe hadn't held many babies, if any at all. Maybe a long time ago. "Go eat. Relax," he said, then walked to the swing and eyed the screaming infant. He lifted Anthony out then started walking and bouncing. His cries got louder. He had trouble catching his breath, he was crying so hard. So Rafe shifted him up to his shoulder and patted his back.

The crying slowed, bit by bit. Finally he drew a few shaky breaths, tucked his face against Rafe's neck and went to sleep. Rafe felt comforted himself, and happy that he'd been able to calm him.

Kirsten wandered in, a bowl in her hands, a

smile on her face. "He must like men's voices better than women's. Thank you. Can you stay until Jeremy gets home from the hospital?" She laughed.

"Won't he sleep for a while?"

"If you hold him. If you put him down, all bets are off."

Rafe sat in a rocking chair, the baby's warm body against his, a living reminder of what he'd expected to have with Melina. Four kids *at least,* they'd decided. They would've had two by now, if all had gone to plan. He was surprised at the depth of emotions he felt thinking about it. It'd been off his radar for so long, he'd forgotten.

"You're a natural," Kirsten said, taking a seat on the sofa, pulling out baby clothes from a laundry basket to fold.

Eventually Jeremy returned. They talked for a little while about the medallion's connection to the Fortune family, then Rafe maneuvered the baby into Jeremy's arms, feeling an instant loss of warmth—and peace.

Rafe headed for Melina's, parking on the side street as usual. Maybe this wasn't the best time to have a talk with her. He hadn't realized how cheated he'd felt for all these years since their plan had gone awry.

Then again, maybe a little clearing of the air was just what the doctor ordered.

Melina was more edgy than on any of the other nights since Rafe had started coming over. Before, she'd been excited and anxious. Now her nerves felt close to the surface and prickly.

The plan was to talk. Would she learn things she didn't want to know? Would he? Would tonight move their relationship forward or push it back?

Maybe it would end it.

The idea made her breath catch. If they talked, if they were honest with each other, he might walk out and never come back.

That fear escalated when he knocked. She tried to steady herself, then went to the door, her knees shaking. He slipped inside her house quickly, as always, and shut the door.

He looked different. More serious. As apprehensive as she, his emotions just as close to the surface as hers.

She set her hands on his chest and looked him in the eye, something indefinable driving her to change their plans. "I think we should talk later."

He didn't even answer, but swept her into his arms and headed up the stairs with her.

With so much raw emotion between them, sex could either be mind blowing or devastating.

But life without risk wasn't life at all....

He laid her on her bed, followed her down and kissed her, not giving either of them time to come to their senses or change their minds. She felt no hesitance from him, no second thoughts, just need mixed with urgency. He was more aggressive and more driven, which was just fine with her. Soon, he let her take charge, her need just as powerful. She explored him. Cherished him. Welcomed him...

Couldn't get enough of him.

She tasted, taunted and teased, enjoying all the textures of his body, all the hitched breaths and sounds of arousal. How powerful that was, to bring about such a response.

She lingered, making the experience last, running her fingertips over him, following with her mouth, taking him almost to the brink several times, until he hauled her on top of him and helped her to lower herself onto him. She loved the sounds he made and the attention he paid to her body, so exposed to him. But he didn't last long after that. Nor did she. It was a wild ride of abandonment, tempered with fear and doubt and a tiny bit of hope. Nothing like it had happened before, not to this degree.

Would it ever happen again?

She ended up draped over him, his arms around her, their slick bodies adhering.

"Would you like to spend the night?" she asked, quietly, apprehensively.

Then came the answer she'd dreaded. "Before we go that far," he said. "Let's do what we intended to. Let's talk."

She rolled onto her side, facing him, dragging her fingertips along his neck, stalling.

"You smell like baby powder," she said.

"I just came from visiting Jeremy and Kirsten." He put a hand on hers, stopping her exploration. "The baby needed calming. For some reason, he took to me."

"Just like Elliot."

"Melina." His expression was so serious. "Why are you evading?"

Because I'm scared. "I don't know."

He got out of bed, grabbed her hand and pulled her up. When they were dressed, they settled in on her couch downstairs. She sat at the opposite end, facing him, her knees up.

"On the subject of Elliot's attachment to you," she said, finding a safe place to start. "I called Q when I got home, then I spoke with Elliot's parents. Elliot knows about Asperger's in theory, but he doesn't really understand the complexities of it, so his parents work with him issue by issue as they come up. Baseball is a big-picture issue—physical, mental and emotional elements come into play."

"So, nothing can be done about his strong connection to me? It's too complicated to try?"

"They'll talk to him about how it looks to the other kids when he's not fully involved in the game, so that would be your cue. Remind him what his goal is. It should work. If not, we'll try something else. It's important that he doesn't obsess about you, because it's very hard to break an obsession, which you've probably guessed from how he's always quoting your stats."

"His parents sure have a lot to deal with."

"Parents are the unsung heroes of the world, for so many reasons."

"Even temporary ones, like Kirsten and Jeremy taking care of a baby they have no ties to."

"Your mom would've done that," Melina said. She rested her chin on her upraised knees, looking at him directly, wondering once more where this conversation—this long-overdue conversation—would take them, while still aching pleasantly from their lovemaking. "She seemed happiest when she was taking care of everyone."

"As do you."

His tone sounded matter-of-fact, and yet his body language was at odds with that, not nearly as relaxed. "I'm not totally selfless," she said.

"People like to talk about you to me," he said, his eyes smiling at the absurdity of it all. "You are the champion do-gooder of Red Rock."

"Is that a compliment or a criticism?"

"I guess it's somewhere in the middle." He held up a hand. "I know. I have no right to make those kinds of comments."

She thought that over for a few seconds. "It seems to me that this *is* the time for that, now that our initial sexual attraction has settled down."

His brows went up. "Settled down? That's what you call—" he pointed toward the ceiling "—that?"

"You know what I mean."

"I don't think I do. I want you as much now as I did our first time. Probably even more than then. It's far from settled down for me. And I haven't detected any lessening of desire from you. Just the opposite, in fact."

"Wow. Okay. This really is going to be a

serious discussion," she said, even more worried about the outcome. "Yes, I want you even more than ever. But, there are walls between us, Rafe."

He nodded. "I'm looking to start the next stage of my life, Melina. I didn't know that when I made the decision to come home. I thought it was to help my dad, and certainly that was number one in my reasoning, but I'm making a new life here. A complete life. I hadn't realized how shallow my existence had been these past few years. As I told you, I'd had one goal in mind—success. I liked the money and prestige. I have a knack for buying and selling, and I don't even know where it came from. It's just instinct."

"How'd you manage to take the time to help Elliot?"

"I made time. Put off some other things."

"*Why* did you?" she asked, since it didn't seem to fit with running a successful law practice.

He was quiet awhile, then, "Because you asked. I haven't done anything I haven't been paid to do for a long time. Maybe never. I don't remember."

"It's incredibly rewarding. Helping people," she added. "If I hadn't taken care of my grandmother for that year, I never would've

known about this field of work—or how good
I would be at it."

"Tell me about that."

Showtime, she thought. The beginning of
what had become the end of their relationship. "You were with me when I got the news
about her stroke. We'd been at Ann Arbor for,
what, three months? Mom and Dad talked me
out of coming home until Christmas break."

"Then you never went back to college."

"I couldn't. You saw that. Gramps wasn't
in the best of health, so he couldn't assume
the load. My mom worked full-time. Angie
and Stephanie were too young." She leaned
across the space between her and Rafe and
touched his arm. "I missed *you,* but I found
I really didn't miss college."

"I loved every minute of it."

"I know. I did, too, once I found my calling and started studying in the right field.
Not that caring for Grandma Rose was easy.
It wasn't. It was really, really hard, physically
and emotionally. Plus Gramps was difficult to
deal with. He was so afraid he would lose her.
A year later, when she did die, he went into
such deep mourning we thought he'd never
come out of it. As I'm sure you've heard, I
stayed on at his house for a year more."

"He seems to be okay now."

"He put up quite a fuss when I told him I was moving out, but it was past time. Mom and Dad have offered to have him live with them, and I imagine he'll do that at some point. I'm not sure how well Mom will make that transition." Melina smiled at the idea. Her father was hard enough to live with. "It was good of you to invite your father to live with you."

"It's hard to see your parent become scared, or worse, dependent." He laid his hand on her feet and squeezed. "I guess I finally understand what drove you to take such a drastic step, to quit college to care for your grandma."

"Do you? I don't think I even really understood then. I just knew someone had to help, and I seemed to be the only one available. It wasn't until a couple of weeks ago, after you got back, and I started reflecting on it all, that I realized once and for all that I wasn't cut out to be a lawyer. I wouldn't have been any good at it. I rationalized my leaving school because of my grandparents, when it was just as much my own desire." Her eyes stung at the admission. "See? I'm selfish, after all."

She took a breath, then said what she'd been needing to say for years. "Being away from you was hard enough while I was helping them 24/7, but having you break up with me at the same time just about did me in."

He let go of her feet. His jaw went hard. "A lot of people have alluded to the fact I broke up with you. Melina. I've kept quiet about it because I wasn't the one living here, and I understood you wanted to keep people's good opinion of you. But since we both know that's not how it happened, maybe it's time you at least acknowledge that for me, if no one else."

His anger was palpable. She felt the heat of it travel to her, adding to her own. "What do you mean, you didn't break up with me?"

"You think I did?"

What a ridiculous question. "Of course I do. I even have proof."

He sat up straight. "Okay."

"Okay, what?"

"Prove it."

"You don't know? Seriously?"

"If I knew, I wouldn't ask. You say you have proof. I want to see it."

She pushed herself up, her muscles bunched and taut. "I'll be happy to," she said, then she ran upstairs as her heart pounded.

The time had come.

Chapter 12

Rafe got up, as well, then didn't know what to do with himself, so he went into her kitchen and poured a glass of water, standing at the sink to drink it.

This hadn't been what he'd had in mind when he'd suggested they just talk tonight. He'd wanted to know about the past ten years. He'd wanted to know about her work. He hadn't wanted to dig into the painful ending of their relationship....

Except it had to come out sometime, and the no-strings-affair wasn't working. It wasn't enough. So, it was time to clear the air—even if it muddied the waters.

She came down the stairs and directly into

the kitchen, handing him a picture frame. But instead of a photograph inside it, there was a typed note, a letter from him to her.

Melina, I don't know any other way to get through to you. I've been patient long enough. You've made decisions without taking me into consideration, and that says it all to me. So, I give up. I'm done. You made your choice. Good luck with that. Rafe

He remembered every detail of the note now that he'd seen it again, reliving every emotion. Anger and betrayal surged through him anew as he realized what he held. "You framed it? You framed my note?"

She crossed her arms. "Darn right I did."

His jaw hurt, sending shards of pain down his body. "I see I was wrong. Your silence back then didn't say it all. *This* did." He handed it back to her, then walked toward her door, not looking back.

Suddenly she was there, behind him. "Oh, sure. Walk out. At least this time it's in person, not by letter."

He spun around, trying to rein in his temper. She'd framed his note. Of all the— "That letter was a damned sight more effort than you ever put in. The least you could have done was return my calls. Even just one call."

Her brows drew together. "What? When?"

"Oh, come on, Melina. Be honest, at least. I called for weeks."

"Only a couple of times."

Fury teemed in him. No one ever questioned his integrity. "Many times. Why would I lie to you? You didn't own a cell phone then, but I left messages. I talked with your grandfather. *You* never called me back. Not to tell me what was going on, or how your grandmother was doing, or even when you were coming back to school. Nothing."

She shook her head. "My grandfather would have told me. I only remember two calls."

"I *called.* A lot. Then when I gave up and sent you the letter, all you did was send me back the promise ring in the mail, with a note that just said *okay,* I might add."

She crossed her arms. "I was too hurt."

"You think I wasn't? I went through hell."

They stared at each other, tension crackling between them.

"I guess it shows how wrong we were for each other," she said, voicing aloud what he'd just figured out. "It would've ended at some point. Maybe not that soon or painfully, but sometime."

"Unlike you, I never saw my future without you in it," he said honestly. "You were all I wanted."

"You think I didn't feel the same? I applied to Michigan because of you. I didn't want to leave home, but, even more, I didn't want to leave you."

His gut clenched. "Why is this the first I'm hearing about that? Why didn't you tell me?"

She threw up her hands. "I was young and in love. You convinced me that it would be an adventure, and it was, but not in a good way for me. And, honestly, I would've made a lousy lawyer."

"So you grasped at the first opportunity to come back home instead of telling me, and letting us deal with it together?"

"I was eighteen years old! I'd been sheltered all my life, Rafe. I got scared. You were enjoying yourself, and I wasn't. I could see myself getting clingier all the time. You even made a comment about it."

Rafe thought back, recalling a vague memory that she'd become more and more dependent on him. "I didn't know it was that serious."

"I didn't know, either. I couldn't make sense of it. I just knew I was worried all the time. So, yes, I guess I did use my grandmother as an opportunity to come home again. But I loved you, and missed you."

I loved you. Past tense. He didn't know why it hurt so much to hear it put like that. "So you're saying you were too immature?"

"Without a doubt. Not that I acknowledged it then, but I've done so much soul searching since you came back. In retrospect, a lot has come clear to me. All these things I've just told you are new to me, too. I don't think I wanted to look back, and having you here forced me to."

He saw desperation in her eyes, as if willing him to understand. As if begging to be held, too, but he was careful not to touch her, not knowing how he felt now. He looked at the framed letter again, and the stab of pain returned in full force. She'd kept the damn letter—*framed.* Who did that?

"I need time to sort this out," he said and saw her retreat, not physically, but emotionally. "I know we'll see each other because of Elliot."

"Whatever." She turned away.

He had to go. Had to get away from…everything. He didn't even say goodbye, but left. Outside the cool air felt good against his skin. Too restless to go home, Rafe drove to

Red, hoping to catch his brother, not knowing his schedule for the week.

When there was no one up front to greet him, Rafe took a seat at the bar.

Wendy Fortune moseyed over. "It's a slow night. Marcos is running the bar as well as managing. He's in the kitchen, but he'll be out in a sec. Do you want something to eat?"

Did he? Even a drink didn't sound good, but he probably could use both. "How about a half order of nachos with chicken, please?"

"Sure thing." She grinned at Marcos over her shoulder as he reached the bar, then she headed for the kitchen, her hips twitching a little more evidently.

"When are you going to admit you've got a thing for her?" Rafe asked his brother as he pulled a cold draft.

"The day you admit you've still got a thing for Melina."

Rafe hesitated, then said, "Well, then you'd better start figuring out where to take Wendy on your first date."

Marcos said nothing, but his mouth tightened. He waited as Rafe took a long sip.

Rafe finally set down the glass. "Remember when you said I should give you something harder to figure out?" he asked his brother.

Marcos leaned both arms against the bar. "I do."

"Women, Marcos. I don't understand women."

"What's going on?"

"I don't want to talk about it. I just want words of wisdom. Go ahead, speak in generalities."

"Can't live with 'em. Can't live without sex. One of 'em has to give."

"You're not helpful."

"Give me specifics."

Wendy came up with his order of nachos. "Woman trouble, Rafe?" she asked, her eyes full of sympathy.

Rafe stared back.

She patted his hand. "You men have perfected the look. Hangdog, you know?"

Hangdog? Him? That made him straighten up. She patted his hand again, turned a sparkly gaze on Marcos for a minute then strode off, humming to the classical guitar music always playing in the background.

"Don't start," Marcos said. "Wendy and I had an argument right before you came in. She's impervious to criticism. She says no one has given her less than a twenty-percent tip, so she must be doing her job well."

"If no one's complained, why do you care?"

Marcos stared off in the direction she'd

gone. "Beats me. Something about her drives me crazy. But let's get back to you."

Rafe realized he needed to think things through for himself, not get feedback in generalities. He'd learned more about Melina in a couple of hours tonight than in the weeks they'd been seeing each other.

After a while he went home. Tonight they'd each revealed the truth as they'd seen it. Who was right? Both? Neither?

Did it even matter any more?

How did someone recover? Maybe it wasn't possible.

And maybe it was just time to accept that and move on.

Melina didn't sleep after he left, not well, anyway, or deeply. When her phone rang the next morning, she knew it would be him.

"I didn't sleep much," he said.

"Me, either."

A few unbearable seconds of silence followed, then, "I need to step away," he said, breaking her heart. "I want to move forward, Melina. A sex-only relationship with you isn't going to make that happen."

"I understand," she said, not really understanding. But it was her turn to give him space. Maybe it would turn out differently from when *she'd* needed space all those years ago. "I'll see you at the ballpark."

He didn't say anything, so she said, "Goodbye, Rafe," her throat aching and eyes burning.

"Bye."

"I love you," she whispered after she'd hung up. "I'll always love you." He was her mate, had always been her mate. It had taken time to see that, and some pain, too, but she couldn't deny the truth any longer. She loved him as a woman, not a girl. Forever. She wanted more than just sex, too.

She wouldn't settle for less.

Now she had to figure out how to win him back.

Chapter 13

When Melina arrived at her grandfather's house later that morning, he told her he was driving his truck, and she couldn't argue. He'd rigged a step device that let him to climb into the vehicle, then he could pull it into the cab and stow it in the backseat.

Melina settled into the passenger seat, Rafe still on her mind.

"What's got your ears floppin', missy?" her grandfather asked as he started the engine.

"I'm okay."

"Nope. I've seen the signs before. I'd say it's man trouble."

The way he said it, dragging out the word "man," made her laugh. "Maybe it's lack-of-man trouble," she said. "As in, being twenty-nine years old and not having a man."

"Maybe. Doubt it, but maybe." He navigated his driveway and started up the street. His truck was an automatic, so he didn't have to use a clutch. Melina wasn't sure he could have.

"Been a while since I drove ol' Trigger," he said. "I forgot how heavy-handed he is."

"You're the only man I know who doesn't refer to his vehicle as a she."

"Some vehicles are *shes*. Some aren't. This one's reliable and powerful. Can't be female."

Melina laughed again, the knots in her stomach loosening. "Do you feel ready for your driving test?"

"Don't have much choice, do I? It's two days off. Now or never. And I sure don't want somebody having to take me grocery shopping or whatever forever. Wouldn't feel like much of a man then, that's for sure."

"We all wish you'd take Mom and Dad up on their offer to have you live with them."

"Everyone except your mom and dad." He gave her a sly glance. "Oh, sure, they offered. What decent son and daughter-in-law wouldn't? But they've only had an empty nest for a year. They're still on their second honeymoon."

Melina hadn't thought of it like that. "You're very wise."

"Supposed to be by now. Your grandma accused me of arrested development for a long time, but I think I finally grew up."

He reached the downtown, where traffic was a little more congested and he had to make decisions rather than just drive. He was doing better than when he drove her car. Maybe it was the familiarity.

"Want to head to San Antonio?" she asked. "You should probably get some freeway time in."

"I know my limitations. I'll drive in Red Rock but no farther. No sense tempting fate."

She wondered what had gotten into him. He was much more mellow today, was even seeing his future clearly. Maybe driving his truck again had been enough to restore his confidence.

He pulled into the grocery store parking lot. "I need a few things. Okay with you?"

"You can use your hour however you want to, Gramps."

He aimed for a space close to the front of the store, then shut off the engine. Before she opened her door, she said, "Did Rafe come to see you?"

"No. Why would he?"

After a minute she shrugged. She'd hoped Rafe had come to the same conclusions she had during the night, especially once she'd calmed down enough to realize that he wouldn't lie to her. If he said he'd called, he had.

"Something you want to talk about, missy?"

Her heart started to pound hard, but she had to know. "When I was living with you and Grandma, did Rafe call me? Did he leave messages?"

"'Course he did. I told you."

"More than twice?" she asked, although she didn't think his answer would surprise her much.

He stared out the windshield. "Maybe a few more. But you specifically told me you didn't want to talk to him."

"Not forever. I just needed some time to adjust." She'd known that Rafe would try to talk her out of staying. She hadn't wanted to argue with him. She'd had enough on her plate.

"How was I supposed to know that?" Gramps asked.

She looked him in the eye, saying nothing, accusing him but also acknowledging her own part in what had happened.

"Okay," he said. "I didn't want you to leave us. I couldn't help Rose on my own. I figured

you'd hightail it back to school—and Rafe—
as soon as you could. I know it was wrong."

"You think?" She thought of the framed
letter, and humiliation washed over her. She'd
been such a fool. She hadn't trusted him. How
differently things would've turned out if she'd
talked to him.

And yet, maybe not. He was right that she'd
never called him, but had selfishly waited for
him to do the calling—and then had thought
he hadn't bothered. Maybe talking wouldn't
have made any difference at all. She hadn't
wanted to face the truth—that she didn't want
to go back to college.

They'd both been so young and foolish,
with no life experience yet, no romantic experience except with each other.

"Are you and Rafe fighting because of what
I did?" Gramps asked. "I'll go to him. Talk
to him."

"No." She tempered the harsh word with,
"Please don't. Promise you won't. This is between Rafe and me. Period." What her grandfather had done was part of the problem but
not all of it.

He look relieved. "I can promise you that."

He spent the rest of his hour making nice to
her, even being cooperative about following
her directions to take a different route home,

seeing if he could do it without getting lost. He did fine.

When they reached his house, everything was okay between them again.

"You're a good girl. Thank you for helping me," he said.

"My pleasure, Gramps." She kissed him goodbye and went on to see Big John, hoping he was in as mellow a mood as her grandfather. She really didn't feel like coaxing him today. She had too much on her mind. For example, now that she knew the truth about what had kept her and Rafe apart, what difference did it make? She'd already come to realize that they were both vastly different people now. Maybe they would've been like June and Wade, getting a divorce, having outgrown each other.

Time would tell.

Later that afternoon Rafe met Debbie Anderson in the sports complex parking lot as usual. Elliot hopped out of her car.

"Hi, Rafe Mendoza!" he shouted as he ran around the rear of the car.

"Please tell Melina we talked to him," Debbie said. "Keep reinforcing the fact he needs to remember he's on a team and they're counting on him, okay?"

"Got it. Hey, sport," Rafe said to Elliot, who smiled more spontaneously than Rafe had ever seen. "All set?"

"Ready, set, go!"

"Bye, sweetie," Debbie called out.

"Bye. Let's go, Rafe Mendoza."

"Here comes Melina. We always wait for each other, remember?" Rafe didn't know what he could say to her. The fact she hadn't believed that he'd called her so many times weighed heavy. He'd thought they had a relationship based on trust. Everything he'd been learning lately indicated there was no truth to that. She'd never told him how she felt, how much she'd hated college. He didn't understand why she didn't feel she could tell him.

The problem was—he still wanted her. His need hadn't diminished since he was fourteen years old. He should have gotten past that by now. He could control everything else in his life except his desire for her.

It's one of those relationships that's only physical, he decided. No more, no less. And physical could be conquered, although probably only by not being around her. Which was impossible, given their connection through Elliot.

"Hi, guys," Melina said, a little too brightly, as she jogged up to them, her gaze on Elliot.

"Let's play," Elliot said. "Can I go to the field myself?"

Because he would be in their line of sight the whole time, there was no reason not to let him run, to be like the other boys—except it would leave Rafe and Melina alone. "Sure," Rafe said, not willing to deny Elliot's request. "We'll catch up."

Elliot took off running, not a smooth lope but a determined one. He'd already matured just in a few weeks.

Rafe and Melina walked silently side by side. He had nothing to say.

After a minute Melina said, "If you want to go ahead, feel free."

"Thanks." Relieved, he took off running. They had only two more team practices before opening day. He needed to focus on Elliot now. Only Elliot.

"Trouble in paradise?" Beau asked as Rafe reached home plate, where Beau stood, watching the boys warm up but obviously aware of tension between Rafe and Melina.

Rafe ignored him, peripherally aware of her settling in the dugout, where she pulled her cap low and tossed a ball into her glove, again and again and again, her usual activity during practice, even though she'd created a solid pocket in her glove by now.

"We need to talk about the boy," Beau said, bringing Rafe to attention.

"What about him?"

"It doesn't look to me like he'll be ready next week."

Rafe watched Elliot doing stretches with the rest of the team, his expression serious. Single-minded. "He'll be ready. And you need his bat. He's the best hitter you've got."

"He also has to play defense for at least a couple of innings every game."

"He's working hard, Beau. Give him a shot."

"I need to win. You know that."

"You need to have a heart, too. Just playing is a win for Elliot."

Beau crossed his arms. He looked at the boys, not Rafe. "The other kids haven't taken to him."

"I know. Relating is a tough skill for him. But I've seen some changes, and expect there will be more."

"We'll see."

Rafe started to walk away when Beau said, "It really was an accident, me hitting him. Because of my injury. I didn't want to admit it was hindering my game, even at this level."

Rafe wasn't feeling sympathetic at this point. "Yeah? Well, don't use a kid as your scapegoat again." He leaned close, tired of his life spinning out of control, needing to take action, to do something. "If you deny Elliot the right to play, you can expect to see us in court. I'll file a civil suit so fast your head will spin. Wouldn't be good PR, either, no matter how it ended."

Rafe didn't feel any better for having chewed out Beau. Maintaining his cool was something that Rafe had gotten good at. Really good at. For all his good intentions, he wasn't moving forward, wasn't finding peace. It had all been made worse overnight, it seemed.

And there she sat in the dugout, a visible reminder of the havoc one woman could wreak on a man's life.

He needed to do something about that.

Melina barely watched the practice. She jabbed at the dirt floor with the toes of her sneakers, kicking up dust.

"Someone's not happy." June took a seat beside Melina, eyeing her thoughtfully.

The last thing Melina wanted was for the town crier to have more gossip to spread. "Just restless. I wish I could be out on the field."

June's brows went up.

"I know," Melina said with a sigh. "In high school I was the world's biggest klutz. I've been helping Rafe work with Elliot. Sometimes I can even catch a fly ball." She smiled at the memory of her one catch, which had taken everyone by surprise—all of her family and Rafe's, who'd been recruited to help act as a team.

"That *would* be newsworthy," June said, grinning.

"Ha-ha. So, are you still working on the story about Beau?"

"Yes. I've been able to take my time because the editor isn't running it until the season opens next week. He decided to put out a special issue just about Red Rock baseball. I've got most of the bylines."

"Good for you, June."

"You know what I've learned? There are four kids known to have Asperger's playing on various teams."

Melina did know that. Two of them were Q's patients, but since they didn't have Beau as a coach, they didn't have as much to prove, plus they'd all played ball before. Just as important, they'd been living in town when registration closed, which seemed to be key to Beau.

"I'd like to do a story about it, but I've

run up against total resistance from all the parents. Which I understand," June added quickly. "The kids don't want to be seen as different. But I was thinking maybe I could do a story on you, and incorporate information about autism and Asperger's."

"My partner is the one to talk to. It's his specialty. I work mostly with stroke and accident victims—and also the elderly who want to continue to live alone. *That* would be a good story, I think. Timely. There's a huge, aging population trying to figure out how to stay independent."

"Let me run it by my editor. Sounds good to me."

They sat side by side without talking for a while.

"So, Rafe got ticked at me for doing a little online speculation that you two were back together," June said, "but you haven't said anything."

Her sister Stephanie had been the first to point out the item to Melina, but not the last. She hadn't taken the bait. "We're not back together." Melina could say that honestly now. "Elliot's a team endeavor, that's all."

"Yeah, I heard that Rafe didn't leave town this week, as usual. I wondered if that would hurt his business."

Leave town? Melina didn't want to seem ignorant, but she had no idea what June meant. "It's nice to be your own boss."

"But it doesn't really matter, does it? You're still always working for someone."

Melina couldn't disagree with her.

June fidgeted. "So, the reason I asked about Rafe is that I didn't want to step on any toes. I'll be honest, Melina. He interests me."

Dread filled Melina's body from top to toe. She felt frozen in place. "I thought you were interested in Beau."

"He's pretty messed up. Rafe's got his head on straight. And he likes kids, which is important, since I've got two."

Melina hesitated, then said, "You know, I've heard from a whole lot of people that you should take a little time for yourself when a relationship ends. Time to heal."

"I'm not looking for serious. Just someone to hang out with."

Well, Rafe's looking for serious, Melina thought. He's ready to get married and start a family. So it wasn't really fair of June to—

She stopped the thought cold. Rafe was a big boy. He could take care of himself, make up his mind just fine on his own.

She searched the field for him, spotted him hunkered down in front of Elliot, talking to him, Elliot nodding back. Maybe Rafe *had* agreed to help because of her, as he'd said, but he was fully invested in the outcome now, and their common cause would keep them tied together for the two months of baseball season, so there was no hope of breaking all contact.

I want him. Need him. Love him. The words hammered her brain. She couldn't bear for June—or anyone else—to have him. She couldn't give up. Now that she knew the truth about what had kept them apart, now that they'd both grown up and knew their own minds better, it could be so different for them. Not sex only, but the whole deal.

She watched him running beside Elliot, encouraging him. What a wonderful father he would make—

What if she took a different tack altogether? What if instead of trying to avoid him, she put herself squarely in front of him at every opportunity? What if she acted as if nothing had happened between them? What if she became superfriend? Dazzle him with confusion.

She felt laughter bubble inside her. She wouldn't mind seeing him confused by an all-out assault of happiness.

She took a quick look at June, who had suddenly become the competition. Melina was up for a little competition, needed some, actually. Her life had become static, going nowhere. She went to work each day, then met Rafe secretly at night. What had that resulted in? Great sex? Sure. What else?

Not much. But they hadn't given it a chance, either, beyond her bedroom.

So before she gave up altogether, she needed to give it one last shot—on her own terms.

With a little luck, he would never know what hit him. She'd given up on him before. He deserved to know she didn't want to give up now. He could make up his mind from there.

She laughed then, feeling good, feeling free of all the pressures of the past weeks. She'd already survived losing him once. She could do it again, if she had to.

But this time she planned to win.

Chapter 14

Five days later, Melina and her mother were slicing tomatoes and onions for the hamburgers that her father was grilling on the patio. It was Elliot's last day of training in her family's backyard, and they were feeding thirteen people—everyone who'd been helping form a practice team.

However, this day was different from the rest. It was all for fun. Melina knew that Rafe's goal was to get Elliot to loosen up, to laugh, deciding that would help him more in the long run.

Melina hoped so. Tomorrow would be the final team practice, when Beau would make his decision, and the next day, his first game, if he passed muster.

"You look happy," Patsy Lawrence said to her daughter.

"I am happy, Mom," Melina answered. She'd barely stopped smiling for days. Rafe was utterly confused. Melina loved it. "Elliot's in the home stretch, Gramps passed his driver's test, Q and I both have full caseloads. Life's good."

"You didn't mention Rafe." Patsy pulled a head of lettuce apart and rinsed the leaves. "Is he part of your happiness quotient?"

"He's the unknown-X factor."

Patsy eyed her. "That's the first time you haven't denied there was something between you."

"Because hope triumphs over reality."

Her mother seemed to let that sink in. "So, you want something to happen, but it's not happening?"

"Yet."

Patsy laid a hand on Melina's arm. "Haven't you been hurt enough?"

"Things are different this time, Mom." She had already decided not to tell her parents what Gramps had done. That was then, and this is now. "There's really no one else for me but Rafe."

"Of course there is, honey. There are a lot of people in this big world we can love."

"Rafe's my mate. For life."

"Does he know that? Does he feel the same?"

"Deep inside, yes." She just had to mine down that far. Drill past the barriers. "But don't worry. I'm not being patient. I'm going for it. It's now or never."

She would've made more progress by now, too, except that he'd left town for the weekend. She'd had a moment's ridiculous worry that he'd gone away with June, then she'd seen June at the grocery store. Melina hadn't really believed he would jump into a situation like that right away, anyway, but sometimes the heart asked questions instead of the head. The point was, she was determined not to live with regrets for not trying.

"You're *chasing* him?" Patsy asked, sounding appalled.

"I seem to remember a story you told me once about how you had to chase Dad to catch him. And don't you dare say that was different. The approach may be different, and the particular circumstances, but the goal is the same. I want to marry him. I want children with him." Every time she drove by the old Crockett building they'd decided years ago to buy, she wanted a life with him even more.

It was a small building but it loomed large to her for what it represented.

And at Angie's wedding reception, he'd wondered why it hadn't been demolished by now.

Maybe ten years had passed, and maybe they'd both changed, sought different career paths, but they were at their cores the same people with the same values. They both worked hard, cared about others, wanted a family of their own. Even if old buildings didn't mean the same thing to both of them.

Melina heard her mother sigh.

"What can I do to help?" Patsy asked.

Smiling, Melina hugged her. "Try to keep Dad calm when I openly flirt with Rafe."

"Oh, sure. Give me the easy job."

Melina laughed.

"Ready out here!" her father called from the porch. "You ready in there?"

"Tell everyone to come wash up!" Patsy called back.

As people cleaned up and were walking back outside, they were given something to carry. Two picnic tables and a few extra chairs were enough to hold everyone—all of Melina's family, Rafe's and Elliot's. Elliot's mother had made cupcakes decorated to look like baseballs. Lemonade flowed, as did conversation and laughter.

Melina carried her plate to where Rafe sat with his brothers and father and took the empty seat next to him, bumping shoulders as she settled in.

"Mind if I sit here?" she asked Rafe, after the fact, smiling at his family then at him.

He subtly maneuvered his body away from hers enough not to touch. "Make yourself at home."

The dry way he said it made her laugh. When she made eye contact with Marcos, he grinned, too.

"Food's good," she said, digging into her potato salad.

"I haven't been to a family barbecue in a long time," Marcos said. "As good as the food at Red tastes, nothing beats a homemade burger. So, how was the trip to Ann Arbor?" he asked Rafe.

"Productive."

He'd gone to Michigan? Was that what June had been talking about? Did he take a "usual trip" to Ann Arbor? Was there a woman—

"I'm closing up my office there," he added. "I can fly up occasionally, if necessary, but there's little I can't do by phone and email.

Teleconferencing is easy these days, even with video. Saves us all time and money."

Melina let the conversation drift around her, piecing together the facts. Apparently, before he'd moved home, he'd promised three companies in Ann Arbor he would spend a week every month in town. It was easy to figure out that he hadn't gone north for a week this month because of his commitment to Elliot, one that would continue for two more months.

He hadn't said a word about it, hadn't even hinted at it. He'd accepted Beau's rules, knowing he wouldn't be able to meet his other obligations, the ones that paid him.

After dinner, Rafe's brother Javier played guitar and sang, joined by Melina's grandfather. They sang old cowboy songs, bringing back childhood memories for Melina, who still sat next to Rafe.

"There's room over here with us," her father said, patting an empty spot on the bench next to him.

"I'm good, thanks," Melina said. Her mother whispered in his ear. He frowned, looked at Melina then Rafe and frowned a little more, but he didn't repeat the offer the rest of the night.

Rafe's back was to her as they listened to

the music. She ached to lean against him, to slip her arms around him. Instead she just leaned close enough that her breath would dust his neck when she spoke. "They're really good together, Gramps and Javier. Who would've guessed it?"

He looked over his shoulder. "Good thing you and I aren't singing."

She laughed. Neither of them could carry a tune.

It seemed like an easy summer evening, yet it was late March and a school night for Elliot. His parents took him home under protest, then the others started drifting away, too. Kitchen cleanup went fast. Melina expected Rafe to have left by the time she was done with the dishes, but he still sat in the backyard with his father.

"I'd forgotten how nice these family events are," his father said. "Elena always planned our parties. I miss them."

"I'll get a barbecue up and running soon, Dad," Rafe said.

"Thank you. You are a good son, Rafe. A good man."

A moment of silence followed as Rafe reached for his father's hand and squeezed. Melina felt like an intruder into their private moment, but then his father stood.

"Well, this old man needs his sleep. Good night." He made his way across the yard to the driveway and disappeared.

Rafe and Melina were alone. She wondered why her father wasn't hovering, then decided her mother was probably making him stay inside.

"This was nice," he said.

"Yes."

"You seem to be doing okay, Melina."

She smiled. "I am." She decided not to ask if he was okay, too, but to let him tell her what he wanted to. She'd found a storehouse of patience within her determination to have him again. "So, tomorrow we find out if Beau will allow Elliot to play," she said. She rested her arm on the table, her hand an inch from his. She could almost feel him. Almost.

"I'm not worried about it," he said, looking at their hands then back at her.

"Do you think Beau's going to let him play?" she asked.

"I do."

"I know Elliot's come a long way, but he still has a lot of trouble in the field." She felt Rafe's fingertips brush hers—or had they? It might have been wishful thinking on her part. "His catching has improved, but he can't throw the ball in far or straight."

"He needs more practice, that's all." He moved back a little. "June came to see me."

Her hopeful mood made a U-turn. "Oh?"

"She wanted me to represent her in her divorce."

"Oh, really?" Melina couldn't keep the sarcasm out of her voice. So *that* was how June was playing it? Everyone knew Rafe didn't do family law. "Are you going to?"

"No. Not my specialty, although that hasn't stopped some other people from seeking me out lately. Like you."

Melina couldn't get a handle on him. Was he trying to entice her with elusive touches, or was that a diversion while he talked to her about another woman?

"Technically, *Angie* did that," Melina said, starting to cross her arms, then remembering her goal was to win him back. "I never would have."

"Things have a way of working out. It was an interesting conversation with June, however. Apparently she has your blessing to ask me out."

Well, how...blatant of the woman. "All I did was tell her no, that we weren't together."

"Do you think I'd be interested in a woman newly separated from her husband, Melina? A man I consider a friend, by the way."

"Did you hear what I just said? I only answered her question. No, we aren't together." She made herself seem unperturbed by the conversation. She even smiled. "I think you and I have both learned the hard way that honesty's the best policy, and all that."

"Plus, you knew I wouldn't be interested in June."

Which wasn't entirely true. "No, I didn't. I don't know what kind of woman you go for these days. Other than for sex, that is."

She waited for several long seconds for him to respond, but all he did was stand. "I should get going."

She walked with him, grabbing her purse from the back stairs where she'd left it. Her car was in the driveway. His was at the curb. They stopped next to her driver's door.

"You're up to something," he said.

"I am?" Her smile widened.

"The Cheshire-cat grin doesn't fool me. I know you too well."

If he knew her that well, he would know she'd fallen in love with him again. He would know that her heart and future were in his hands. "I'm just being myself."

He stared into her eyes, murmured goodnight, then walked away, hardly making a sound.

She felt instantly lonely.

And just a little bit more hopeful than she had this morning.

Rafe hurled his mitt into his trunk, slammed the lid shut then climbed into his car, all the while watching Melina back out of the driveway then take off down the road. He could almost hear her whistling happily as she went.

He'd had a hell of a week.

First had been his decision to step back from Melina, then his threat to take Beau to court if he didn't leave Elliot on the team. Then June had put the moves on him, leaving him in the awkward position of turning her down when she was most vulnerable. And then he'd had to ask for a weekend meeting with his Michigan clients to tell them he wouldn't be as available as he'd been. To top it all off, his flight home had been delayed for six hours, so he'd barely had any sleep last night.

And now Melina was changing right before his eyes. She was way too…happy. Like the Melina he used to know, not the one he'd met since he came back. Apparently, ending their relationship was a good thing for her.

He wanted her more than ever.

Rafe had to drive by her house on the way

to his. He could see her taillights ahead of him and slowed to a crawl as she parked and walked toward her courtyard, turning at the last minute, staring in his direction, lifting a hand in a tentative wave.

He took off, angry at himself. What would she think? That he was stalking her?

He was too tired. Too confused. Too much in demand. He needed to slow his pace, his goal when he'd first come home. He needed to make some life decisions, too.

Rafe headed for his shower as soon as he got home. He stood under the spray, his hands pressed to the wall, water pounding his neck and shoulders...missing her.

He'd been missing the Melina he'd seen tonight, the bright, infectious woman he'd fallen in love with. That Melina hadn't made many appearances the past few weeks. Sexy, yes. Dedicated, yes. But the woman who'd loved life and lived it so joyously had been AWOL since...

Since Ann Arbor, ten years ago.

He had noticed she wasn't happy when they'd started college, but he'd chalked it up to being homesick, to the pressures of college courses. He hadn't looked deeper than that because he hadn't wanted to. He'd been having fun. His world had expanded in immeasurable ways. Hers had narrowed.

He hadn't paid attention.

Tonight she'd been the girl who'd graduated from high school with him, fun and flirtatious, but now also independent. That was what was different. She'd been dependent on him at college, for companionship, for studying together, for social connections—totally unlike the Melina of high school.

And now? Now she was like that Melina, but more. So much more. Since they'd started their secret relationship he hadn't been looking at the big picture, but pieces of it. Sex had blurred the lines too much.

Rafe turned off the shower, dried off, then dragged himself to bed, the lost sleep from the previous night catching up.

But as he lay in bed he realized something critical had happened tonight—his doubts about the future had dimmed. He'd needed forward momentum, something to drive him, instead of just spinning his wheels.

He'd needed to break up with Melina in order to start over.

He'd done that. Now he only needed a new plan.

It was as simple—and complicated—as that.

Chapter 15

Melina arrived at the final practice the next day earlier than usual, intent on advancing her plan to change Rafe's mind. She sat in her car, watching the parking lot entrance, waiting for him to arrive, optimistic about seeing him again.

He didn't show. Nor did Elliot.

Worried, she called Rafe's phone but only got his voice mail. Frantic, she got out of her car and jogged to the field, her heart in her throat. Where could they be? How could both of them not show up? Practice started in two minutes. They were always there ten minutes before it began.

She clenched her phone, ready to call Elliot's parents, then spotted the boy in right field. Rafe stood about twenty feet away.

Relieved, she slowed down. Then annoyance hit her full force. He had to have known she would notice his car wasn't there, since the three of them always waited for each other to walk down to the field together.

So much for optimism. Apparently all bets were off. Not only did he have no interest in working things out, he didn't even care about the friendship anymore.

Melina sank onto the bench in the dugout. It was the last place she wanted to be, especially when Beau moseyed over and leaned a shoulder against the dugout post. "So, Melina, I have it on good authority that you and Rafe aren't dating," he said casually.

That *good authority* probably being June, Melina thought. "We never said we were."

"Did you know there are bets being placed around town about you?"

She jumped up. "What?"

"Yep." He looked out over the field thoughtfully, then zeroed in on her, taking a long look at her standing there, flustered beyond speech. "A couple of 'em. One's for when you go out in public together for the first time. One's for when you get engaged."

She couldn't speak. They'd been so careful, too. Damn June Adams. She had to be the source of it all.

"Cat got your tongue, Melina?"

"It's too ridiculous to comment on."

"Uh-huh. That's why you sprang out of your seat like a rocket, and your face is bright red." He cocked his head. "How's that saying go? The lady protests too much?"

She fumed silently, needing to protect her own image, but also protecting Elliot, whose future was in Beau's hands today. Today, of all days, wasn't the time to irritate him.

His grin was wide and leisurely. "By the way, I've invested in both pools, but I picked the same day for them to happen. Tomorrow. Don't let me down, okay?" He touched the brim of his cap and strode back out to where the team was gathered, waiting for him to fire his opening salvo about this being the last practice, the last chance to ask questions or improve a skill.

Melina made herself calm down enough to watch the practice, because it was the most important one of Elliot's young career. She found herself holding her breath as each grounder came toward him. He missed all of them.

Come on, Elliot, shine. Please shine, she urged him silently. Rafe seemed sure that he would make the team, but Melina thought Beau was a loose cannon, given to overreaction and delusions of grandeur. So she sat in the dugout, knees bouncing, fingers laced and numb from squeezing, her heart lodged in her throat.

Elliot got up to bat four times, connecting three times, and openly unhappy at himself for missing the fourth, drawing the gazes of the other kids by kicking the dirt and muttering to himself. However, Rafe called Elliot's name then gave him a run of hand signals, and he straightened his shoulders and went to stand next to his teammates waiting to bat, encouraging them by clapping, as the rest of the boys did.

Tears filled her eyes. How far he'd come. How very far. And it was all thanks to Rafe. She couldn't take any credit, nor could Beau as coach. Everything Elliot had learned about baseball, except for hitting, had come from Rafe.

Melina finally relaxed, her thoughts heading in a different direction. She wondered if Rafe knew about the bets.

She also wondered how many people had actually put money on them. She wished she found it funny, but mostly it was humiliating. Especially if she and Rafe didn't work things out—which looked more like a possibility now than it had before the practice started. Why hadn't he called and let her know he wouldn't be meeting her in the parking lot?

A total change in routine generally meant something.

As the practice wrapped up, Melina started winding up again, too. She was irritated at Rafe and annoyed at Beau—well, the whole town, actually, or at least those who'd placed bets on her and Rafe's hearts. Because that was what was happening—people were betting on whether or not she and Rafe would find love again—or break each other's hearts again.

Practice ended. She joined the team and coaches for their final pep talk. After, Beau pulled Rafe aside and said something privately to him. Rafe shook his hand, then started walking to the parking lot, inviting her along with his gaze.

"Elliot's all set for the big game tomorrow," Rafe said.

She wanted to whoop, jump and do the happy dance, but she couldn't, since Elliot hadn't known he might not be allowed to play. Nor could she hug him, because that kind of physical contact made him squirm.

"I'm looking forward to the game myself,"

she said. "Elliot, you've worked really hard. I'm so proud of you."

He grinned. They reached the parking lot.

"Where's your car?" she asked Rafe, trying to keep her cool.

"At home. I walked. Needed to blow off steam."

"And you didn't think to let me know of your change?" Okay, maybe she wasn't being so cool now.

He raised his brows. "It didn't occur to me. You found us."

"You always wait. Or I wait. We go together."

"I'm sor—"

"Did you know people have placed bets on us?" she asked, interrupting his apology, everything coming to a head for her.

He glanced at Elliot, who'd turned around and gave them a worried look. "I did hear that, yes," Rafe said quietly.

"You *knew?* And you didn't bother to tell me? How could you not tell me? I found out from *Beau,* of all—"

"Stop it," Elliot said, putting his hands over his ears. "Stop yelling."

She hadn't been yelling. In fact, her voice was barely raised, but he, like many Asperger's kids, got sensory overload quickly, especially from sound. And especially when that sound was an argument, not a cheer.

He didn't wait for her apology but raced ahead to where his mother waited in the parking lot.

"What's wrong?" Debbie asked as Elliot stormed past her to climb right into the car and jerk the door shut. "Was there a problem? Did he not make—" She put a hand to her mouth.

"He's in," Rafe said immediately. "He made it. Melina and I were having a disagreement, and he got uncomfortable. I apologize."

"Me, too," Melina said. "It had nothing to do with Elliot, or even baseball. All my fault."

"Heavens, Melina." Debbie hugged her hard. "He hears us argue. It's another life lesson."

"Well, he needs to hear people apologize, too," Melina said, then opened the car door. He was already buckled in and staring out the windshield. "I'm sorry I raised my voice, Elliot. I'm sorry it made you uncomfortable."

He gave her a quick glance. "It's okay."

"Thank you. I'll see you tomorrow for the game. Would you mind if my family come? And probably Rafe's? Everyone would like to cheer your team on."

He thought about it for a few seconds. "That would be okay."

"Great. I'll see you then." She closed the door.

"Big day tomorrow," Debbie said.

"A very big day. He's ready," Rafe said.

Debbie hugged them both. "Thank you so much." She waved, hopped in the car and drove off.

"I'm sorry you were worried," Rafe said right away. "But, really, Melina, don't you think you overreacted?"

Of course she had. Her emotions were bubbling, her thinking not clear. Overreacting was par for the course under those circumstances. But she didn't like how paternal he'd just sounded, either.

Plus, she should've been on his mind. When it came down to it, *that* was what bothered her most.

"I can see where you might think that," she said, lifting her chin.

He smiled. "We're at an impasse about this. Can we just let it go?"

She didn't want to let it go. She should've been on his mind! But before she could find a point to argue, he said, "You've been at all the practices. What do you think? Is Elliot ready?"

"Skillwise, I know he still has a lot to learn,

which he will. But it's his self-control that's impressed me. What were the gestures you made when he was about ready to blow his top?"

"A reminder to calm down. I discovered he loves when the coaches give their run of hand signals when they're at bat. The more complicated, the better. He learned them faster and more consistently than the other boys, frankly. I added a couple just for him, but I bury them in decoy signals just for fun."

She clamped her mouth shut and contemplated him for a few long seconds. "Do you ever do anything wrong, Rafe?"

"What's that supposed to mean?"

"It's a simple question. You never seem to make a misstep. You say the right things. You sacrifice for a boy you don't know. You take care of your father."

He leaned close. "I make love pretty well, too."

She caught fire just from his words and the way he said them. "You're not exactly humble."

"See? Not perfect. My fatal flaw. Are you happy now?"

No. No, she wasn't happy. She'd thought she was getting there last night, but now she felt miserable. *You forgot about me,* she wanted to shout at him, but he'd already decided it was no big deal. Trying to convince him that it *was* a big deal would be useless. As far as he was concerned, they'd broken up. He wasn't obligated to do anything for her.

Disheartened at the thought, she said, "I should get going."

"Me, too." He was entirely too cheerful. "See you."

Off he went, leaving her with her teeth clenched and her irritation still brewing. So this was how it was going to be with them? He no longer sees when she's upset? And she gets upset easily?

This would require some thinking on her part.

She headed for her car then spotted Beau on his way to the office building. "Beau! Wait up."

She reached him quickly. "I just wanted to thank you for including Elliot on the team. It means a lot to all of us."

He lifted his cap and scratched his head. "Well, Melina, I don't think the boy's up to speed, but I can't fight city hall, you know? I've got a lot on the line here. I couldn't afford the press."

"What do you mean, you can't fight city hall? What press?"

"Rafe left you out of the loop? Well, isn't that interesting. Okay, then, I'm happy to tell you. He threatened me with a civil suit if I didn't leave the boy on the team. I can't afford a lawsuit, financially or professionally." He walked away, then turned back. "Rafe's got the kid under control, so you can sit in the stands during the game, if you want, instead of the dugout—or don't even show up, if you don't want to."

He left, his stride taking him a long distance in a brief time, as she stood watching him, thinking about what he'd said. When had Rafe threatened him? Yet another thing he hadn't discussed with her.

She got in her car and headed home, then spotted him walking down Main. She pulled over, lowered the window. "Want a ride?"

"I'm good, thanks." He kept walking so that she had to move slowly alongside him.

"I'd like to talk to you, Rafe."

"You're just going to chew me out. I'll pass."

She frowned. Today was the first time she'd been openly angry at him. She didn't think it was fair for him to act as if it was something she did all the time.

"I have things to tell you," she called out to him. "Need to tell you. Especially about my grandfather."

"I figured it out. It doesn't matter, Melina. Nothing from the past matters."

Blood drained from her head so that she was a little dizzy, because it did matter to her. The past and the present mattered.

And certainly the future.

When a car honked behind her, she picked up speed, but she didn't go home. Instead she drove to his home and pulled in the driveway. She was sitting on his front porch when he came up.

He eyed her, took out his keys and unlocked the door without saying anything, although he did leave the door open.

"I haven't seen your house yet," she said, following him inside, but he was already out of sight. She followed sounds until she found him in the kitchen, his head in the refrigerator.

He tossed her a Coke, got a second one for himself. "Want some chips and salsa?" he asked.

"Sure." She sat at the counter, popped open her soda and took a sip. His kitchen was gorgeous, all stainless steel and granite, maple cabinets and beautiful tile.

"What do you think?" he asked, setting bowls on the counter, taking the seat beside her.

"Money well spent."

He clinked cans with her and took a long drink, then set down the can. "So."

"So?"

"You have things to say, I guess."

He seemed amused. And calm. And...tolerant. "Gramps admitted—"

"In the past. Choose another topic," he said.

She pursed her lips. "Beau told me you threatened him with a lawsuit."

"I did. Next question?"

Meaning, that was all he would say on the matter. Actually, Melina kind of admired him for that. He'd dealt with a situation that needed to be dealt with. Action did speak louder than words.

"Why didn't you tell me about the betting pool?" she asked.

"I figured it would tick you off."

"You decided I didn't need to know something that...infamous about myself?"

"I found out the day after we'd broken things off. I figured it wouldn't be relevant."

"After *you'd* broken things off," she said.

"I stand corrected."

She couldn't get a handle on him. He didn't seem happy she was there, but he also didn't seem angry. She finally just ran out of steam. He hadn't responded in a way that furthered their conversation. Now she was stuck sitting at his kitchen counter with nothing to say. She dipped a chip in some salsa and ate, the crunch sounding cannon-fire loud. So did he. They went through the bowl of chips without conversation. Then she was at a loss.

"I guess I should go," she said.

"Would you like to see the rest of the house?"

She still couldn't figure out his mood. He hadn't touched her, but hadn't given her the cold shoulder, either. "Yes, I would, thanks."

The tour didn't take long. He hadn't invested in dining room furniture yet, and had only a few pieces in the living room, wanting to wait until they'd finished repairing, staining and painting. His home office held only a desk and chair.

Upstairs, two bedrooms were empty and in sore need of fresh paint and window coverings. Another bedroom was furnished so that his father could stay overnight. Then came the master bedroom, which was remodeled and spectacular, the headboard tall and hand carved, the bedding colorful and inviting.

"I tore down the wall between this room and a bedroom beside it to make the master bath and walk-in closet," he said, letting her peek into both spaces. "Come see the view out the back window."

From there she could take in his entire backyard, a sprawling mess.

"I've lined up a crew to relandscape," he said. "They start next week. But picture this—a big deck with built-in barbecue right off the house. A swimming pool and spa over there. Lots of lawn."

"A place for a vegetable garden?" she asked. "And a dog or two?"

"It wouldn't be a home without them."

If Melina stayed in his bedroom for one more minute she would haul him off to his king-size bed and have her way with him.

He looked at his watch. "I've got a meeting I need to get ready for."

Just like that her decision was made. Or rather, taken away. She should be grateful, but...

"I'll see you at the game tomorrow," she said, even though the words hurt as they dragged along her throat. He'd been able to turn off the attraction switch way too easily.

They walked downstairs together. He opened the front door, held it as she passed by him. He didn't follow her to the car, but also didn't shut the door until she'd backed out and waved goodbye.

If his intention had been to let her know he was over her, he'd succeeded. He'd been nice—a horrible word, in this case. He'd invited her in, gave her food and drink, took her on a tour, then sent her on her way, all of it done in a nice, polite way.

She'd never been more discouraged in her life.

Sometimes what was broken couldn't be fixed—like this relationship. Giving up was foreign to her, but it looked as though she had to. He hadn't wanted to hear any details about Gramps. He'd already given up.

And there was no changing Rafe Mendoza's mind once it was made up.

Chapter 16

The last day of March brought beautiful spring weather, the perfect start for the new baseball season. Seeing the stands filling up, Melina was torn between sitting in the dugout or on the benches with everyone else.

In the end, she was honest with herself, deciding that Elliot wouldn't care whether she was in the dugout or not. Plus the view was better from the stands.

People wandered into the complex, carrying hot dogs and popcorn, licorice and churros, the scents mingling in the air, adding to the excitement. Melina sat with Elliot's anxious parents. Soon her family arrived, then Rafe's father and brothers. Everyone who'd had a hand in helping Elliot had made time to come and support him.

His team, the Orioles, took the field to much applause and whoops, the boys acting cool, as if they didn't hear the cheering, and looking sharp in their brand-new uniforms and caps. Melina pressed a hand to her stomach.

"Me, too," her mother said, doing the same thing.

"Me, three," Elliot's mother said, laughing.

Melina already knew Elliot wouldn't play in the field until the fifth inning of the six-inning game, but every boy was in the batting lineup from the beginning to the end of the game. He would hit in the fourth spot, cleanup, which meant Beau counted on him to get base hits, to bring in the players on base ahead of him.

It was a lot of pressure. Elliot knew what hitting fourth meant.

The game started. Elliot stood at the chain-link fence of the dugout, watching, calling out support, with Rafe beside him, doing the same. There were hits and strikeouts, great throws and errors, shoestring catches and dropped balls. The sun was in the eyes of the left and center fielders, causing missed catches, missed opportunities. Nerves showed.

Coaches encouraged but also used errors as a time for instruction.

Elliot came up to bat, swung at the first pitch and missed. He looked for Rafe on the sidelines, got his it's-okay signal and stepped back into the batter's box. He hit the next ball over the shortstop's head, driving in the base runner at third to score, the stands exploding as people jumped up and hollered.

The game moved along, one team leading, then the other. Twice more Elliot came to the plate, getting two more singles, two more runs batted in. He went out to right field in the fifth inning but never had a ball hit to him.

Then came the bottom of the sixth and last inning. The Orioles were down by one run. There were two players on base. Elliot's batting average was .754, which meant he usually struck out or flied out once every four at bats. He was coming up on his fourth at bat. They needed him to connect now to at least tie the game.

The pressure intensified. Melina watched Elliot listen to Rafe, who was right in his face, before he headed to home plate. The crowd went quiet, too quiet.

Melina cupped her mouth with her hands and yelled, "You can do it, Elliot!"

Others followed suit—except his parents, who clutched each other and could barely watch.

"Strike one!" the umpire called.

Elliot backed away, looked at Rafe, got his signals.

Melina shouted, "Shake it off, Elliot. Shake it off."

He looked toward her for just a second. And in that moment she knew that *she* mattered to him, too, not just Rafe. She plopped back down and pressed a hand to her mouth, overwhelmed. She was so glad he'd come into her life.

And because of him, she'd had Rafe for a while, too.

"What's wrong, honey?" her mother asked.

"Nothing, Mom. Everything's good. All good."

Another pitch. "Ball!"

Elliot stepped out but didn't look at Rafe, then he approached the plate again. "He calmed himself," Melina whispered excitedly to Elliot's mother. "He didn't rely on Rafe."

Debbie Anderson squeezed Melina's hand, knowing the importance of the moment. "We were blessed to find you and Rafe."

Melina grinned. "I don't know. You've been adopted by our families. You may regret that. We're big and we're noisy, you know."

"And Steve and I are grateful."

Elliot moved into the batter's box again. He set himself. His bat waggled a little then went still. The pitcher threw. Crack! The ball flew right at the second baseman, hit the tip of his outstretched glove and kept going into the field between center and right. One run scored, a second run scored. They won the game.

The stands erupted. Elliot's teammates mobbed him. Melina looked for signs of it being too much for him, but he was grinning and jumping up and down just like the rest of them.

Melina caught sight of Rafe watching the boys, a smile on his face, looking as proud as a father might. He lifted his gaze to hers, gave her a small salute, then dragged his cap down over his face for a minute, bringing tears to her eyes.

She wished she could wrap her arms around him and never let go.

Wouldn't that give everyone in town something to bet on? she thought, and finally laughed about it. Where else but in Small Town, America, could something like that happen.

And she was very glad she lived there.

Melina came to a decision—she was not

going to give him up without a fight this time. If she was going to lose him, it wouldn't be because she hadn't made the effort. Time for one last hurrah before she called it quits.

Even if she had to do the proposing. At least then she would have answers.

Postgame pizza was a tradition after the first and last games of the season. After a little while, the noise proved to be too much for Elliot, whose parents decided to take him home before he was overwhelmed.

Rafe followed them to their car. "I'll see you at practice, okay, sport?"

Elliot nodded, then they did the seven-part handshake they'd made up. Steve and Debbie tried to thank him, but Rafe gave Elliot the credit and said he'd been privileged to give him some help along the way.

Rafe felt good. Worn out, but good. The game had sent him on a sentimental journey, especially hearing Melina yelling from the stands. It might as well have been him at the plate instead of Elliot, the memory was so vivid.

He headed back into the pizza parlor intending to tell people goodbye. He needed to make some phone calls, finalize some plans. The sooner, the better.

His cell phone rang—Ross Fortune.

"I figured you'd want to be kept in the loop," he said. "My brother Flint came to town this afternoon. He's had his DNA test already, so we should know soon if he's baby Anthony's father."

"Any word from Cooper?"

"No. He goes where the work is, and sometimes he doesn't get in touch for months. But the other big news is we just got a call from the Haggerty, Texas, police department. Seems they've got a homeless man with amnesia who may be William Fortune. Jeremy and Andrew are on their way now."

"So Jeremy was right to keep the faith about his father. That's great news." He saw Beau open the pizza parlor door and look out. Rafe waved him over. "Thanks for letting me know, Ross."

Rafe slipped the phone in his pocket and waited for Beau.

"You were right," Beau said seriously.

"So were you, Beau."

"About what?"

"He wasn't fully ready, except for hitting."

"But you're going to keep working with him, right?" Beau asked.

Rafe nodded. "You're a good coach, Beau.

I've had my share of coaches, and you're one of the best."

Beau cleared his throat. "Thanks."

"And you were right about something else, too. I *was* jealous that you went to the show."

"You seem to have done okay," Beau said, smiling. "Besides, I heard you had offers after college."

Rafe didn't like to dwell on it. He'd stuck with his plan to go to law school, and most of the time could convince himself that he'd made the right choice. "A couple offers. I'm sorry about your injury." He didn't add any platitudes, knowing it wouldn't help.

"Me, too. But what are you gonna do, huh? Life goes on."

Rafe decided to change the subject. "I hear you started a betting pool on Melina and me."

Rafe's old rival grinned. "Some harmless entertainment. She looked a little peeved when she found out."

"You could say that."

"I noticed she's been short on feistiness lately, Rafe. Figured she could use a boost."

"Thanks."

Beau laughed at Rafe's dry tone, then he turned serious. "I'm thinking about bringing on a partner. Interested?"

Rafe wondered how much it cost Beau

to ask. "Not in a partnership, but I've got a good head for business, and I'd be happy to do some consulting work for you. You've got something unique in how you're running the complex. I think I could help you grow it, maybe even franchise it. First thing you'd have to do is give up micromanaging. It'll take a lot of pressure off you."

Beau stuck out his hand, but seemed incapable of speech. Rafe shook it, then watched him return to the restaurant and his noisy, victorious team. Before the door shut all the way, Melina slipped out.

"I wondered where you went," she said, approaching him. Like many of the parents, she'd bought an Orioles T-shirt. The yellow color suited her. "Is Elliot okay?"

"He's pretty wiped out, I think." He'd wanted to get away without talking to her. He had places to go and people to meet, and he was afraid he'd get swept up into something with her before he was ready to. "I am, too. I'm going to go."

Her brows went up. "You can't even talk to me for a minute? I'm that repulsive to you now?"

"Repulsive? What the hell are you talking about?"

"You couldn't wait to get me out of your

house yesterday. You didn't say one word to me after the game. And now you were going to leave without even saying goodbye or discussing Elliot for a minute—our common cause who will continue to be one until baseball season ends?" She crossed her arms. "What else am I supposed to think? You can't stand to be around me."

"You're wrong about that, but I don't have the time or energy to debate it with you right now. I have things to do, Melina. Important things." And the clock was ticking.

Hurt settled in her eyes. "I see. Well, at least you admit I'm unimportant."

He couldn't stand it. "You're important," he said. "Too important."

"How can someone be too important? I don't even know what that means. I don't see how the way you've been acting the past few days shows that I'm important in any way."

Melina was goading him on purpose. She'd been sitting in the pizza parlor watching people look from her to Rafe and back again constantly. Everyone wanted to know where things stood with them, but even she didn't know. And she was tired of being left in the dark herself. She was losing sleep and losing weight. She wanted to know where she stood and be able to move on.

If she proposed to him, she would know, one way or another. Except she hadn't planned on starting an argument, hadn't planned on him not wanting to spend even a second with her.

He glared at her. "You don't think you're important, Melina Lawrence? I'll show you how wrong you are."

He grabbed her hand and pulled her along, heading toward his car, unlocking it and waiting impatiently while she got inside. People were gathering outside the restaurant door, a hum of excitement running through the ever-enlarging crowd.

"You're ruining everything, you know," he said, grinding out the words. "What happened to the patience you're so famous for? Two days. You only needed to wait two days." He slammed her door shut, ran around to the driver's side and got in.

Melina decided not to say anything. It seemed she'd unintentionally interrupted a plan he'd made, and she was now going to pay for it. Once again, had she hurt her own cause?

Usually when he got mad, he got quiet. He would speak without emotion, always being logical. Now he was acting so irrationally she didn't know what to make of it. Except that she recognized she'd chosen the wrong moment to force him into some kind of action where she was concerned. Apparently he'd had a strategy in mind....

He drove a few blocks, turned onto Main, pulled up alongside a rundown wooden-sided building. The old Crockett building. *Their* building.

"Recognize this place?" he asked.

"Of course I do."

He stared at it. "This used to be our future."

"At Angie's wedding reception you said you thought it should've been torn down by now."

He frowned. "No, I didn't. I said I was surprised it hadn't been." He angled toward her. "I bought it. Or more accurately, I'm in the process of buying it."

"Why?"

"Because I'm opening an office in Red Rock. Right here."

He got out of the car, so she did, too. He shook his head at her, probably because she hadn't waited for him to open the door, then he led her to a window and peered inside.

"If you'd been patient for a couple more days," he said, annoyance in his voice, "I would've had it cleaned up, and a nice table set, and an elegant meal brought in. After dinner, I would've pulled out a black-velvet box, gotten down on one knee and asked you to marry me."

She barely reacted to his words, not fully comprehending them, her own goal crowding out his. Her plans had gone awry, too. "Yeah? Well, I was going to propose to you, then I got scared, so I got mad."

They faced each other like duelists.

"Wait. What?" she asked. "You were going to propose?"

"The right way. The romantic way." He shoved his hands through his hair. "I can't believe I just let that happen. I should've walked away at the pizza parlor. Done things the way I wanted to, was planning to."

She crossed her hands over her chest, which ached. "I love you, Rafe." She took a step toward him, happiness pouring into her, out of her. "I love you with all my heart."

He took her by the shoulders. "I love you more, Melina. Once I let go of the anger, love filled the empty space so fast I could barely breathe. I thought you only wanted sex, and I wanted that, too, but I also only wanted *you*. Anyway I could get you." He looked amused and surprised at the same time. "*You* were going to propose?"

She laughed joyously. "I'd already waited

years for you. I didn't want to wait a second longer. And I wanted a definite answer, not more could'ves and should'ves."

He kissed her then, softly, tenderly but thoroughly. "So, marry me today."

"Today? Rafe, really—"

"We've lost too much time already. We'll fly to Vegas."

Melina threw her arms around him, laughing and crying, happier than she'd been in such a long time. "Not today, but very soon. I want a real wedding, with our families and friends. Not a big one, but a proper one. I've dreamed of it since I was fourteen."

He threaded his fingers through her hair. "I'll give you a month. Let's go tell our families."

"That's a deal. I can— Oh, no! No, we can't get engaged today." She looked around, wondering if anyone had seen them—then could barely count the number of cars that had pulled up. "The bet, Rafe. The bet."

He eyed the street and the people standing outside their cars, watching. "I love this woman!" he shouted. "I just asked her to marry me and she said yes!" Then he bent her over his arm and kissed her most publicly, most exhaustively.

"Pay up, people!" came Beau's voice out of the melee.

Car horns honked. Cheers went up.

"Bells are ringing," Rafe said, holding her tight. "For me and my girl."

"Our song." She framed his face with her hands, cherishing him, sorry that she'd taken away his big proposal moment. She would make it up to him. "Let's go tell our families before the grapevine beats us to it."

"I love you," he said, taking her hand to walk her to his car, to start their lives together.

"I love you more," she said, echoing him from earlier.

It was a good start.

* * * * *

THE AWAKENING

"A tender, hilarious, intense love story. . . .
Everything Jude Deveraux readers expect from her
passionate pen. . . . This is a keeper."

— *Romantic Times*

WISHES

"In *Wishes,* one of Jude Deveraux's most enchanting
stories, she blends a pinch of magic, a dash of Cinderella fantasy, and spoonfuls of fun into a stunning
romance."

— *Rave Reviews*

"Jude Deveraux always spins a gripping tale. . . .
Plenty of passion—and the plot never slackens."

— ALA *Booklist*

"This Jude Deveraux fairy tale about a Cinderella in
Colorado and her unlikely Prince Charming is amusing and suitably fanciful."

— *New York Daily News*

THE PRINCESS

"The Princess is unadulterated Jude Deveraux. She delivers a humorous, enchanting, and romantic tale."
— *Rave Reviews*

THE MAIDEN

"This one has it all—depth of character, adventure, well-developed plot, steamy love scenes, and all the other attributes that make a Deveraux offering such a reading pleasure."
— *Rendezvous*

"Jude Deveraux creates enchanting and mysterious medieval characters and landscapes as well as situations that illuminate the differences between men and women. . . . *The Maiden* resonates with a deeply felt longing for a union of souls, not merely bodies, when men and women find each other."
— *Publishers Weekly*

"The Maiden is a truly beautiful, funny, tender, and magical love story that is destined to become a favorite of every Jude Deveraux fan."
— *Rave Reviews*

Books by Jude Deveraux

Published by POCKET BOOKS

Jude Deveraux

The Conquest

POCKET BOOKS

New York   London   Toronto   Sydney   Singapore

This book is a work of fiction. Names, characters, places and
incidents are products of the author's imagination or are used
fictitiously. Any resemblance to actual events or locales or
persons, living or dead, is entirely coincidental.

An *Original* Publication of POCKET BOOKS

POCKET BOOKS, a division of Simon & Schuster, Inc.
1230 Avenue of the Americas, New York, NY 10020

ISBN: 0-671-64447-5

First Pocket Books printing February 1991

20 19 18 17 16 15 14 13 12 11

POCKET and colophon are registered trademarks of
Simon & Schuster, Inc.

For information regarding special discounts for bulk
purchases, please contact Simon & Schuster Special Sales
at 1-800-456-6798 or business@simonandschuster.com

Front cover illustration by David Loew

Printed in the U.S.A.

The
Conquest

Chapter One

England
1447

The old castle, even from a distance looking run-down and in need of repair, stood surrounded by a clean, deep moat. Outside on the grounds many men trained, practicing with swords and lances. Some fought on foot, some on horseback.

Overseeing the training were two men, both big, both muscular, both wearing looks of intense concentration on their handsome faces. These were the two remaining Peregrine brothers, the others having long ago been killed in the three-generations-old feud with the Howards.

"Where is Zared?" the older Peregrine brother, Rogan, shouted. Sun glinted off his dark hair, showing the red he had inherited from his father.

"Inside," Severn, the younger brother, shouted back, and he met his brother's eyes. "I saw Zared go," he said, not using the feminine pronoun "she," not letting the men around him know Zared was female.

1

Rogan nodded and looked back at the men fighting near him. He had already lost four brothers to the sneaking treachery of the Howards, and two years before he'd almost lost his wife. He did not mean to lose his little sister to the skulking rats, and so he checked often on her whereabouts.

He glared at the men near him. "Are you women that you fight so softly? Here, I will show you." He took a pike from a knight and attacked. Within minutes the knight who'd tried to fight against him was on his knees. Disgusted, Rogan glared down at the man. He raised the pike as if to strike but instead tossed it to the ground and walked away.

How could he protect his family, protect what little land the Peregrines had left, when the men who fought for him were so weak?

He mounted his horse and started toward the castle, but Severn halted him.

"You mean to see to her?" Severn asked belligerently when they were alone. He was angry that his brother had not taken his word that their young sister was safe.

"She is disobedient," Rogan answered, scowling. Three weeks earlier Zared had decided to go swimming and had ridden out alone, unescorted, unprotected. At seventeen she had a youth's belief that she could come to no harm.

"I will see to her," Severn said, trying to relieve his older brother of at least one responsibility.

Rogan nodded, and Severn reined his horse away. Severn knew all too well how his sister felt, for he, too, had felt the weight of his family's hatred of the Howards on his shoulders. Over the years he'd watched the Howards kill his family one by one. He'd seen his older brothers killed, his father and stepmother starved to death by the Howards. He'd seen

Rogan's agony when his first wife and later his beloved second wife had been held captive by the Howards.

Since the birth of Zared, the only girl born to their father, the family had bonded together to protect her. From the first they had let no one know that anything as fragile and as vulnerable as a female had been born to the Peregrines. They had spread the news that a seventh son had been born.

After Zared's mother had died, starved in a castle besieged by the Howards, Zared had been raised by her six older brothers. They raised her as they would have another brother, dressing her as a boy, giving her her first sword when she was four, laughing when she'd fallen off horses. Never had they allowed Zared the luxury of believing herself to be a weak, delicate female.

But now the brothers seemed to be paying for having raised her as a male. Zared acted as independently as any boy of seventeen. She felt that if she wanted to leave the castle grounds, she had that right. She strapped a sword to her belt, hid a dagger in her boot, and thought she could protect herself from an army of Howards.

Both Severn and Rogan had tried to reason with Zared. As much as the girl liked to think she was strong and skillful with weapons, she was, in fact, merely a puny girl. Rogan's wife, Liana, had had something to say about Zared, but then Liana seemed to have something to say about everything, Severn thought.

"How could you raise her with a sword in her hand and then one day tell her to sit in the solar with her sewing and think that she would be content to do so?" Liana had asked. "She is the hardheaded know-it-all that you have raised her to be."

Severn grimaced in memory and thought for the

3

thousandth time that Rogan ought to take a hand to his wife. Her tongue was too sharp by far.

So now, as if he and his brother didn't have enough to worry about, they had constantly to see about Zared, to make sure she had not taken it into her head to wander about the fields alone.

As Severn's horse clattered across the drawbridge he smiled. Two days past he'd had an idea about how to get Zared away from the danger of being watched constantly by the enemy Howards, and how to win himself a rich wife at the same time. He had already told Rogan of his plan, and all that was left was telling Zared. He smiled more broadly when he thought of Zared's reaction. For all that she dressed as a boy and swaggered like one, she had a girl's way of showing her pleasure over the smallest things. And Severn knew that what he had planned would give his little sister pleasure.

Of course, first he had to tell Liana what he intended. She would, no doubt, give him some difficulty, but he knew he could handle her. "A sight better than Rogan does," he muttered, for he thought his brother much, much too soft on the woman. "Ask Liana," Rogan had said when Severn told of his plans for Zared. *Ask* a woman? "I shall *tell* her," he said firmly as he dismounted and started up the stairs to Liana's solar.

Zared stood to one side of the doorway, her cheek against the rough stone and silently watched Liana's women. They laughed and giggled and whispered to one another while sliding dresses of gorgeous silks and velvets over their heads. Now and then Zared could catch a whispered word as they talked about the men of the castle. Zared stood a little straighter when she

4

heard Ralph's name mentioned. He was a young knight her brother Rogan had recently hired, and never had a man affected her as Ralph did. Just walking past him made her heart beat faster and the blood rush to her face.

"Would you like to try this gown?"

It took Zared a moment before she realized the woman was speaking to her. She was one of Liana's prettiest ladies, her hair encased in a net of gold, her body corseted and wrapped in velvet, and she was holding a gown of emerald satin toward Zared. Although the secret of Zared's femininity had been kept from her brothers' men, Liana's women knew the truth—that Zared was a girl.

Zared almost reached for the gown, but she drew her hand away sharply. "Nay," she said, with as much disdain as she could put in her voice. "I have no need for frivolities."

The woman, instead of looking as if she'd been put in her place, gave Zared a look of pity.

Zared tried her best to look haughty and turned away. What did she care for women's finery? For women's gossiping chatter?

Zared ran down the steep stone stairs and then paused at the second level, stepping back into an alcove when she heard Liana's voice. Zared held her breath as Liana passed.

In the two years since her oldest brother had taken a wife many things had changed in the Peregrine household: The food was better, the beds cleaner, and there were women all over the place. But Liana had not changed Zared. No amount of arguing with Zared's brothers had softened them into allowing Zared to change. For her own protection Zared must remain disguised as the youngest Peregrine son.

5

Of course, Zared told herself, she wouldn't want the confinement of being a woman. She wouldn't want to be like Liana, always confined within the castle grounds, never allowed to ride free, to gallop across a field. Women such as Liana and her ladies had to sit and wait, wait for a man to come to them. But Zared didn't have to wait for anything. If she wanted to go riding, she did so; she didn't have to wait for some man to help her on a horse and then accompany her.

But sometimes, just sometimes, she wished she could have a woman's wiles. She had been in sword practice with Ralph when one of Liana's ladies had walked past. Ralph had turned away to watch the woman. Zared had been so angered that she'd struck Ralph on the side of his head with the flat of her sword. He'd fallen to the ground, and the men around them had laughed. After that Ralph wouldn't practice with her. Nor would he sit with her, nor, if he could help it, would he remain in the same room with her. Severn said Ralph might think Zared was a boy, but she bothered him just the same.

After a week of Ralph's hostility Zared had considered asking Liana for a gown, but she couldn't bring herself to ask. If she wore a dress, she might get Ralph's notice, but her brothers would be mightily displeased. If she wore a gown she knew her brothers would no longer allow her outside the castle walls. Was gaining Ralph's favor worth the loss of her freedom?

She was thinking so hard that at first she did not realize that the voices in the next room had grown much louder.

"You cannot think to do this," Liana was saying in a voice filled with exasperation.

Zared knew her sister-in-law had to be talking to

6

Severn, for the two of them were always butting heads. Liana had a way of getting anything she wanted from Rogan, which was one of the things that enraged Severn. Whenever Severn spoke to Liana there was an undercurrent of hostility in his voice.

"She is my sister, and I will take her," Severn said with anger. "I do not need your permission."

Zared's ears perked up as she listened.

Liana's voice grew calmer, as if she were reasoning with the village idiot. "You are barely able to keep her safe here, yet you mean to expose her for all the world to see?"

"She will be my squire. *I* will protect her."

"While you court the Lady Anne? Will Zared sleep with the other squires? Or in your tent with you while you take your whores to bed? Zared is no Iolanthe to stand by and watch while you bed other women."

Zared sucked in her breath. Liana had gone too far. Iolanthe was the beautiful woman who had lived in the rooms above the kitchen. She had been married, but her old, senile husband had let her live with Severn—or maybe he hadn't known where his wife was. When the old man died Severn had asked Iolanthe to marry him, but she'd refused. She said she loved Severn, would always love him, but he was too poor for her to marry. She'd returned to her husband's house and within a year was married to a fat, stupid, but very rich man. She'd asked to see Severn again, but he'd refused to see her. Now Iolanthe's name was never mentioned.

Zared couldn't see Severn, but she knew he was no doubt trembling with rage.

"Severn," Liana whispered pleadingly. "Please listen to me."

"Nay, I do not listen to you. I must go to get a wife. I

7

do not want a wife, for I have seen how a wife can change a man, but the coffers must be filled if we are to win the war against the Howards, if we—"

"Cease!" Liana shouted. "I can bear no more. It is always the Howards. I have heard of little else since I married into this family. I eat with the Howards, sleep with them. They never leave me. How can you risk your sister's life in your hatred of them?"

Zared held her breath. Severn wouldn't strike his brother's wife, would he? If he did, Rogan would kill him.

Yet how could Liana speak so lightly of their enemies? How could she dismiss what the Howards had done to them over three generations?

Zared released her breath when Severn spoke again. At least he could control himself enough to refrain from striking Liana. Zared knew what her brother was talking about. A month before a herald had come issuing an invitation to a huge tournament to be held in honor of the marriage of Lady Catherine Marshall. There were rich prizes to be won, including a large emerald, but the herald had hinted that the richest prize was the younger daughter, Lady Anne. She was eighteen, just returned from years spent at the French court, and her father was seeking a good English husband for her.

At supper, after the herald had left, Severn had announced his intention of going to the tournament and returning with the rich Lady Anne as his wife. That had started a loud argument between Liana and Severn. Liana had said he thought a great deal of himself if he believed he could win a lady of manners and education merely because he could unhorse a few brawny, battle-scarred men. Severn had said Rogan had gotten himself a rich wife, and he planned to do so, too. Liana pointed out that *she* had chosen Rogan, not the other way around, and she doubted very much if Anne would choose an unshaved, dirty, full-of-himself knight like Severn who also happened to be in love with another woman. Severn dived across the table, going for Liana bodily, and Rogan had had to leap on his brother to prevent him from harming Liana.

There hadn't been much peace in the Peregrine household after that, and Zared thought the continuing battle was Liana's fault. Ever the organizer, Liana had started to prepare Severn for the tournament. She ordered new garments, embroidered hangings for his horses, planned Severn's tent, planned even the decorations for his helmet. But the more Liana planned, the more Severn dug in his heels and refused to comply with her wishes. After three weeks of arguing he told Liana that if he had to, he'd sling the Lady Anne over his horse and force her to marry him.

"You'll have to do that," Liana said. "Force is the only way you'll get her to marry you after she gets near enough to smell you."

So Severn was planning to leave in two days for the tournament, and he was refusing to take the finery Liana had had made for him. "She will take me as I am."

"She will not have you at all," Liana had snapped.

But now he was telling Liana that he planned to take Zared as his squire. Zared smiled in anticipation: to see the world, to hear the music, taste the food, to . . .

"She can *not* go," Liana was saying. "Do you forget that for all her disguise she is a female? What if her sex were discovered? What is to keep some drunken man from her body? She will not be much of a marriage prize without her virginity."

Marriage? Zared thought. No one had mentioned marriage to her.

Liana's voice lowered. "What of the Howards? They will know that two of the Peregrines attend the tourney. Will they not try to take one of you? And will it not be the younger, smaller one?"

"Even the Howards would not offend the king, and he will be there."

"On the journey there and back, then," Liana said angrily. "Severn, please listen to me. Do not endanger the child's life. Do not let your anger at Iolanthe cause the death of your sister."

Zared realized that her hands were made into fists, her short nails cutting into her palms. She wanted to show herself to Liana and shout that she could take care of herself, that if any man tried to touch her, she'd use a knife on him. How could Liana think she was so weak that she must be protected like the puniest female? She was a man, not a woman!

"I mean . . ." Zared whispered, and to her horror she felt tears coming to her eyes. She was *female,* but she could take care of herself.

"She will go with me," Severn said, and his tone made Zared know that he meant to discuss the subject no further.

Zared pushed away from the wall and ran down the stairs before Severn saw her. Damn them all, she thought. One minute she was on the training field with Rogan yelling at her to hold her sword higher, and the next she was hearing Liana say she was too weak to fend off some drunk's advances. Was she a knight or a puny female? Was she a man or a woman?

She kept running down the stairs until she reached the courtyard below, and there stood Severn's stallion saddled and waiting for him. Cursing her whole family for confusing her, she jumped on his horse and thundered across the drawbridge, ignoring the shouts behind her.

She rode as hard and as fast as she could, not caring where she was going. The castle and the Peregrine lands disappeared behind her, and she spurred the horse harder and faster. She was some miles from home when the three men fell in behind her. A quick look back showed that they wore the Howard chevron and the Howard colors.

Her heart leaped to her throat. Rogan had warned her that the Howards watched them, that the Howards sat in wait for one of the Peregrines to go unprotected.

All her life she had been warned about the Howards. From the time she had been born the treachery of the Howards had been drilled into her. Generations earlier a Peregrine duke, old and half senile, had taken for his second wife a young, pretty woman from the Howard family. The woman was ambitious, and she had persuaded her old husband to change his will to leave all—the money, the title, the estates—to her weakling of a son, a son that many whispered was not the duke's get.

The only way the Howard woman could persuade the old man to disinherit his grown sons was to make him believe he and his first wife had not in truth been married. The old man, his mind clear one day and foggy the next, had requested that the parish registers that recorded the marriage be brought to him, as well as the witnesses. But no registers were to be found, and all the witnesses had died—some of them all too recently.

The old man, dying and in great pain, had declared the sons of his first marriage bastards and had given everything to his wife's waiting family.

Since that time the Peregrines and the Howards had fought for the wealthy lands that the Howards controlled. Over the years the losses on both sides had been heavy, and the hatred was very deep.

Zared looked back at the Howard men chasing her, then rode harder than she ever had in her life, her head down to the horse's neck, the mane whipping at her eyes. The horse's hooves pounded on the hard, rutted dirt track, past people and carts and animals. But it wasn't long before she could feel the tired horse losing ground and feel the Howard men gaining on her.

"Come on, boy," she said to the horse. "If we make it to the king's forest, we'll lose them there."

She spurred the horse on, her heart beating hard with the horse's.

They almost made it, but moments before they reached the forest, when Zared could see the concealing safety of the trees ahead, the horse stepped in a hole and went down. Zared hit the ground and went rolling head over heels across the dusty road. When she stopped rolling and looked up three men were standing over her, swords pointed at her throat.

"It's the youngest Peregrine," one man said, as if he didn't believe his luck. "We'll be paid well for this."

"Stop counting your money and tie him up. I don't want him escaping before we can get him back."

One man grabbed her arm and pulled her up. "Little thing, he is," he said, feeling Zared's arm.

She jerked out of his grasp.

"Don't fool with me, boy, or I'll give you a taste of my knife. I don't guess Howard will mind whether a Peregrine is delivered to him dead or alive."

"Quiet!" the first man said. "Put the boy on your horse, and let's leave before his brothers come."

The mention of the elder Peregrines sobered the

men, and one threw Zared up into a saddle and mounted behind her.

All Zared could think of was that now the feud would start afresh, and before it ended she would lose more of her brothers. She closed her eyes against tears of regret. As long as possible she must make them continue believing her to be a boy. She didn't like to think what could happen were men like these to discover she was a female.

Tearle Howard stretched his long, muscular legs, gave a great yawn, and leaned back on the sweet grass by the side of the little stream. The sun was warm on his body, and the flies droned lazily. To his left he could hear the low murmur of his brother's three men.

Tearle meant to fall asleep, meant to idle the day away dozing in the sun, but the men's voices kept him from sleeping, for the voices reminded him of his brother's obsession.

Until two months ago Tearle had lived in France, had spent time at the court of Philip the Good. Under his mother's direction Tearle had lived a life of education and refinement. He'd learned the finer aspects of music, dance, the arts. His life had been one of ease and plenty, spent in a place where conversation was an art.

But six months earlier his mother had died, and with her death Tearle's main reason for living in France disappeared. At twenty-six years of age he'd found himself curious about the family he'd never known and rarely seen, so when Oliver demanded his young brother's return Tearle had been pleased and intrigued. Tearle had made the journey back to England in the pleasant company of friends and had greeted his brother and sister-in-law warmly.

The warmth had soon cooled when Tearle found

that Oliver wanted him to wage war on a family named Peregrine. Oliver had been horrified to find that Tearle had not been taught from an early age to hate the Peregrines. According to Oliver, the Peregrines were devils on earth and should be eradicated at all costs. Tearle was just as horrified to discover that the elder Howard brothers had been sacrificed to this long-running feud.

"Isn't it time to cease all this?" Tearle had asked Oliver. "Isn't the cause of the feud that the Peregrines believe our estates to be theirs? If we own the estates and they do not, would it not make more sense for the Peregrines to attack us instead of our attacking them?"

Tearle's words had so enraged Oliver that his eyes had glazed over and spittle had formed at the corner of his mouth. It was at precisely that moment that Tearle began to doubt his brother's sanity. Tearle could never get a full answer regarding the true cause of Oliver's hatred of the Peregrines, but after piecing together bits of castle gossip he suspected Oliver's hatred had something to do with his tired-looking wife, Jeanne.

Whatever the cause, the hatred was far too ingrained in Oliver for Tearle to be able to dislodge it. So while Tearle did his best to stay out of his brother's way, life with Oliver was dull at best. As far as Tearle could see, all of his brother's energies went into his hatred of the Peregrines, and nothing was left over for the finer things in life like music or pleasant society.

So there he was, idling the day away, sent out on a fool's errand by his obsessed brother.

"Go and watch them," Oliver had said, as if when Tearle saw the Peregrines he'd see not men but devils with red scales for skin. "Go with my men and see them."

14

"You post men outside the Peregrine castle?" Tearle had asked. "You watch them on a daily basis? Do you count the cabbages they buy?"

"Do not sneer at what you do not know," Oliver had said, his eyes narrowing. "Two years ago the oldest one went with his wife alone into the village. Had I but known, I could have taken him. I did take that wife of his, but she . . ." He stopped and turned away.

"She what?" Tearle asked with interest.

"Do not remind me of that day. Go and see what I fight. If you see them, you will understand."

Tearle was beginning to become curious about the Peregrines, so he went off with one of the four groups that Oliver planted about the Peregrine castle.

Tearle had not been impressed by the sight of the crumbling old castle. Some effort had been made to patch the worst of it, but nothing could disguise the poverty of the place. Tearle sat on a hill some distance away and watched through a spyglass as the three remaining Peregrines trained daily with their men. The youngest was a mere boy.

For three days Tearle sat there and watched the Peregrines training. By the end of the third day he felt he knew them all. In addition to the two men and the boy there were two illegitimate brothers who were awkward with their training, as if the weapons were new to them.

"Their father's by-blows," Oliver had said in contempt. "Had I known—"

"You would have killed them," Tearle said tiredly.

"Beware you do not try my patience too far," Oliver warned.

The Peregrines in their poverty took in illegitimate brothers, but Oliver, with all his riches, constantly threatened to toss Tearle out. Wisely, Tearle did not make that observation to his brother.

By the fifth day Tearle had no more interest in watching the Peregrines. He was itchy for exercise and wished he could join the training. "I could take the blond one," he said to himself as he watched Severn down yet another man. He gave the spyglass to one of the men and walked away. He had to figure out a way to get away from his duty as spy.

He wasn't aware that he was drifting into sleep until the thundering hooves of horses woke him. Oliver's men were gone. Tearle was on his feet instantly. He grabbed the spyglass from the ground where it'd been tossed and looked. The Peregrine men were in confusion, the oldest, Rogan, shouting as he mounted his horse. The slightly younger brother was already galloping away. But no one seemed to know exactly which way to go, so they split off in four directions.

"The boy," Tearle said. Once before he'd seen the boy ride away from his protective brothers, but Tearle had not told Oliver's men. Let the boy meet his village sweetheart, he'd thought, and then he worked on keeping the men's attention until the boy was safely returned.

Tearle ran to his horse and rode after Oliver's men. Obviously they had seen the direction in which the boy traveled. It took Tearle a while to find the men, and at first he thought he was too late. A stallion he knew to be Severn's led behind them, the men were already heading toward the Howard lands.

Tearle's heart sank. The capture of the boy would mean open warfare—and the Howards would be at fault. Damn Oliver and his obsession, he thought.

The men reluctantly halted when they saw Tearle. Their ugly faces were shining with triumph in having captured one thin, weak boy, and they looked at Tearle in expectation of praise.

Before one of them, sitting rigidly in the saddle, was the boy. Tearle could hardly bear to look at him.

When at last Tearle could meet the boy's eyes his mouth dropped open in shock. For he didn't look into the proud face of a boy, but into the fiery eyes of a girl.

In astonishment he looked back at the men.

"We caught him, my lord," one man said. "Do we take the boy to your brother, or do we kill him here?"

Tearle could only gape at the men. Couldn't they see that they held a girl? Couldn't they tell the difference between girls and boys?

"My lord?" one of the men asked, his voice anxious. "The Peregrines will be here soon."

Tearle regained his composure. He didn't think those Peregrine brothers would stop to talk when they saw their little sister held captive.

"I will take the . . . child to my brother," Tearle said. And get the girl out of the hands of these louts, he thought.

The men hesitated.

Frowning, Tearle tossed them a bag of coins. "Here, take this. I will deal with this Peregrine myself."

The men's eyes laughed. They had what they wanted, and they couldn't care less what Tearle did with the boy, or what happened to Tearle, for that matter.

One of the men rode beside Tearle and half shoved, half dumped Zared into his saddle. Tearle winced when he saw how tightly the girl's hands were tied. "Go!" he commanded the men. "Before they find you."

They hesitated not a second longer before they spurred their horses toward the Peregrine lands. Tearle fastened his arm around the girl's slim waist, hugged her body close to his, and rode hard and fast into the king's forest.

Chapter Two

T earle lost himself in the forest, leaving the paths that centuries of villagers' feet had carved, and slipped deep into the dark recesses between the giant oak trees. As he rode he held the girl before him, feeling her slim back against his chest, her slim, strong legs against his. Once a low-hanging branch threatened to hit her, and he put out his hand to protect her, the branch painfully cutting into the back of his hand. Another time, as he leaned forward to duck a branch, he put his face in the curve of her neck, her soft hair on his face.

He smiled as they rode. Oliver thought he knew all there was to know about the Peregrines, yet he'd never guessed that the youngest son was actually a girl. The Peregrines were right for keeping her gender a secret, for Oliver seemed to be particularly fascinated by the Peregrine females.

He pulled his horse up sharply when he entered a

secluded glade. He dismounted, then pulled the girl down before him. Her hands were still tied behind her back, and she was alone with her enemy, but her eyes showed no fear.

He put his hands on her shoulders and looked down at her. Her worn, dirty tunic reached to mid-thigh, and from there down her legs were encased in tight knit hose, her little feet in soft boots that reached to her knee. Her dark hair, showing red even in the shadows of the forest, was shoulder-length, curling under at the ends, and she wore a jaunty little cap with a feather on one side.

For the first time since leaving France he was feeling some interest in life. What an intriguing female she was, he thought, remembering watching her train with her brothers. He suddenly felt an overwhelming urge to remount his horse and take her back with him to his brother's estate. The place was so big he could no doubt hide her there.

Zared looked at the man who held her by the shoulders, a big man with dark hair and eyes—and the unmistakable look of a Howard about him. The men who had captured her had called him lord, so he must be the long-missing youngest Howard brother.

Zared had heard stories of this younger brother, so evil he'd had to be sent away to France with his she-devil mother when he was just a boy. Looking at him she could believe all the stories about him. On the ride into the forest he'd felt her body as though to see if she were plump enough for roasting. And his beady little black eyes were glittering as though he meant to have her for a feast.

Lunatic, she thought, and she would have crossed herself in protection if her hands hadn't been tied.

While he stood there looking at her as a starving

man might look at a meal, she tried to make a plan. She could never have escaped three of the Howard men, but she had a chance with one madman. If she could get him to untie her hands, perhaps she could get to the knife hidden in her boot. With a weapon she could, perhaps, fight him off. He was big, true, but he might be as lazy as his brother, and his large size could be attributed to fat instead of muscle.

"What is your name?" he asked.

"Peregrine!" she hissed at him. If he did not untie her, if he meant to kill her, she would not disgrace her family by dying a coward.

"Your Christian name," he said softly, his eyes gentle.

What trick is this? she thought. Did he think to make her believe there was anything but evil in him? "My brothers will kill you," she said. "They will take you apart piece by piece."

He smiled a bit. "Yes, I imagine they would." He took a jewel-handled dagger from his belt, and Zared took a step backward involuntarily.

"I don't mean to hurt you," he said, talking to her as though she were a frightened wild animal.

He was stupid as well as crazy if he believed she'd ever trust the word of a Howard, she thought.

He took her by the shoulder and turned her around, then used his knife to cut the cords that bound her hands. As he turned her back around, in one deft movement she had practiced many times, she pretended to stumble, went to the ground on one knee, removed the knife from her boot, and slipped it inside her sleeve.

"Are you hurt?" Tearle asked, helping her to her feet. "I fear my brother's men were over-rough with you."

21

He had his hands on her shoulders again, and, not seeming able to help himself, he pulled her to him and kissed her gently on the mouth.

Zared was outraged! No man had ever kissed her before, and that this man, this evil, hated enemy of hers, should dare to touch her was more than she could bear. She dropped the knife from her sleeve into her hand and plunged it into his ribs.

He stepped back from her, looked down at the blood forming on his tight-waisted velvet tunic, and looked back at her in surprise.

"Death to all Howards," she spat at him, and she ran to the horse nearby.

"You are free," he whispered. "I never meant to keep you a prisoner."

She mounted the horse and glanced at him. He was growing pale, and the blood at his side was spreading wider. She kicked the horse forward and left the glade, putting her head down as she and the horse raced through the forest.

She had to find her brothers and tell them she was safe. She had to prevent them from attacking the Howards. At all costs she must stop what could become open war.

It was when she was at the edge of the forest that she realized that there could yet be war between the Howards and the Peregrines, for she had, perhaps, just killed the youngest Howard.

She rode on. Of course she hadn't killed him. She had merely wounded him. She had not hit vital organs. Had she? The image of his pale face swam before her. What if he lay there and bled to death? Oliver Howard's three men would know that once again a Peregrine had attacked a Howard. The Howards would attack, and because of Zared more of her brothers would be killed. Perhaps this time Oliver

Howard would succeed in wiping out all of the Peregrines.

At the edge of the forest Zared halted. She had to go back. She had to see that the man didn't die. But what if he regained his strength enough to hold her captive and take her to his brother?

Zared put her hands to her head as though to still her thoughts. All her life her brothers had made decisions for her. She knew that both Rogan and Severn would be so enraged at a Howard taking their sister that they would joyfully destroy the youngest Howard. Should she go to her brothers and tell them what had happened? Should she add fuel to their hatred? Renew all the old hurts and rages?

Yet it was her own fault for having been taken. Both Severn and Rogan had warned her again and again that the Howards' men lurked just outside the grounds.

She *had* to return. She had to keep the man from bleeding to death and thus causing a war. She would take his sword and, if need be, tie his hands and feet to prevent his overpowering her. She had to do what she could to prevent a war.

Tearle watched the girl go with regret. He guessed he'd never see her again. Peregrines and Howards rarely socialized, he thought with a bit of a smile.

He looked down at his side, at the spreading blood, and pulled up his tunic to examine the wound. His ribs had deflected her blade, and he was glad she wasn't experienced enough at knifing humans to have known how to injure him more severely.

He looked about the glade, realizing she had taken his horse. Was he supposed to walk back to his brother's? He calculated how long it would take the three men to get to Oliver, then how long it would take

Oliver to mount a body of men and come in search of Tearle and his Peregrine prize.

Four hours, Tearle thought. Within four hours his brother would be there. Until then he might as well rest and give the wound time to stop bleeding. He stretched out under a tree and was asleep very soon.

Zared dismounted and left the horse some distance from the glade. Then, knife in hand, she crept back to where she'd left the man.

Dead, she thought when she saw him stretched on the ground. He was already dead, and she was too late to save him.

Tearle heard her coming from some distance off, knowing by the lightness of her step that it was she. He had to prevent himself from smiling. So much for the cruel, inhuman monsters his brother spoke of. This Peregrine, at least, had a much softer side to her. Whatever he did, he must not frighten her away. He must seem helpless and keep her near him as long as possible, he decided.

He moved just a bit and gave a groan of pain.

Zared jumped at the sound, then gave a sigh of relief that he was still alive. Cautiously she moved forward, creeping nearer to him. With her knife at the ready she nudged him with her foot. He gave another little groan.

"A priest," he murmured. "Get me a priest."

Zared lost her caution at that. She had to save him. She went to her knees beside him, slit his tunic away, and examined his wound. She had hit his ribs, but she couldn't tell how deep her knife had gone. There wasn't much flesh over his ribs, just skin and muscle, but he seemed to have lost an extraordinary amount of blood.

She glanced at his face and saw that his eyes were closed and that he wore a pained expression. Were

Howard men so weak that they died from such slight wounds? She'd seen her brothers hurt that way and continue fighting for a full day before the wound was dressed. Yet the man was calling for a priest because of a mere cut.

She cut away more of his tunic and sliced a long strip of his linen shirt away. She wadded a piece of his shirt against the wound, then tried to wrap the linen strip around his big body.

He was an inert weight, and lifting him was impossible. She could have as easily lifted a dead horse. She leaned across him and tugged. She put her arms about his neck and tried to lift him. She heaved against him with her shoulders, but he just lay there, oblivious even to her presence.

"Wake up!" she commanded.

He stirred but didn't open his eyes.

Zared gave him a few sharp smacks on his cheeks, and at last he opened his eyes. "I am trying to get this bandage about you. You must lift yourself up."

"You must help me," Tearle said in a hoarse whisper.

She gave him a look of disgust, then leaned over him and helped to pull him up. He was very weak and ended in clasping her to him, his body heavily against hers. Zared had difficulty reaching around him to pull the bandage about his ribs, and holding him up was straining her back, but she managed to dress the wound.

"Lie down now," she said. The man really did seem to be quite stupid. She had to tell him the simplest things. She eased him back to the ground, but he had to have Zared's help all the way, and she had to peel his arms from around her body when he was lying flat once again.

"You will be all right now," she said. "The wound is

25

not deep. Stay here and rest. Your brother will come soon. He is never far from Peregrine lands." She started to rise, but he caught her hand.

"You would leave me? I will die here alone."

"You won't die," she said in disgust. Perhaps the Howard had been sent away as a child not because he was evil but because he was such a weakling that his family was embarrassed by him.

"Wine," he whispered. "There is a bottle of wine on my horse."

Zared gritted her teeth. Her brothers were no doubt frantically searching for her, yet she was playing nursemaid to a sniveling Howard. Reluctantly she went to the horse, removed the hard leather bottle, and handed it to him. But he was too weak to sit up without Zared's support; he couldn't even hold the bottle to his lips.

This is the enemy? Zared thought. This cowardly, weak, trembling, oversized child is something to fear?

She took the wine bottle from his lips. "I must go," she said. "I will leave the bottle here and—"

"Stay," he said, clasping her hand in his. "Please stay with me. I am frightened."

Zared rolled her eyes skyward. She was sitting on the ground, and he was leaning against her as though he could not support himself.

"I will die if you do not stay."

"You won't die," she snapped. "You ought to at least try to have some courage. The bleeding's stopped, and besides, I have to leave. My brothers will be searching for me, and it's best if they don't find me . . . here."

"Ah. You mean with a Howard. Do you know that I am a Howard?"

"We know much about the Howards. You are our enemy."

26

He sighed and leaned limply against her. "Surely *I* am not your enemy."

"If you are a Howard, you are indeed the enemy of all the Peregrines."

"Yet you returned for me."

"I came back to prevent a war. Had you died, your brother would have attacked my brothers." She tried to move out from under him, but he had her trapped by his weight.

"You returned only because of your brothers?"

"Why else?" she asked, genuinely confused.

He lifted her hand to his lips. "Perhaps you know all of us, but it seems we do not know all about the Peregrines. We did not know the youngest was a daughter and a lovely young woman." He kissed first one fingertip and then another. "Did you not perhaps return because of our kiss?"

It took a moment for the words to sink in, but then Zared began to laugh. Still laughing, she squirmed out from under him, stood, and looked down at him. "You think I care for a kiss? You think a kiss from a Howard could make me forget my four brothers your family has killed? You think me shallow enough to betray my family for anything a Howard could give me? I could slit your throat now, but your death would mean open war, and that I do not want."

Her laughter was changing to anger. "You Howards are less than nothing to me. Did I not show you what I thought of your kiss?" She nodded toward the bloody bandage on his side.

She stepped away from him and gave him a look of contempt. "I would feel a kiss that was from a *man,* but not from a spineless weakling such as you. Oliver Howard is no doubt greatly ashamed of his youngest brother—and well he should be."

She crossed to the horse and mounted. "I will free

27

your horse at the edge of the forest, for I do not want my brothers to see me on a Howard animal. I will not tell them of your men's skulking treachery or of your touching me. My brothers have killed men for less."

She gave him one last look. "Even the Howards do not deserve such a half-man as you."

Tearle was on his feet by the time she'd turned the horse, but she was out of the glade before he could catch the bridle.

Rage gave color to his pale face. Half-man?! His brother should be ashamed of him? A spineless weakling?

He? He, Tearle Howard, a weakling? In France he had won tournaments since he was a boy. He beat all comers. Women threw themselves at him. Women begged him for his kisses, yet this . . . this boy-girl had said his kiss was not that of a *man!*

As though she knew one kiss from another. As though she were such a lady of sophistication that she knew anything about kisses—or anything else, for that matter. All she knew were swords and warfare and . . . and horses. She'd have to be a *woman* to know if a kiss came from a man or not. She'd have to—

Abruptly he stopped his silent tirade and began to chuckle. Perhaps he had appeared to be a little too helpless. But it had been nice having her lean across him in an attempt to lift him. When her chest had been against his he had felt a hard padding and guessed she must bind her breasts down in her attempt to appear a boy.

And what a futile attempt that was, he thought, for her every movement screamed that she was female. How anyone could believe her to be male was beyond his understanding.

A boy wouldn't have come back to see if his enemy

was all right. Of course, Tearle wouldn't have kissed a boy and thus prompted the stabbing, but either way, a boy would not have returned.

He leaned against a tree and closed his eyes for a moment. What an intriguing girl she was, all passion and fury, yet softness underneath. She was so unaware of how she could affect a man. She was so different from other women who were coy and flirted and gave promises. The young Peregrine would never flirt, never tease. She would always say what she meant.

He moved away from the tree. He would probably never see her again, he thought.

He started walking. Maybe, he thought, he'd see his brother's men soon. If anyone knew what the Peregrine family planned, it was his brother. Oliver would no doubt be pleased when at last his young brother began to take an interest in the enemy family.

Zared stared out the small stone-cased window and watched the people on the grounds far below. Two days locked in the tower room with nothing but bread and water was her punishment for scaring her brothers half to death. Severn had yelled at her for a solid hour after she'd come limping back home. Rogan's anger had been worse, for he'd looked at her in such a way that she felt small enough to slide between the stones of the fireplace.

At least Severn's yelling had made lengthy excuses unnecessary. Zared had merely mumbled that she'd wanted to ride, Severn's stallion had thrown her, and she'd had to walk back. She much regretted the loss of Severn's horse, but only she knew how very much worse it could have been. All considered, two days locked away was a slight punishment. Her biggest fear was that her brothers wouldn't allow her to go to the tournament.

"If the Howards keep me from that pleasure," she muttered, "I will kill that whining, cowardly worth-nothing with my bare hands."

She jumped when she heard the door open behind her. Turning, she saw Liana enter with a cloth-covered basket. Zared repressed a smile, for Liana, underneath her efficient exterior, was as soft-hearted as a human could be. No doubt she feared that Zared would starve in two days without meat and wine.

"I have brought you something to eat," Liana said. "Not that you deserve it, for what you did endangered all of us."

"And I am most sorry," Zared said, reaching for the basket. "You are more than kind to bring me food when I do not deserve it." She moved to sit on the edge of the filthy bed.

"I couldn't let you starve," Liana said, taking a seat on the one chair in the room and looking about. "This place is not fit for humans."

Zared didn't think the room was so bad—a few fleas here and there, a few rats, but not unlivable. Speculatively she looked at Liana. She knew that Liana had power over whether or not she went to the tournament, for Rogan listened to his wife, and if Liana said Zared should not be allowed to go, then Rogan would forbid it.

"Do you not think it is time for me to have a husband?" Zared asked as she bit into a thick piece of pork.

Liana looked startled. "I have thought so, but I did not think you or your brothers gave much thought to the idea."

"I have been considering it lately," Zared said. "Perhaps I should have my own home, children. Perhaps I should get away from this." She waved her hand. "And the Howards."

"Oh, Zared, I could not agree more. Your life would change so much if you had your own family. Perhaps it would help your brothers get over their hatred of the Howards if they were allied with another family."

"Ah," Zared said. "Then you have someone in mind for me to marry?"

"No," Liana said slowly. "We are so isolated here that we see no one. But perhaps my stepmother would know of someone." She was quiet a moment.

"Perhaps Severn will meet someone at the tourney," Zared said, as though it didn't matter to her. "Or perhaps *I* could look the men over there."

Liana didn't say anything, and when Zared looked at her she was smiling.

"I see," Liana said. "Perhaps if you, say, went to the tournament as Severn's squire, you could find yourself a husband?"

Soft-hearted, true, Zared thought, but awfully clever. "Liana, please. Please allow me to go. I have never been anywhere in my life but here. I should like to meet some people who are not my relatives or hired by my family."

Liana's face showed her agony of indecision. "It's so dangerous for you. The Howards—"

"Bah!" Zared said, standing up. "The Howards! Those spineless cowards! They aren't worth considering."

"What do you know of the Howards to call them cowards? What happened when you rode away on Severn's horse? There was blood on your hose but no cut on your leg."

"Must have been the horse's from when it fell," Zared said quickly.

"I'm not sure I'm hearing all of the truth."

"What else could there be? Do you think I was captured by the Howards?" Zared gave a little laugh.

"They captured me, but out of the goodness of their hearts they released me. Very amusing idea."

"I've seen you use a knife," Liana said softly. "Perhaps you could have escaped were you captured."

Zared walked across the room, grabbed a chunk of bread, and filled her mouth. "This is *delicious* bread. When I'm married I hope I can be half the housewife you are. That is, if I can find a husband, or, rather, if Severn can find one for me. I'm sure he will pick a good husband for me."

"All right, keep your secrets," Liana said. She'd lived with the Peregrines long enough to know that they revealed nothing about themselves unless they had to. She sighed in resignation. "Severn will no doubt choose a man who is best able to help fight the Howards, some man with years of war experience." She looked at Zared. "You need less war and more love."

"Love?" Zared said with a snort. "I have my brothers, I have God, I need no more love."

Liana looked up at her pretty young sister-in-law. She was sure Zared would someday love a man. If she knew nothing else about the Peregrines, she knew they were people of passion: They hated with passion, fought with passion, loved with passion. Zared seemed to think it didn't matter who she married, but were she bound to a man she couldn't respect, or worse, one she held in contempt, she would hate him until, if the man had any sense, he would fear for his life.

Liana also knew that all she had to do was tell Rogan that Zared should not go to the tournament and Zared would not be allowed to go, but something held Liana back. Zared would be safer at home, true, but what if Zared's passion should turn to hate: more hate for the Howards, who prevented her from leaving her home-prison, and possibly hate for Liana as well.

"You will stay near Severn?" Liana asked softly, wondering if she'd ever see Zared alive again.

"Yes, oh, yes," Zared said, her face filled with joy.

"How I wish I could go with you! I'd order some gowns for you, greens and blues. You could be quite pretty if your hair weren't always in a snarl. Oh, Zared, a tournament is so lovely. You give your favor to a man, and he—"

"I'd rather fight," Zared said. "I'd rather mount a horse, hold a lance, and knock a man off his horse. I would not like to sit and watch."

"No, I guess you wouldn't." Liana put her hands on her big belly. She was too soon due with her second child to be able to leave. Perhaps it was better if she didn't see her husband's young sister acting as a squire, mucking out stables, currying horses, running between combatants to deliver fresh lances.

Liana stood. "I do not feel it is the best thing to do, but perhaps you will be safe enough. Perhaps Severn is right and Oliver Howard will not dare attack while the king is there. I will tell Severn he has his squire." She started for the door.

"Liana," Zared said. "When you met Oliver Howard, what was he like? Is he a very great fighter?"

Liana smiled. "Not at all. He's much older than your brothers and gone to fat. But then he does not have to fight, for he's very rich and can hire as many men as he needs."

"And what of his brother?"

"Brother? I heard nothing of a brother. I'm afraid I don't know the Howards as well as your family does. Zared, what do you know of a brother?"

"Nothing. Nothing at all. It's just that . . ." She

looked at Liana. "I have not seen much of the world and know only of my brothers. They are such fine men." She smiled proudly. "They are strong and handsome. No one could beat them on a battlefield. Are they such unusual men? Or are there many men like them?"

Liana took a while to answer. "I don't believe there are *any* other men like your brothers, but Zared, there is more to a man than a strong right arm. You do not choose a husband by physical strength alone. There are other qualities such as kindness and unselfishness and whether he will love you and your children or not."

"And protect his family from enemies."

"Yes, that's important too, but . . ." She didn't know how to explain to this girl that there was another way of life besides what she'd known. All her life Zared had lived in a private war with another family. She'd been raised as a boy to protect her. She knew nothing of sitting in the sunshine with a handsome young man while he played a lute and sang to her. She'd never had a man kiss her hand and tell her how lovely the sunlight in her hair was. Zared had never giggled with the maids or flirted with a boy, or done any of the things other girls did. Zared knew swords and horses and could sing all the vulgar songs with the men. But she didn't know satin from brocade or ermine from sable. Worst of all, she knew no men except her brothers.

"You'll find no husband like your brothers," Liana said softly.

"Then I shall never marry," she said with all the confidence of youth. "I shall remain a virgin until my death."

That made Liana laugh and the baby kick. A Peregrine remain a virgin? That was a good one. She knew, much better than her brothers did, that when Zared discovered sexual feelings she was going to be impossible to restrain. If Severn did not keep close watch on her at the tournament and she met some splendid man who took her fancy . . .

Liana did not like to think of the possible consequences, for Zared's brothers would kill any man who touched their little sister. "I am sure I am making a mistake in allowing you to go."

"I will be good," Zared said. "I will obey Severn and stay near him, and I will get into no trouble. I swear it, Liana. You have my word as a Peregrine."

Liana smiled and sighed at the same time. "Peregrines were born to be in trouble. I'm sure both you and your brother will get into a dreadful mess. Swear to me that you will not allow Severn to kill anyone and you will not come home with child."

Zared's mouth dropped open. "With child?"

"Swear to me. You cannot go otherwise."

Zared grimaced. Her sister-in-law understood nothing. Severn was going to get a wife, not to kill anyone, and she was going to see the sights. Besides, people thought she was a boy, so no man was going to try to impregnate her. A brief memory of the youngest Howard kissing her crossed her mind. He'd known she was female, but that was probably because he was half female himself, fainting over a little cut!

"I swear," Zared said.

"I guess that shall have to do. Now get a good night's sleep, because tomorrow you leave with your brother."

Zared grinned broadly. "Yes, I will, and thank you, Liana, thank you. I will do the Peregrine name proud."

"Don't say that or I'll think you mean to return with a dozen heads on pikes. Goodnight, Zared. I will pray

35

for you every day." Liana left, shutting the door behind her.

Zared stood where she was for a moment, then jumped high, her hands hitting the cracked plaster ceiling. She felt as though the next day her life would truly begin.

Chapter Three

For two days Tearle listened to Oliver rant about the Peregrines. Most of what he heard was useless information, but Tearle listened just the same. He found out that the girl's name was Zared, and it was Oliver's opinion that the "boy" would never be the equal of his brothers.

On the afternoon of the second day Oliver received the news that Severn Peregrine was to enter the Marshall tournament, and it was rumored that he was going to try for the Lady Anne's hand in marriage.

Oliver had been quite jovial at the idea. "I shall take him prisoner while he is there."

"With the king watching?" Tearle asked, yawning. "I don't imagine Anne's father would like this feud of yours taken onto his land."

"Anne, is it?" Oliver asked, his ears perking up like a hunting dog's. "You know the woman?"

"Only by sight. She lived in France for a while."

"Then you shall go."

"To the tournament? To spy on the man as he goes courting?"

"Yes." Oliver's eyes were feverishly bright. "You will see what they do, watch them, report to me about—"

"Them?" Tearle sat up in the chair. "Who is to go besides the second son?"

"The boy is to be his squire." Oliver snorted. "He cannot afford a true squire, so he has to use his own brother. He will be a laughingstock, for they are a dirty, crude lot, and the Marshalls are people of great refinement. Would that I could see the Peregrines' humiliation."

"I will go," Tearle said.

Oliver grinned. "You will fight him. I shall *have* to go. I must see this. On the jousting field a Howard will down a Peregrine. The king—the world—shall see that a Howard—"

"I'll not fight him," Tearle said. He knew that he would never have an opportunity to spend time with the youngest Peregrine were he to announce himself as a Howard. "I shall go in disguise." Before Oliver could open his mouth Tearle continued. "I shall spy on them," he said, feeding Oliver's obsession. "No one in England knows I have returned. I shall attend the tournament as . . . as Smith. I shall watch and learn more about the Peregrines than I could if I announced myself as their enemy."

Oliver looked at his brother, and his expression changed. "I was not sure you understood," he said softly. "But I should not have doubted our blood."

Tearle smiled at his brother. He did not feel the least bit guilty for deceiving his brother, for Oliver's hatred of that family did not deserve respect. I shall protect them, he thought. I shall see that no harm comes to the Peregrines, no misaimed arrows, no pieces falling from the roof, no cut saddle cinches. I shall see that for once they are safe from Howard hatred.

"No, you should not have doubted me," Tearle said. "I have always been as I am. I have never changed."

Oliver frowned a bit at that but then smiled. "Yes, I see. You have always been a Howard. When do you leave?"

"Now," Tearle said, and he rose. He wanted to hear no more of Oliver's venom, but most important, he wanted to get to Anne Marshall. He hadn't told his brother the truth when he'd said he barely knew Anne. He'd tossed her on his knee when she was a child, had kissed her tears away when she'd fallen, had told her ghostly stories at bedtime and then received tongue-lashings from her mother for causing Anne to wake screaming in the night. An adult Anne had comforted Tearle when his mother had died.

Tearle knew that if he was to appear at the Marshall tournament in disguise, he had to get to Anne first and tell her of his plans.

Tearle sat on top of the garden wall and watched Anne and her ladies walking. One lady was, as usual, reading aloud. Tearle had often teased Anne for her scholarly ways; she seemed forever buried in a book.

He leaned back against a branch of an old apple tree and smiled at the sight. The women in their bright gowns, their elaborate headdresses trimmed with jewels and gauze veils, were a beautiful sight, but Anne stood out even from those women. Anne was a beauty among beauty. She was tiny, barely reaching a man's shoulder, and she was vain enough that she always surrounded herself with tall women. She looked like a precious jewel, and the towering women were a setting for that jewel.

As she and her women moved forward he had no doubt that Anne would see him. The other women would probably never look up, but Anne didn't miss anything. If possible, her brain was even brighter than her face was lovely. And, Tearle thought with a wince, her tongue could be as sharp as a blade. Too often he'd been on the receiving end of her barbs, and he knew how they could sting.

When Anne glanced up and saw him, only for a second did she look startled. Startled, but not fearful, for it would take more than one mere man to frighten Anne Marshall. Tearle gave her a smile, and she looked away quickly.

Within moments she had dismissed her women, sending them all away on errands, and she stood below Tearle, looking up at him.

He jumped lightly to the ground, took Anne's small hand, and kissed it. "The moon has no beauty compared to you. Flowers hide their faces in shame when you walk past. Butterflies close their wings; peacocks do not dare show themselves; jewels cease to sparkle; gold—"

"What do you want, Tearle?" Anne asked, pulling her hand away. "What causes you to skulk about my father's garden? Are you in love with one of my maids?"

"You wound me," he said, his hand to his heart as, stumbling as though he had been stabbed, he sat on a stone bench. "I have come merely to see you." He looked up at her with a bit of a grin. "I would forgive your accusations were you to sit on my knee as you used to do."

Anne's beautiful face relaxed its sternness, and she

smiled as she sat beside him. "I have missed your silver tongue. Do you not find these English a sober lot?"

"Most sober. My brother is . . ." He didn't finish.

"I have heard. My sister has filled my ears with naught but gossip. Your family is at war with another family."

"Yes, the Peregrines."

"I have heard much of them," Anne said. "My sister attended the wedding of the eldest son to Lady Liana." She gave a delicate shudder.

"They are not so bad." He was on the point of telling Anne about Zared but stopped himself. It would not do to tell anyone she was female. If a person could not tell by looking at her, he did not deserve to be told. "The second son is coming to the tournament and means to win your hand."

Anne turned to look at him, astonishment on her beautiful face. "To win *my* hand? A Peregrine? For all your family's feud with them, you must not know much of those men. They are a filthy, ignorant lot. The oldest brother did not attend his own wedding feast. He was too busy counting the gold his bride brought him. When Lady Liana's stepmother was justifiably so angry she threatened to dissolve the marriage, he took his virginal bride upstairs and . . . and . . ." She stopped and looked away. "He is more animal than man."

"All hearsay," Tearle said in dismissal. "I have seen the men fight. The one who comes will do well in your tournament."

"He can beat you?"

Tearle smiled. "I don't plan to find out. I do not enter the games. I have come to ask a favor of you."

"Ah, so you have not come merely to see the flowers bow down in shame at my beauty?"

"Of course that was my first reason." He reached for her hand, but Anne pulled away.

"I would think more of your compliments if I hadn't heard you use the same ones since I was eight years old. Really, Tearle, you are too easy in your lovemaking. You need a woman who will not give in to you at hearing your same old tired flattery."

"A woman such as you? I could be happy if you would marry me."

"Ha! I shall marry a man who uses his brain instead of his brawn. I want a husband to whom I can talk. If I tried to speak to you of something besides armor and lances, you would fall asleep snoring."

He smiled at her sweetly. She didn't know him at all if that was what she thought most interested him. "I swear I would not fall asleep were I married to you. And I would give you something to do besides talk."

"Your bragging is wasted on me. Now tell me what favor you have to ask of me."

"I plan to help the Peregrines, and I do not want them to know I am a Howard. I shall pose as a man named Smith."

Anne gave him a cool look. She had dark hair, mostly hidden under her headdress, dark brows, and dark eyes that could burn a man when she chose to do so. "You ask me to endanger a man who will be a guest at my father's house?" She rose, glaring at him. "I had thought better of you than this."

He caught her before she'd gone two steps. "I said I meant to help them, and I am telling the truth." He said no more, just looked at her, praying she would believe him.

"Why?" she asked. "Why do you wish to help filthy beasts like these Peregrines? Isn't it true that they believe all your lands to be theirs? You wish me to

42

believe you would help men who would make you a pauper?"

"It is difficult to believe, but it is true. I do not even know these brothers. I've seen them only from a distance, but I have no hatred for them as my brother does. I merely wish to . . ." He couldn't tell her more and couldn't think of an excuse for why he wanted to help the Peregrines without telling her of Zared.

"There is a woman involved," Anne said.

Tearle blinked. Clever brat, he thought. "A woman? How could a woman be involved? There are two brothers coming—an older one to compete and a younger one to be his squire. Can I not do something out of my love of mankind? My brother hates these Peregrines, and I am sick of the talk of hatred. Could I not merely wish for the end of this hatred? Perhaps I wish only to make peace between our families."

"What is her name?"

Tearle narrowed his eyes at her. "I recant my marriage proposal. I have known you since your birth, yet you doubt my good intentions. You dishonor me and my family."

Anne smiled at him in a knowing way. "Are you in love with her as much as you loved that young count's wife?"

"That was something altogether different. She was a woman married to a boy. And I told you, this has nothing to do with a woman." Tearle vowed to go to confession as soon as possible. "I am hurt that you think so little of my character."

"All right," Anne said. "You win. I will keep your secret, but I swear to you that I will find out why you wish to dupe this poor stupid Peregrine man."

Tearle didn't answer her because he had no answer to make. He had no idea why he was interested in a

43

JUDE DEVERAUX

girl who dressed as a boy, a girl who was the daughter of a house that had been at war with his family for generations. Her brothers had killed his brothers. By rights he should hate the girl, should have been glad his brother's men had captured her.

But he hadn't been glad, and later, when she'd tried to dress his wound, he'd wanted her to remain with him.

He looked back at Anne and smiled. Perhaps it was merely that the Peregrine girl was a novelty. He'd had many beautifully dressed women, so perhaps it would be different to bed a woman who might fight him for his clothes in the morning.

"There is nothing to find out," Tearle said, looking innocent. "I but want to help some poor, misunderstood people."

Anne gave an unladylike snort. "You may keep your secrets, but keep those Peregrines from me. I do not wish to be the fool Lady Liana was. Now leave here before someone sees you and tells my father."

Tearle gave a nervous glance toward Hugh Marshall's big house. "Thank you," he said, quickly kissing her hand and bounding over the garden wall out of sight.

Anne sat on the bench after Tearle had left and smiled. It was so good to see a person who could laugh, a person who could take life less than seriously, people such as she had known in France. Anne's mother had taken her daughters home to France when Anne was only five years old and her sister Catherine six, and Anne and her sister had grown up with their mother's family. They'd been surrounded by laughter and learning and beauty. Their mother's family's household had been a place where they'd felt free to say whatever they wanted, where they were encouraged to use their wit and intelligence. They were

44

praised for their beauty, their skill at cards, their talents on a horse or when they read aloud. It was almost as though they could do no wrong.

Looking back, Anne knew she had not been appreciative enough of those wonderful years of freedom and happiness. They seemed so long ago and far away.

When Catherine was seventeen and Anne sixteen Hugh Marshall had demanded that his wife bring his daughters back to England, saying it was time to get them husbands. Since neither Anne nor her sister could remember their father, they felt no fear. Instead they looked at their journey with anticipation, and they whispered excitedly about the idea of husbands.

But Hugh Marshall's demand had sent their mother into a decline. Overnight her face had lost its sparkle, her hair its sheen. At first the girls were too caught up in their own excitement to notice their beloved mother's misery, but by the time they boarded the ship for England they saw that their mother was wraithlike in her thinness, and her face had no color in it.

It didn't take two weeks at their father's house to learn the cause of their mother's misery. Hugh Marshall was a humorless, uneducated bully of a man who ran his rich estates by terror and brute force. He also tried to run his wife and daughters that way.

After the women returned to England there was no more laughter, and certainly no more praise. Hugh Marshall made no attempt to hide his disappointment in how his wife had reared their two daughters.

"You give me nothing but daughters," he bellowed at his wife, who seemed to lose weight daily, "and then you fill their heads with books. They try to *defy* me!" he yelled.

When Catherine had told him she didn't like his choice of husband for her he'd blacked her eye, then locked her in a room for two weeks. Tearfully Catherine had finally agreed to the odious old man her father had chosen for her. Her father, already a rich man, wanted more riches, but more than that he wanted power. He had visions of grandsons who sat at the king's right hand. So he was marrying Catherine to an earl who was a distant relative of the king and enjoyed some society at court.

Six months after they'd returned to England their mother had died. Hugh Marshall had shown no regret at the loss, saying she was never a wife to him, that she'd been able to bear only worthless daughters. He'd allowed her to go to France when he was told she could bear no more children. She was useless to him as a wife if she couldn't give him sons. Since she was dead he planned to get himself another wife, one who could give him a dozen sons or more.

Anne had stood at her mother's grave and felt deep, deep hatred for her father. He had killed her mother as surely as if he had taken a knife to her throat.

After her mother's death and her sister's betrothal Anne had declared war on her father. There was a part of her that didn't care what happened to her, so she dared to defy him and to make some demands of her own.

Anne knew that her father would use her as a pawn in his life game, just as he'd used Catherine, but Anne planned to do better than her sister had. Anne used all her knowledge, used everything she'd ever learned, to talk Hugh Marshall into giving a tournament at Catherine's wedding. At the tournament Anne planned to choose her own husband and to use her powers of persuasion to get her father to marry her to a man who would make her a proper husband. She was not going to allow him to marry her off to a man like himself, as he was doing to Catherine.

She looked up at her father's house and narrowed her eyes. From that point on it would be a battle between her father's brawn and her brain. And how she fought the battle would determine the rest of her life. If her father had his way and married her to a man like himself, she would spend the rest of her days in an even worse hell than she'd known since she had returned to England.

At the tournament she would see what England had to offer, and she would find a man who would please both her father and herself.

She turned when she saw her ladies returning, and she remembered Tearle's visit. She was glad Tearle wasn't going to enter the tournament. Her father would no doubt like Tearle. He was second in line to his brother the duke, and his family was very, very rich.

But Anne had no desire to marry Tearle. He was young, handsome, rich, and suitable, but he was too glib for her, too much a ne'er-do-well. Were they to marry they'd probably kill each other within a year.

"My lady, you have had bad news?"

Anne looked up at her maid. "Nay, I have heard nothing I have not heard before. Come, let us walk. Or better yet, we shall ride. I feel in need of exercise to clear my brain."

Zared stood to one side and watched her brother's men straining to push the big cart out of the mud. They had been traveling since the day before, and now they were within hours of reaching the site of the tournament. Zared was so excited she hadn't been able to sleep and had, instead, pestered Severn with hundreds of questions. Usually he would have snapped at her to be quiet, but he didn't seem able to sleep either. At one point Zared thought perhaps he was excited, too, but she knew that couldn't be. Severn had been to lots of tournaments—hadn't he?

"Did you win the others?" she'd asked.

"What others?"

"The other tournaments you've entered. Have you won all the prizes?"

Severn looked at his little sister's eager face in the moonlight. He'd never attended a tournament in his life. His youth had been spent fighting the Howards. "Of course not," he said, and he watched Zared's face fall. "Rogan won some of them."

Zared laughed. "They must be wonderful, with all the men in armor. They must look splendid."

"No more of that!" Severn commanded. His voice lowered. "How am I to keep you safe and to prevent others from knowing your gender if you look calf-eyes at every strutting ass whose armor catches your eye?"

"I have more sense than that," she hissed. "I would never—"

"And what of Ralph?" he asked mockingly. "The poor boy thought he was beginning to lust after my brother."

"Lust? Are you sure? What did he say?" She stopped at her brother's infuriating chuckle. "His lust is not my concern," she said haughtily. "He is naught to me."

"Umm hmm," Severn said smugly. "You are to behave at this tournament. Do not make a fool of yourself, and do not dishonor the Peregrine name."

"You honor our name on the fields, and I will do my part," she said, a bit angry that he'd think her capable of dishonoring their family name, but then she relaxed. "Tell me of a tournament. Are there many people there? Liana said the people wear beautiful clothes, that even the horses are garbed most wonderfully. Perhaps we should have taken the garments she had made for us."

"Ha!" Severn said. When Liana had shown him an embroidered cloth that his horse was to wear he'd scoffed at her. What did it matter what a man wore when he fought? What was important was whether he knocked his opponent to the ground or not. "I want them to see me, not my horse," he'd told Liana, and he walked away. He wasn't going to let a woman tell him how to dress, *nor* was he going to let her know he had no idea what a knight wore to a tournament. And he wasn't going to let his little sister see his ignorance.

"The men who can't fight need to dress up their horses," Severn said firmly. "I do not need to wear cloth of gold to make me a man." He took a breath and expanded his chest. "It is my experience that the better a fighter a man is, the less he has to dress as a peacock to impress others."

Zared was thoughtful for a moment. She was sure her big brother was right—Severn and Rogan seemed to be right about most things—but there was still doubt in her mind. "If the other men's horses are dressed, will not the Peregrine horses look plain?"

This had crossed Severn's mind, too, and a couple of times on the journey he'd wished he had taken the pretty garments Liana had offered him. The helmet with the plume on it or that black velvet cloak might have looked good on him. He caught himself. No, he thought, he was a fighter, not some London playactor.

"The Peregrines will stand out as a haunch of beef on a table loaded with fancy sweets." He smiled as he said that, liking the image. "You will see, people will remember the Peregrines."

Zared smiled in the darkness. "We need only Hugh Marshall to remember us so he will award you his rich daughter. Do you think your wife will be like

Rogan's?" Her voice was hopeful, for she liked Liana very much and especially liked all the things she'd done to horrible old Moray castle in the past two years.

Severn grimaced at his sister's words, for he hated what Liana had done to his older brother. He didn't like the way marriage had changed Rogan, the way it had softened him. Before marriage Rogan had been a man of fire, a man ready to fight, but since then he constantly preached caution. Instead of fighting he'd rather sit with his wife and listen to ladies singing. Now he found more pleasure in his little son's first steps than he did in training. Severn was sure that someday the Howards were going to attack and kill them all while Rogan was tickling his wife.

"My wife will *not* be like Rogan's!" Severn snapped. "Now let me go to sleep, and no more of your foolish questions. You'll find out what a tournament is like when we get there."

Zared didn't ask him any more questions, but it was a long time before she could go to sleep.

The next day she stood watching the men pushing at the mud-jammed cart. They traveled with four knights, and four servants to do the mundane work, and two big carts full of armor and weapons and a couple of tents. Grazing under trees were Severn's precious warhorses, as well as the riding horses and the nags to pull the carts.

Severn and the men had been working for an hour to clear the carts, and Zared watched them impatiently. They were very near the Marshall estate, and she was eager to get there and set up their tents. During the three days of the tournament all food was to be provided by Hugh Marshall. In the morning the procession would be held, and all the knights would ride their splendid horses before the stands to greet Hugh Marshall and his daughters.

Zared wondered what the Lady Anne was like and how she would fit in with Rogan and his wife. It never crossed Zared's mind that Severn would fail to win Lady Anne's hand. She believed that whatever her brother wanted, he would get.

Zared was the first to hear the rider approaching. She knew what she had to do. She gave a low, piercing whistle to Severn as she ran for a nearby tree. Grabbing the lowest branch, she swung herself upward.

Sometimes it annoyed her that her brothers made her hide at the least sign of danger, but after her recent encounter with the Howards she was not about to be disobedient.

Zared was high off the ground by the time the rider came by, and she gave a look of disgust to see some fool of a lady tearing below her. She'd lost the reins to the horse and was hanging on for all she was worth. Zared would have climbed down, but she didn't dare until Severn had called that it was safe.

She looked through the branches at Severn and the men, swords drawn, ready to fight.

Severn was muddy from head to foot, but Zared could see the way he looked at the approaching woman. That idiotic look he wore could only mean that the woman was pretty. She rolled her eyes, thinking she'd probably be up in the tree all afternoon while Severn wooed the woman.

Zared watched without much interest as Severn ran straight at the horse. The horse reared, but Severn ducked the hooves to catch the reins.

"He'll be killed!"

Zared was so startled at the sudden voice from beneath her that she almost fell from her perch in the

51

tree. Below her were three ladies and two men, all dressed in velvets and furs. She had been watching Severn so intently that she hadn't heard them approach, and she cursed her lack of wariness.

"What does it matter?" one of the men said. "He's only some farmer."

The other man turned. "His death will matter very much if . . ." He paused. "If my lady's gown is splattered with blood." They all laughed.

Before she thought, Zared slipped the knife from her boot and prepared to jump. Some tiny bit of common sense stayed her. She sat rigidly and glared down at the people, trying to see their faces and memorize them.

"Oh, look," one of the women said, "he has caught the reins. He's braver than any farmer I have seen. Do you think Lady Anne will reward him?"

Zared looked through the leaves to the woman on the horse, but her back was to her. Severn's face looked even stupider than it had a moment before, so she guessed this Lady Anne was quite something to look at. She wished her brother's face didn't have quite so much mud on it because, from the way Lady Anne was leaning away from him, she didn't seem to find Severn exactly appealing.

"Thank you," Zared heard Lady Anne say.

"It was a pleasure to save such a beautiful neck."

"Why, the insolent dog!" the man below said. "I'll teach him—"

"He doesn't look as though he'd take kindly to a whipping, and have you not noticed those four buffoons lurking in the trees?" the other man said.

Buffoons! Zared thought. She very much hoped the soft-spined men would face Severn on the tourney field the next day. They would find out he was no farmer!

"Come to me on the morrow at the tournament, and I will reward you," Lady Anne said.

"I shall be there, and I shall collect my reward," Severn answered, eyes twinkling.

She reined her horse away, and Severn went back to his men. Lady Anne rode back to the people under the trees.

"Fine lot of help you are!" Anne snapped. "You left me unprotected with that . . . that . . ."

"He seemed much taken with you, my lady."

"I do believe he would have touched me if I had given him any encouragement." She shuddered. "As it is, I shall have to boil the reins to rid them of his touch."

"He did save you, my lady," one of the women said softly.

"I am aware of that!" Anne snapped. "And now I must reward him. What shall I give him?"

"A bath?" one of the men said, laughing.

Lady Anne did not laugh. "Perhaps, John, I should let *you* bathe him. You seem more fit for women's duties than for men's when you cannot help a lady in danger of falling to her death." She kicked her horse forward.

Zared stayed in the tree and stared after the people for a long while. So that was the Lady Anne, the woman who was to become her sister-in-law. She didn't seem very promising as a woman who would make the Peregrine lives easier, as Liana had done. In fact, the woman seemed like a real shrew, a mean, ill-tempered shrew.

"Can you not hear me?"

Startled, Zared looked down at her brother as he grinned up at her.

"I have called you, but yet you sit there." He turned away to lean against the tree as Zared climbed down.

"Did you see her? She is beautiful. She is as beautiful as a rose."

Zared dropped to the ground. "Roses have thorns."

"What does that mean?"

"I was but stating a fact. You said she's like a rose, and I said roses have thorns. Maybe beauty isn't all there is to a woman."

"And you know so much of women and life?" He was smirking at her.

"More about women than you seem to."

He looked as though he would get angry, but then he ruffled her hair and grinned. "I forget how young you are. Come, help us make camp."

"Camp? But tonight we go to the tourney grounds, and tomorrow we ride in the procession."

"We will ride in the procession as planned, but I do not want the Lady Anne to see me before we enter. She will be most surprised when she sees that it is I who saved her."

"Hope she has her reins washed by then," Zared muttered. "Are you sure?" she asked, louder. "Maybe she won't be so glad to see you. Not as glad as you think."

Severn put his hands on her shoulders and wore the expression of an older, much wiser man talking to a simple but well-meaning child. "You could not see her face. The way she looked at me . . ." He chucked her under the chin. "There are things men and women share—a look, a gesture—things you do not know, but which I as a man of some experience do know. The woman—ah, well, how can I put it? The woman wants me."

"For what? Scrubbing her horse? Look you at yourself. She could not see your face for the mud. She will not recognize you in the procession if you are clean."

Severn dropped his hands and his patronizing expression. "Do not talk to me of things you do not know. I know what I saw in the woman, and I saw lust. Now get to the camp as I said."

Zared obeyed her brother. Maybe he was right. Maybe Lady Anne had looked at Severn with lust, and she only said those things to her people to make them believe she didn't like a man who was covered with mud. She shrugged. She was sure Severn knew much more about ladies and tournaments and lust than she did.

Chapter Four

Zared sat on her horse with her back utterly rigid. She was sure that if she didn't remain absolutely stiff, she would fall into a heap of tears.

Before her, on his war horse, sat Severn, wearing sixty pounds of armor, and she couldn't tell what he was thinking or feeling. Around them, huddled close, were the men who had come with them, but outside their group was a laughing, jeering crowd of peasants.

That morning Zared had ridden proudly behind her brother, proud to carry the eight-foot-long Peregrine banner, but as they neared the Marshall estate and the field for the tournament they had halted.

Before them rode long lines of gorgeously attired knights. Their armor, partially covered with fur-trimmed, richly embroidered garments, was painted with beautiful designs, or else had been dipped in silver and flashed in the sunlight. Plumes or models of beasts and fowl decorated the knights' helmets.

Zared gaped at the men and boys before her, then looked at the Peregrine group. Severn's armor was dented and rusted, and his horse wore only a saddle, no sparkling cloths. The armor his men carried was in even worse condition, and as for Zared, her old tunic was threadbare in places and dirty most everywhere else.

"We cannot enter the procession," she whispered to Severn.

He threw up his face guard and glared at her. "Fine clothes do not make a good fighter. You are a Peregrine—remember that." He slammed down his guard and turned away.

Yes, I am a Peregrine, she thought, and she straightened her spine. Severn would beat them all in battle, so what did clothes matter?

Severn raised his hand, and the Peregrine knights fell in behind him as they started riding toward the tournament grounds. Along the road the peasants, who had come from many miles away to see the spectacle, had stopped to gape in awe at the sumptuously clad men.

When they saw the Peregrine knights they pointed and laughed. Zared kept her eyes straight ahead, not daring to look at them. What did they matter? she thought. Only the coming games mattered.

At the entrance to the grounds all the participants halted, and a Marshall herald called off the name of the first challenger to go before the Marshall family and the king.

Zared had assumed that the procession was just that, a parade of men riding before the Marshalls. But what she saw made her mouth fall open. She was as awed as the peasants.

The first knight to enter was named Grenville. He was dressed in black velvet over armor painted gold, and he was surrounded by half a dozen young pages also wearing black and gold. Before him went four trumpeters announcing Grenville's arrival. Behind the trumpeters were fifteen pretty young girls wearing saffron-yellow gowns, baskets in their arms as they spread rose petals on the ground for Grenville's horse to tread upon.

"The horses will make a mess of the roses," Severn said, and Zared joined him in his ridicule. She wanted some way to feel superior, but as Zared looked about and saw merchants dressed better than the Peregrines she wished she had not been allowed to attend the tournament.

As the procession continued Zared realized that Grenville's show had been one of the tamest. Some men entered with plays being performed before them. Others had entire orchestras. One man had a long, flat wagon pulled by six beautiful black horses, and on the wagon was a man dressed as St. George who was trying to slay a twenty-foot-long green dragon that hissed at him.

With each entry Zared sank a little lower in her saddle. Perhaps if she closed her eyes and wished hard enough she would find herself safe at home, away from the humiliation she was going to face. The people in the stands were applauding each entrant as he rode past. Would they laugh when the Peregrines came by?

"You!"

Zared turned to see a boy near her own age looking up at her. He was holding a lovely tunic of red velvet up to her. "What is this?" she asked.

"It's from my master," the boy said angrily. "He said to give it to you."

Charity, Zared thought, and the steel returned to her spine. "Tell your master I want nothing from him."

"From the look of you, you need everything."

Zared didn't think what she did, but she took her foot out of the stirrup and hit the boy in the chest, sending him sprawling.

"Behave yourself!" Severn bellowed at her, taking his anger about the procession out on her.

"But he offered me—" she began, stopping when she saw a man bend to help the boy from the dirt. He was the most beautiful human she'd ever seen: blond hair, white skin, blue eyes, armor of silver that was draped with white silk embroidered with silver roses.

Zared's mouth fell open as she stared at the man.

"Forgive my squire," the man said, and his voice flowed over Zared like hot honey. "I sent the tunic. I thought perhaps, through an accident, all of your garments were lost. I meant only kindness."

"I . . . we . . ." Zared could only gape, not able to say a coherent word. She didn't know men could be so beautiful.

"We need no charity!" Severn bellowed at the stranger. "We have all we need to fight. I am no popinjay who must wear flowers in order to fight," he said sneeringly.

The boy whom Zared had knocked down turned into a fighting cat. "You know not who you speak to!" he yelled. "This is Colbrand. He will knock you off your horse before you enter the lists."

"Jamie!" Colbrand said sharply. "Leave us."

The boy Jamie gave Zared a defiant look, then turned away. "Forgive him," Colbrand said to Severn. "He is young, and this is his first tournament."

Severn didn't answer, just glared.

Colbrand smiled at Zared, and she nearly fell off her horse. His smile was like a ray of sunshine on a rainy day. "I did not mean any offense. Good luck to you all."

She watched as he turned away. He bolted into the saddle of a white horse that was clothed in white that had been embroidered with more silver roses.

She was still gaping at him, her chin down about her waist, when Severn hit her on the shoulder so hard she almost fell out of her saddle.

"Get that look off your face," he growled.

Zared tried, but it wasn't easy. She watched Colbrand enter the procession. Before him went six men carrying hand-held harps. Behind them came six more men with trumpets. Then came six knights on white horses carrying Colbrand's weapons. Colbrand rode alone, his squire and more retainers behind him.

All of Colbrand's people, from musicians to knights, wore white and silver. Zared thought his group stood out splendidly from all the colorful spectacles that had gone before him. She sighed, for not only was he beautiful, but so were his horse and his clothes and his—

"We ride," Severn said, and Zared could tell from his voice that he was angry. She straightened. It was better to get it over with, she thought.

Severn was indeed angry. Theirs were the last name to be called to enter the procession, and already he could see that some of the people in the stands were beginning to leave. It was time for dinner, and they'd looked down the line, seen that the Peregrines lacked the sumptuous attire of the others, and decided they were not worth seeing.

Anger raged through him. People were judging men on the sparkle of their clothes and not on their skill at arms. Since when was a man's worth based on what he wore instead of how he acted?

The act of charity from that man, that Colbrand, had been the final straw. Severn couldn't wait to flatten that softling on the lists. He imagined standing over him and laughing.

Severn motioned for his men to fall in behind him, and he waited for the herald's signal that the Peregrines could at last go before the stands. Severn saw the herald watching the stands and saw that he was waiting for the Marshall family to leave before he allowed the Peregrines to go.

It was when Severn saw Lady Anne rising to leave that he decided he wasn't going to wait. Even if no one else wanted to see him, he knew she did. Hadn't she promised him a reward for saving her?

He tossed his helmet to the ground, then spurred his horse forward, ignoring the shouts of the herald, ignoring the laughter of the people around him, concentrating only on getting to the beautiful Lady Anne.

At the sound of the thundering hooves of his war-horse everyone halted and turned to look. Severn had an impression of a man standing beside Lady Anne, but he didn't look at him. Severn bent to the right, his thighs holding onto the horse as his armor-clad right arm caught Lady Anne about the waist and pulled her to him. He tried to kiss her, but he was so sweaty from sitting for hours in the sun in his helmet that his face merely slid across hers.

At the far end of the grounds he halted his horse, then triumphantly set her on the ground. "I have taken my reward," he said loudly to all the people that he knew were watching.

Lady Anne's eyes were alive and bright, and she looked as though she wanted to say something, but he didn't give her a chance before he rode away. Later there would be time for her to whisper love words to him. He rode away without looking back to see the impression he'd made. But there was no laughter. He had shut them all up.

As Zared watched her brother break the rules and gallop ahead and snatch the Lady Anne from beside her father she prayed to be struck dead on the spot.

Her prayer was not answered.

What was Severn about? She knew next to nothing about tournament etiquette, but she could see that what he'd done was awful, truly awful. They could have quietly paraded past the stands, and perhaps their worn, dirty clothes would have caused little comment, but after that . . .

She looked at Lady Anne, standing where Severn had left her, her hands in fists at her side. Zared knew fury when she saw it, and Lady Anne was murderous.

All around her the people were silent, too stunned to make a sound. Then, to her left, came one loud, sneering laugh. Zared turned and saw it was the boy Jamie. He was standing there in his white tunic and hose, so clean and neat, and Zared's own rage came to the surface.

She reined her horse toward the boy, lowered the staff of the Peregrine banner as though it were a lance, and charged. The boy's eyes widened in horror as he began to run.

Zared never reached him, for the long banner trailed on the ground, tangled in her horse's feet, and made it stumble. Zared, leaning forward in her charge, kept going forward even when the horse stopped. She went flying over the horse's head, landing flat on her back. For some moments she could neither breathe nor think. She just lay there looking up at the sky.

The first thing she heard was the roar of laughter.

Standing over her was Jamie, his hands on his knees

as he looked down at her and laughed. To her right she could hear hundreds more people laughing.

She was too dazed to move, or to do anything but lie there.

"Cease!" she heard someone say, and she looked up to see Colbrand bending over her. In his white and silver he looked like an angel.

"Are you hurt, boy?"

Zared managed to shake her head, and when he held out his hand to help her up she smiled at him.

"Good," Colbrand said, smiling back. "Let me look at you."

He put his hands on her shoulders and turned her about, dusting off the back of her. Zared thought she might die from the pleasure of his touch. She looked at his face, at his blue, blue eyes, and felt her knees go weak.

"I think you *are* hurt," Colbrand said, and to Zared's disbelief, he swept her into his arms.

It was too much for Zared. She fainted.

Anne Marshall bathed her face in cool water and looked in the metal mirror on the wall. Her face was still red from the scrubbing she had given it when she'd tried to remove that man's sweat from her body. Her ribs still ached from where he'd pulled her off the ground, his armor digging into her, bruising her skin.

For a moment her ears seemed to ring with the laughter of the people after that . . . that . . . She could think of no name for him. He had humiliated her, made her an object of ridicule before hundreds of people. Even that odious old man who had married Catherine that morning had laughed at her.

She looked in the mirror and saw her eyes change from rage to tears. If only she could have remained in

France with her mother . . . If only she had never come to the barbarous land where men were little more than animals. If only—

She didn't finish the thought, for the door to her chamber burst open, and her father entered. He didn't bother to knock, never bothered to show the least respect to either of his daughters.

"People are below eating, and they want to see my unmarried daughter," he said.

"I am not well," Anne said truthfully. "I cannot eat."

"You will eat if I have to force you. I'll have no daughter who sulks because a man touched her."

Anne's self-pity left her. "A *man!* That barbarian, that pagan! You call that animal a man? I have encountered dogs with more sensibilities than that one."

"You don't know a man from a dog." Hugh snorted. "You women took tournaments, these preparations for war, and turned them into showings of fashion. Were it up to you, the man with the most feathers or gold embroidery would win the prizes. The Peregrine boy isn't—"

"Peregrine!" Anne gasped. "Is that who he was? I should have guessed. He is brother to that man who married poor Lady Liana. It is no wonder—"

"Married two years and she's given him one son, and another due any day. The father of these Peregrines bred nothing but sons."

"There is more to life than sons!" Anne spat at him.

Hugh Marshall took a step toward his daughter, but Anne didn't allow herself to flinch. "I would not look down my nose too much at him. You will perhaps join this Lady Liana in breeding Peregrine sons."

"No," Anne said under her breath. "Please . . ." she began, but she stopped. She wasn't going to beg her father for anything. She straightened her shoulders. Remember, she thought, it was her brains against his power. "If you wish grandsons who are stupid, then by all means marry me to the man. No doubt the king will want one of these Peregrines at his table. What I saw today assures me of the suitability of a Peregrine at court. But perhaps that means naught to you. You would no doubt like to see your grandsons jeered at when they parade before the king. Perhaps you should ask His Majesty if he plans to invite this Peregrine knight to sit above the salt with him."

Hugh glared at his daughter. He hated clever women, hated it when a woman said something he had not considered. Her mother had been like that, her tongue moving twice as fast as his brain. When she'd asked to leave and return to her people in France he had been more than happy to let her go.

But at no cost was he going to allow his too-clever daughter to know that her words had confused him.

"If I see you show your displeasure to this man, you will regret it," he said, then he quickly left the room. If he had no other considerations, he'd marry the witch to the roughest man he could find, he thought. She needed a man who'd curb her tongue. But she knew that Hugh wanted grandsons. He'd not been able to get sons on a woman himself, so he must look to his puny daughters to give him grandsons. Much as he hated to admit it, the girl was right. He did not want grandsons who would be laughed at at a tournament. Even the king had chuckled at the sight of the dirty Peregrines.

Hugh grimaced. Damn the girl. If there was anything he hated more than a clever female, it was a female who was right. He stormed down the hall to the stairs. In the next three days he'd find a husband for the girl and get rid of her. He wasn't going to put up with her sharp tongue and sharper brain. Let another man deal with her.

After her father left Anne breathed a sigh of relief. She was going to be able to handle him—for the moment, anyway. But even as she hurriedly finished dressing she knew she would not always have the words to control him. He was as stupid as he was mean, and at one point he would forget about reason and act only on instinct. What Anne knew she had to do was to choose a man and get her father to approve of him. She had to find a man who could replace that filthy Peregrine in her father's mind.

She lifted the three-foot-long cone-shaped henna and slipped it on her head, arranging it at the perfect angle so it was tipped far back. The heavy wire loop on her forehead that held the weight of the henna cut into her skin, but the pain soon lost its bite. She adjusted the soft, transparent silk veil over the henna and gave herself one last look in the mirror. She wanted to look her best because she was going hunting. Hunting for a man.

When Zared awoke she was lying on a cot in her brother's tent, and through the open flap she could see that the sun was low in the sky. Feeling groggy, she didn't try to sit up. The last thing she clearly remembered was Colbrand picking her up in his strong arms.

She smiled up at the tent roof and remembered the look of him, the smell of him, the sound of him, the—

"So, you are awake."

Languidly she turned her head to look at the man standing over her. But the light was behind him, and she couldn't see him very well. "Is there anything to eat? I'm hungry," she said.

The man snorted. "It is, no doubt, hard work making a fool of yourself."

"A fool of myself?" In puzzlement she squinted at the man. He seemed somewhat familiar, but she couldn't quite place him. He moved out of the bright light, his back to her, and she absently listened to dishes clattering and a noggin being filled. Her mind was full of Colbrand. Perhaps she had dreamed him. Perhaps no man alive could be as he was.

"Eat this," the man said, and he thrust a wooden platter of meat and bread before her.

She took the food, sat up on her elbow, and began to eat. The man sat on a stool beside the cot. Outside a clash of arms sounded. "It has begun!" she said, sitting up. "The fighting has started. Colbrand will need me." She started to get up, but a big hand pushed her chest just below her throat, and she sat back down.

"What do you think—" she began, then her eyes widened as she looked at the man before her. It was the youngest Howard! "You!" she said under her breath, and immediately she reached for the knife hidden in her boot.

"It isn't there," he said calmly. "I have removed all your weapons, and I must say I enjoyed looking for them."

She put her head down and rammed him in the chest. He made a little *woof* sound, but then he caught her in his arms and easily held her.

"Severn!" she shouted.

He put his hand across her mouth. "Your brother is on the field." He paused. "As is Colbrand, the weakling."

Zared stopped struggling against him. "Colbrand is not a weakling."

"And you know so much, do you? Seen him fight a hundred times, have you?"

"Let me go. My brother will chop you into little pieces. He'll—"

"Yes, yes, you've said this."

Zared realized that he was toying with her as she struggled against him, as a child and a parent might play. But his hands were roaming over her hips and thighs. With a push she shoved away from him to land back on the cot. She put her chin up and looked at him.

"Take *me,* but do not sneak up on my brother. I will go with you and be your prisoner if you will not harm my brother. I will . . . do whatever you want if you will but keep your army from attacking my brothers."

Tearle looked at her a long while, knowing she meant every word she said. For all her boy's hair and clothes, there was a woman underneath, a woman capable of sacrificing all for love.

"I am here to harm no one. Your brother believes I am called Smith and that I have been sent here by Lady Liana."

Zared gaped at him, her mouth opening and closing like a fish. "Liana sent you?" she gasped.

"No, of course not. Eat your food, and I'll tell you all."

"I'll eat nothing a Howard gives me."

"That is your choice, but you will perhaps get hungry, as I am to care for you and your brother for the next three days."

"Care for? A Howard care for a Peregrine? You mean to poison us." She started to get up, but he pushed her down again, and she didn't fight him. "Where is Severn?" she whispered. "If you have harmed him, Rogan will—"

"You are a bloodthirsty wench. I have harmed no one. Your brother is on the fields waiting his turn to knock some fool off his horse."

"As he will knock you down," she said. "You have

68

seen what a Peregrine blade can do," she said, referring to the cut she had given him.

"And it still pains me. You owe me much for that, as
well as for saving your brother's name."

"No Peregrine owes a Howard," she said. There was
a noise outside, and as Tearle turned to look Zared
leaped from the cot and headed for the door. Tearle's
foot tripped her, but he caught her before she fell.

"Where are you going?"

"To get my brother. To escape you. To fetch the
king. Anyone!"

"If you call your brother and he kills me, an
unarmed man, then my brother will attack that heap
of stones your brothers own and kill all the Peregrines." Tearle gave her a bored look. "Go. You are
free to call your brother. Get my death over with, but
please, beg him to use a very sharp sword. I do not
wish to die a lingering death."

Zared stood there blinking at him and felt as though
she'd lost the war before the first battle. Everything
he'd said was true. If Severn did kill the man, it could
mean the deaths of all the Peregrines.

Feeling very heavy, she sat down on the edge of the
cot. "What do you want?" she whispered. "Why are
you here?"

"I have come to help," he said brightly. "From what
I had heard of your family, I correctly guessed you
would come to the tournament in rags."

"We do not wear rags," Zared said indignantly.

He curled his upper lip as he looked at her worn and
greasy tunic. "Rags," he repeated. "Days ago I sent
one of my men to my brother to fetch clothing. I
regretted he did not return in time to prevent this
morn's disaster, but now your brother wears more
suitable clothing."

69

Zared was beginning to recover from the shock of waking to find a Howard bent over her. She went to the tent doorway and looked out. Standing near the lists was her brother, and he was wearing a black tunic over his armor. She could not be sure from a distance, but it looked to be embroidered in gold.

"My brother," Zared spoke slowly and evenly. "My brother is wearing clothing given him by a *Howard?*"

"Yes, but he doesn't know that. He believes it comes from his lovely sister-in-law."

Zared sat down again. "Tell me all," she whispered.

"After you made a fool, an ass, a laughingstock of yourself yesterday over that colorless, weak, simpering Colbrand, I—"

"When I want a Howard's opinion, I will ask for it. Tell me what treachery you have done."

"Treachery? I? I have been kind and generous while your Colbrand— All right, I will tell you. After you lost your senses I came to your rescue and took you from that spineless—"

"You touched me? A *Howard* touched me?"

"I have been touching you since I met you."

"I shall have to bathe."

"Whatever accomplishes that is worth it."

"Continue!" she spat at him.

He smiled at her. How easy she was to provoke to passion. "There was no Peregrine tent, so I took you to another."

"To Colbrand's?" she asked eagerly.

"Nay, not there. I would rather have thrown you into a pit of vipers than take you there."

"With a Howard I would rather go into a pit of vipers."

Tearle snorted. "I knew I had much to do and you would be a hindrance to me, so I gave you a draught of—"

"You have poisoned me," she whispered. "How long do I have to live? I must go to warn my brother. Does he die also?"

She was almost outside before Tearle caught her. He grabbed her shoulders and put his nose to hers. "Do you not hear? No one is hurt. I have not come to hurt you. I gave you a drink to make you sleep so I could do my work without your hindrance."

"Without my sounding an alarm," she said, jerking out of his grip.

"That, too." His voice softened. "Come, sit down. Eat."

"I would never eat what a Howard touched."

He took her plate from the cot, tore away a piece of bread and ate it, then cut off a piece of meat. "The food is not poisoned."

Zared was still not convinced even though she was very hungry. "Why are you here?" she repeated.

"I came . . ." He trailed off, for he didn't know why he was there. Some part of him said he wanted an end to the hatred, but another part knew that if it weren't for that angry young woman, he wouldn't care what happened between his brother and the Peregrines. He had no idea why he was so interested in her. There were many other women prettier. Others who were richer. Nearly all women were sweeter-tempered than she was. Yet there he was, and he didn't think he could leave if he wanted to.

"I came to end the feuding," he said at last.

"To end . . ." Zared was so stunned she sat on the cot.

"You see, my brother is obsessed with the hatred between our families. Your entire family is concerned with little else. No, do not deny it. It is all you talk of, and I have seen the way you are prisoners in that falling-down castle of yours."

71

Zared was amused at the idea of ending the feud. She knew him to be cowardly and weak-fleshed, but was he stupid also? "How do you propose to stop the fighting? To give us back the land your family stole from us? Will you give my brother Rogan the title of duke that should be his?"

"Why, no," Tearle began, and at that moment he had an idea. "I shall end the feud by marrying a Peregrine to a Howard. We will join our families."

"Do you have a sister hidden away who you plan to marry to Severn? Some drooling idiot of a sister you will try to foist on my handsome brother?"

He smiled at her. "I thought perhaps I would marry you."

Zared made the mistake of trying to breathe and laugh at the same time. She choked rather spectacularly.

Tearle pounded her on the back and handed her a mug of watered wine. She gulped the wine while trying to move out of his reach.

"Me?" she said at last. "Marry me? Me marry a Howard?"

Tearle stiffened. "What better could a Peregrine hope for? You have no dowry." He looked her up and down. "You are not even a full woman."

"Woman enough to want a man," she shot back at him. "Do you know how my brothers would take my saying I was to marry a Howard? My brother Rogan would—"

"Yet you considered Severn marrying a sister, if I had one, which I do not." He had talked of the marriage on impulse, but since he'd said it, he didn't like her laughing at him. After all, it was an excellent idea, the best part being that he'd get his hands on her slim little body.

Zared knew the man was stupid. "If my brother

married a Howard, the woman would come to us. If I married you, a mere second son, I would go to live under your brother's rule. Do you think Oliver Howard would treat me well? Or do you think he would enjoy having a Peregrine to torture?"

Tearle blinked at her. He could see his brother laughing in glee at the prospect of having a Peregrine under his roof. What he would do to Zared would increase the feud, not dampen it.

"So you came to marry me," Zared said, still laughing at him. "How did you get past my brother?"

"I have told you. I brought clothes." Tearle didn't feel jubilant any longer. He'd never proposed marriage to a woman before, and he had certainly never been turned down. What more did a woman want? He was the brother of a duke, he was handsome, he was—

"Surely you did not think I would be fool enough to agree to marry you," she said. "It would be the same as turning myself over to you as a prisoner. I want the truth of why you are here."

Tearle tried to recover his self-esteem. He grinned and shrugged. "You cannot blame me for trying. I told the truth when I said I wanted to end the feud. I am tired of hatred, and I thought perhaps I could befriend your brother and stop the hatred."

"Befriend? How can a Howard be a friend to a Peregrine?"

"I have made progress already. I brought clothes, and I brought your brother a splendid suit of silvered armor. It is mine. We are nearly the same size." He meant to point out to her his own strong, muscular body and to let her know he wasn't the weakling she seemed to think he was. But she didn't seem to hear.

She stood and walked to one side of the big tent. "You came bearing clothes and armor—Howard clothes and armor—and my brother accepted it all without question?" Zared was having some doubts about her brother. Severn had said he'd been to lots of tournaments, yet he hadn't known about the procession. He said he knew all about women, yet he hadn't known Lady Anne would hate being picked up in front of everyone.

"It was easier than I'd hoped. Your brother seemed to be expecting clothes from Lady Liana."

"Not expecting them, but Liana . . ." She stopped. She wasn't going to tell that man, that enemy, anything. It wasn't like Severn to believe a stranger, but perhaps he had been embarrassed this morning, too.

Zared's head came up. "So you are to be a servant to my brother? Is that what you told me? He is to call you Smith, and you, a rich man—falsely rich, for your land belongs to my family, but a rich man nonetheless —you are to fetch food for us? Shall you empty the chamber pots?"

"I'll see that those lazy servants of yours do the work."

She didn't believe him, not one word he said. "Now that the Howards know there is a Peregrine female, is it I you plan to take?"

"I have told no one that you are female. I have told no one that I am a Howard."

"Someone will recognize you. Someone will point you out as a Howard, and then my brother will kill you and your brother—"

"Cease!" he half yelled. "I am not the evil monster you portray me to be. I am a simple man who does not want to spend his life hating. I saw a way to befriend the Peregrines, and I took it. No one knows me here except Anne, and she—" He stopped because he'd said far too much.

"Anne? *Lady* Anne? The woman Severn is going to marry?"

74

"Anne marry your uneducated lout of a brother? She'd rather—"

Zared slapped him across the face, and it was a good, hard slap.

"Why, you little—" he said, going for her.

"You are awake," Severn said from the doorway, his eyes adjusting to the dim light. "Have you met Smith? Liana sent him." He walked toward the cot and picked up Zared's plate, but before he could get a bite to his mouth Zared grabbed the food from him.

"That's mine," she said. "I mean it was meant for me."

Severn looked puzzled. "All right. Smith, get me food."

"No!" Zared yelled, dropping her plate. Food fell to the ground as she ran to put herself between Tearle and the food that stood on a little table.

"What is wrong with you?" Severn asked, frowning.

"Uh . . . uh . . ." She couldn't seem to think quickly enough.

"I believe the boy is concerned that this food isn't as good as what the Marshalls are serving. This is cold and greasy, while in the hall hot soups are being served."

Severn still looked puzzled. It wasn't like Zared to care about food. As long as the meat didn't have maggots on it and the weevils in the bread had been baked and weren't still crawling, the Peregrines didn't pay much attention to food.

"I want you to have the *best*," Zared said. "To keep up your strength for the fighting."

Severn rumpled her hair. "All right. I'll go up to the hall. You stay here with Smith and sort out the clothes Liana sent. See if there's something in there for you."

"My clothes are more than suitable for a Peregrine." She looked at Severn's tunic of thick black silk.

There were gold and silver dragons embroidered along the edge. "We need not all look like peacocks."

Severn gave her a hard look. "Do not disgrace me. Smith, see to my squire." With that, he turned on his heel and left the tent.

Zared turned to look at Tearle. "Once in my life I get to see the world, and I am put in the care of a Howard. Now I shall have to stay with you every minute to see that you do no harm to my brother."

"Every minute?" Tearle smiled, liking the prospect.

Chapter Five

Zared watched as the Howard man went outside and rummaged through the cart that contained the clothes and weapons he had brought. Her belly growled with hunger, and in the distance she could hear the clash of weapons and the shouts of the crowd as the combatants met one another in the joust. Had Severn fought yet? Who had he fought? Had Colbrand fought yet?

She didn't know because she had been drugged by a Howard and had slept the day away.

Watching the man with his black hair and black clothes, she knew that what was to have been a pleasurable time for her was going to be a nightmare. Do Howards mean to ruin *all* my life? she thought. Was she to have no time when she was free of them? On her own land she could not ride out alone without being snatched by a Howard. And it looked as though she wouldn't even be allowed to enjoy herself at the tournament.

She watched him pull out a garment of ruby-red velvet, the hem trimmed in gray fox.

He had proposed marriage to her. Marriage between a Howard and a Peregrine. How absurd the idea was. Her brothers would never allow her to live under Oliver Howard's power. Not to mention the fact that the Howards would probably chain her to a wall and starve her.

As she watched the Howard she knew he would not have strength enough to fight his older brother. A marriage to him would mean being a prisoner to his brother. The weak man who had nearly died from a small cut was not man enough to stand up to someone like Oliver Howard.

"This," he said, holding out the dark red tunic to her. Across it was draped a pair of finely knit hose.

"I will—" She started to say that she would not wear anything a Howard gave to her, but then Colbrand went striding by. He was as beautiful as she remembered, perhaps even more beautiful. Again he was wearing white. A white as pure and as clean as a mountain lake. His hair shone in the sunlight. Rays sparkled off his armor. His eyes—

Tearle shoved the tunic into her chest so hard that Zared took a step backward. "Put it on," he growled.

She felt the velvet, looked at the fur. Perhaps Colbrand would like her better in pretty clothes. "I will wear them, but not for you," she snapped at Tearle, turning back into the tent. "Stand here so that I can see where you are," she ordered.

With one eye on her enemy's back she quickly changed into the new clothes. She stretched out her leg, pleased that there were no holes in the hose, no

78

grease stains. There was soft fur about the neck, and she rubbed her cheek against it.

"Are you dressed yet?" Tearle asked impatiently from outside. "Your brother rides against his first opponent."

Zared shoved past him to go outside and ignored the way he looked at her. "Come, I would see my brother. You are to stay near me."

"I will force myself to do so," Tearle said, chuckling.

But Zared never made it to the lists. Not far from the dilapidated Peregrine tent she could see a tent of white sendal, a white banner embroidered with silver leopards flying from the crown. As though she had no control over her feet, she turned toward the tent.

"Your brother—" Tearle said from behind her, but Zared kept walking.

Before the tent sat Colbrand's squire Jamie, ineptly trying to sharpen a sword on a round, pedal-powered whetstone.

"You," Jamie said, looking up at Zared with the hovering black shadow behind her. Jamie had decided he hated the Peregrine boy because he had been the cause of a severe tongue-lashing from Colbrand. "What do *you* want?" Jamie sneered.

Zared opened her mouth to reply, but then Colbrand came out of the tent. He no longer wore his armor, but his big, muscular body was covered in a short white tunic, his legs encased in pale gray hose. She could only stare at him speechlessly.

Colbrand did not at first see the Peregrine squire. His eyes were on Jamie. "That is not the way to hold the blade," Colbrand said in a tone, as though he'd said it a hundred times. "You have not your mind on the task. I will show you."

"I can do it," Zared said, and she walked to Colbrand, her eyes big as she gazed up at him.

Colbrand smiled at her. He was used to young boys hero-worshipping him and this boy was no exception, he thought. He was always kind to the boys, for who knew if in a year or two he might not meet one in a joust. But then Colbrand was kind to most people because it was his nature.

"I would be pleased if you would show my squire," Colbrand said.

Zared took a step forward, but a big hand clamped on her shoulder. "He has to attend his brother."

"Oh, then you must go."

Zared turned and narrowed her eyes at Tearle. "My brother can take care of himself. *All* the Peregrines can take care of themselves, including *this* one." She jerked her shoulder from his grip, then turned and smiled back at Colbrand. She was still looking at him as she took the sword from Jamie.

"I'll get you for this," Jamie whispered as he relinquished Colbrand's sword.

Zared ignored him as she sat on the stool before the whetstone. When she'd been growing up her brothers had despaired of making her as strong as a boy might have been, so they gave her many peripheral tasks, such as sharpening swords and banging dents from armor. She was good at putting an edge on a blade, and she used all her knowledge to put a perfect, sharp edge on Colbrand's sword.

When she was finished she held it up to him, looking at him as a puppy might when it hoped for praise from its master.

Colbrand took the big sword and ran his thumb along the edge. "Excellent," he said, and he smiled so warmly at Zared that she was sure she was going to faint again.

At that moment a vendor came by, a big tray on a ribbon about his neck.

"Work such as this must be rewarded," Colbrand said. "Are you boys hungry? No," he said, laughing, "boys of your age are *always* hungry." He gave the vendor a coin and told Zared and Jamie to choose the tarts they wanted.

Zared chose a cherry tart, and for a moment she just stared at it. It was from Colbrand, and she had an urge to save the tart, to keep it forever. But hunger won out, and she ate it, but slowly.

"Have you fought yet?" she asked Colbrand.

"Once," he answered, smiling fondly at the boy who looked up at him with such naked worship. The boy had no doubt heard of his reputation, of the many prizes he had won over the years.

"And he won," Jamie said belligerently to Zared. "He scored four times. Colbrand has *never* been knocked from his horse."

"Now, Jamie," Colbrand said. "We should not tempt fate. Perhaps at this tournament I shall be downed. There are some new men here, such as your brother. He is good with a lance?"

Zared bit down on a cherry pit, and instead of spitting it on the ground she sucked it dry, then slipped it into the top of her hose. "He is very good," she said. "But perhaps with your skills and practice you will show yourself well against him."

"Show himself well!" Jamie said, coming to his feet. "Colbrand will knock your brother to the ground." Jamie didn't like the way his beloved master was paying attention to the too-pretty boy. He was angry that the boy could sharpen a sword better than he could. He didn't like the way people were saying that for all their dirt, the Peregrines were brilliant fighters. He knew Colbrand expected him to display good manners at all times, but the bragging of the Peregrine brat was too much for him. He leaped on Zared.

Tearle's first instinct was to let the two of them fight it out. Zared had been making a fool of herself over Colbrand, and he didn't like it one bit. How could she be so starry-eyed over a man who was too stupid to see that she was a girl? How could she be so dumb as to fall for a pretty face on top of some shiny armor?

Neither Colbrand nor Tearle had time to interrupt the brawl because Severn, wearing armor, his hair plastered to his head with sweat, came storming up to them and grabbed both Jamie and Zared by the necks of their tunics and pulled them apart. He didn't so much as look at Jamie but flung him aside as though he were a used rag. Zared he held on to, and he pulled her with him as he hauled her through the tents, past the watching eyes of the many people on the grounds, and led her to their tent. He shoved her inside, shoved her so hard she nearly went through the other side.

She knew Severn was angry, and when one of her brothers was like that she knew better than to open her mouth.

"You are my squire," he said in a low voice that Zared knew meant he was really, truly, deeply angry. "Your duties are to bring me fresh lances, to care for my horses, to give me drink when I need it. Yet you sleep the day away, and when you wake, do you come to help me? No, you make an ass of yourself over that puffed-up, strutting—"

"Colbrand isn't—" Zared stopped herself. It was not the time to argue with her brother.

He advanced on her, and she stepped back in fear. While her brothers often pummeled each other, they'd never hit her in the same way, but she didn't trust him to hold his temper. "I am most sorry, Severn," she whispered.

"I've a mind to return you to Liana."

"Oh, no, please don't," she whispered. "I will help you. I swear it."

"How? By playing the fool to that Colbrand? Don't you realize that he also tried for the Lady Anne's hand? At dinner it was said that she favors the man, as does her father."

"I didn't mean any harm. His squire is stupid. He doesn't even know how to sharpen a sword. I had to show him all that you have taught me, and—"

"You sharpened *his* sword?" Severn's eyes were popping, he was so angry. "A sword he is to use against *me?* Has your loyalty changed so completely? Do you wish to see him shed my blood?"

"No, Severn, please, I meant no harm. I was only trying to help. His squire cannot even sharpen a sword."

"And *my* squire cannot even get out of bed. What is it you want from this Colbrand? Do you wish to see him beat me?"

"No, Severn, of course not. I just . . ."

"What?" he demanded.

"I . . ." What could she say? That she found Colbrand beautiful beyond words? That when she was near him her skin tingled?

"I believe she desires him in her bed," Tearle said calmly from behind Severn.

"I do not!" Zared bellowed. "What do you know of my wants? What do you know of anything? You are—"

"She?" Severn asked. "You told someone of your sex?" He sat down on a stool, his head in his hands. "Liana was right."

"I didn't tell him anything," Zared spat. "He knew."

Severn looked up at Tearle questioningly.

Tearle was quite calm. "Look you at her. Would *you* believe her to be male? She is so hot for this Colbrand she can barely stand when he is near, yet the fool thinks her to be a boy. She argues as a girl; she speaks as a girl; she walks as a girl; her voice is that of a girl. How could I not know?"

Severn's mind was reeling. If it became common knowledge that Zared was female, that knowledge was sure to get back to Oliver Howard. He seemed to have taken a vow to capture all Peregrine females, and Zared would be no exception. How could Severn possibly protect her if he was always on the jousting field? That day, when she should have been where he could see her, she was instead dallying with a man who was competing with him for a woman's hand. How was he to know that perhaps Colbrand wasn't paid by Oliver Howard?

"You must return to Rogan," Severn said at last. "You are in danger."

"No!" Zared and Tearle said in unison.

Tearle knew that if she left now, he'd never see her again. "I will see to her," he said quickly.

"You?" Zared said, sneering. "You, a—"

"A what?" Tearle asked, daring her to tell Severn he was a Howard.

Zared looked at her brother. "He's a coward and a weakling, and he can't look after anyone."

At another time Severn might have been puzzled by his sister's animosity toward the stranger, but he had too much on his mind. "Liana sent him; she chose him." His opinion of his sister-in-law was rising by the hour. He should have listened to her and taken the clothes and left his sister at home, he thought.

"Liana didn't—"

"Didn't what?" Severn asked.

"Didn't know what he was like. He's too weak to

protect anyone. If the Howards attacked, he'd probably deliver me to them." That was as close as she could come to telling her brother the truth.

Severn looked at the man Liana had sent and couldn't reconcile his sister's words with what he saw. The fellow Smith was a bear of a man: big, thick, muscular. While Zared had slept Severn had seen just how strong the man was when he'd helped unload weapons and armor. And twice Severn had seen him hold a sword in a way that told Severn the man had had some training.

"Will you pledge your life to protect her?" Severn asked.

"I will," Tearle answered, and there was truth in his eyes.

"No! Oh, Severn, no, you cannot do this to me."

"You have done it to yourself," Severn said, rising, feeling much better. "See that she does not let the world know she is female. Keep her out of fights, and for the sake of all of us, keep her out of men's beds. I promised Liana I'd return her with her virginity intact."

"I will protect her always," Tearle said. "You have my word."

"Good," Severn said, standing. "She is yours to guard. See that no one knows the truth of her. Now I must watch the jousts. I must weigh my opponents' abilities." He turned and left the tent.

Zared stood where she was, staring after her brother. Never in all her imaginings could she have conceived of where she was. Her brother had just put her under the care of their family's sworn enemy. A Howard was to protect her from the Howards.

"Do not look at me so," Tearle said when Severn was gone. "I have told you again and again that I will not harm you. I will protect you."

"Your family has killed mine for three generations, yet I am to believe that a Howard is now my friend? No," she said tauntingly, "you are to be my husband."

Tearle winced at her words and again asked himself why he did not leave. Perhaps her words weighed on him, and he felt the sins of his ancestors and his brothers on his shoulders. Perhaps his ancestors *had* stolen the Peregrine lands.

"It is time for supper," he said, "and you must serve your brother and his men."

"I must what?"

Tearle smiled at her. She carried the title of squire, but she also bore the name of Peregrine. Usually when a boy reached about seven years of age he was sent to foster with a family other than his own. People had known for centuries that a boy would gladly take lessons from strangers but would learn nothing from his own family. Zared, who was used to eating beside her brother, was balking at fetching his meat and wine.

"I have told your brother I will care for you, and I mean to see that you do your duty. If you have more work to do, you will have less time to make a fool of yourself over Colbrand."

"I have had more than enough of your orders." She strode to the open tent flap. "I am going to supper by myself."

Zared had to elbow her way between two squires to get the hunk of meat Severn had told her to fetch for him. She was trying to keep her temper, but it wasn't easy. Severn had very much liked the idea of his little sister serving him, and he also wanted to punish her a bit for having neglected him earlier in the day. He'd point to joints of meat on other tables and command her to get him a piece.

"Get your brother a napkin," the Howard man told her.

"Why? He will not use it," Zared had retorted.

Of course Severn had then decided that the thing he wanted most in life was a napkin, so Zared had had to run and find one for him.

With every move she made she glared at the Howard man. Severn had seated him at his right hand, and they looked for all the world to be old friends. Friends who had a common enemy, she thought. Me.

It was a long meal, and Zared was so busy she never had a moment even to look about her. She'd had such dreams about going to the tournament with her brother, and so far all of it had been a disaster.

At long last the meal was over, and the men, the Marshall family, the king, and the guests began to file out of the enormous hall and go about their evening's entertainment. Some of the young men invited Zared to go whoring with them, but she declined. She tore off a big chunk of beef, took half a loaf of bread and a flagon of wine, and left the hall.

"I have waited for you," Tearle said as soon as she was outside.

Zared nearly dropped the wine. Was there no reprieve from the man? "Leave me," she said.

"I have sworn to your brother to protect you."

"From what? From yourself? Can you not see that I do not want you near me? Go and find another to inflict yourself upon. Leave me to myself."

Tearle looked at her, and quite suddenly he wondered why he was forcing himself where he was not wanted. His brother wasn't going to come after her, not while Tearle was at the tournament. He looked around, and there were hundreds of people milling about, and groups of boys teasing groups of girls. There were ladies in their long gowns being escorted

87

by gentlemen in fur-trimmed tunics. There were vendors hawking goods, acrobats climbing on top of one another, singers and musicians.

"Go," he said. "Go, but do not stay so late that I have to come looking for you."

Zared practically ran from him, hurrying into the crowd to get away from him as fast as she could. She ate her food as she walked about and looked at what was for sale, at the performers, at a dog baiting a chained bear. The sights were all wondrous and new, and they kept her attention for quite some time.

But her good mood fled when a pretty young village girl began flirting with her. Zared glared at the girl, but instead of leaving she came up to Zared and asked if she'd like to go for a walk. Zared turned on her heel and left the girl.

Some other girls, daughters of rich merchants, walked by in their lovely gowns, jeweled headdresses twinkling, and Zared tried to memorize everything they wore. She'd like to wear something like their gowns with their trailing skirts, she thought. She watched the girls glance over their shoulders at a group of boys, and the boys follow like dogs answering a whistle.

"Come with us," one of the boys called to her.

Zared stepped back and shook her head.

"He's one of those Peregrines," she heard one of the boys say, and they all laughed.

Zared turned away, feeling as though she didn't belong anywhere. She didn't belong with the girls, and she didn't belong with the boys. And their entrance into the tournament had made the Peregrine name a source of laughter.

"Tomorrow Severn will fix that," she whispered to herself, vowing to help her brother in any way that she could. She wouldn't allow the Howard man to drug her so she slept the next day away.

The people and the commotion had lost its appeal to her, and all at once she wished she were at home. She would go up on the battlements of Moray Castle and look out across the fields to the trees in the distance. She wished she could sit in Liana's solar and listen to one of her ladies sing.

She wondered where Severn was. "Probably with some woman," she said in disgust. Her brother never seemed to have trouble acquiring women.

She kept walking away from the noise until she reached the stream in the trees that ran near the Marshall estates. There seemed to be a couple of grunting people under every bush, and as Zared sidestepped them she felt lonelier than ever. She couldn't go with the girls and didn't want to go with the boys, so there was nowhere for her to go.

She followed the stream, stepping over bracken, moving around trees. It was almost full dark, but the moonlight was bright. Ahead of her she heard splashing and stepped through the trees expecting to see a deer. Instead, what she saw halted her and made her draw in her breath.

Standing in ankle-deep water, his back to her, was Colbrand, and he wore not a stitch of clothing. A warmth flooded her body as she looked at him, his white skin looking silver in the moonlight. Her mouth grew dry as she looked at him, and her knees grew weak.

He turned to look at her over his shoulder and smiled. "Young Peregrine. Come and wash my back."

Zared tried to swallow the lump in her throat as she waded into the icy water. She didn't bother to remove her shoes for, truthfully, she didn't remember that she wore shoes. Her eyes were only on Colbrand's bare body.

She took the soap he handed her and lathered his back. Her hands spread out over the muscles in his back, down his arms, to the small of his back and lower.

Colbrand laughed. "It seems you are better at many things than my squire. Why is it you are not out kissing girls as Jamie is?" he asked.

"I . . ." She couldn't speak when she was touching him. She seemed to change from a thinking person to one who could only feel.

He turned toward her, and Zared gulped. Would he realize she was female? Would he kiss her?

"Fetch the bucket that I may rinse," he said, and Zared obeyed him.

He had to kneel before her so she could pour buckets of water over him, and as she did so her heart pounded in her ears. He was so close to her.

"My thanks to you," he said, standing and walking to the bank, where he began to dry off.

Zared just stood in the water and gazed at him. Was there any other man on earth as splendid-looking as he? Golden hairs glistened on his muscular forearms.

"Will you stay in the water all night?" Colbrand asked, smiling.

"Ah, no." She left the water and didn't notice that her feet were half frozen. She just stood there and watched as Colbrand began to put on his clothes. "You . . . you are seeing someone?" she managed to ask. I will rip out her eyes, she thought.

"The Lady Anne," Colbrand answered. "Her father has invited me to talk with him of the morrow's games, and I believe the Lady Anne is to be there."

"She is beautiful," she said, and there was resignation in her voice.

"And rich," he said, laughing. "Now I must go. If you see my squire, tell him to sleep some tonight, as I'll need him fresh on the morrow." He gave Zared a little wave, and then he was gone.

She stood staring after him for a while, then sat on the cold bank and looked at the water. How did she have a chance with Colbrand when her competition was Lady Anne? She couldn't offer more beauty, more money, more anything than Lady Anne. "Except maybe a sweeter temper," she said aloud, remembering Severn's encounter with the woman.

She sat there for a long time, completely lost in her thoughts, and didn't hear the man behind her.

"I have searched for you," Tearle said.

Zared was feeling so low that she didn't even curse at him. She just kept looking at the stream.

Tearle had tried to occupy himself at the tournament but, unlike Zared, he had been to many a similar gathering in France, and there was little to hold his interest. A few women had cast their eyes at him, but he'd looked away. For some reason it seemed that only red hair interested him. It was no doubt the challenge Zared represented to him. After an hour or so without her he'd begun to search for her and had become concerned when he couldn't find her.

He had at last swallowed his pride, found Colbrand, and asked if he had seen the young Peregrine squire. Colbrand had said that Zared had helped him bathe, and that news had sent a current of rage through Tearle. It hadn't taken him long to find her after that.

He wanted to lecture her, wanted to tell her again that she was making a fool of herself, but there was a look on her face that stopped him. He sat down beside her.

"It is time for bed," he said. "Your brother will be on the lists early tomorrow."

Zared kept looking at the water. "I will be there."

"What plagues you?" he asked softly.

She turned toward him, her eyes sparkling. "You!" she snapped. "Why do you know I am female if no one else does?"

"I do not know. If you refer to Colbrand, he does not know because he is stupid. He's like an animal, clever enough to fight but not clever enough to think."

"Why do you hate him so? Because he can do manly things that you cannot? Are you jealous of all men who are *men?*"

She started to rise, but he caught her arm and made her sit back down.

"What defines a man to you? Fighting skill? You fainted for Colbrand before you ever saw him fight; you have not yet seen him fight. How do you know him to be a man? You step into the water with him, run your hands over his nude body, and he is not smart enough to know that a woman touches him—a woman who lusts for him. Is stupidity what makes a man to you?"

"You are jealous," she said in wonder. "You are jealous of Colbrand. Why? Because he can have all the women, and you can have none?"

"None?" He looked at her, then stood, looming over her. "Can you not see me? Can you not forget that I am a Howard long enough to *look* at me?"

She looked up at him, but he was right. The fact that he was a Howard blinded her to all else.

He turned away, his hands in fists, for he saw that his words made no difference to her. What did he care? he asked himself for the thousandth time. What did it matter what this one young woman thought of him? Why wasn't he enjoying himself? He could be laughing and drinking, with a buxom wench on his lap and another beside him, but instead he was standing in the dark trying to make one hardheaded imp of a girl see that he was as handsome as an idiot like Colbrand. He, Tearle, was handsome, rich, strong, educated, yet this girl treated him like a farrier's son.

He turned back to her. "Come, we will return to your brother's tent. He will worry if you are not there."

"Severn will not spend the night alone. He will spend it with a woman."

She said this with such heaviness in her voice that he smiled, realizing that she had been sitting there feeling sorry for herself, no doubt because Colbrand hadn't known she was a female.

He could not bear to see her feeling sorry for herself, and he knew enough about her to know that her pride was stronger than her self-pity.

"Peregrine," he said with mock severity, "were you to don the most beautiful gown on earth, Colbrand would not notice you. You could not be a woman no matter what you wore. You could not entice any man."

She reacted as he'd hoped. She shot up to stand in front of him. "I could have any man I wanted. Liana says I'm pretty."

"A woman has told you that, but not a man?" He was chuckling at her.

But Zared didn't realize he was teasing her, and she felt herself close to tears. He was saying all the things she'd felt. "A man would tell me that if he knew I were a woman. Lots of men would like me if—"

Abruptly Tearle's teasing spirit left him. She *could* entice any man she wanted, but whom would she want to entice? "Such as Colbrand?" he said with some anger. "He doesn't even notice you when you run your hands over him. Why do you think he would notice you if you wore different clothes?"

"I hate you," she whispered. "Hate you." She turned away from him and started up the bank.

He stopped in front of her. He had not meant to make her cry, but her lust for Colbrand was more than he could bear. "Would it mean anything to you if *I* said you were pretty and as feminine as any woman I have met?" he asked softly.

She looked away from him. She would not let him see her cry. "Your words mean less than nothing to me." She stepped around him and walked away, trying to keep her shoulders back.

Tearle watched her go and felt rotten as he followed her back to the tent. In his teasing of her he had only hurt himself.

Chapter Six

There were three cots in the main Peregrine tent, with Severn's men sleeping in the secondary tent. Zared was already on one cot, the light blanket pulled up to her chin, when Tearle returned. He didn't say anything, just undressed down to his loincloth and got into bed.

He didn't go to sleep right away but lay awake and looked at the tent ceiling. The girl was doing something to him that he didn't like; she was making him into someone he didn't know. Where was the man who could kiss and caress a woman, the man who teased and laughed with women? The girl, somehow, made him feel little except anger.

He went to sleep vowing that he would not get angry again, that no matter what she did, he would not become angry. He woke only slightly when Severn came in and fell facedown on his cot.

Just before dawn Tearle awoke, his eyes wide, his

95

senses alert, and he knew that something was wrong. He lay there quietly, listening to the silence outside the tent, trying to sense if there was some danger. His first thought was that his brother was outside, and his hand slipped down to the sword he kept by the cot.

After a moment of listening he realized that the apprehension he felt came from inside the tent and not outside. He threw back the cover and went to stand over Zared. She made no sound, but he knew she was crying. He sat on the edge of her cot and pulled her into his arms, realizing as soon as he touched her that she was still asleep. Did she often cry in her sleep? Did she always cry so silently?

He held her body, wrapped only in one thin layer of linen, against his bare chest and cradled her to him. Like the child she was not far from being, she snuggled against him, her hot tears wetting the mat of hair on his chest. If he had not felt her unbound breasts pressing against him, he would have thought her to be a child.

He held her securely while she cried, stroking her hair and wondering what made her weep so in her sleep.

Severn had awakened before Tearle. He knew his sister cried, for she often wept in her sleep, just as her mother had done, but he didn't go to her. He lay awake, silent, ready to go to her if she needed him, but he did not try to stop her weeping.

When he heard the man Smith stir, then saw him rise from his cot, Severn put his hand on the sword by his cot. What was the man doing sneaking about at night? When Smith went to Zared Severn almost drew a knife on him, but he hesitated and watched as Smith pulled Zared into his arms.

At first Severn gaped in astonishment. How had he heard Zared's weeping? No one except Severn knew how she cried in her sleep. None of her other brothers had ever been aware of Zared's tears, yet that man had heard.

Severn relaxed against the cot as he watched the two shadowy figures. Liana, he thought. His sister-in-law knew more than he had given her credit for. She had chosen Smith, perhaps knowing he was the right man for Zared.

Severn watched Smith hold his sister, and he remembered all too well those years when Zared's mother had cried. His brothers had hated hearing the woman's loud unhappiness, and in their way they had tried to comfort her. For a year or so they had allowed her to cry and had not complained, but in the second year of her marriage to their father they had told her to cease. Their words seemed to make her cry more.

It was Severn who had made an effort to stop the woman's tears. He was already a big, sturdy boy of ten years, and his own mother was long dead, but his stepmother's tears awakened a need within him. At night he would creep down the stairs and go to her room and climb in bed with her. Her own child, Zared, the only daughter born to his father, had been taken from her at birth. She used to cling to Severn, hold him so tightly he thought she might break a rib or two. But in the end she did not hurt him; in fact, he found he slept better on those nights when he slept near her.

He had been very afraid of what his older brothers and father would say when they found out that he had gone to comfort a crying woman, but his stepmother had never told anyone, and during the day, on the rare occasions when he saw her, she made no reference to the fact that sometimes he came to her.

Yet sometimes he'd find a piece of fruit in his room, or perhaps a sweet beside his bed. And in 1434, when he was so ill, she had sat up day and night nursing him, feeding him mugs of hot broth and spoonfuls of vile-tasting herbs. He hadn't fully recovered his strength when she went off with his father and his oldest brother William to Bevan Castle.

The Howards had laid siege to Bevan Castle, and she had starved to death there. His stepmother, his father, and William all dead at the hand of the Howards.

Afterward Severn and his remaining four brothers had decided to raise Zared as a boy to protect her from the Howards. Perhaps it was the memory of that poor, crying woman starving to death that had influenced them. They could not bear to think of their failure to protect one weak female. Perhaps Zared's pretty face with its long lashes, her bright hair, her smiling ways, reminded them too much of their failure.

There were times when Severn knew they were working Zared too hard, but a year after Zared's mother was starved by the Howards Rogan's first wife was taken prisoner. Severn shut his eyes in memory, for the fight to get her back had killed both Basil and James.

When there were only three brothers left Rowland, then the eldest, had doubled his vigilance against the Howards, and the brothers' training had also doubled. Rowland intensified his watch over Zared, forcing her to train as hard as her brothers. If he saw even a hint of softness in her, he stamped on it.

When Rowland was killed by Howard's men four years before, both Rogan and Severn had been devastated. Rowland had been their guiding light, the foundation of what was left of their family.

It was after Rowland's death that Zared began crying, just as her mother had done. The first time

Severn had heard it he'd thought it was the ghost who haunted Moray Castle, but on the second night he got up to see who it was. Zared, half asleep, half awake, lay in her bed on a wet pillow. She was thirteen years old, but she felt frail to him when he pulled her into his arms. She had begged him not to tell about her crying, and he'd sworn he would not.

After that she didn't cry aloud, but sometimes he went to her and saw that she cried while she was sleeping. At first he thought her tears were from grief—she had seen many deaths in her short life—but he came to realize there was more than grief. He suspected that Zared didn't know why she cried, but he guessed that she was lonely, as deeply lonely as a person can be.

Severn had once mentioned to Rogan that he thought perhaps it would be all right to allow Zared to show that she was female. But while Rogan pondered the idea Oliver Howard had kidnapped Rogan's wife Liana, and the Peregrine vigilance had been renewed.

For Zared's own safety she had to remain in disguise.

Looking at Smith holding Zared, Severn smiled. To him, Zared was so obviously female that he could never believe that others believed her to be male. He and Rogan always teased her because she got angry like a wet cat, all claws and hisses. Yet the men who worked for them never seemed to question who the young lad was. As far as he knew, no one had ever guessed that Zared was a girl. Even Liana, his smart sister-in-law, had had to be told.

Until Smith. The man said he had known from the beginning that Zared was female, and Severn believed him. He knew Liana would not tell anyone outside of her ladies. She knew too well the danger the Howards posed to Zared's safety. Yet the man had known.

Severn watched Smith put Zared back in the bed and then go to his own cot. If Zared were to marry and go away with her husband, she would be out of the Peregrine–Howard war. She could live elsewhere in peace and contentment. She could wear pretty gowns and let her hair grow down her back as it had when she was a child. Severn thought he'd like to see his sister as a sister, with a fat baby on her hip and a smile on her lips. It would be pleasant to see her doing something other than beating boys at sword practice.

He smiled again. It looked as though Liana had chosen well.

Tearle awoke early, but not as early as the Peregrines. They were already out of the tent, and he could hear low voices outside and the splash of water. The sound of water reminded him of Zared washing Colbrand the evening before. Already, before he was even fully awake, he could feel his anger rising. He pulled on his stockings and started to pull his linen shirt on over his head, but he paused. Perhaps it might do Zared some good to see another man besides Colbrand.

He went outside the tent, bare from the waist up, yawning and stretching. Severn was sitting on a low stool just outside the tent, also bare from the waist up and Zared was washing his back.

"Good morn," Severn said to Tearle, and he smiled at him.

Tearle didn't look at Zared but instead smiled at her brother. "You are ready to fight this day?"

"I fear I have not brought enough lances to cover all that I will break this day," Severn said, boasting.

Zared poured cold water from a basin over Severn to rinse the soap away as he ran a rough and not-too-clean cloth over his body.

"Have a seat, Smith," Severn said as he stood and motioned to the stool. "My squire will wash you."

"I will *not!*" Zared said, but then she looked at her brother, saw the way his eyes narrowed.

I should have stayed at home, Zared thought once again as the Howard enemy sat on the stool before her. She soaped her hands and ran them over his back. She was cursing him to herself, cursing all men everywhere, since it was her brother who had made her do the disagreeable task, when he spoke.

"It is like bathing Colbrand?" Tearle said softly over his shoulder. "I hear that you washed him also."

"I washed him, but I *enjoyed* that," she said under her breath.

"And you do not enjoy touching me?"

"How could I? You are my enemy."

"But first I am a man."

"If man you can be called. A weak-limbed, puny thing like you."

"Puny? I?"

Zared hated when he taunted her, but then she hated everything about him. He *was* a weak-limbed . . . She looked down at the body under her hands. There was nothing small or weak about the muscles that moved under his skin. He wasn't quite as large as Colbrand . . . or maybe he was. Maybe he was even more muscular.

She straightened and moved away from him. Perhaps he had the look of a man, but she knew he was but a soft, weak, spineless demi-man. All his muscle was fat. He was—

"Do you waste my time dawdling?" Severn snapped at her. "Have you no armor to clean? No horse to see to? Do you sharpen only the swords of my enemy?"

Zared threw cold water over Tearle, threw a dirty drying cloth in his general direction, and began to run to get ready. She was not going to be accused of being a laggard.

Within an hour she had Severn dressed in his armor and mounted on his war-horse, ready to go. All morning he was to face competitors at the lists.

A low wall of wooden planks had been built before the stands, and the jousters were to run at each other, wooden lances tucked under their right arms, and try to break the lances against each other. Points were awarded to each man according to where he struck his opponent's body (no hitting below the waist), the number of lances broken, the number of courses each man ran, and the number of times a man was struck, whether the lance broke or not.

Severn, riding toward his first opponent, had to move aside to miss being struck at the same time that he broke his lance giving a clear, solid hit to the other man's body. If at all possible, it was best to maneuver so that your opponent's lance struck your saddle or your horse, for demerits were given then.

A cheer went up at the first loud thwack of lance hitting steel. Severn rode to the far end, and Zared was waiting with a fresh lance as Severn rode again.

Severn rode again and again and again, knocking men from their horses and breaking several lances against his opponents' armor.

"He is good," Tearle said to Zared. "The people like him."

"Yes," she said, her voice full of pride. "They care not that he wears no plume on his helmet, and they do not remember the procession. He is heroic now."

Tearle had to agree with her as, with each pass Severn made, the cheers of the crowd grew louder. Only Colbrand received as much attention.

"Who will you want to win when your brother fights Colbrand?" Tearle asked.

"My brother, of course," she said, but only after a moment's pause. She looked away.

There were other jousters besides Severn, and between turns he would stand by Zared, downing huge mugs full of beer, while he watched the other men, trying to ascertain their weak and strong points.

"He will not win the Lady Anne," said a spiteful voice in Zared's ear.

She turned to see Colbrand's squire, Jamie, sweaty, just as she was, from running to fetch lances and help his master.

"My brother may not want the woman," Zared said haughtily, too well remembering Lady Anne's words about Severn.

"Ha!" Jamie said. "The lady's father approves of my master. He does not care for the filth of a Peregrine."

Zared's anger that had built up over the last days came to the surface. Severn's sword lay propped against a nearby post, and she grabbed it, going after the boy as though she meant to kill him.

Tearle caught her about the waist and lifted her off the ground. "Release it," he said.

"I have had enough of his taunts and mean to silence him," she yelled.

Tearle's big arm squeezed her waist until she could no longer breathe. With his other arm he took the sword from her. He dropped her so that she barely caught herself before falling. "Go back to your master," Tearle growled at Jamie, and the boy scurried away.

Tearle turned to Zared. "Do you always greet anger with a weapon? Do you not know how to think?"

"As well as you do," she snapped. "That child—"

"Is just that," Tearle interrupted, then he sighed. "I

103

should be grateful you did not agree with him and hope for Colbrand to win."

"Over my brother? Colbrand will no doubt beat the other men, but he will not beat a Peregrine."

Tearle was glad Zared was not ready to betray her brother for the stupid Colbrand. He didn't say more as he turned back to the field.

At noon the jousting was halted, and all the participants were to leave the grounds to go into dinner. Zared knew it would be another long meal serving her brother. "You are ready?" she asked Severn.

He looked down at her, then at Smith behind her, and he remembered the way the man had held her in the night. Severn wondered if Zared remembered what had happened. He ruffled his sister's hair, knocking her cap askew. "Go you with Smith and see what the merchants have to sell," he said.

"Leave? But who will serve you? Who will—"

"I will not starve. Now go before I change my mind."

Zared didn't waste a moment in making up her mind. She turned and was off the tournament grounds almost before Severn had finished his sentence. She almost ran into a man who had two dead pigs slung across his back.

Tearle's hand clamped on her shoulder.

"Leave me," she snapped at him. "I do not need a keeper."

"Will you enjoy this visit among the people as much as yesterday? You left early to go and sit alone in the woods."

"I wanted to do that," she said, her chin stuck out. "I was tired of the crowds, and . . . and . . ."

"Mmmm," he said, obviously not believing her. It didn't take a great deal of work on his part to figure out why she cried at night. Were he made to dress as a woman he would do more than weep.

"If you will allow me, I will accompany you."

Zared didn't want to agree to go with him, but she, too, remembered the night before, when she'd felt so alone. Perhaps a Howard was better than nothing—not a great deal better, but better than being alone.

"All right," she said. "You may come with me."

"You are very kind to me, Lady Zared," he said softly.

"Lady" Zared, she thought, and she rather liked the sound of the words.

She hated to admit it—oh, very much hated to admit it—but she enjoyed the Howard man's company. He led her through the tents of vendors set up near the tourney grounds and showed her everything. At a booth selling religious objects she stared in awe at bloodstained splinters from Christ's cross. The Howard man showed her that some of the blood wasn't even dry yet, and he pointed to a wooden tent post that was suspiciously missing some large splinters.

He took her to a goldsmith's booth, and when Zared would have stood to one side to look at the beautiful objects the Howard man bade the goldsmith show them all his wares. At a cloth merchant's booth he had the man pull down all the luscious fabrics so that Zared could see and feel them. At another booth he showed her children's toys, bidding the merchant to demonstrate each one.

The few hours they had before the tournament began again went by much too quickly, and Zared was reluctant to return.

"A woman at heart," Tearle said, laughing. "How have you resisted purchasing? If nothing for yourself, then a gift perhaps for your lovely sister-in-law."

"The Howards stole our fortune," she said, hating being reminded of her poverty.

Tearle's handsome face lost its smile. He had only meant to tease her, not to remind her of her family's poverty. "Here," he said. "See what this man sells."

Zared lost her anger when she looked at the man with the big tray suspended from around his neck. On the tray were beautiful embroidered gloves. They were of white or tan leather, or of colored silk, and the embroidery was so bright it flashed in the sunlight.

"You may touch them," Tearle said, smiling. "Smell them."

"Smell?" she asked, and she picked up one soft, beautiful pair. The gloves smelled of roses. She turned to him, delight on her face. "How?" she whispered. In her experience leather smelled of horses and men's sweat.

"Before the gloves are cut the leather is buried for months in flower petals. Do you have jasmine?" he asked the vendor.

The man, watching the strange pair, dug through the pile and took out a pair of yellow leather gloves heavily embroidered with gold thread. For all the world, he thought, these people talked as a man and his lady, but what the vendor saw was a big, handsome, obviously aristocratic lord and a pretty red-haired boy who had a smudge of dirt on his cheek.

"Choose the one you want and one for Lady Liana. Or perhaps a pair for each of her ladies."

"Liana would love these," Zared said, looking at the colors, feeling the softness of them. She put the gloves down and stepped back.

"Choose," Tearle urged her.

She glared at him. She didn't want to admit before the vendor that she had no money and couldn't afford something as frivolous as one pair of gloves, much less several pairs as gifts.

Tearle understood her thinking. "I mean to purchase all that you want."

Her fists clenched; her back teeth locked together. She was so angry she couldn't speak but turned on her heel and stalked away.

Tearle grimaced. He was beginning to understand the Peregrine pride. He lifted his tunic edge, felt for the drawstring bag hanging from his waist, and pulled out a gold coin. He flipped it to the gaping vendor, then took the gloves—all of them—shoved them down the front of his tunic, and went after Zared.

She was walking so stiff-legged that it was easy to catch her. He didn't try to reason with her but grabbed her arm and pulled her into a narrow place between a thatch-roofed hut and a stone wall. He blocked the exit with his big body.

Zared glared at him, her arms crossed over her chest. "Peregrines do not take charity from a Howard. We do not take charity from anyone. Even though our lands were stolen we—"

She broke off because he kissed her. He didn't pull her into his arms but just leaned forward, head turned, and kissed her firmly. When he stood upright Zared could only look at him, blinking. It was a moment before she could recover the use of her senses. She wiped her mouth with the back of her hand and stared at him.

"It is good to see you have no words," he said.

"I have words for you," she answered, and tried to push past him to get out of the confined area. "Let me pass."

"Not until you listen to me."

"I will hear nothing you say."

"Then I shall kiss you again."

Zared stopped and looked at him. His kiss had not been unpleasant. In fact, it had made her feel a little warm. "I will listen if it puts an end to such degradation."

He smiled at her so knowingly that she looked away. "Say what you must."

"First, see this," he said softly, and he pulled a pair of red silk gloves out of the inside of his tunic. They were embroidered with bumblebees and yellow buttercups.

In spite of herself Zared took the gloves from him. Before, in front of the vendor, she couldn't try the gloves on, but now she did, slipping her small hand into the silk. They were beautiful, soft and bright, glistening as she turned her hand to look at them. "I have never seen anything as beautiful," she whispered.

"Not these?" he asked, withdrawing another pair. "Or these?"

She took them one by one, but as he pulled more and more pairs from his tunic she began to laugh. "What have you done? Stolen them?"

"I gave him a gold Howard coin," he said, watching her.

Her face lost its laughter. "Take them. They are yours."

He made no effort to take the gloves, and he could see that Zared wasn't about to drop them in the dirt.

"I take no charity."

"If Howard lands belong to the Peregrines, then perhaps the gold I gave him is, in truth, Peregrine gold. You have purchased the gloves yourself."

Zared had to think about that a moment. Was he jesting with her? But then there was some truth in his words. The Howard lands *did* belong to the Peregrine family. She shifted her arms, and the leather gloves

108

sent up a heavenly scent. A wave of longing went through her. She would like to own something as beautiful, something as feminine as a pair of the gloves, and she would very much like to give gifts to Liana and her ladies. Liana's ladies had often looked in pity at Zared, for they knew she was female even if her brothers' men didn't. If Zared gave the ladies such lovely gifts as these gloves, their faces would change.

Tearle could see her thinking the matter over and had to work to keep from laughing out loud. For all her boy's clothes and hair, she was feminine throughout. "Which pair is your favorite?"

"I . . . I do not know," she answered, looking at them. The pair on top was white leather embroidered with black and yellow butterflies.

"Perhaps you should keep them all. We will purchase another gift for your sister-in-law."

"Oh, no, one is enough, as I cannot wear them."

"Can't . . . oh, yes, I see. What will you do with your pair?"

"Hide them. I have a . . . a secret place, a loose stone in the wall. I shall wear them when I am alone."

He frowned, guilt flooding him, for it was his own brother's obsession with the Peregrines that made the young woman have to hide away a pretty garment. At that moment he had an idea. Perhaps later at the tournament he would have an opportunity to give her what she so clearly wanted.

He reached out to touch her cheek, ran his finger down the side of her face. "I should like to see you wear the gloves."

She should, she thought, spit in his eye, but she didn't. Was it her imagination, or was he better-looking than when she had first met him? She remembered him as having beady little eyes, but his eyes were rather nice, actually, she thought.

"I . . . I think I'd better get back," she said softly. "Severn will need me."

"Yes," he said, and he moved his hand down her cheek to her shoulder, then pulled away from her. "Here, I will take the gloves. Were you to tuck them away you would add to what you work so hard to conceal."

It took a moment for her to realize that he was referring to her breasts. She could feel the blood rushing to her face, and she ducked her chin down to keep him from seeing her red cheeks, but when he'd taken the gloves and she looked up he was smiling at her in an especially infuriating way.

"Let me pass, Howard," she hissed at him.

"Aye, my lady," he said under his breath, then he bowed to her as she pushed past him.

As they started back to the tournament grounds Zared walked ahead of Tearle. Something had happened in the few hours since they'd left the grounds, and she wasn't sure what it was. When they'd left she would have as soon put a knife in the man as look at him, but at the moment he seemed part human to her. He had been very kind to her as they'd looked at the merchants' wares. He'd explained everything to her, and never once had he acted annoyed or been impatient with her lack of knowledge.

He certainly was different from her brothers, she thought. Severn and Rogan always seemed to be impatient with her, as her other brothers had been. They grew angry when she would stand in one spot and watch a sunset. They ridiculed her once when she'd made a crown of flowers and put it in her hair. They had no patience with her when she was too slow. They had no time for anything but war and training for war.

Since Liana had come into their family their lives

had softened, but still neither Severn nor Rogan had much time to give to her. Rogan spent his time with his wife, Severn with his mistress, and Zared had been alone.

She turned to look back at Tearle, walking backward as she went. "In France, did the women wear such gloves as these? Is that where you learned about their scent?"

"English women wear them also. I would think Lady Liana has a pair or two of scented gloves."

"I do not know. I have not smelled them." She looked at him not as her enemy, but as a man. He did not look feminine, but how did he know so much about women's clothes? Her brothers knew nothing of women's clothes, she thought. Wasn't that how men were supposed to be? "Did you spend your time in France with the women? Is that why you know of women's goods and not of men's?"

"I know of men's goods," he said, puzzled and somewhat defensive. She always made him feel as though he were defending his masculinity.

It was very confusing to her. She recalled that Liana had said that there was more to a man than his fighting ability, but was this the kind of man Liana had meant? This man knew of women's gloves and fainted from small wounds. Were men divided into two categories? Men like her brothers and Severn on one side and men like the Howard on the other?

"Why do you look at me so strangely?" he asked, pleased that she was looking at him at all.

"You are not a man, yet you look to be one," she said thoughtfully.

"Not a man?" He was aghast.

"No. You do not fight as men do. You faint from the smallest of wounds. You are large, yet I, much smaller than you, fought you and won."

"Fought me and won?" he said under his breath, at first having no idea what she was talking about. Then he remembered the first time they'd met, when she'd drawn the knife on him. He'd planned to release her from the moment he saw she was female. Yet suddenly he knew she thought she had "forced" him to release her.

"Yes, I fought you. Had someone pulled a knife on my brother, he would have destroyed his attacker."

"Even a bit of a female?"

"Perhaps not a female, but he would not have been beaten so easily. No, not my brothers or"—she thought for a moment—"nor do I think Colbrand would have been beaten so easily."

"But then Colbrand would not have the brains to know you were female," he said tightly.

"Perhaps not. You do have a mind, it seems. You seem to know about . . . about unmanly things such as women's gloves, and how to tell the quality of emeralds. It is just men things you know nothing of."

"Oh?" He was trying to keep his temper. "And what assures you I know nothing of what men do?"

She looked surprised. "You would be entered in the tournament if you could. You would not spend your time playing nursemaid and servant if you could hold a lance. Liana said Oliver Howard was so rich he could hire men to fight for him. Perhaps in France you hired men to joust for you while you sat with the ladies." Her face brightened. "Yes, that is it. That is how you know so little of men and so much of women."

Tearle could not speak for a while. She was still, like a kid, walking backward, and she was smiling as though she'd figured out some great problem. She had decided that because he knew so much about fabrics

112

and jewels and ladies' clothes that he could not be a man. It had not occurred to her that there were more men like him than men like her brothers, who cared *only* for warfare.

He opened his mouth to tell her—as though words could change a lifetime of her ideas of what men should be—but he saw a man behind her trying to control an unruly horse. The horse, angered by several strokes from its master's whip, broke free, running and kicking toward Zared, who had her back to the animal.

Tearle didn't think; he just leaped for Zared and flattened her to the ground, his big body completely covering hers. As the horse ran at him, hitting him again and again with its steel-shod hooves, he tucked his head down, trying to protect his head and neck by hunching his shoulders.

Within seconds there were shouts, and men scared the horse away, but not before it had done a great deal of damage to Tearle. He lay still a moment, taking deep breaths. He couldn't yet tell if his ribs were broken.

Beneath him Zared began to squirm as she tried to push out from under him so she could breathe.

"You are hurt?" a man above them yelled.

"Fetch a cot," another man yelled. "We will carry him."

Tearle painfully rolled away a little to let Zared out from under him, and as he looked at her face he knew he could not allow himself to be carried away. He could give her no more reason to think him less than a man.

He took a deep breath and rolled onto his side.

"I will fetch Severn," Zared said. She could think of nothing else to say, but she knew that a Howard had probably just saved the life of a Peregrine. She would fetch Severn, and he would know how to deal with an injured man.

"I am well," Tearle said, speaking with difficulty. The right side of his body felt as though it had been crushed. "I have merely had the wind knocked from me."

"Severn can—"

"No!" he said, closing his eyes against the pain. Using all the effort he could muster, he sat up.

"You are hurt," Zared said. "I will fetch help."

"No!" he said again.

By then there was a crowd around them, all of them gaping at the man who had been brutally kicked by a horse but was rising as though he had not been injured.

It took all Tearle's effort to come to his feet. He slowly took a couple of deep breaths, and as far as he could tell, his ribs were unbroken. "We must return," he said to Zared.

"You have to—"

"To what?" he asked, glaring down at her.

"Nothing," she said angrily. "There is naught I want you to do. If you were hurt, you would no doubt cry to high heaven for relief. I have to return to help my brother."

She turned away from him, leaving him to follow or not. She hated the way her knees felt a little weak after what had happened. The Howard man's body had so completely covered hers that she had been able to see nothing of the horse, but she had felt the impact of the hooves on his body as the horse hit him.

Yet he had shielded her. Why? What did that Howard want of her?

She glanced back over her shoulder to see him following her. He was walking, but stiffly. He said he was unhurt, yet how could he be? Should she go to him and demand that he let her see his wounds?

She, a Peregrine, demand to help a Howard? Yet he had saved her. *Why* had he saved her? Why hadn't he allowed the horse to trample her? It would have eliminated one Peregrine on earth.

There had to be something that he wanted. There must be a reason that he wanted her alive. He had talked of marriage between them, a marriage that would join their two families. What if the documents saying the Peregrines were true owners of the lands the Howards held had been found? Perhaps Oliver Howard had found the papers and sent his young brother to court the only Peregrine female. That would explain why the man so much wanted her to stay alive. If the only Peregrine female were dead, the families could not be united, and if the papers were found, Oliver Howard would lose all he had killed to keep.

The weakness began to leave her knees. Everything was beginning to make sense to her. The Howard man wanted her alive and well, and he wanted her to marry him willingly. That explained why he had purchased the gloves for her. The gloves were an attempt to endear himself to her.

It will not work, she thought. He will not be able to win me no matter what he does. And if he is hurt, it is because he has his own selfish motives. She straightened her shoulders and hurried toward the tournament grounds. She no longer felt guilty because a Howard had protected her.

Chapter Seven

Tearle managed to walk back to the tournament grounds keeping his head high and his back straight. What kind of woman was she? he thought. A man had just risked his life protecting her, and she did not so much as acknowledge the deed.

He went back to the tent only long enough to leave the gloves, then went to the field. On the grounds Severn was dressed for the joust, and he was in a foul mood, obviously angry about something that had happened at dinner. He snapped at Zared for being late, and the first man to run against him was hit so hard by Severn's lance that he went sprawling in the dirt. The crowd cheered, but Severn's mood didn't lighten.

Tearle stood to one side and watched as Zared scurried to and fro fetching lances and trying to do enough to please her brother. Only once did he try to speak to her, and for his attempt he got a tongue-lashing.

"Do you think to impress me, Howard?" she hissed at him. "Do you think I will marry you now and unite our families? Do you hope to assure yourself of keeping the lands that belong to my family?"

Tearle stood there, the entire right side of his body screaming in pain from having saved her underdeveloped little body, and she was talking to him of land and estates. He could only gape at her as she went running off to help Severn as he mounted to ride against Colbrand.

He watched Zared smile sweetly at Colbrand even as she helped her brother. "I nearly die for her, and I receive not even thanks, but Colbrand receives all from her for doing naught," he muttered.

He stood to one side and watched Severn and Colbrand run at each other. They were both excellent fighters, and he could see that unless one of them had luck on his side, the match would be a draw. By the fourth run Tearle was sick of watching Zared hold her breath at each pass, her eyes on Colbrand, afraid he might be harmed. "She cares naught for horses' hooves on my back but all for a light wooden lance against his steel-covered body," he muttered.

When Severn broke his fourth lance against Colbrand just as Colbrand had broken his fourth lance against Severn, Tearle waved Zared away and took water and a lance to Severn.

"He lowers his lance too much," Tearle said to Severn while he drank. "And he holds it wide to the left. If you were to swing in to your left and lift your lance, I think you might take him."

Severn gave Tearle a hard look. "My sister watches this Colbrand. Do you have a wish to see him downed?"

"I should like to see his guts in the dirt," Tearle answered with feeling.

Severn grinned, then lowered his faceplate. "I will do my best," he said, adjusting the lance Tearle handed him.

It was the only run in which Severn's lance broke but Colbrand's did not, thus giving Severn the higher score.

Tearle could not resist gloating to Zared. "It seems your invincible knight can be brought low," he said smugly.

"By my brother," she said, "but only by a Peregrine. There is no other man here who could beat him. No other man in England."

"I—" Tearle began, then he stopped.

"You what?" she asked, glaring. "You were not about to say that *you* could beat him." She smiled at him. "Howards can only hide and kidnap. Howards do not make open fights."

She turned away from him and went to Severn as her brother went back to the Peregrine tents. Suddenly it was all too much for Tearle. He had always had more women than he knew what to do with. Never had obtaining the affections of a woman been a hardship for him, yet this scrap of a girl was beginning to make him doubt himself.

He stopped a boy passing by, gave him a copper coin, and told him to deliver a message to Lady Anne in the stands. Moments later he saw Anne listen to the boy, then say something to her father before leaving the stands. Tearle followed her at some distance as she went back into the house. He watched as she mounted the stairs, and he was soon behind her. On the second floor he saw the edge of her skirt disappear inside a doorway. He followed her into the room and shut the door.

"You are in danger?" Anne asked.

"Danger of killing a woman," Tearle said.

"And I a man," Anne answered.

"Colbrand?"

"Nay, it is your enemy, that Peregrine."

"Severn?" Tearle asked as he unbuckled his belt and began to remove his tunic.

"What do you do?"

"A horse stepped on me, and I would have you look at the wound. What has Severn done?"

Anne began to help her friend undress. "Do you know he plans to marry me? To him there is no question. Today at dinner my father seated him next to me, and this Peregrine told me he had journeyed here for the express purpose of marrying me. He seemed to consider this a great honor for me—as does my father, now that he has seen this man on the field."

Tearle felt sympathy for Anne, for if her experience with a Peregrine was as bad as his was, she deserved sympathy. When Tearle pulled off his linen shirt Anne gasped.

"You are black and blue and bloody. Tearle, no horse merely stepped on you, you have been kicked—and hard. How far does this extend? Get the rest of your clothes off. I would see all of you." She went to the door and told a passing servant to bring rags and hot water.

Behind her Tearle smiled. This was how a woman was *supposed* to act, he thought. Women were supposed to be sweet, gentle creatures. They were supposed to stroke a man's brow and murmur soothingly to him when he was in pain. Proper women did proper things. They knew about gloves and satins, and they did not sharpen swords.

Tearle removed all his clothes except his breech-cloth and stretched, facedown, on the bed in the room. Anne, beautiful, sweet, proper-woman Anne, bathed his wounds and applied salve to them.

"Tell me of her," Anne said softly.

Tearle started to say he could not, that there was too much danger, but he knew he could trust her. After all, he was already trusting her with his life. If Anne told who he was and Severn heard, Tearle had no doubt that Severn would kill him instantly.

The whole story came tumbling out. Tearle told Anne everything from the beginning, about Oliver's men kidnapping the youngest Peregrine and Tearle realizing they held a girl. He told her about Zared cutting him, about his obsession with her and how he'd arranged to be near her.

"But she has fixed on Colbrand," he said bitterly. "I throw myself over her body and protect her, yet still she does not acknowledge that I am a man."

"You could beat Colbrand. You could take Severn also. How I'd like to see him fall," she said, her eyes glittering. "After dinner today he tried to kiss me." She smiled. "I applied my knee to his brain."

Tearle snorted. "It seems we have opposite goals. Your father would not force you to marry a man who could not win the tournament." He smiled. "And I would love to beat Colbrand; I should greatly love to see him brought low."

"Were it not for this silly disguise you've adopted you could fight them. You could bring them both down. I have seen you fight, and you are better than either of them."

"Yes," Tearle said sadly, sitting up so Anne could bind his ribs. "If only I didn't need to remain as Smith—" He broke off and stared at her. "I could fight now."

"Yes," she said eagerly, "there is no reason you

cannot be seen. Announce yourself as a Howard and enter the next two days. That Peregrine would not dare harm you while under my father's roof."

"No," Tearle said thoughtfully. "I will not stoop to my brother's level. Too many people have seen me with the Peregrines, and they will see them as fools for having had a Howard in their midst."

"They *are* fools," Anne said vehemently.

Tearle looked at her exquisite face. Was she protesting too much? "Severn does not strike me as being unattractive to women."

"He is a boor, an unmannered boor who believes a woman is his for the taking—not for the asking, mind, but for the taking."

"But not unpleasant to look at," Tearle said. "He sits a horse well."

"I should like to see him fall to the ground. I should like to hear him laughed at. I should like him seen as the fool he is. I should—"

"I understand," Tearle said, unable to keep the amusement from his voice.

"If you dare to laugh at me, I will—"

"I?" Tearle said in innocence. "I, a man sorely wounded in the cause of the Peregrines, laugh at another's ill wishes for them?"

Anne's lovely face relaxed. Tearle had known her too long and well, she thought. When that awful man, smelling of sweat and horse, had pulled her into a dark corner, she had at first responded to his kisses. There was something so very basic about the man. He seemed to take it for granted that she would be willing, even eager, to marry him. Throughout dinner he had talked easily to her father, as though they were already kin, and her father had responded in kind. Anne had sat between them, ignored. The Peregrine man had repeatedly reached across her for food, and she'd had to lean away from his elbows. He had talked across her and over her as though she weren't there.

And all the talk had been of weapons and warfare. As far as she could tell, there wasn't a finer sentiment in the man's body. At least Colbrand, the other man her father favored, had beautiful manners and had noticed when her gown matched her eyes. There were no compliments from the Peregrine. He had looked at her once as though appraising her, and as far as she knew, he hadn't glanced at her again.

After dinner he'd gone off with her father. Anne would have left them, but her father had ordered her to accompany them to the mews where he had some hawks to show the Peregrine. Anne and a couple of her ladies had followed the men, not speaking or being spoken to.

It was at the mews that the man had pulled her behind a shed and kissed her. Perhaps it was because she was so full of anger that at first she kissed him back, but it didn't take long for her to recover her senses. She'd raised her knee and brought it up between his legs. He had pushed her away from him, his face furious. Anne didn't want him to know how much he frightened her, so she had stood her ground.

He didn't say anything to her for a moment, then said, "Go back to your father," and he turned and left her. She had to admit that his reaction wasn't what she would have expected, but she was pleased she had made him so angry. Perhaps he would drop the suit for her hand.

"I shall appear in disguise," Tearle was saying.

"In disguise?"

"Yes, as . . . as the Black Knight. Can you find armor for me and have it painted black? I will challenge the men who have the most points so far."

"That will be Colbrand and this Peregrine. No one seems able to touch them."

Tearle remembered the way Zared looked at Colbrand each time the man came within sight of her and felt a surge of strength flow through him. "I will beat them," he said softly. "For you I will beat Severn, and for myself I will make Colbrand sorry he was born."

Anne smiled at him. "I will find the armor. Come to the garden tonight at midnight, and I will see that you have what you need. And I will see that all is arranged with my father. He will like a mystery knight to act as his champion."

Tearle rose, his wounds feeling much better. "And what if he gives you to me as my prize?"

Anne, sitting on the edge of the bed, looked up at him. He was wearing only the smallest piece of white linen, and as he moved muscles played under his skin. "I would accept," she said softly.

He turned to look at her. She was so lovely, so perfectly featured, and he knew her dowry would be enormous. Uniting the Marshalls and the Howards would be a very wise thing to do, and he knew his brother would heartily approve the match. Oliver could use Anne's dowry to buy more weapons to try to destroy the Peregrines.

As he looked at Anne's face, at her perfect loveliness, he began to see Zared's face, her prettiness nothing to compare with Anne's beauty, but there was an innocence to Zared that Anne could never have. Tearle remembered the look on Zared's face when she'd tried on one of the gloves. There was a world of new and different things he'd like to show Zared.

Perhaps it was her lack of experience that fascinated him, he thought. Perhaps because he had seen and done so much in his years on earth, Zared's freshness was a delight to him. Even the open, adoring way she looked at Colbrand intrigued him. Anne, and women like her, who were used to courts full of handsome men, would never show their feelings so openly. Tearle knew that if Anne loved a man she would not tell him so unless it was suitable for her to do so. But Zared, Tearle thought, smiling—if Zared loved a man, she'd protect him with her life.

"Then I should be most honored," Tearle said, smiling as he lied.

Anne smiled, too, knowing he lied. "Get dressed. I will leave first so no one sees me alone with a half-dressed man—even if you are old enough to be my father."

Tearle smiled at her knowingly. He was pleased to have her look at him as a man. After Zared, it was pleasant to have any woman look at him. "At midnight, then," he said as she reached the door.

She nodded and left the room.

Zared left the tournament grounds more confused than ever. Too many things were happening to her. She kept remembering—feeling—the Howard man on top of her as the horse stomped on him. She could feel the blows through his body to hers. Yet later he had refused any help from her.

Had he saved her for some ulterior reason? Did he want to unite the Peregrines and the Howards? If his brother had found papers proving the Peregrines owned the land held by the Howards, Oliver Howard would merely have burned the papers. He wouldn't need to send his brother to join the two families.

She put her hands to her ears as though to stop the raging thoughts. What did the man want from her? Why didn't he just go away and leave her to herself and to . . . to Colbrand?

At the thought of the beautiful man Zared decided to go to his tent. Perhaps the sight of the blond man would make her forget the dark one who was beginning to haunt her.

But at Colbrand's tent she was greeted with abuse from Jamie, his squire.

"Do you come to gloat?" he sneered at her.

"No, I . . ." What? she thought. Just wanted to see Colbrand?

"Your brother had luck on his side. My master's horse slipped."

"It did not. Severn is just a better fighter, that's all."

"He is better at naught than my master!" Jamie shouted. "My master fights better. He is a better man. Colbrand will win in the end, for he will win the Lady Anne."

Zared was too upset by the day's events to control her tongue. "My brother is to marry Lady Anne."

Jamie smiled nastily. "The Lady Anne hates your brother. She sneers at him when he does not look, but others see. Today after dinner she struck him."

Zared glared at the boy, knowing that what he said was true, but at the same time hating him for saying what he did. He was a scrawny thing and quite young. She thought she could quite likely beat him to a pulp.

She made a move toward him, but Colbrand put a hand on her shoulder.

"Fighting again?" he asked, bemused.

"I have told him of your intent to marry Lady Anne," Jamie said smugly.

"Ah, yes, the lovely Lady Anne. Her father wants a strong man for her husband."

"Then her father will want a Peregrine," Zared said evenly.

"Then he will have made a good choice in your brother," Colbrand said.

Zared smiled at him. Beautiful, kind, as well as gracious, she thought.

Zared would have answered him, but at that moment Severn came by, angrily grabbed her ear, and pulled her toward their tent. "What are you doing?" she demanded, but he wouldn't answer her.

Once inside the tent he released her. "Where is Smith?"

Zared was rubbing her painful ear. "I do not know. He is my keeper, not I his."

Severn poured himself wine. "I have heard what happened today, that he saved you, and in protecting you he was trampled by a horse."

Zared turned away. "He had his reasons for what he did."

"Aye. He believes himself in love with you."

Zared looked back, wide-eyed. "In love?" she gasped. "With me?"

"You are no more surprised than I, but he looks at you with lovesick eyes just as Rogan looks at Liana." And I vow never to look that way at a woman, he thought.

"Your brain was knocked from your head," she said. "The man cares naught for me."

"He has known always that you are female. He goes to you when you weep at night, and now he has saved your life."

Zared was horrified by the conversation. She had never spoken of love—or any emotion, for that matter—with her brothers. "What would you have of me?" she asked suspiciously.

"I believe Liana means for you to marry the man. She must have sent him here to court you."

"Liana did not—"

"Did not what?"

126

"Does not mean for me to marry him," she said, unable to tell him any more of the truth. "What matter is it to you who I marry?"

"The man knows weapons. He gave me advice so that I beat Colbrand."

"I see," Zared said coolly. "You want me to marry him so you can have someone to help you beat other men in tournaments."

"To help our family beat the Howards."

"He'll not help you there!" she snapped, then, to cover herself, she attacked. "Why do *you* not marry to help our family? Are you pushing me to marry because you think you may not get the Lady Anne? I hear she struck you."

Severn's face turned red with anger. "What I do with a woman is not your concern."

"And my life is yours? You cannot get a wife, so you are foisting me on some man you know nothing of?"

"I know he wants you, which no other man does," Severn snapped.

It was true, all so painfully true, she thought. Only one man desired her, and he was her family's sworn enemy. She pushed past Severn, jerking from him when he tried to hold her, and left the tent. As soon as she was outside she started running, and she didn't stop until she reached the stream.

She sat down on the bank, put her head on her arms, and began to cry. Why couldn't life be simple for her as it seemed to be for everyone else? Of course, other people seemed to be sure whether they were male or female.

She didn't know how long she sat there crying as quietly as possible, but the moon rose, and still she stayed there.

At one point, when she wiped her nose on her

sleeve, she jumped to see the Howard man next to her. "Have you no work to do?" she snapped.

He stretched out on the bank beside her. "Nay, I have none. I am of the worthless Howards, do you not remember?"

Zared looked at him. Severn said the man desired her, she thought.

"I remember how your brother took Rogan's first wife, Jeanne, and later he took Liana."

"You could have been no more than a babe," he said. "How could you remember Jeanne? She is the best there is about Oliver."

Zared looked at the moonlight on the water. "Liana speaks highly of her." Her voice lowered. "Does she love your brother Oliver very much?" Zared had never told anyone before, but the story of Rogan's first wife fascinated her. Her oldest brothers had chosen Rogan as the one to take a wife because they needed the dowry a wife would bring. Rogan had married a young woman named Jeanne, but mere months after the marriage Oliver Howard had taken her prisoner.

The Peregrine men had fought long and hard for the return of Rogan's wife—so hard that two of their brothers had been killed. It was after their deaths that the Peregrines found out that the captive Jeanne had fallen in love with Oliver Howard and was carrying his child.

A child herself then, Zared only remembered the quiet rage of her three remaining brothers. Her parents and her brother William had died the year before, and Zared remembered being afraid that one by one her brothers would leave her.

"I believe that Jeanne loved him once," Tearle said, bringing her back to the present. "But I am not so sure now. My brother is bitter at having no sons to pass his wealth to."

"Rogan has a son," she said, smiling in memory of the baby with red-gold curls.

He didn't say anything for a moment, then, very softly, he said, "Why do you cry? Why do you weep in your sleep and now, here, alone, as well?"

Zared was on her feet instantly and starting back to the camp. But he came to his feet quickly and caught her by the shoulders. "Release me or I will make you regret your hold of me."

"Oh?" he said, smiling at her. "Will you draw a knife on me again? Will you call for your beloved Colbrand?"

"He is not my—" she began, then she wrenched away from him and took a step forward before he caught her again.

"So this is why you cry? Did he ignore you? Did you again make a fool of yourself before him? Did he again fail to recognize you as female?"

She tried to twist away from him, but he wouldn't release his grip, and after a moment she stopped struggling. "What do you want of me?" she hissed at him. "Why do you not go and leave me to myself? Are there no other women to interest you? We are enemies! Do you not understand that? Since you cannot conquer us in battle, do you mean to conquer us with your pretense of friendship?"

Her eyes were blazing, and he was so close to her. "Nay, I do not want friendship," he said in a husky whisper before drawing her into his arms.

At first she struggled against his lips touching hers. She pushed against him, tried to turn her head away, but his hand held the back of her head, and she could not move away. Realizing that it was no use fighting him, she allowed her body to go limp, thinking that as soon as he lightened his grip she would escape him.

But when she stopped struggling the oddest thing

happened. He loosened the hold on her head, and his lips on hers softened, and the feeling was . . . was something Zared had never felt before.

She just stood there, her eyes wide open, as he kissed her, and she could feel her body growing warmer by the second. He used his hand to turn her head sideways. Zared felt her body being pulled against his, and it was as though she melted into him, her head going against his thick, hard shoulder.

His lips opened over hers, tempting her into opening them. She closed her eyes and leaned against him as his body covered hers, and she felt as though she were drowning. He moved his lips off of hers to kiss her cheeks, her temple, her neck, moving down to her throat.

Zared leaned against him, her body a mass of sensations. Her life had been entirely without affection. To be touched so gently, to be held, to be kissed was almost more than she could bear.

Tearle leaned back from her and looked at her in his arms. She was leaning on him fully. If he released her she would no doubt fall to the ground. No woman had ever put herself into his care so completely. He touched her hair, smoothed it back from her temple. When she loved a man, she was going to love him with all her being—and he meant to be that man.

"My name is Tearle," he whispered as he kissed her forehead, and the old name, meaning one who is without tears, sounded like a caress.

"Tearle," she whispered against his neck.

He smiled down at her, for there was the softness he'd always known she possessed. "I should like to take you away with me," he said softly, touching the hair at her temples. "I would make love to you all night and into the morning."

She moved closer to him and put her face up to be kissed again.

Tearle kissed her slowly, softly, a gentle kiss for a virgin. "Now, my love, I must return you to your brother."

"Mmmm" was all Zared could say as she put her face in his neck, her lips on his skin. She'd had no idea that touching a man could be so pleasant.

Tearle pulled her away from him, and the look on her face made his body grow hot. He could take her if he wanted; he knew that. "We have to return," he said. For leaving her a virgin that night he was sure that in heaven he would be given a crown of gold.

He put her hand in his and started leading her back toward the tents.

They had gone only a few yards when Zared's senses returned to her. She shook her head as though to clear a fog from it, then jerked her hand from his. She had just given herself to the enemy. Instead of remembering that she was a Peregrine and the man her family's enemy, she had lost all memory and allowed him to touch her. Allowed him? She would have allowed him much more if he'd wanted it—which he had not. He had broken from her when she would have gone on.

She drew the little eating dagger from her belt, turned, and held it out as though she meant to thrust it into him. "If you ever touch me again, I will kill you," she said.

He, the hideous, odious man, smiled at her.

Zared lunged at him, but he easily caught her wrist and pulled her into his arms again.

"I have a half-healed knife cut and a bruised side because of you. I do not want more wounds."

"I will cause you a great deal more pain if you force yourself on me again."

"Force?" he said, still smiling, then he bent his head as though he meant to kiss her again.

Zared turned her head away. "No," she whispered.

He released his hold on her, and when Zared ran from him she could hear him laughing behind her.

Chapter Eight

She ran all the way back to the tent, and when she arrived she was shaking. Severn was lounging on his cot eating an apple, and he turned to look at her when she entered.

"Someone chasing you?" he asked. "Colbrand's squire after you again? I do believe the boy senses your sex. He seems to have the brains his master lacks."

"Haven't you something to do?" she snapped. "No swords to sharpen? No women to court?"

"I have won all the women," he said smugly.

"Except the Lady Anne."

He finished his apple and swung his feet to the floor. "Where is Smith? Did you see him with another woman—has that put you in an ill temper? Beware, little sister, that you do not play *too* hard to get."

"You know *nothing!*" she yelled at him. "Nothing!"

He chuckled at her as he left the tent.

Zared sat down on her cot, her body stiff with anger. She was angry at her brother for being able to see nothing, at the Howard man for coming into her life, and at herself for the way she had acted.

"It would have happened had any man kissed me," she whispered aloud. "Had Colbrand touched me . . ." She trailed off, remembering the way it had felt to be touched by the Howard man. By any man, she corrected herself. It would have felt wonderful to have been held and kissed by any man at all.

"Yes," she said, standing. She was a Peregrine, and as her brothers liked lots of women, she, no doubt, liked many men. It was a shame, perhaps, that her family's sworn enemy could make her react, but that was the way of the world.

She just had to keep her wits about her and not allow the man to make her lose sight of what was really important, she decided. He was a Howard, and he had put himself in the Peregrine camp for a reason. Since Zared was the only one who knew who he was, did he mean to seduce her so that she would begin to believe him?

She didn't yet know what he hoped to gain from his disguise, but it was her duty to protect her family.

"And that does not mean succumbing to his kisses," she told herself. It won't happen again, she thought. She wouldn't allow him to touch her, and if he did happen to touch her, she was *not* going to fall against him like some peasant girl. "I'll take my knife to him before I allow him to touch me again," she said, chin in the air.

Hours later she was in bed, her eyes tightly closed as her brother and her enemy came to the tent. From the way they laughed and staggered she thought they must have shared about half a hogshead of beer.

"Sssh," Severn said loudly. "Can't wake my little sister."

"I'll take her back to bed," Tearle said even louder, and both men dissolved in laughter.

Zared slammed her fist into her pillow and turned onto her side. Her anger and indignation kept her from sleeping—and if anger hadn't kept her from sleeping, the drunken snores of her brother and that man would have.

She was just about to go to sleep when she heard the Howard man rise very quietly from his cot and leave the tent. She looked at Severn and saw he was still sleeping, so Zared got out of bed, slipped her tunic on over her head, and followed the man.

Severn was awake the moment Tearle put his foot to the floor, and he lay there watching as the man took his sword and left the tent. For all that Severn liked the man, he was always cautious, and Zared's continued animosity made him less trustful of Smith than he might normally have been.

He and Smith had gotten drunk together—or at least Severn had pretended to get drunk. He hoped to pry some secrets out of Smith, to find out how he knew of weapons yet didn't fight, and where Liana had found him. But Severn had discovered nothing about the man. He was very good at not answering questions and at revealing nothing about himself.

When Severn saw his little sister slip out after the man he relaxed. He was glad Smith liked Zared, and Severn knew he could trust Smith to protect Zared, just as he had when the horse had nearly trampled her. He lay back on the cot and went to sleep.

Zared followed Tearle as he made his way through the people who were still awake. She watched as he slipped in and out of shadows; it was easy to see that

135

he did not want to be seen. Twice Zared had to slip into darkness to keep him from seeing her.

After many twists and turns he slipped through a door in the stone wall that surrounded the Marshall castle. Zared could not follow him without being seen, and it took her a while to find a tree that she could climb to see over the wall. She had to climb slowly to keep from being heard, and when at last she was high enough to see she gaped in openmouthed astonishment.

The Howard man hugged Lady Anne, then he whirled her about, her pretty skirt belling out around her. He set her down and soundly kissed both her cheeks.

Zared wanted to see no more. She climbed down from the tree.

For a while, as she walked back to the tent, she couldn't think clearly. She had discovered the reason for the Howard man's interference in the Peregrines' lives. He wanted to prevent the Peregrines from marrying into the wealth of the Marshall family. He wanted to make sure the Peregrines were never wealthy enough to conquer the Howard stronghold.

She went back to bed, but she did not sleep. When the Howard man at last returned to the tent her body grew rigid, and she lay there awake all night, not sleeping until nearly dawn.

In the morning two things happened: one, the practical jokes started, and two, the Howard man disappeared.

Severn overslept, and when he awoke to find Zared still asleep and the other cot empty he was annoyed with Zared, saying she had done something to anger Smith. Severn said he needed Smith to give him advice on the day's fighting, and he was sure Zared had done something to make Smith leave.

Zared had no way to defend herself. She had kept too many secrets for too long to begin to reveal them. Her only consolation was imagining telling Severn the truth when they were once again at home. She hoped her brother would have the courtesy to apologize to her for his accusations.

But for the time being all she could do was clench her fists at her sides and repeat that she had no idea where "Smith" was.

It was once they were on the tournament field that the "jokes" began. Severn put on his helmet and found that the inside of it had been coated with mud. At his first charge his lance broke away in his hand before he ever reached his opponent. Someone released bees from a hive, and while the bystanders swatted at them they came to land on Severn because parts of his armor had been coated with honey. When the Peregrine banner had been unfurled, instead of a white falcon on a red ground the banner had been replaced with cloth that was painted with a picture of a satyr chasing a nubile young girl—and the satyr looked remarkably like Severn.

With each of these harmless but mean little jokes the crowd laughed, and their laughter increased until at midday the mere sight of a Peregrine caused gales of laughter.

Zared looked into the stands and saw Lady Anne and her father laughing and pointing. Zared was glad the king had left the day before, but she had no doubt he would hear of how the Peregrine knight had been made to look the fool.

Severn instructed one of his men to stay with his armor at all times to see that nothing more was done to it. Zared had to ask other knights for lances, for all of Severn's had been sawed nearly through during the night. Colbrand sent his smirking squire over with an armful of new lances, and Zared forced herself to say thank you to the boy.

Severn took it all quietly, never saying a word as Zared washed mud off his face and out of his helmet. But the fact that he would not bend down to her, so that she had to climb on a short barrel to reach him, showed how enraged he was. He said nothing while she scrubbed honey off his armor. He did not comment while she frantically rerolled the banner that should have been the proud Peregrine falcon.

With each new thing that made the crowd laugh Zared was more and more sure that the Howard man was behind the jests. It would suit him, she thought. He seemed to like to spend most of his time laughing at her, and he was making everyone laugh at her brother as well.

And this laughter, she thought with anger, would assure that Lady Anne would not marry a Peregrine. She doubted if an old war-horse like Hugh Marshall would allow his daughter to marry a man who was the butt of such jokes.

"He has what he wants," she whispered to herself, watching as Severn knocked another man from his horse. It looked as though the Howard man would be able to keep the Peregrines from using the Marshall wealth to regain their lands.

Would he marry the lovely Lady Anne himself? she wondered. Again she remembered seeing him kiss her. What would he have done if Zared had accepted his marriage proposal? Added something else to his list of what there was to laugh at the Peregrines about? Would he sit with his fat older brother and laugh that the youngest Peregrine had agreed to marry him?

"That is one pleasure I will deny him," Zared said under her breath.

When the games were halted for dinner Severn did

not go to the castle to eat, and he would not allow Zared to go either. Not that she wanted to, for she could not bear to hear more laughter. Severn sent one of his men to fetch food, and Severn and Zared sat alone on stools outside the tent and ate without speaking.

At one point Zared asked her brother who he thought was playing the tricks.

"I will kill whoever it is," Severn said softly, and he continued eating.

Zared knew he meant just that. Were she to tell him she was sure that the man he seemed to think so highly of, Smith, was actually a Howard, and that he was making the Peregrines look like fools, she knew that Severn would kill the man. And then what? Would Severn be executed? Would Oliver Howard retaliate by laying siege to Rogan and Liana and their child?

Zared just kept eating and said nothing.

After dinner Severn did not return to the lists. He was not due to fight again until late in the day, and he did not care to see the men he had beaten earlier. He went into the tent and stayed there.

Zared decided to go to see the other jousters. As she neared the lists she straightened her back, preparing herself to be the object of ridicule.

As she drew closer to the lists she realized that something new had taken the crowd's attention, for no one even glanced her way. All eyes were on the jousting field. She could see the people in the stands, saw the way their eyes were wide, their bodies leaning forward.

She moved through the crowd of spectators and found herself near Jamie. He barely glanced at her and showed no sign of even remembering the Peregrine humiliation of the morning.

"What is it?" she asked. The crowd was quiet, as though waiting for something.

"There," Jamie said, pointing to the far end of the field.

At the end of the field was a man on a black horse draped in black silk, wearing black-painted armor, his face covered, a black plume on top of his helmet. It was not at all rare to see black armor, and she could find nothing unusual about the man.

"That is what you gape at?" she asked.

Jamie gave her a look of contempt, as though she were too stupid to comprehend even the smallest thing.

"He is the Black Knight. No one knows who he is, and he has come to challenge all. So far he has knocked every man from his horse."

"So has my brother," Zared snapped.

Jamie snorted. "Your brother is likely to smear them in honey and the bees knock a man from his horse."

Zared put her hand up to smack the boy, but Colbrand stepped between them and smiled down at her. Zared's anger melted away as she looked up at him.

"The man is a mystery," Colbrand said.

"Who is?" Zared asked, smiling up at him. His golden hair waved back divinely from his temples and his eyes were very blue.

"The Black Knight," Jamie snapped. "Is all your family stupid as well as foolish?" he hissed across Colbrand so only Zared could hear him.

"I will make you eat those words," she said, and she started for him, but the shout of the crowd got her attention. The Black Knight was about to ride against his opponent.

His heavy horse thundered down the field, and the

140

man kept his body tilted forward, his lance held low. When he hit the armored man on the other side of the low fence the blow was so hard that the man fairly lifted out of his saddle and hit the ground, landing with a crash of armor.

"He is good," Zared said under her breath.

"Better than anyone except Colbrand," Jamie said, but there was doubt in his voice.

"Who is he? Where does he come from? What does he want?" she asked.

"He was announced as the Marshall challenger, to fight all comers, and his identity is to be kept a secret."

"People have reasons for keeping secrets," Zared said with some bitterness. "What does he want?"

"To win the emerald," Colbrand said above their heads. "What else could he want?"

"All that the Lady Anne possesses," she snapped. "Power. The notice of the king."

Colbrand looked down at her with vacant blue eyes that had no understanding in them, and suddenly she didn't think they were such handsome eyes.

She shrugged and turned away. She had more to think about than whether or not Colbrand was handsome, for there was something wrong. Why had the man waited until the second day to enter the games? Why keep his identity a secret?

She moved away from Colbrand and Jamie and made her way to the Black Knight's end of the field. There were half a dozen boys crowding around the knight, handing him new lances, wetting his horse's nose, and in general worshiping the mysterious man who was such a good fighter.

Zared watched the man through two more runs before she realized there was something familiar about him. At first she thought he might be her oldest brother. He was the same size as Rogan, but he did not move as Rogan did. Nor was he one of her father's illegitimate sons, for she knew them well.

She stepped closer to watch the man, and when she did so he turned his head toward her. She could see none of his face through the grid of his face mask, but the way he moved his head, even when it was encased in steel, made her draw in her breath.

Howard, she thought, and she knew without a doubt who was inside the armor.

She turned away before he could see the expression on her face. She walked back to stand by Colbrand and watch the man joust, but she looked with new eyes.

There was the man who had nearly died when her knife had grazed his ribs. *Had* nearly died? Or had just pretended to? He had lain there on the grass and told her he was afraid to be alone, and she, fool, had believed him. She had left him, yet she had returned because she feared he was dying.

Lies, she thought. The man was composed of lies. He pretended to be a weakling; he pretended to be who he was not; he pretended to want to marry a Peregrine; he pretended to be a friend.

"Do you think your brother can take him?"

It took her a moment to realize that Colbrand was speaking to her. And it was another moment before she realized that her body did not vibrate at being so near the beautiful man. Beautiful, yes, but so were the gloves Tearle had bought her, and Colbrand's eyes looked as though they held as much intelligence as the gloves. She would have very much liked to talk to someone about the mysterious knight, but as she looked up at Colbrand's handsome face she knew he would not be the one. She sensed that he would not be able to understand the finer points of a conversation that involved logic and deduction.

"My brother will kill him," Zared said softly.

"With mud or honey?" Jamie said, smirking.

She did not react to his words at all but turned a blazing face to the boy. "Go and fetch my brother."

Jamie didn't hesitate, for he knew a command when he heard it. He turned and started running.

Zared stood beside the field and watched as the Black Knight downed one man after another. Her ears rang with everything she'd said to the Howard man, how she'd taunted him about being soft, about knowing of women's clothes yet not knowing of men's weapons.

How he must have laughed at her, she thought. How he must have chuckled over her every word. Did he laugh at Zared while Lady Anne was in his arms? He had admitted that he knew her in France, so perhaps they had planned their marriage while there. What had happened? Did Lady Anne's father dislike the notion of having a Howard son-in-law—and had he forced his daughter to choose another man? Had Hugh Marshall chosen Severn?

But the Howard man had eliminated Severn from competing for Lady Anne's hand. The crowd laughed whenever they saw a Peregrine, laughed even at the Peregrine banner. So now the Howard man caught the crowd's fancy by dressing as a mysterious knight. He fought no better than Severn had, but in the end, when he revealed himself, he would not be a man the crowd had laughed at. With the glory of the Black Knight strong Hugh Marshall would no doubt listen to a Howard petition of marriage.

Zared watched the man who called himself the Black Knight with increasing concentration. Severn *must* beat him, she thought.

It was a while before she realized Severn was standing behind her.

"What do you think?" he asked softly.

"You can take him," she said. "He has intimidation on his side. Half these men *expect* to be knocked down by him. He scares them. He has weight and strength on his side, but he is no larger or stronger than you."

"You seem awfully sure."

She turned to glare up at him. "I *am* sure." She saw something in her brother's eyes and realized that the laughter of the morning had hurt him. "He is the one who put the mud in your helmet, the one who released the bees."

Severn stared at her. "You are sure?"

"Aye," she said with conviction. "It is not skill he uses as much as fear. Why else appear in disguise? He knew he could not beat you, and he knew he could not make you afraid, so he tried to break your spirit with laughter."

She could have told her brother that the man in the black armor was Smith, the man Severn had believed to be his friend, but she did not. She wasn't sure why she didn't tell Severn the truth; perhaps from fear of his rage at such a betrayal, or perhaps because if she gave more than the necessary information, it might lead to more questions, and Severn would discover Tearle's true identity.

Severn straightened and looked at the man on the black horse, and as Zared watched his eyes changed. Her brother was returning. She saw again the man of supreme confidence, and no longer were his eyes filled with doubt.

"Aye, I can take him," Severn whispered.

Knock him down for me, Zared thought. Beat him to repay him for his humiliation of me. She turned and went back to the tent with her brother to help him dress.

An hour later she walked with her brother to the

lists. Upon seeing Severn the crowd began to smile and poke one another in the ribs. Zared soon found out that the Black Knight had knocked Colbrand to the ground and had then challenged him to fight on foot with axes. Colbrand had refused the challenge.

"If the Black Knight can beat Colbrand, he can beat anyone," the people said as Severn walked past, clanking in his armor.

"Remember the bees," Zared said as she handed Severn his lance once he was mounted.

Severn nodded and slammed his face guard down. When the herald blew his horn he thundered forward.

Both men broke lances at the first pass. Even score.

At the second pass both lances broke. Still even.

"Remember the mud," Zared said.

Severn broke his lance against the Black Knight at the third pass, but he managed to dodge the knight's lance. A point scored for Severn.

"I believe he means to have Lady Anne," Zared said, giving her brother water. "He wants to make people laugh at you so he can gain her hand and her money."

Severn's eyes blazed as he slammed his faceplate down. He charged the Black Knight as he would charge a man on a battlefield. He was out for blood. He sat firmly in his saddle, leaned forward, held his lance in his gauntleted hand, and charged.

Everything happened too quickly for Zared to understand. One moment her brother was charging, and the next he was on the ground. The crowd's roar of approval for the Black Knight's win was deafening as she ran under the barricade to help her brother.

Severn, humiliated beyond words, pushed his sister away and stomped back to the tent. Zared followed, carrying his helmet.

"What happened?" she asked once they were alone.

145

"He bested me," Severn answered. "The better fighter won."

"I do not believe that. You are better than he is."

Severn picked up an apple from the little side table and crushed it in his strong fingers. After a while he turned to Zared, his handsome face showing his rage. "My saddle cinch slipped. He never touched me. *I fell off my horse.*"

Zared swallowed. The Howard man would pay for this, she thought. She would make him pay if she had to die trying.

Chapter Nine

∞

Tearle swam underwater, only coming up to the cold surface of the lake when his lungs were bursting. He swam on his back for a while, smiling as he moved. He doubted he'd ever felt so good in his life. He was tired, sore, hungry, and he wasn't sure he'd ever be able to replace all the water he'd sweated out, but he felt very good.

He had done exactly what he'd set out to do: He had proved to Zared that he was a man. He was sure she'd recognized him, for he'd seen her eyes widen. He wondered what had given him away, but perhaps she just sensed who he was, as he had known she was female the first time he'd seen her.

He turned onto his stomach and swam easily across the lake. She would change toward him now, he thought. No longer would she doubt him. No longer would she think him less than a man.

He swam to the edge of the lake and walked onto

the shore. Two of his brother's men were hidden in the trees. Throughout the tournament they had stayed dressed as merchants, and Tearle had paid them well to keep his secret. They had helped him dress and undress, and they had hidden his horse and armor.

He dried himself and began to dress, smiling all the while. It had not been easy beating all the contestants. By the time he got to Severn his body was screaming with pain. The bruises where the horse had kicked him, combined with the jarring his body took when his lance met steel, was almost more than he could bear.

But any amount of pain was worth it, he thought, for he had beaten them all. Colbrand had been difficult, and only sheer will power had kept him on his horse. By the time he got to Severn he wasn't sure he would succeed. Severn was good, very good, and after Severn's lance broke Tearle had been sure Severn was going to beat him. But on that last run, almost by magic, Severn had flown out of his saddle and landed on the ground.

It had been a bittersweet moment for Tearle because he could not savor his triumph. He could not remove his helmet and show the roaring crowd who he was. He had only a moment to watch Zared run to her brother before the crowd reached him. The people meant to see who the mystery man was. Tearle had turned his horse and thundered away before they could reach him.

He had ridden into the forest a few miles, his brother's men behind him, then tiredly dismounted at the side of the lake. He'd stood while the men unfastened his armor, then he'd removed his sweat-soaked clothes and waded into the water.

An hour later he was feeling better. He was eager to

see Zared's pretty little face. She placed so much importance on skill at arms, unlike most women who liked soft words and flowers, and now he had shown her he was even better at arms than her brother.

As he mounted his horse he smiled again. At last the woman was going to look at him as something other than an enemy.

Zared had no experience at soothing a melancholy man, for in her lifetime her brothers had mostly been full of rage. She had seen them overcome with grief when death struck their family, but that grief was usually tinged with anger, for most Peregrine deaths had been caused by Howards.

However Severn's anger was different this day, for his confidence seemed to be broken. She had never known her brothers when they were not utterly confident. The way Severn sat silently inside the tent, not speaking, eating alone, seeing no one but Zared, caused her more concern than anything she'd ever experienced.

When the Howard man entered at sundown she turned to look up at him, and for a moment she could not keep her hatred for him from her face. For what he had done to Severn she could easily have killed him. She looked away quickly. She would not let him see her hatred because she planned to revenge herself on him. She didn't know how she was going to do it, but she was going to make him pay.

"There was an illness in my family," Tearle said, looking from one to the other. He had carefully rehearsed the excuse for his absence, but the look in Zared's eyes made him forget everything. If he'd thought he'd seen hatred from her before, that had been nothing compared to what was there now.

149

"You missed the final humiliation of the Peregrines," Severn said, sitting on the cot.

Tearle looked from Severn's ravaged face to the back of Zared's head and knew that something was very wrong. Did Severn take one defeat so hard? he wondered. Tearle had thought more of the man than that.

Tearle filled a plate with food, then sat on a stool to eat. Zared didn't look at him. "I hear there was some excitement today," he said, his mouth full. "Something about a mystery knight."

Severn, after one angry glance at Tearle, left the tent. Zared, glad she had not identified Tearle as the Black Knight to her brother, left quickly to follow Severn.

"Return to our camp," Severn said to her when they reached the edge of the forest.

"People should be told," she said. "They should know that that man did not knock you from your horse. Had not the cinch been loosened, you would have beaten him."

Severn turned on her. "I am to cry foul play? That will cause more laughter." He turned away. "You do not understand. I have failed."

"You have *not* failed! You have an enemy at this tournament, and he has taken the victory from you."

"Aye, we Peregrines have an enemy, but Oliver Howard is not here. Do you not see that this is the end of our hope to regain what we have lost?"

"What do you mean?" she whispered.

"I had hoped to show myself well at this tournament and catch Hugh Marshall's eye. And after the humiliation of this day no man would give his daughter to a Peregrine. The word of this tourney will spread from one end of England to the other. If I do not get a rich wife, we will never be able to afford what is needed to beat the Howards. We will never get back what they have stolen from us."

Zared could not bear to hear the words, for all of this was her fault. If she had told Severn from the first that the man he trusted was actually a Howard, this would not be happening. She remembered all too well seeing the Howard man with the Lady Anne.

"You shall marry her," Zared said softly. "If it is possible, you shall marry the Lady Anne."

She turned away and left her brother. She had some serious thinking to do.

As Zared walked back through the crowd to the Peregrine tent many people stopped to look at her and smile. Everyone was once again laughing at the Peregrines.

Once inside the tent she saw the Howard man asleep on his cot. She did not hesitate as she picked up Severn's sword in both hands and prepared to bring it down over the man's neck.

Tearle rolled away as the sword swung downward. He hit the floor and came to his feet in one movement, then leaped across the cot to land heavily on Zared, throwing her to the ground and pinning her under him.

"You could have killed me," he said into her face.

"I meant to," she spat at him. "Even if I die for ridding the world of you, it would be an honor."

He looked down at her. She had always looked at him with anger, but there had also always been an underlying softness. Now there was no softness. Had he been fully asleep when she attacked, he would not be alive, for she would have severed his head from his neck.

"What has happened?" he asked softly, easing his weight off of her but still pinning her with his arm, a leg thrown across hers.

"What your brother could not do, you have done. Yet he uses a *man's* weapons, while you use treachery and deceit. My brother thinks you are a . . . a friend." She nearly choked on the word.

He didn't dare release her, for the look in her eyes told him she'd attack again. "What do you know?"

"I know all. You want the Lady Anne for yourself. You—"

"Anne? I want Anne?"

"You conspire with her. You—"

Tearle could only look down at her. She was saying he wanted Anne. If Anne was angry at a man, she wouldn't grab a sword and try to behead him, she'd dress in some beautiful gown and seduce him into doing what she wanted. No, Tearle did not want Anne. He'd much rather have Zared, who spoke and acted honestly, with no hidden meaning, no hidden treachery.

He had not heard all of what Zared was saying. "Why would I want Anne?"

"She is a rich wife for a second son."

"True." He moved his hand down her arm and moved closer to her.

"Do not touch me!" she yelled, fighting against him, but he held her easily, although he grunted when she hit a sore place.

"I do not want Anne," he said, and he put his face against her neck.

Zared let her body go limp. Then, when the man relaxed, she rolled away from him, and as she did she kicked him hard between the legs.

Tearle groaned and grabbed himself with one hand and Zared with the other. "Sit!" he commanded, shoving her onto a cot. He hovered over her, trying to recover from the pain, and when he could at last breathe again he bent over her. "I want to hear all. I want to hear all that is in your head."

"I will tell you nothing," she said, firm-jawed.

"If you do not tell me, I will tell your brother who I am."

"He will kill you!"

"As he did today?" he asked mockingly, then he wished he hadn't. He had not meant to admit he had disguised himself.

"You loosened his cinch," she screamed at him. "You humiliated him! You want the Lady Anne!"

Tearle had to hold her to keep her on the cot while he thought about what she'd said. Perhaps there had been no "magic" to Severn's being unhorsed. Perhaps he had slipped. After all, Tearle's lance had barely touched him.

"Someone loosened Severn's cinch?" he asked softly, fearing his brother's hand. Since the king was gone, Oliver might dare much.

"You should know. You put the mud in his helmet, the honey on his—"

"What?" Tearle straightened and looked down at her. "I put mud in his helmet?" he asked indignantly.

"The people laughed at Severn," she said, and misery at the memory of that laughter was replacing her rage. "Severn will not get his rich bride now, and it will be my fault. If I had told him about you at the beginning, he could have killed you. Better that he was executed than suffer this humiliation."

Tearle couldn't seem to think for a moment. He had meant merely to dress in black armor to impress a girl, but instead of impressing her he had somehow caused her family humiliation and dishonor.

"What would you have of me?" he asked softly.

"Shall I go? Shall I leave here and never see you again?"

"Yes," she said, putting her face in her hands. "You have ruined all. Severn will never marry his rich bride."

He put his hand lightly on her hair. "You must believe that I meant only good for you and your brother. I never meant—"

She jerked away from his touch. "Go! Leave me. I never want to see you again. You have ruined all for my family."

Tearle turned away from her, not really understanding, but hearing the deep sorrow in her voice. He left the tent and intended to leave her life, but first he wanted to find out what she meant when she talked of mud in a helmet.

It didn't take Tearle long to hear the story, for it was all the people on the grounds could talk of. As he listened to each recounting of the story of bees and mud and broken lances a suspicion began to grow inside him.

"Hugh Marshall won't be giving his lovely daughter to a Peregrine," one man said, laughing. "He wouldn't want a fool for a son-in-law."

"The Black Knight is who Marshall wants. I hear he's offering a reward to anyone who can tell him who the man is."

"The reward being the Lady Anne," someone else said, laughing.

Tearle didn't listen to any more but walked away. He paid a boy to go to the hall and deliver a message to Anne that he would meet her in the garden at dark.

A few hours later, when he arrived in the garden, Anne was there waiting for him, and her beautiful face was radiant in the moonlight.

"You were magnificent," she said, holding his shoulders and kissing both his cheeks. "Really magnificent, and Tearle, it worked so well. My father no longer speaks of that Peregrine man. Now all he talks of is the Black Knight, who, of course, will never be found."

"And this pleases you, that Severn is no longer considered by your father for marriage?" he asked softly.

"It pleases me very much. He is a dreadful man, and I could not bear to spend five minutes' time with him."

"Have you done so? *Have* you spent five minutes with him?"

Anne stopped smiling and gave him a hard look. "What is on your mind? Are you not pleased with your victory?"

He turned away from her. Pleased? He had meant to show Zared he was not the weakling she believed him to be, but instead he had made her hate him and had caused a good man like Severn great humiliation.

He looked back at her. "Who put the mud in Severn's helmet?"

Anne looked away, but not before he saw her smile.

He grabbed her shoulders and turned her to face him. "Who, Anne? Who made the people laugh at him?"

She jerked away from him. "I will *not* marry him. He has humiliated me publicly. Did you see what he did to me at the procession? He picked me off the ground in front of everyone. Twice he has tried to kiss me."

"He wasn't like the fawning men at court, was he?" he asked softly. "Severn wrote no love poems to your beauty. He did not woo you with words."

155

She glared at him. "I do not like your tone," she said, lifting her skirts and starting to walk away.

Tearle caught her arm. "Severn is a good man. His manners may have little polish, but he is a good man. He cares about his family and his honor. He is a man with a great deal of pride."

At that Anne broke. She put her hands over her face to hide her tears. "And I have no pride?" She looked up at him as she tried to control the tears. "Yes, I humiliated him. Yes, I made people laugh at him. But tell me, what else could I do? What other ways of fighting are open to me? I have told my father I do not want to marry this man. I have told Peregrine I do not want to marry him, but no one listens to me. Don't you understand that I had to *do* something?"

Tearle had no answer for her. He gave a sigh, and when he spoke it was softly. "Who does your father favor now that Severn has been made to look a fool?"

Anne sniffed. "My father chose my sister's husband based on his connection to the throne. For me he says he wants a strong man."

"A wise father," Tearle mumbled.

"He favors Colbrand or—"

"Colbrand!" Tearle gasped. "The man is an idiot. He has no sense."

"He has lovely manners and is beautiful to look at."

"And easy to manage," Tearle answered. "If you married Colbrand, you'd eat him alive. He is no match for you."

"And who is?" she snapped, recovering herself. "That filthy Peregrine?"

"A better match for you than anyone else I've seen. Severn wouldn't allow you to control him."

"I have no desire to control him or even so much as look at him." She put her hand on Tearle's arm. "This Peregrine may be a friend to you, but to me he is rude.

156

He never speaks to me. At dinner he talks to my father, not me."

"And wisely so—as you have just said, he must court your father and not you."

She gave Tearle a look of exasperation. Could he understand *nothing?* "Colbrand spoke to *me*. He—"

"Colbrand!" Tearle said through his teeth. "I have heard enough of the man to last all my life. He is too stupid to tell girls from boys. Within a year of marriage you'd hate Colbrand."

She glared at him. "I do not need a year to hate this Peregrine. If you love them so much, you marry them, but not I. I thank you for helping me rid myself of my father's urging me to marrying one of them, but I do not feel I owe you any reward. You got what you wanted."

"What I wanted? Pray tell me, what did I want?"

She looked at him in astonishment. "Why, the same as I wanted: to humiliate the Peregrines. All of England will laugh at them after today, and when it is known that it was a Howard who beat this Severn even the animals in the fields will laugh. You will have no more worries of war with them, for they will be too afraid to stick their noses out their doors." She smiled. "You and I have done a fine job indeed. Your Severn will be hard pressed to find a bride at all, rich or poor."

She lifted her skirts and left him alone in the garden.

Tearle was too stunned to move from the dark garden. Every word she'd said rang in his ears. He had meant merely to impress a bit of a girl, but instead he had helped to make the Peregrines a laughingstock.

He knew that Anne was right; the identity of the Black Knight would eventually be found out. Too many people knew for it to remain a secret forever.

Some of his men knew, Anne knew, and Zared knew. Before long word would get out, and as Anne had said, all of England would laugh that a Howard had beaten a Peregrine.

Tearle thought of his brother Oliver and knew that Oliver would be filled with glee at the knowledge of what Tearle had done. Oliver would see to it that the news of a Howard beating a Peregrine was spread all over the country.

Tearle sat down heavily on a stone bench. Zared was correct: He had destroyed the Peregrine family. Through good intentions he had accomplished what three generations of his family could not do with their weapons.

He lay back on the bench and looked up at the stars. Was there any way he could right the wrong he had done?

Zared didn't sleep much that night. She lay awake trying to figure out a way to keep her promise to Severn and make Lady Anne marry him. She thought of going to Anne but remembered too well the way the woman had reacted when Severn had caught her runaway horse. She thought of going to Hugh Marshall and pleading Severn's case, but as Severn said, it would not look good to plead foul play. She doubted she'd be believed anyway.

She lay there and listened to Severn thrash about on his cot. No longer did he spend half the night carousing and teasing the women. He remained in the tent, not even spending time with his men—which was good, since the men weren't exactly proud of riding under the Peregrine banner.

Morning came, and Zared went to get them some food. Severn was not to joust until afternoon, and she did not think either of them would leave the tent until then. At midmorning she went outside to the privy, and as she was leaving a hand was placed over her mouth and nose.

She kicked and clawed at the arm about her waist but could not escape. When she thought she was going to die from lack of air the hand moved away from her face, and she gasped for air. As she did a cloth was stuffed into her mouth, then a cloak thrown over her body.

She was picked up, thrown across the saddle of a horse, and taken away. Howard, she thought. Once again she had been captured by a Howard.

They rode for some while before he stopped the horse and pulled her down, then removed the cloak from over her body. She was not surprised to see *him*.

"Do not look at me that way," Tearle said. "I mean you no harm."

Once the cloak was gone Zared started running, removing the gag as she ran.

He caught her within a few yards, grabbing her and landing hard on the ground so that she fell on him. He held her against him as she struggled.

"Do not kick me, I beg of you," he said tiredly. "You have stabbed me, I have been trampled by a horse while protecting you, I have nearly killed myself on the tourney field, you tried to cut my head from my body, you have perhaps removed all hopes of my having children, and last night I slept not at all. Please, I beg you, give me a moment's rest."

He sounded so genuinely tired that Zared nearly laughed. She didn't laugh, but she lay still on top of him. He was so very warm and comfortable, and she, too, had not slept much for two nights.

"What is it you want of me now?" she asked.

He pulled her head down against his chest. "Please do not struggle. I am too weak to protect myself from your knives and your swords . . . and your feet."

"Weak!" she snorted. "You downed Colbrand."

"Easy," he said. "Very, very easy."

"Release me," she said, pushing against him, but he wouldn't let her go. "I shall scream for help."

"I shall kiss you then."

"No!"

He smiled at the fear in her eyes. "Will you marry me if I get Lady Anne to marry your brother?"

She lost her lethargy at his words and began to struggle against him in earnest.

With a sigh he released her, but when she tried to stand he put a big hand on her shoulder and made her sit by him.

"I would not marry you were you the last man—"

"Even to bring Anne's riches into your family?"

"I wouldn't marry you . . ." She looked at him stretched lazily before her. "Her father will not allow her to marry a Peregrine. You have seen to that. You have made all of England laugh at us."

"I did not make anyone laugh at your family. I did not put honey on Severn's armor or remake your family's banner. If I want to beat a man, I do so with a sword or lance." He smiled at her. "You have seen that."

"I know you could not beat my brother, so you loosened his cinch to make it seem that you could beat him."

"I could beat your brother were I to lose an arm."

Zared's face turned an unbecoming shade of purple, and she leaped on him, ready to strangle him.

He chuckled and rolled with her, tossing her back and forth in his arms, moving his head when she tried to claw him.

160

After a few moments Zared realized he was playing with her, and her body went rigid. When his hands loosened their grip she moved off of him.

"I will not marry my enemy." She looked away from him.

"I thought you cared for your family name," he said, rolling to his feet. "I thought it mattered to you whether the Peregrine name is a great source of humor." He started walking toward his horse, but Zared put herself before him.

"You know *nothing* of family pride," she spat at him. "You live on stolen land. Your brother is insane. If you fight, you must do so in disguise."

"I disguised myself to protect your family name," he said, aghast. "I did not want people to know a Howard beat a Peregrine."

"*You* beat my brother?" she yelled. "You had to loosen his cinch to—"

He bent and kissed her.

Zared turned her head away, hating the way he made her feel. "It is because I love my family that I would not marry a Howard," she whispered.

"A marriage alliance would end the feud."

She looked back at him, recovered again. "Your brother would—"

"I would live with you," he said. "Wherever you wish. I will go with you to live with your brothers."

She blinked at him. "Rogan would kill you," she whispered.

"I doubt he can."

"You are a fool."

"Probably," he answered, shrugging. "I may be a fool, but I am not without honor. I did not loosen your brother's cinch. I can beat him without such low tricks."

"Ha! You could not—" She stopped because he

161

looked as though he might kiss her again. She turned away. "It matters not. It is done now. Lady Anne will not marry a man who causes laughter."

"Then you will not do what you can to stop the killing, or to help your family bring a rich bride into the family. I understand." He took the reins of his horse.

"I would do all that I could to protect my brothers. I would do *anything.*"

"Oh?" he said, one eyebrow raised. "It does not seem so to me."

She looked at him, eyes narrowed. "How do you plan to get Hugh Marshall to allow his daughter to marry a Peregrine?"

"You leave that to me."

She gave him a slow, humorless smile. "Do you plan to throw a cloak about her head, put a gag in her mouth, and kidnap her? Howards are masters at kidnapping defenseless women. Will you force her to marry my brother? Do you mean to start a feud between the Peregrines and the Marshalls? Do you plan to unite with the Marshalls to wage war on us?"

For a moment he was quiet, just standing there and blinking at her. "Do you think of naught but war? Do you believe there exists no other motive for a deed besides war? I do not plan to force Anne Marshall to do anything. Her father will give her in marriage to your brother."

"And you are sure of this?"

"As sure as one can be about the future." He smiled at her. "But I will not go to the trouble to arrange your brother's marriage if I am not to get what I want in return."

"And you want a Peregrine," she snapped. "You will not go to my brothers' house to live as you have said. You will force me to go to the Howard house.

What then? Torture for me? Or do you use me as a hostage to force my brothers to do your bidding?"

"I have told you I will not take you to live with my brother. I will live with you and your family, just as I do now, as Smith."

Zared could only stare at him. Was he stupid? "The Howards watch us. They will see you with my brothers, and they will betray your identity. When my brothers know who you are they will kill you. And your brother will—"

"Yes, I know," he said, his voice full of disgust. "There is no more use in our talking. Go back to your brother. Ask him to propose marriage to Colbrand for you. Marry him. See if on your wedding night he can tell that you are a woman." He mounted his horse and looked down at her. "Give my farewells to your brother."

As she saw him start to ride away all she could think of was that her worries were at last over. She was at last free of the hideous burden of keeping his identity a secret.

But as he turned his horse away she called after him. "Wait!"

He halted and looked down at her.

"What of Lady Anne?" she asked. "How do I get her to marry Severn?"

"The problem is that your brother is an object of laughter, and Hugh Marshall will not allow his daughter to marry him."

"And you can change his mind?" she asked nastily.

He turned his horse away, but she caught the reins.

"Tell me how!" she demanded. "You owe me this after the way I have kept your secret."

"And you owe me for saving you from my brother's men, and you owe me for saving you from the horse, and you owe me for—"

"Tell me!" she yelled, smacking him on the calf with her fist. "It is all to my family and nothing to you."

"You know my price," he said quietly.

She put her forehead against the neck of the horse. "I cannot marry you," she said slowly. "You are my enemy, and I hate you."

"If you think you hate me, it is nothing compared to what Anne Marshall will feel when she's made to marry your brother."

Zared smiled at that and looked at him. "Before the games her horse bolted, and though Severn saved her, she sneered at him. She said she needed to boil the reins before she could touch them again."

"That sounds like Anne."

"You know her well?"

Tearle wasn't sure, but he thought he detected an undercurrent in her voice. He didn't dare hope it was jealousy he heard. "Well enough," he said.

He took a deep breath, for he meant to make her decide. No longer could he bear the indecision about his future, and since it was the last day of the tournament, it was now or never.

"I will get your brother the wife he wants," Tearle said. "Hugh Marshall will give Lady Anne to Severn, but I will not do it nor tell you how unless you agree to marry me."

"You will not succeed," she said. "Hugh Marshall will not do the bidding of a second son."

"Then you have no cause for worry, do you? If I fail, you will not have to marry me." He looked at her. "But I will not make the attempt if you do not swear to what I want."

She dropped the bridle and walked away to look at the forest. To marry him? To marry a Howard? How would her brothers react if they discovered that their new brother-in-law was actually a Howard? Severn

164

might hesitate in killing him since he liked him, but Rogan wouldn't blink before running him through. And then Oliver Howard would bring an army to kill them.

On the other hand, all of England was laughing at the Peregrines. Only Severn's marriage to Anne Marshall would stop the laughter.

Zared put her hands to her ears. He was like the devil tempting her, and he looked like the devil, too, sitting atop the big horse with his black hair and eyes. Marry him? she thought. Marry him and live forever under the rule of a family that her family had hated for generations?

"I cannot," she whispered.

Tearle reined his horse away.

"Stop!" she screamed. Not looking at him, her fists clenched at her sides, she said, "I will."

"I did not hear you."

She didn't look at him. "I will marry you," she whispered.

"I still didn't hear you."

She looked up at him, her eyes sparkling with anger. "I will marry you," she shouted. "If you can get Lady Anne to marry Severn, I will marry you." Her lips tightened. "But I will *never* go to live at your brother's. I will *never* be put under Oliver Howard's rule."

He looked down at her, and his face softened. "I will live wherever you do until you are willing to follow me wherever I go."

"Ha!" she said. "Ha!"

But Tearle just smiled at her, turned his horse, and rode away.

165

Chapter Ten

Zared walked back to the tents, her body shaking with both anger and fear. What in the world had she done?

"You were gone long enough," Severn snapped at her.

She almost let him have a piece of her mind. How could he be ill-tempered with her after what she'd just done for him? Agreed to do for him, she corrected herself. So far none of the horror that *could* happen *had* happened.

The thought cheered her a bit. Perhaps nothing bad was going to happen. Perhaps she and Severn could stay in the tent until his last run on the tourney field, then they could go home and pretend nothing had happened. Perhaps people would forget all about the mysterious Black Knight, and about the mud in Severn's helmet, and about the banner with the satyr on it.

Sure, she thought, and God will give me angel's wings tomorrow.

Severn dropped his dagger, and Zared jumped half a foot.

"What ails you?" he asked.

"Nothing. I am fine. I have no problems. My life is a joy."

Severn smiled. "Missing Smith, are you?"

"It is good you have bone in your head, for you have no brain to hold your helmet off your neck."

"I'll brook no such insolence from you," he said, and in one lunge he was across the tent after her.

Zared didn't try to escape him as she usually did. Instead she felt like having a good, rousing fight, so she put her head down and rammed Severn in the stomach. He grunted, then grabbed the back of her clothes and pulled her away.

"What the hell's wrong with you?" he asked just before she swung her leg and kicked him in the shin.

"Why, you little—" he gasped, tossing her to the cot.

Severn had every intention of teaching his little sister a much-needed lesson, but in walked Smith, a tearstained, richly dressed woman held firmly to his side. Severn looked up from Zared and caught both her elbows in his ribs. With a grunt he cuffed her one across the head and sent her rolling off the cot.

"What is this?" Severn asked, rising.

Zared rolled away from the side of the tent, shook her head to clear it, and stood, narrowing her eyes at the Howard man as soon as she saw him.

"Tell him," Tearle said to the woman.

She began to cry, then she lowered her head and shook it no.

Tearle tightened his arm about her waist. "I will give you to him," he threatened.

167

The woman gave a quick look at Severn, and there was fear in her eyes.

"My brother is not—" Zared said, meaning to say that he was not to be used as punishment, but Tearle cut her off.

"Tell him!" he ordered.

The woman sniffed. "She will kill me."

Tearle didn't say another word to the woman, but then he didn't have to. His look was quite enough for the woman.

Zared watched the woman cry a bit more. When she spoke, at first her words were so soft she could barely be heard.

"Lady . . . mud . . . armor . . . banner."

Zared looked in puzzlement to Severn and saw he also was straining to hear.

"Louder," Tearle said.

The woman put her chin in the air and glared at Severn as one might glare at the face of the devil.

"My lady does not want to marry you. She arranged for the mud in your helmet, the honey on your armor. She paid a man to paint your—"

She stopped because Severn was advancing on her, but Tearle protectively put the woman behind him.

"She is not the one," Tearle said. "Lady Anne played the tricks on you."

"Anne?" Severn asked in wonder, and Zared knew what he was thinking. Usually women liked him, usually women did what he wanted and were pleased to be allowed to do so. By any reckoning Severn was a handsome man. Were he not her brother, Zared might even believe him to be as handsome as Colbrand, so the news that Anne had done those things to him was shocking.

"Lady Anne did these things?" Severn asked.

"Aye," Tearle answered. "She has her heart set on

Colbrand, but she knew her father favored you, so she made sure you were no longer a contender for her hand. She made everyone laugh at you."

Severn looked at Tearle. "A woman did this?" he whispered. "This was no Howard trick?"

"I can guarantee it was no Howard trick." Tearle glanced at Zared. "Perhaps Lady Anne thought it was a great joke."

Zared could see blood staining Severn's neck as his anger seemed to rise from somewhere deep inside himself.

"A joke?" he said. "I have been made to look like less than a man, and she believes it to be a *joke*? She has made even the lowest of the low laugh at me. *Me!* A Peregrine. Who is *she*? Naught but the rich daughter of a trumped-up merchant, while I . . ." He trailed off, no longer able to speak.

"Where is she?" Severn managed to croak out after a while.

"Eating dinner, I believe," Tearle said cheerfully. He released the woman from his grip, but she did not move.

"I will show her what it means to be laughed at," Severn said.

"My lord," the woman cried, "you cannot—"

Severn pushed past her and left the tent, the woman following him, begging him not to harm Lady Anne.

"What have you done?" Zared hissed at Tearle.

He smiled innocently. "I do not yet know what I have done, but based on your brother's temper, I can guess."

Zared didn't waste more time talking to him but ran after her brother. Maybe she could stop the worst of whatever Severn planned to do. Maybe she could prevent him from making the Peregrine name more of an object of ridicule.

Zared ran, Tearle right behind her. "I'll kill you for this," she yelled over her shoulder at him. Why in the world had she ever believed him when he'd said he could get Anne Marshall married to a Peregrine? After Severn made his accusations to Hugh Marshall people were going to laugh at them even more than they had.

She reached the Great Hall just as Severn reached the high table where Hugh sat, his daughters on either side of him. Hundreds of men and women ate and drank at the long tables set up in the hall.

Zared started to run to her brother to stop whatever foolishness he intended, but the accursed Howard man grabbed her about the waist, put his hand over her mouth, and pulled her into a shadow. No one would have noticed had he torn her arms off, for *all* eyes were on Severn, his handsome face enraged as he glared down at Anne.

Severn didn't look at anyone else in the hall except her. He leaned across the table, grabbed her by the shoulders, and pulled her up. She screamed at him, and more than a dozen men drew their daggers and started for Severn, but Hugh Marshall put his hand up to halt the men. He was fascinated and eager to see what the big man was planning for his daughter.

When Anne was halfway up Severn caught her waist and dragged her across the table. When Anne saw that her father was going to allow no man to rescue her she began to fight for all she was worth. She beat Severn with her fists and kicked out at him, trying to hit him, but she succeeded only in knocking over wine pitchers, goblets, platters of meat, trays of vegetables.

"Unhand me!" she screamed. "Father!"

When the guests realized the performance was sanctioned by Hugh they sat back down and began to enjoy the spectacle.

Once Anne was on Severn's side of the table he

tucked her, screaming, kicking, clawing, under his arm and hooked his foot over a bench. He pulled the bench to the middle of the space between tables—the space left for acrobats and other such performers—and sat on it.

"Help me!" Anne screamed. "Someone, I pray you, help me."

Severn tossed Anne across his knees, flung all but one of her petticoats over her back, and applied his hand to her firm little buttocks.

Whack! "That is for the mud in my helmet," he said. Another *whack!* "And that is for the mud on my face."

It was at that moment that the diners began to understand what it was about. They knew enough about the slovenly Peregrine ways, and they had had ample time to observe the too-fastidious ways of the beautiful Lady Anne, and all they had to do was put one and one together.

Hugh Marshall was the first to laugh. It was a joy to him to see his too-clever daughter brought low in such a way.

"And for the sawed lances," Severn said, applying his hand at each sentence he spoke. "And the honey. And the banner."

Anne stopped struggling at the first sound of laughter. Her fear was replaced by anger and hatred. She clenched her fists, gritted her teeth, and refused to cry at her humiliation. For humiliation it was. He was not hitting her hard, just enough to sting—and that, if possible, made her even angrier.

The huge old Great Hall echoed with laughter, the laughter of everyone: guests, servants, entertainers, children, even the dogs started scampering about.

At long last Severn pulled Anne's skirts down and stood her upright before him while he still sat on the bench. The crowd quieted as they waited to hear what Severn had to say.

"That should teach you to play tricks on men."

With him sitting and Anne standing they were nearly at eye level. He wore a smug look of triumph. She spit in his face.

The crowd hushed.

Severn, after a second's anger, grabbed her by the back of the neck and pulled her to him, and after a second to look at her he put his mouth on hers.

The crowd began to laugh and applaud, and when Severn continued holding Anne and didn't break the long, hard kiss they began to stamp their feet in approval.

Anne fought him throughout the kiss, but she was no match for his strength.

When at last he pulled away from her Severn picked her up in his arms, walked toward the table, and proceeded to drop her, bottom first, onto her father's half-eaten plate of food.

"I suggest you keep closer watch on your daughter," Severn said loudly, then he turned to leave the hall.

The people were laughing again, but now, he thought, they weren't laughing at *him*.

Throughout Tearle had been holding Zared against him. He hadn't had to hold her mouth to keep her quiet, and he probably hadn't had to hold her at all, but he refused to release her.

As Severn started to leave, the beautiful Lady Anne left behind on a large plate of pork, Zared jerked away from him. "Now Hugh Marshall will *never* allow his daughter to marry a Peregrine," she hissed.

"Halt!" Hugh Marshall shouted, and the entire hall grew quiet instantly.

Severn stopped where he was, his hand ready to go

to his sword in order to defend himself. Zared stepped from the shadows, ready to fight beside her brother.

Slowly Severn turned to look at Hugh Marshall.

Hugh stood, and when Anne tried to get off the table he pushed her back down.

"I have something to say to you, Peregrine."

"I can hear you."

There wasn't a sound from any of the hundreds of people in the big room. They held their breaths. Would the fierce old Hugh declare war on the poor Peregrines for the way his daughter had been humiliated?

Anne turned and glared in triumph at Severn, her arms across her chest, her bottom in pork roast, her feet in cabbage stew. She hoped her father would order a particularly vile death for the man.

"It is my wish," Hugh said into the silence, "that you . . ." He took a breath and looked about the room. "I would be honored, sir, if you'd take my daughter in marriage."

The roof nearly fell in at the explosion of laughter.

Zared's mouth fell open as she watched her brother's chest swell in pride. Swaggering, Severn made his way to the high table, then leaned across Anne as though she weren't there, tore a leg off a roast pig, sat on the table near Anne's head, and began to eat.

"How much gold do you give me to take the wench off your hands?"

The crowd was laughing so hard they could hardly stay on the benches, and how Severn loved it! He was going to take his time in the wedding negotiations and enjoy this moment when the crowd wasn't laughing at his family.

Zared stood where she was, watching as Severn bargained with Hugh over Anne's dowry, and she knew that the Peregrine reputation would not suffer from the bargaining. She could see men's heads nodding in approval as Severn asked for more and more gold if he was to take on the burden of Lady Anne.

Zared had some sympathy for Anne, but not much when she remembered how hard everyone had laughed at Severn. But one look at Anne's face, red with rage, and she sensed that perhaps Severn wouldn't have the last laugh, for she doubted that Anne would be an easy person to live with.

After a while she grew tired of the noise and left the hall. There would be much to do to prepare for Severn's wedding.

Outside there were very few people, for they'd all heard of the excitement and jammed into the hall to hear Severn bargaining for the uppity Lady Anne.

A hand clamped on Zared's shoulder. "Do you forget our bargain?"

Zared turned to see the Howard man, and she remembered everything.

"What bargain?" she said, stalling for time. Her mouth was growing dry.

Tearle smiled at her. "I have given your brother his rich bride."

"You gave her to him? You had nothing to do with it. My brother got the woman by . . . by . . ." Humiliating her? By making people laugh at her? "You had nothing to do with it," she finished.

"I caused it all. I told your brother that Anne played those tricks on him."

"Yes, but that is not what made Hugh Marshall offer his daughter. My brother did that on his own, without your help, so there is no bargain between us." She turned away, but he caught her shoulder and turned her back.

174

"I arranged all. I know your brother's temper, and I know that when he is angry he has no control, he—"

"He can control a sword, and if he were here now, he'd control it through you!"

"Oh?" Tearle asked, not at all perturbed. "He could not control his temper today, as I knew he would not be able to. Had Anne another father, not one such as Hugh who values strength above brains, I would not have told Severn what Anne did. But I rightly guessed that Severn would do something such as he did, and that Hugh would be pleased by it. I, little wife, arranged their marriage."

"Wife?" she said under her breath. "I am not your wife and will never be. I cannot keep a bargain that was not fulfilled. You could not have known what would happen. Severn could have killed the woman—he was angry enough to do so—and then where would we be? Or her father could have—"

"I took note that Severn does not hurt women. If he did, you would have bruises aplenty, for I have never seen a woman deserve chastising as much as you do."

"You know *nothing*. Hugh Marshall could have ordered Severn killed for what he—"

"It is a sad but true fact that Hugh cannot abide his younger daughter. She has more brains in one foot than he has in all his body, and he resents that. Also, I have heard it rumored that he was not her father. He's the sort of man to want to repay Anne for rumors she could not help."

"You mean for me to believe that you knew all this, and that this is why you brought the maid to Severn?"

"No, I brought her to Severn to give him the wife he wants so that I may have the wife I want."

She could only look at him, unable to say a word. After a moment she recovered herself and turned away. "You could not have known what would happen, therefore you did not bring about this marriage, therefore my bargain with you is void." She started to walk away.

She walked about ten yards before she stopped. What would he do now? she wondered. Go to his brother and raise an army to attack the Peregrines? Challenge Severn to a combat to the death? Tell Severn who he was and cause a war?

She looked back and saw that he was walking in the opposite direction. She ran after him. "What are you planning now?"

"Planning? I plan? You have just told me that I am incapable of planning."

"What are you going to do to us?" she asked, teeth clenched.

"Do to you? Why should I do anything to you?"

"Because I'm not keeping my bargain. I mean," she said quickly to cover her error, "what are you going to do to my family because I won't marry you because your bargain was false?"

"I will do nothing," he said, smiling.

"Oh, I see. Your *brother* will do all. Do you go to him to plan war now? Will you use what you know against us?"

Tearle's eyes widened. "I would never tell my brother or anyone else that a Peregrine refused to fulfill a bargain. I would want no one to know that a person who bore the proud, ancient name of Peregrine was so lacking in honor."

"We Peregrines do *not* lack honor," she screeched at him.

"I know that to be true of one brother, but you . . . Tell me, is your brother Rogan like you or like Severn?"

She tightened her fists until the skin turned white. "We are *all* honorable. I am most honorable."

"If you say it, it must be true."

She wanted to kill him, to run a sword through him and watch him bleed. "I will marry you," she shouted.

"No," he answered, moving away.

She stepped in front of him. "No? But our bargain was for me to marry you if you got Anne to marry Severn."

"Severn did that himself. I did not have the pleasure of paddling the beautiful Lady Anne; he did that himself."

"But you told him Anne had played the jokes."

"What did that have to do with paddling her lovely bottom?"

The man was truly stupid, she thought. "If you had not told him, Severn wouldn't have known, and if he hadn't known, he wouldn't have gone to Hugh Marshall's Hall and taken Lady Anne—" She stopped.

"Yes? Are you saying that if I hadn't told Severn, he wouldn't be betrothed to Anne now?"

She refused to speak to him.

"So if I did have something to do with the betrothal taking place, then perhaps I did fulfill my part of the bargain."

She refused to speak, but she gave a tiny, curt nod.

"So it seems that I kept my end of the bargain, but you do not wish to keep yours. I understand now. Good day, Lady Zared." He smiled at her and started walking.

She caught his arm. "Where are you going?"

"Home to the evil brother you so fear." He smiled. "You seem concerned that I plan some revenge because you will not keep your word. It is my idea that breaking an oath is revenge enough. You must live with this on your conscience the rest of your life. Were it me, I could not bear myself, but then you are a

Peregrine, not a Howard, so perhaps your name means less to you than mine does to me. However, it is your choice. I will not force you to honor your own word. It is my belief that one has honor or one does not. In this case it seems that you do not. Therefore—"

"Cease!" Zared yelled at him, her hands to her ears. "I will marry you."

"I could not ask that of you, for you seem to doubt that I kept my end of our bargain."

"You kept it!" she hissed. "I have told you so. Do you wish me to shout it from the rooftops?"

"It might be pleasant were you to tell your brother you wish to marry me."

"Wish to marry you? You are the last person I would *wish* to marry."

He started to walk away.

"All right! I'll tell Severn I"—she swallowed— "that I wish to marry you. He would be suspicious otherwise."

"How kind of you," he said, smiling. "Shall I meet you in the church in two hours?"

"Two . . . two hours?"

"Of course, if you would rather not fulfill your part of the bargain, I can leave now. If you can live with your dishonor, I am sure I can."

"I will be there," she said, then she angrily turned on her heel and left him.

Tearle smiled at her back. He was *very* happy.

Chapter Eleven

Zared sat rigidly on her horse, trying not to look at the man who rode beside her, the man who was her husband. They had been married for two days, and she was still a virgin. She was glad, of course—glad that the Howard man had not touched her—but some part of her, some part deep within her, resented the fact that he had not made her his wife.

But then she had said a few things to him that seemed to make him quite angry.

After she had agreed to marry him he had lost no time in going to her brother to ask his permission for the marriage. Severn, still involved in his own marriage negotiations, had not wasted much time in thinking about giving his permission. He liked Tearle, and he thought Liana had sent him, so Severn quickly consented. Zared had been hurt at how little attention her brother had paid to the matter of her marriage. Severn had given her a perfunctory kiss on the forehead and gone back to counting coins with Hugh Marshall.

Zared hadn't said a word to Tearle as they walked to the church, and her mumbled replies to the priest in answer to his questions could hardly be heard. After the ceremony she had stood rigid as Tearle had bent and kissed her cheek. There were others in the church, and they were snickering, for it looked as though the big man was marrying a slim boy. Zared kept her head up, refusing Tearle's arm as they left the church and went to their waiting horses.

She mounted and then tried to still her growing fear. What did the Howard plan for her? Did he mean to take her back to his brother's place, to the place for which Peregrines had died? Would he turn her over to his brother to use against her brothers?

"I am not the devil," Tearle said as he mounted his horse. "You need not look at me as though I mean to torture you."

She hadn't answered him. She didn't ask him where he was leading her or what he planned to do with her. Of course, he had said that he was going to take her back to her brothers and that he would live with the Peregrines, but she was not sure she believed him.

They left the Marshall lands, taking only what they could carry on their horses, and outside the grounds they were met by three men—Howard men.

Zared knew then that she had been betrayed by him. She cursed herself, for she knew that her marriage was going to cause the deaths of her two remaining brothers. She rode beside the man who was her husband, but she did not speak to him. Several times he tried to talk to her, but she didn't answer him. It took all her strength and all her courage to hold back her tears. She tried to think of ways to kill the three knights who rode with them, but she didn't think she could do it. She had to face what she knew was going to happen.

It was on their wedding night that all her fears and misery came out. The Howard man hired a room at an inn. At supper Zared sat silently by him. She did not speak, and she ate very little. Several times she glanced at Tearle and saw that he was looking at her with gentle eyes, almost as though he understood what she was feeling, but she wasn't going to let herself soften toward him.

When it was time to go to bed she braced herself, but instead, with a polite concern, he sent the landlady up with her. But Zared didn't undress. Instead, she sat rigidly on the bed and waited for him.

Some time later Tearle came to the room, and by the light of a single candle she stared at the bed hangings while she heard him undress. She heard the loud rustle of the straw-filled mattress as he climbed into bed beside her. And then he reached out to touch her.

At his touch all of Zared's fears and rage came leaping to the surface. Later she couldn't remember exactly what she had said, but she used words that would have earned her a beating had she used them around her brothers. She told the Howard man what she thought of his treachery, of his lies. She told him that the souls of the Peregrines would come back to haunt him. She called him every name she could think of and said that she would shed her own blood if he so much as touched her.

Days later she could still remember the look on his face. He seemed to be stunned by her accusations, stunned by her hatred. He got out of bed and pulled on his braes, then he turned to look at her.

"I was in error. I thought perhaps that—"

"You thought what?" she spat at him.

"I thought that we could be a man and a woman. But I seem to be wrong."

"We are a Peregrine and a Howard," she said. "How could we be anything else? Did you expect me to love you because a few words were spoken by a priest? Did you expect to wipe out three generations of hatred with a few moments in a church? I told you I hated you. Did you not believe me?"

He was silent for some time as he looked at her. "I do not think I did. I have had . . . feelings for you since I first saw you. It was vain of me to think that those feelings would ever be returned." He pulled on his linen shirt, then gathered his other clothes over his arm and went to the door. "I will see you in the morning," he said, then he left the room.

For a moment Zared was too stunned to speak. She sat on the bed and stared at the closed door. What manner of man was he? Had a woman spoken to one of the Peregrine men as Zared had just spoken to Tearle . . . well, her brothers would have done just what Severn did to Lady Anne. But when she had cursed the Howard man he did not return her rage but instead left his bride on her wedding night.

She didn't sleep much that night, and in the morning she went downstairs to where the Howard men were already waiting for her. Her husband did not help her onto her horse as he usually tried to do, nor did he speak to her during the day.

That night they stayed at another inn, and he did not so much as come to her room. Zared was too tired to stay awake, but when she awoke in the morning she tried to stamp down the resentment that she felt. She rode beside him and found his silence as annoying as she'd once found his constant talking.

"Where are we going?" she asked, and the words came out more belligerently than she meant them.

He gave her a hard look. There were dark circles under his eyes and whisker stubble on his cheeks. Had Zared not been so caught up in her own misery she would have wondered at the look of him. She had no way of knowing that Tearle had spent the previous two nights alone and awake, drinking and cursing himself. He had congratulated himself in being so clever in persuading the woman to marry him, but he'd not thought beyond the ceremony. Perhaps he'd been foolish enough to believe that after the words were said she'd turn to him in love. But the mere ceremony of marriage had not changed her. Even knowing her as he did, he had been unprepared for the vehemence with which she had attacked him on their wedding night. He had won her, true, but what had he won? A woman who hated him with all her heart and soul.

"I am taking you to my brother so that he can throw you in the dungeon and torture you. I am going to allow him to use you in his war against your brothers. I, like he, have a great desire to own that decaying castle of yours. It is my greatest wish to see your brother Severn dead and to be married to a woman who hates me."

She looked away from him. "Where are we going?" she asked in a much softer tone.

"To my house. I do not often stay with my brother. The house was owned by my mother."

She gave him a look of surprise.

"Does it surprise you that I had a mother? Or have you been taught that all Howards come directly from hell?"

"I have never thought about your mother. Your brother starved mine to death in a siege when I was but a child."

Tearle looked away from her. "Yes, Oliver would do that."

183

She didn't speak for a while, and then she asked him about his mother, saying that she thought he had grown up in France. He told her of living with his mother in France but added that every other year she would come back to the place that had been her father's house to see to the people on her land. Tearle would travel with her.

There was another long period of silence, then he looked at her. "Do you know why I wanted to marry you?"

"No," she answered honestly. "I do not know."

"Part of the reason is that I want to end this feud. It has gone on too long. Unlike you, I have not been raised with this hatred between the Howards and the Peregrines. I know that there is a dispute about who should have the title and the land. My brother has no children, and from looking at him, I would guess that he has not long to live."

"Then you will be the duke," Zared said softly.

"Yes, I will become the duke. I thought that if I were to marry a Peregrine and a son were to come from that union, then the child could one day inherit the title and the lands. That way both the Howards and the Peregrines would own what they both want."

"No!" she said sharply. "It is Peregrine land. It has always been Peregrine land. My brother Rogan should be the duke, and his son should rule after him. No Howard should own the land or the title."

He arched an eyebrow at her. "It would be your son who became the duke. Would you not want that?"

There was no decision for her to make. "My son would not deserve the title. Nor do you. It belongs to my brother Rogan." She looked at him. "You married me to ensure the title for yourself and your son?"

At that Tearle sighed and shook his head. "Will you forever believe the worst of me? I am not my brother. I saw a way of ending the feud, and yet you believe only that I want power. What can I do to prove to you my worth?"

"When you inherit, turn it all over to my brother."

Tearle's eyes widened. "Your grandmother was never legally married. It is only legend that they were married. Your family is a lot of bastards. Even the king declared it so."

"That's not true!" she yelled at him. "My family is the true owner of all that your brother holds. Why do you think he fights us so hard if it isn't true?"

"It might have to do with your brothers killing my brothers," Tearle said softly, then he paused a moment. "If our marriage and our producing a child will not settle the feud, then I see no reason for our being married."

"Nor do I," she answered, looking straight at him.

Tearle looked at her a while, and then he smiled. "I have done foolish things in my life, but nothing like this. Lady Zared," he said, sweeping off his cap, "I apologize for having forced you into marriage with me. I apologize for thinking that I could make you care for me. I see now that I was a fool. The Peregrine hatred is stronger than the Howard love. Since there seems to be no way to compromise in this feud—since both sides ask for complete surrender—then I suggest that we end this marriage."

"H-how can we do that?"

"I shall petition the king. I am sure that with a little land deeded to him he will allow the marriage to be annulled. Then we can all go back to where we were. Your people can spy on my people, and mine can spy on yours. Does that suit you?"

"I'm not sure," she said hesitantly.

"Not sure? What alternative is there? You hate me, and you'd rather die than allow me to touch you, so there can be no hope of children. For myself, I would like to have a few brats. My proposal is that we stay at my mother's house until we have heard from the king. I do not think that I would like to stay with you and this formidable brother of yours, nor do I think that you would like to stay with my brother."

"No!" she said quickly. "I don't want to stay with the Howards."

"Then it is settled. That is, if this is all right with you. I no longer want to be accused of forcing you—of forcing you to marry me, of forcing you to go to bed with me. As you said, you'd rather mate with a . . . what was it you said? A three-legged hunchback with the mark of the devil on his cheek. Do I have it right?"

Zared looked away, her face red. She had said many things on their wedding night and didn't remember half of them. She would have said *anything* that night to keep him from touching her. She nodded.

"Good, at last we seem to agree on something. The sooner we get the marriage annulled, the sooner we can get away from each other, and the sooner I can find myself a few willing women." He smiled in a way that Zared had not seen before. His whole face softened. "At the tournament there was the prettiest little green-eyed blonde. She had hair . . ." He stopped and cleared his throat. "Well, then, it's settled. Shall we clasp hands on the bargain?"

Zared took his hand and quickly and firmly clasped it, then she looked away, frowning. She had what she wanted, but for some reason she wasn't happy at all.

The sight of the house owned by her husband's mother made Zared even more unhappy. It was a house—not a fortress protected by high walls, but a beautiful, large house made of pink stone. There were trees in the large park surrounding it, and she saw deer roaming under the trees. Everything was clean and tidy and utterly beautiful.

Part of her said that the house was useless in defense, that it could be taken by anyone who wanted it, but another part loved the beauty of the place.

When they rode up to the courtyard their horses' hooves clattering on the cobblestones, people came out of the house to greet them. There were three older women, all exquisitely dressed in brocade, their head-dresses sparkling with jewels.

Tearle introduced her to the ladies who were kind enough and polite enough to make no reaction to her boy's clothes. Zared had planned to dismount and curtsy to them, but she bent only a little before Tearle caught her arm and held her upright. He told her that the lovely women were to be her maids, that they were to care for her just as they had for his mother. She was to go with them, and he would see her at supper.

As Zared looked at the women, looked at their beautiful gowns, she felt something akin to fear. Until that moment she hadn't considered what it was going to mean to her life to dress as a woman. She had been so involved with her anger at her husband that she had not considered the issue. She thought of wearing a silk gown and felt some excitement, some part of her wanting to feel the fabric against her skin, but another part of her was terrified. With longing she looked back at the Howard men. They were no doubt going to the stables or to the men's quarters to drink beer and brag to one another about the tournament. How she would have liked to have gone with them! She would feel more comfortable with those bragging, belching, scratching men than with the ladies.

She looked from the men to Tearle and saw that he

was watching her. For the first time she didn't look at him as though he were her enemy; he was the most familiar person to her. She gave him a little smile.

He didn't return the smile and seemed to be puzzled by hers.

"This way, Lady Zared," one of the women said to her.

Zared gave Tearle a look of pleading, silently asking him to help her, to allow her to go with the men.

Gradually he seemed to understand her meaning, and he smiled at her. "I will come to you soon," he said.

The words made Zared blush, for they sounded as though she couldn't bear to be parted from him. She put her nose in the air and followed the three ladies. She'd show him that she didn't need him.

Upstairs it was worse than she had feared. The women seemed to think that she was dressed in boy's clothes for protection and that she was dying to put on a silk gown. They apologized for not having made her room ready.

Zared looked at the large oak-paneled room and wondered what could have been done to make it more ready. There was no room in her family's castle that was half as nice. She went to the big four-poster bed and tentatively touched the hangings.

"Shall we help you bathe and dress, my lady?" one of the women asked.

Zared did not want to show her ignorance. "No, I . . . I will do it myself." She saw the women look from one to the other and knew that she had done wrong.

"Very well, then, we shall have your bath sent to you."

Zared gave a silent nod, and the women left the room. Within minutes four men carried the big wooden tub into the room, and women followed with hot water, soap, and towels.

The bathwater felt good, and Zared was glad that Liana had shown her enough about bathing so that she wouldn't look to the Howard maids to be more of a fool than she already did. She soaped her body and her hair, then ducked under the water to rinse. When the water was cool she stepped out of the tub onto the cold stone floor and picked up the drying towel. It was of a finer quality than she was used to, and it was warm from the fire. For a moment she buried her face in its softness and smelled it. No matter how much her home castle had been cleaned, she thought, it could never smell as good as this house and everything in it.

When she was dry she looked for her clothes, but they were nowhere to be found. Instead, on the bed was a clean linen shift and a long, soft velvet robe. She put the shift on, then slipped her arms into the robe. It was of a deep blue with tiny gold fleurs-de-lis embroidered on it. She hugged her arms about her and closed her eyes for a moment as she rubbed her cheek against the lush softness.

At that moment there was a soft knock on the door, and then one of the maids entered. Zared thought her name was Margaret.

"My lady," the woman said, and it took Zared a moment to realize that the woman was speaking to her. "Lord Tearle asks that you join him below for supper."

Zared opened her mouth to say that she would be there soon, for she was quite hungry, but then she realized that she had no clothes. "I would like my clothes returned to me," she said as haughtily as she could manage.

"If you would be so good as to tell me where your

baggage is, I will see that your garments are sent to you straight away."

There was nothing to reply to that, for Zared had no baggage. "Tell him"—she wasn't sure what to call her husband—"that I am not hungry and will not eat with him."

"Then I will help you into your nightdress."

Zared knew that she didn't have any nightclothes either. In her family night apparel had been an unnecessary expense. Her brother bought her a suit of clothes, and she wore them night and day until they either wore out or she was too tall for them. "No," she told the maid, "I will see to myself." She breathed a sigh of relief when the woman left her alone.

With a sigh she looked at the bed. There didn't seem much else to do except to go to bed with her stomach rumbling. She was startled when, a few minutes later, four men came and took the tub of dirty water away.

Moments later, when she was standing by the fire warming her hands, running them across the velvet of her robe, another knock sounded. This time, again before she could speak, the door opened, and her husband entered.

"You carry this too far," he said to her. "Do you hate my company so much that you will starve yourself?"

"Why, no," she said in surprise. "I do not—"

"Ah, then you plan to have all your meals alone in your room."

"I did not request a meal in here." The truth was that she didn't know that she could request a meal brought to her room. It was not something that had ever been done at her brothers' house.

Tearle went to her and put his hands on her shoulders. "You cannot do this. You cannot starve yourself. If it is my company that you so despise, then

I will see that you have your meals here alone. No one will bother you, but below I have music and entertainment. Can I not persuade you to sit with me at supper?"

She gave him a look of disgust. "I have no clothes, you fool. What am I to wear while I sit at your table? Those maids of yours have taken my clothes."

It seemed to take him a moment to understand what she was saying, then he smiled at her. He turned away and went to a large carved chest against one wall. "You should have asked. I had you put in this room because it was my mother's. Her clothes are here."

Zared stood back as he rummaged in the chest and withdrew a gown of dark reddish-brown velvet. There was fur of a darker brown on it, and she very much wanted to touch it, but she held back. "How could I ask your maids for clothes? Am I to let them know that I am a pauper? My sister-in-law came to my brother with wagons full of dresses." She wanted to let him know that if she didn't have the proper clothes, she at least knew what she was supposed to have.

Tearle saw the pride in her face. "I will tell them that all you had was lost in a flood. Yes, that you had eight—no, twelve—wagons full of the finest clothes from France, but they were all lost, so now you must make do with my mother's old things." He held out the dress to her. "It is indeed old, but I think it might be a near fit, and the color will suit you."

Zared put out her hand to touch the fur that edged the neck of the dress. "Mink," she said, and she looked up at him and smiled.

"You'll wear the dress?"

She could only nod.

"Then I will call a maid to help you with your hair and help you dress."

"No!" she said, looking down at her hands. "I will

191

dress myself." She didn't want to look like a fool in front of the maids. She knew that they would laugh when they saw that she had no idea how to put the dress on or what to do with her hair. Zared had heard Liana's maids ask Liana hundreds of questions about braids and headdresses and ribbons and stockings, and Zared knew that she would know none of the answers.

Tearle put the gown on the bed, then took her hand and led her to sit down on a bench before the fire. He took a beautiful tortoiseshell comb from the top of a small table and gently began to comb Zared's hair.

"I can do this."

He pushed her hands away. "You and I will not be together long. Do not deny me what pleasure I can find."

She didn't answer him but closed her eyes as he gently combed the tangles from her hair. As a child she had never combed her hair; only when she grew older and began to notice the handsome young men who trained with her brothers had she taken a comb to her hair, and then she had merely dragged it through, tearing at the knots.

"Such a beautiful color," Tearle said. "And as soft as thistledown." He ran his hands up the back of her neck, then over her scalp, massaging it. "There is no silk to compare with your hair."

When he stopped caressing her head she opened her eyes and saw him standing between her and the fire. There was a warmth in his eyes that she hadn't seen before. "It's only hair," she said gruffly, trying to hide the fact that his words had pleased her.

"Will you get dressed now?"

Zared looked at the gown lying on the bed. Surely she could figure it out by herself. Before she could decide what to do Tearle came up behind her and put his hands on her shoulders and began sliding the robe off of her. Instinctively she clutched it to her.

"I will play the lady's maid tonight," he said. "I will help you with the fastenings." He smiled. "Unless you'd rather I called Margaret."

"No, I . . ." She swallowed. "Perhaps I could have supper in this room."

"Zared," he said sternly, "you are going to have to leave this room at some time. You cannot stay in here forever wearing only that one robe. If you do not want me in here, I can call a maid."

He was her enemy but at least he was familiar to her. She had spent days in his company. She released her hold on the robe, and he took the robe from her. Zared snatched the gown off the bed and held it in front of her body.

"Now," he said with the sound of efficiency in his voice, "over the head. No, not that way, the other way. Here, turn this around so the front is this way."

Zared held the gown to her, clutching it so that it did not gape across her bosom. Never in her life had she gone into the light of day with her breasts unbound, and putting on the dress—her breasts without their painful binding—made her feel rather strange.

"Hold still," Tearle said from behind her as he drew the laces down the back of the dress tightly together.

Zared was used to tight lacing, but it usually covered her breasts. This tightness was lower, pulling in her waist. She looked down and saw that her breasts were quite exposed in the deep V of the neckline. She put her hand up to cover herself.

Tearle finished with the lacing then turned her around to look at her. "I think it is a perfect fit. My mother was always very slender." He stepped back to look at her. "Put your hand down. Go on, hands to your sides."

Zared obeyed him, but she didn't look at him until his silence was more than she could bear. Slowly she lifted her eyes to look at him. He wore an odd expression that seemed to make her body grow warmer.

Tearle cleared his throat and dragged his eyes away from her. "Shall we go down to dinner?" He held out his arm for her to take.

Zared took two steps toward him and promptly fell face forward. She would have hit the floor except that Tearle caught her.

"It's the train," he said.

Zared looked behind her and saw that the dress had a great deal of fabric flowing out the back of it. How, she wondered, did one walk with that dragging?

"I think you throw it over your arm," Tearle said, and when Zared gave him a look of disbelief he tried to demonstrate. "I think you do it like this."

She watched as he took a few mincing steps, then made a sweeping bend as though reaching for something. He flipped the imaginary object over his arm. Zared did everything that she could to keep from laughing. *This* was the Black Knight? This was the mysterious knight who felled all comers?

She gave a little frown. "I still do not understand. Will you show me again?"

"I told you that I'm not completely sure how it's done, but the ladies seem to do it with ease. Now walk like this."

She watched as he did his imitation of a lady taking tiny steps.

"Then bend—do this gracefully—pick up the train, and drop it over your arm. There, that wasn't so difficult, was it?"

"I shall try it." Zared took two steps, trying to imitate his walk, then she bent and purposely missed catching the fabric of the train. She looked up at him. "I think you will have to show me again."

He sighed. "All right, but watch carefully this time. Walk. Bend. Lift. Drop." He demonstrated each word, then turned back to her. "Now you try it."

Again Zared made a mess of trying to toss the train over her arm, and she managed to conceal her smile at his frown.

He moved to stand behind her, then put one hand about her waist. "Walk," he ordered, then he bent forward, forcing her to bend also. He took her right hand in his. "Now pick up the damned thing and throw it over your arm."

Zared again managed to drop the train. She stepped away from him and gave him an innocent look. "I seem to be a fool at this. Perhaps you should try on the gown and show me that way."

The look on his face made Zared's laughter erupt.

"Why, you little minx," he said, lunging for her.

With a motion that was almost expert Zared grabbed the train and flung it over her arm before she began to run from him. At first she began to run in earnest, immediately making for the door, but he reached it before she did and put his arm across it so that she couldn't open it. For a moment she was afraid of him. Had she teased her brothers as she had him, making fun of their masculine abilities, they would have made her pay. But when she looked into the eyes of the man she saw that he was amused by her.

She ran from him, holding her train with one hand and slipping around the bedpost with the other. At first it seemed odd to her that she knew he could catch her but that he didn't. She ran toward a table and put it between them, and when she dodged one way he blocked her exit, so she went the other way, and he blocked that way, too. She smiled, and then she laughed and moved back and forth as quickly as possible. But he was always faster.

Zared pushed a chair to the floor and made a leap across it, and he reached for her, but she ran before he could catch her. She ran toward the window seat, and when he made a lunge at her she gave a squeal of laughter and jumped to the floor. He was inches behind her, and twice he caught her, but his hands were loose on her body, and she could easily escape him.

By the time she jumped on the bed she was breathless from laughter and from running, and from something else that she didn't quite understand.

He caught her on the bed. He rolled her about, tickling her until she was dying of laughter, his hands running up and down her body.

"Do you beg me for forgiveness?" he asked, his hands at her ribs. He stopped moving his fingers as he looked down at her. She was on her back on the bed while he sat over her, his thighs straddling her hips.

"Never!" she said, but she was smiling. "I will never beg forgiveness from a Howard."

She had meant no harm by what she said—she hadn't even thought of the meaning of her words—but his face lost its good humor, and he moved off of her. She caught his arm before he left the bed. "I meant no . . ." She didn't know how to finish her sentence.

He sat on the edge of the bed for a moment, then he turned and looked at her. Zared held her breath. Actually, she thought, he wasn't a bad-looking man at all. She smiled at him.

He grinned at her, and Zared thought that perhaps he was the opposite of bad-looking.

He grinned more broadly and made a lunge across

196

the bed for her. "You'll be the death of me," he said as he caught her in his arms.

Zared squealed, her arms together, then stopped moving and looked up at him. His eyes were soft, and she didn't understand the expression.

"You're very pretty, you know." He tucked a strand of hair behind her ear.

"I'm not," she said softly. "I look like a boy."

At that he gave a snort of laughter and lay down beside her, then pulled her into his arms, her back to his front. "I never saw anyone look less like a boy."

"But no one even questions that I—"

"That shows how stupid people are."

She relaxed against him. No one had ever held her like that. There was no physical affection between her and her brothers, and there were few women in her brothers' home. Some part of her brain told her to move away from him, but it felt so good to be held that she didn't move.

His big hand smoothed the hair off of her face. Her hair was still damp from washing, and she felt him bury his face in it. She closed her eyes for a moment.

"You're not beautiful like Anne Marshall," he said softly. "You're more like . . . a two-day-old colt or a pup."

She pushed at his arms, but he didn't release her. "A horse? I look like a horse? Or is it a dog?"

"You know very well what I mean," he answered, and he put his face further into her hair, smelling it. His lips reached her neck and kissed her a few times.

"Mmmm. I understand," she said, her eyes closed. "Men like Anne Marshall. My brother did. He liked her even after all the terrible things she did to him." She moved her head so that he could have better access to her neck. He was placing little nibbling kisses down it. "I wager that you wish you could have had Lady Anne."

Tearle stopped kissing her and pulled her closer to him. "She was offered to me, but I turned her down."

Zared was astonished by that, and she wanted to look into his eyes to see if he was lying. She turned over in his arms so that they were facing each other. "You would not have turned down Lady Anne. She is beautiful, and she is rich. Any man who was offered her would have taken her."

"I was, but I did not." Again he began to touch the hair at her temple. "What fine red stuff this is. Like a spider's web."

"Spiders' webs are sticky. Why would you have turned down Anne Marshall?"

"Because I did not want her. She has a sharp tongue on her, and she is much too clever to live with."

"But what does that matter? Severn will not care for her tongue. He will make her obey."

"As your older brother Rogan has made his wife obey?"

She started to ask him how he knew of her family, but then she remembered that he was a Howard, and that his family spied on hers. But she also remembered that he had been out drinking with her brother Severn, and Zared knew that there were no gossips like men with a keg of beer to share. Instead of cursing him, as was her first inclination, she smiled. "Did Severn tell you of our brother?"

"In detail. He does not know whether to hate his sister-in-law or love her." Tearle ran his hand down her shoulder, his eyes lowered. "However did you hide all of that under your boy's clothes?"

Zared looked down at her breasts, which were pushing out above the velvet of her dress. She put her hand up to cover herself and at the same time started to move away from him, but he held her where she was.

He moved her hand away. "If I cannot touch, at least allow me to look my fill."

She felt herself blushing, and her body tingled all the way down to her toes. "Cannot touch?" she said, her voice catching.

"If our marriage is to end, if I ask the king to annul our marriage, then I feel that I must leave you a virgin. If you are to get another husband, then I would think that he'd want the pleasure of taking your virginity."

"Oh," she said. "Of course." She couldn't breathe very well because his hand was running over the exposed skin of her breasts.

"I hope he is a good lover to you."

"Who?"

"The man you marry. The man who has the right to give you children. The man who has the right to take his pleasure with your beautiful body."

"I am not beautiful. You have just said so. And you said that I was not clever."

"But you have never heard me say that you were not the most desirable female I have ever met in my life, have you?"

"No, I have not." Her voice was very soft. His fingers were slipping down the front of her gown.

"In all the French court I saw no woman more desirable than you."

"A-and how am I d-desirable?" Her eyes were closed. She could smell the strong masculine scent of him, feel the heat of his body so near hers.

"There is an innocence about you. Too many women know all there is to know about men and women before they spend the night together. But you, you are an unmarked slate. A man may teach you what he wants you to know."

Her eyes flew open, and she stiffened in his arms. "I know how children are conceived," she said with some anger in her voice. "I am no ignorant country girl. I may not be a clever beauty like your Lady Anne, but I know a great deal about men and women."

He gave her an infuriating smile. "You know only of the act. You know nothing of what goes before."

"Before what?"

He ran his hand over her bare shoulder. "There is what happens between a man and woman that produces children, and there is lovemaking. A world of difference exists between the two of them."

She was still feeling hurt by his saying that she knew nothing. "Perhaps you should tell me the difference, and I will tell you if you are correct."

He gave a little laugh. "Ah, my little falcon, would that I could show you the difference, but there is my sanity to consider. I think we have had enough of this and that we had better go to dinner."

He dropped his arms from around her and started to move to the other side of the bed, but she caught his shoulder.

"You would tell Lady Anne, wouldn't you? She would be clever enough to understand you, wouldn't she?"

He looked over his shoulder at her. "I imagine that Anne knows all there is to know of what goes on between men and women. If your brother does not please her on their wedding night, Anne will no doubt complain to him and to anyone else who will listen."

Zared moved away from him and leaned back on the pillows, her arms crossed over her breast. "Then I shall complain also. When I have a husband who takes me to bed, if he does not please me, I shall tell him so."

200

He turned back to smile at her. "And to what will you compare his lovemaking? To your other lovers?"

"Why no, I . . ." Her eyes widened. "Do you think the Lady Anne has had other lovers? Severn will not like that."

"Your hotheaded brother may kill her if she isn't a virgin, and Hugh Marshall will no doubt praise him for it."

She didn't understand at all. If Anne Marshall was a virgin, too, then how could she know so much of lovemaking? Zared wasn't sure what the man was saying, but she knew that she felt insulted. Her brothers had always treated her like a child, and this man was treating her like a child as well.

She turned her head away from him and started to get off the bed. She was not going to humiliate herself further by asking more questions.

"Zared," he whispered, pulling her to him.

She started to fight him, struggling against him. She didn't like the way he smirked at her and talked of other women.

He pinned her to the bed with his big body, but her arms were free, and she began to beat him on the back and shoulders. "Release me!" she demanded. "I hate you. I hate having you near me."

He caught her head in his hands and held her steady while he began to kiss her lips. She kept them closed for a moment, but the sensation was very pleasant, and she couldn't resist him for long. He nibbled at her lower lip, and the tip of his tongue very sweetly ran along the crevice between her lips. He kissed her eyes and her cheeks.

It was as though no one had ever touched her before—and in truth very few people had—and she was hungry for physical contact. She forgot that he was supposed to be her enemy, and she opened her mouth to his. It was she who turned her head sideways so that she could kiss him more deeply. Her arms stopped beating on his broad back, and they went around him to hold him as tightly as possible.

Her life had been spent in very physical ways. She was no prim and proper miss who had spent her youth behind an embroidery frame. Instead she had grown up on the back of a horse with a sword in her hand. She was used to exuberance and a great deal of movement.

When she felt desire pouring through her she acted on it with all the enthusiasm that she had been allowed to express in her life. She put her tongue in his mouth and wrapped her legs about his hips, locking her ankles together.

When he seemed to want to pull away from her she went with him, hanging onto him when he rolled over so that she was on top of him.

Tearle had to take her by the shoulders and pull her away from him. He lay on his back looking up at her, and there was an expression of amazement on his face. "Where did you learn that?" he said, and there was barely concealed rage in his voice.

It took her a moment to remember who she was, where she was, and who he was. She was on top of him, her legs straddling his hips, the position he had taken with her earlier. It felt good to be on top of him, rather as though she had wrestled him to the ground and was holding him there. "Learn what?" She smiled down at him.

He did not return her smile but instead threw her to the other side of the bed and got off of it. "Some man must have taught you that. Was it Colbrand? When you were with him in that pond did you do more than bathe him?"

She was taken aback by his words, and she could feel anger rising in her, but then she relaxed against the pillows. "He taught me nothing. I know what I know."

At that he caught her about the waist, pulled her off the bed, and stood her before him. "You may not want to be my wife, but if I so much as catch you looking at another man I will—" He broke off.

"You will what?" she whispered.

He released her and stood there looking at her for a moment. "Put your shoes on and come downstairs. Supper grows cold."

When she was alone in the room Zared hugged herself and twirled around the room, the heavy velvet skirt whirling about her.

"You will have supper now, my lord?"

Tearle gave a start and looked up from his goblet of wine. "Oh, Margaret, I didn't see you. Has she come down yet?"

"No," Margaret said slowly. "I imagine that she will find it difficult to dress herself."

"You do not miss much, do you?" He smiled at the woman who had come to his mother when they were both girls. Tearle's mother had died in Margaret's arms.

"I could not help notice that you are mad in love with her."

"She hates me," he said gloomily.

Margaret nearly laughed aloud at that. "The girl who gave you such a look of longing in the courtyard does not hate you."

"You have not heard her speak to me. Ah, sometimes she desires me, if I kiss her enough and tell her that she is pretty, but she desires that from any handsome man." He snorted. "She desires that even from me, who she thinks is ugly." He looked up at Margaret. "She is a Peregrine."

Margaret's face lost its laughter. She went to Tearle and put her hand on his shoulder. "You were always a good boy. That you'd marry this boy-girl to settle a feud is very noble of you."

"I tricked her into marrying me," he snapped. "And I didn't marry her to settle a feud. I married her because I wanted her."

"Ah, could you not just have bedded her?"

Tearle didn't speak for a while. "Perhaps." He didn't say more but just sat there looking at his wine goblet.

Margaret sat on the chair next to him. He was as near to being a son as she was ever going to have. "I have heard about these Peregrines. Are they as rough as I have heard?"

"Worse."

"Then perhaps some softness in the girl's life would do her good. Perhaps soft music and soft words would win her. Perhaps if you let her see you as you are, she would come to love you."

"I have told her I will petition the king for an annulment. I mean to keep my word."

"Did you tell her when you would send the messenger?"

Tearle smiled at her. "No, I did not. But I did say I would give her an annulment, which means I am not to touch her."

Margaret laughed. "Do you not know that there is much more sensuous pleasure than what goes on in the bed?"

Tearle gave her a look to say that she was half mad.

"The girl moved from me when I but meant to touch her arm," Margaret said. "And she looked at my gown with lust in her eyes. For all her boy's clothes, I think she hungers for what a woman has and wears. I think that roses might win your lady."

"Roses?"

"And music and tales of love and silk and gentle kisses placed behind her ear."

Tearle looked at the woman for a long while, his mind racing with his thoughts. He remembered the way Zared had reacted to his kisses. Perhaps she did not hate him as much as she said she did. If he had not allowed his jealousy to overcome him, what might have happened? Perhaps it was possible to win her with a bit of courting. He smiled at Margaret.

Chapter Twelve

Nothing that Zared had ever experienced had prepared her for life in the Howard house. At supper she sat at a clean table and ate delicious food, and her new husband treated her as though she were fragile and precious.

The calmness of the servants, the general peace of the whole house was new and interesting to her. In her own home it wasn't unusual for her brothers' knights to come storming into rooms demanding that someone come and settle a fight. Her brother Rogan regularly slammed his battle ax into tables to make a point. But at Tearle's the questions were whether she had enough wine or whether her soup was hot enough.

After supper a handsome young man came and played a lute while he looked at Zared with liquid eyes.

"What is he saying?" she asked, since the man was singing in French.

Tearle looked at her across a silver wine goblet. The whole room glowed with the light from the fireplace. "He is singing of your loveliness, of your beauty, and of the beautiful way you move your hands."

Zared looked startled. "My hands?" Her brothers had always complained that she had no strength in her hands, that she could barely lift a sword. She held her hands in front of her and looked at them.

Tearle took one in his own and kissed her fingertips. "Beautiful hands."

"What else is he saying?" she asked, looking away from her husband to the handsome young man.

"He says only what I have told him to, for I wrote the song," Tearle answered, an edge to his voice.

She looked back at him in wonder. "You? You can write songs in another language?"

"Songs and poetry. I can play the songs as well. Should I demonstrate?"

"If you can write, then can you read? Liana can read. Could you read me a story?"

Tearle stopped kissing her hand and smiled at her, then signaled the man to leave them. Another soft command from him and a servant brought five books into the room. "Now, what shall you hear?" When Zared looked blank, Tearle smiled. "I know. I shall read you *Héloise and Abelard*. That should appeal to you."

An hour later Zared was sitting in front of the fire trying not to cry, for the story he had read to her was very sad.

"Come now, it happened long ago, and there is no need to cry." When she kept sniffing he pulled her into his lap and stroked her hair. "I did not know you had such a soft heart."

"I do not think you have any heart at all," she snapped.

He kissed her forehead, then, still holding her, he stood and began to carry her up the stairs. "I think it is time you were in bed."

Zared snuggled against him. He was still her enemy, of course, but at the thought of spending the night with him her skin began to tingle. But when they entered the room he kissed her forehead and left her alone.

She didn't know whether to be glad or enraged. In the end she was just puzzled. She undressed and went to bed and lay awake for a while, thinking about the odd man she was married to. She knew of his idea to keep her a virgin until he could petition the king for an annulment, but how could he keep his word? Her brothers would not have allowed a wife to remain a virgin no matter what the woman said. The more she thought the more puzzled she became. The Howard man was not like any man she had met before.

She woke to find him sitting in her room, a rose on the pillow beside her. He helped her dress in riding clothes, a shorter skirt with no train, but he did no more than kiss her neck as she held her hair up for him to fasten the ties at the back of the gown.

They went down the stairs together, and there were horses waiting and servants bearing trays of fresh bread and cheese and goblets of wine. They rode together, and he talked to her not of war or weapons, but of the beauty of the day. He pointed out pretty birds and once even imitated a bird's call.

They stopped at a lake, and he asked her to go swimming with him. Zared said that she did not like to swim and that she didn't really like the water. She sat under a tree and watched as Tearle stripped down to his loincloth and slowly walked to the water. She looked at him for as long as she liked without his watching her. Over the past few weeks each time she looked at him he seemed to have grown larger. She remembered thinking that he was a puny man, a weak man. There had been that time when she had first met him and thought that he had nearly been killed by a slight knife wound. Then she had thought him to be very weak.

But she looked at him and saw how broad his shoulders were, how thick the muscles in his legs were. There were scars on his body, scars just as her brothers had, scars made by weapons. She wondered if he had been injured in battle or if all the scars had come from practice or tournaments.

She leaned back against the tree and watched him swim. It was all a waste of time, of course. She should be training as she usually did, she thought, but then she smiled. Her training had always been to prepare her for fighting the Howards, but she had married a Howard and was watching him swim in a pool.

He lay on his back in the water, and Zared could not help but notice the deep muscles on his chest. He wasn't as big as her brothers, of course, but he was certainly larger than Colbrand.

She was lazily watching him as he raised his arm to wave at her. She smiled at him, then saw him dive under the water. She sat still and waited for him to resurface. A minute went by, and she sat up. He had not come to the surface.

She waited a few seconds more, and still she did not see him. She got up and walked to the edge of the lake. "Howard!" she called, but there was no answer. She called louder. "Howard!" Still no answer, and still no sign of him.

She didn't think about what she did. She ran into the water. She could swim, her brothers had seen to that, but she had never liked doing it. But she didn't think about like or dislike, she just reacted.

She took a deep breath and dived under the water, her eyes wide as she looked for him. It didn't take her long. He was easy to see, as he was curled under the water, his face against his knees.

Her lungs were already beginning to hurt, but she stayed under long enough to pull him up, putting her arm under his chin and dragging him to the surface of the water. She heard no intake of breath as he came to the surface; in fact, a quick glance at him showed him to be as pale as death.

She swam to the edge of the pool with him, then had to drag him to the shore. He was as heavy as a draft horse, and she had to strain every muscle to get him onto land.

When he was on land, his lower half still in the water, she looked down at him, as pale and cold as death. What should she do? she wondered. "Howard!" she yelled into his face. "Howard!"

He didn't respond. She straddled his stomach and began to slap his cheeks, but it had no effect on him. "Damn you, Tearle," she said, and there were tears of frustration in her voice. "Don't you dare die just when I have begun to think you are worth something."

On her knees she leaned over him, put her hands to his cheeks, and shook his face.

At that Tearle spewed a fountain of water from his mouth. Zared, her face dripping, leaned back from him and stared in astonishment.

Tearle opened his eyes and smiled at her. "I could always hold my breath longer than anyone."

She knew then that he had been playing a joke on her. She sat down hard on his stomach, but he didn't so much as flinch. "You are a horrible man," she said, and she struck him on the chest with her fists.

He caught her fists and rolled over on top of her. "You were worried about me."

"I was not. I only cared that your death might cause a war between my family and yours. Not that that brother of yours deserves the name of family. I care only for my brothers and Liana and maybe Rogan's son, but not for you." He had her pinned to the ground, her hands above her head. She knew that she wanted him to kiss her. She had indeed been frightened for his safety, but she didn't want to admit that to him.

He rubbed his cold, wet face against hers, which was also cold and wet, then he nuzzled her neck. When he released her hands she put her arms around him— and when she did that he rolled off of her.

Zared frowned, for somehow she felt rejected.

"You will freeze if you do not get dry," he said, and there was a smugness in his tone that angered her. It was as though he had wanted to know something and had found it out.

He stood, then pulled her up with him, and when she wouldn't look at him he put his hand under her chin. "Would it be so awful if a Peregrine came to care for a Howard?"

"It cannot happen," she said with as much sincerity as she could muster, but even to her the words sounded false.

He laughed, then picked her up in his arms and whirled her about until she was dizzy. She clung to him, and before long she, too, was laughing.

He stopped twirling her and held her close to him. "Come, my little enemy, and let's get dry. There's a crofter's cottage nearby. Let's see if they can feed us."

She stood by while he dressed, and she allowed him to help her on her horse when they left the lake.

After that things between them began to change. Zared wasn't sure what it was that changed, but she knew that something had. It was as though her attempt to rescue the man had answered a question for him and had freed him from whatever had been holding him back.

She didn't know what he was really like, for she had known him only under the most unusual circumstances, but after that afternoon at the lake she sensed that he began to relax around her. No longer was he afraid of whatever he had been afraid of before, and she began to see the man he really was.

He was as unlike her brothers as night and day. Whereas her brothers tried to get as much work out of each day as they could, Tearle seemed to want to get as much pleasure out of each day as was possible. He trained, just as her brothers did, but he didn't train for many hours at a time, and he had a lighthearted spirit about his training. He laughed when he could. He wagered with his men and paid them when he lost. There was no life-or-death feeling to his training.

At first Zared was annoyed at that attitude of his. She said that he did not understand that training was very important, that men needed to be trained for war. She said that he was so frivolous that even she could beat him with a knife. She knew that she had no chance of winning against him with a heavy sword, but she figured she was faster than he was and more agile.

It didn't take her but minutes to realize that she was wrong on both counts. For all his playfulness he was a very good opponent. He toyed with her, teasing her, making her think that she was winning, then he'd sidestep and take her off balance. As with all the Peregrines her anger rose to blazing in just moments. And when her anger came to the surface Tearle easily took her knife away from her.

"I hope you have learned that a cool head can think faster than a hot one," he said, then, when she meant

212

to try to strike him, he caught her in his arms and kissed her soundly. Zared was embarrassed because of the laughter of the men around them.

Later he came to her and tried to make up. He teased her and handed her a bouquet of flowers and told her she was pretty and that her eyes sparkled more than any jewel. She told him that he was absurd, but she couldn't help smiling. He was an easy man to be near.

The next day he took her to a fair in a town ten miles away. Zared had never been to a fair, for at home she had never been allowed out of her castle, and besides, her brothers did not believe in such frivolity.

The fair was a wonder to her. At the tournament she had not been able to enjoy herself, for she had been under such strain with her brother and her enemy being in the same camp, but at the fair things seemed to be different. Nothing had actually changed, but it seemed that it had. She was still with her family's enemy, but as she glanced at him on his big horse he didn't seem like much of an enemy. In fact, she was beginning to think that he was as big and strong and handsome as her brothers.

The day at the fair was wonderful. All the merchants were glad to see the lord and his pretty lady. It was so different from the tournament, when she had been sniggered at for being one of those dirty Peregrines.

Tearle bought her everything. After having grown up in a household where every penny was treated as though it were gold, it was heavenly to be able to buy pretty things. She ate some of everything that was for sale until Tearle warned her about having a stomachache. When the juice from half a dozen cherries ran down her chin he leaned over and licked the sweet liquid off. She turned red to her toes, but he just laughed at her.

When he saw her watching a beautifully made wrestler bragging that he could beat all comers, Tearle stripped and wrestled the man. When her husband won Zared was bursting with pride, and she held the prize, an ugly knot made of cheap ribbons, as though it were a jeweled ornament won in a tournament.

Tearle stood behind her, his hands on her shoulders as she laughed at a puppet show. When a fight broke out between half a dozen men who'd had too much wine he swept her into his arms and carried her to safety.

There was a booth where a man was selling fabrics from Italy, and Zared paused to look longingly at a bolt of dark green brocade. Tearle ordered the man to show it to them. It was expensive beyond belief, and Zared told the man to put it away. Tearle bought the entire bolt for her. "You can make bed hangings from it," he said.

Some part of her said that she should remember that the money he was spending so freely actually belonged to her family and not his, but all that seemed far away.

He stood with her and watched as she hid her eyes while a man walked across a rope stretched tight between two poles. "That is not so hard. I could do that," Tearle bragged.

"You could not," she answered, and when she saw him moving toward the man she caught his hand and begged him not to do it. It was one thing to wrestle a man, but quite another to walk a narrow rope ten feet above the ground. He could be killed doing that.

She had to beg and beg and beg him to keep him from getting on the rope. In order to stop him she had to tell him that she believed that he could walk the rope and therefore did not have to prove it to her. She had to tell him that he was the best and the bravest knight in all the kingdom. He wanted to know if she thought he was better than Severn, and she said she was certain that he was. He asked if she thought he could beat Rogan, and she assured him that he could. Then he asked if she thought he could beat Colbrand.

"Not in a pig's eye," she said, and then she had the wisdom to start running.

He caught her and tickled her until she admitted that maybe, perhaps, possibly he was better than Colbrand.

When night fell he told her that they had to return to his house, for he was sure that unsavory types came out at night, and he didn't want to risk injury to her. She protested, but she was indeed tired. He mounted his horse, and then one of the five Howard men who had been with them all day handed her up to him, and she rode the ten miles home held in Tearle's arms.

Once they were at home she undressed and waited for him. She was sure that he would come to her bed, but he didn't. As he always did, he kissed her good-night and left her. As tired as she was, she couldn't sleep, and so she got out of bed and sat before the fire.

She leaned back against the chair and felt the warmth of the fire on her face. Sometimes she wished she could go home, for there everything was exactly as it was supposed to be. She knew who were her friends and who were her enemies. She had grown up knowing that she was to hate the Howards, yet her mind was cluttered with a thousand images. She remembered Tearle in black armor knocking all challengers from their horses. She remembered his laughing and teasing her. She thought of his reading to her and smiling at her across the light of a single candle.

She put her hand to her head. Was he the enemy or

215

her friend? He was a Howard, so he could not be her friend, and yet . . .

In the last two weeks they had been together almost constantly, and she had talked to him as she'd never talked to anyone before. In her family, all talk that did not concern war with the Howards was considered a waste of time, but Tearle did not seem to think that any talk was a waste of time.

They talked about things that had happened to them as children, what they liked and disliked, what they hoped would happen in the future. They always managed to avoid talking about the hatred that was between their brothers. In fact, they managed to avoid that issue so well that it was almost as though they weren't sworn enemies.

Tearle had shown her plans he'd had drawn for renovating the dwellings around his mother's house. He took her to meet some of his tenants. At her brothers' house the tenants were not known by their names. Her brothers considered men who could fight to be the only men of importance. But during the many visits Tearle and his mother had made to her home in England Tearle had gotten to know the people who farmed his acres, and he asked about their children, and when there was sickness he saw that the people were cared for.

How could she hate a man who was so kind and who laughed so often? At first she thought that he was pretending to be a man who thought of other people, but the men and women who worked for him were unafraid of him. And the children ran to him, expecting the sweets that he carried in his pockets.

Zared began to ask him more questions about his life, about what he did when he'd returned with his mother to England. "Did you see your brothers when you returned?"

"No," Tearle had answered softly. "My mother felt that she had done her duty and given her husband sons that he could kill in his battle with the Peregrines, so she owed him no more sons and no more of her time. I was the youngest, and she took me with her to France. I lived with her and rarely saw my father or my older brothers."

It took Zared a while to realize that he had not been raised to participate in the feud, that the hatred between the Howards and the Peregrines meant nothing to him.

The more she thought, the more confused she became. If he wasn't interested in the hatred, why had he married her? He had suggested an annulment readily enough when she'd said that she didn't want him to touch her, but he seemed to like her well enough.

She got out of her chair and walked to the fire. *Like* her, did he? She closed her eyes for a moment and tried to think about going back to her brothers' house to live. She would have to return to a place where no one laughed or made jokes, where everything was of the utmost seriousness.

She thought of her oldest brother Rogan and the way his wife had to fight him for every bit of freedom she had. Rogan loved his wife, but it wasn't a love that allowed her to say and do what she pleased. And then there was Severn, who was married to the beautiful Lady Anne. Zared wondered if Lady Anne's temper had caused her brother to kill the woman yet.

She moved back to the chair and sat down hard, her head in her hands. God help her, but she didn't want to go back to her brothers. She wanted to stay with this man, this man who was her enemy, the man her family hated. The blood that ran through him had killed her older brothers, had stolen everything that belonged to them. He was a man she should hate, yet she didn't.

On the table beside her was the ribbon knot that he had won for her. She remembered how proud she had been when she had seen him wrestling that man, how much prouder she had been when he had won. She put the ribbon to her cheek.

What was she going to do? Was there any way that she could have both her family and the man?

She went to bed, but she had a restless night, and in the morning she found herself snapping at people. She was already at the table when Tearle came downstairs. Unlike her, he had no circles under his eyes from lack of sleep.

He greeted her cheerfully, smiling and happy.

Zared looked at him over her mug of watered ale and said, "When will you hear from the king?"

Tearle sat down at the head of the table and cut a large piece of cheese to put on his bread. "You are anxious to have the marriage ended?"

She looked up at him, and for a moment her heart was in her eyes, but she looked away. "It would be best to have it over with."

Tearle was quiet for a moment, so she looked at him. His face showed no expression. When had he grown so handsome? she wondered. When had he changed from being a frog of a man to being the most handsome man she had ever seen in her life? If their marriage must end, it was better that it should end sooner than later. She could not allow herself to grow any fonder of him than she already was.

At last Tearle shrugged. "Who can say what the king will do? I am sure that he will take his own time." He looked at her over his mug. "Perhaps he will deny my petition."

"Deny it?" She held her breath. "W-why would he do that?"

"All in all I would say that ours is a good marriage. We unite two warring families. Perhaps he will not allow us to separate."

Zared's first reaction was to smile. Maybe they could stay in the house forever. Maybe she could have an herb garden. Maybe she could have some new gowns made. Maybe they could breed a few children.

She caught herself and gave a good imitation of a frown. "My brothers will not like my being married to a Howard. Perhaps I should go back to my brothers' house. Perhaps the king will more likely sign the petition if I am home again."

She looked at him and realized that she wanted him to say that he wanted her to stay with him forever, that he wanted her never to leave him. She wanted him to beg her to stay with him.

"As you wish," he said. "Shall I have my men guide you to your home?"

She felt like throwing her food in his face. "If my brothers were to see me riding under the Howard banner, they would attack before questions could be answered."

"Ah, then," he said slowly, "perhaps you should remain here for as long as it takes the king to reply."

It took her a moment to understand him, but then she smiled. "Perhaps that would be best."

They went riding that day, traveling far into the countryside and leaving the men behind them. Tearle took her to see a circle of enormous standing stones that had been built by the ancients. He told her a scary story about human sacrifices being made on the stones, then he lunged at her, pretending that he was about to sacrifice her. She squealed and giggled, but

219

then stopped when he paused with her on the stone, his big body hanging over hers.

He will kiss me now, she thought. He will forget about this talk of annulment and hold me.

But he didn't. He turned away from her and walked to another stone, and when she got down from the stone where he had placed her he didn't look at her. She walked to him, but he kept his face averted, and only after some moments had passed did he look at her.

"It grows dark," he said softly. "We should return."

It was after that day that he began to stay away from her. In such a short time she had become so used to spending time with him that she found that she missed him. She saw him in the courtyard training with his men, so she borrowed some clothes from the cook's boy, dressed in them, and went to join him.

She smiled at him, but he did not return her smile. "You are my wife. You are not to display yourself before my men that way," he said, looking down at her legs, which were covered with no more than thin knit hose.

"What am I supposed to do all day?" she spit at him. "And I am *not* your wife!"

She meant that she was his wife in name only, but he took what she said the wrong way. "You will be free soon enough," he said, and his voice was hard.

Zared turned away from him and from the men around them, who were watching with a great deal of interest in their eyes, and she went upstairs to her room. Her single, lonely room. She had been alone most of her life, and she was alone again, but why did it seem so much worse? It was as though she'd found a friend and lost him.

She flung herself on the bed, wanting to cry but not

able to do so. She should be glad that he was staying away from her, she thought. Who wanted the company of a Howard anyway? She was a Peregrine, and she hated all Howards.

Didn't she?

She thought of what her brother Rogan was going to say when he found out that his little sister was married to a Howard. Rogan would go to the king himself and demand that an annulment be given. Rogan never trusted anyone—he'd probably demand that a midwife examine Zared to be sure that she was a virgin and that the Howard man had never touched her.

"I'm still a virgin," she whispered. "As clean and as untouched as the day I was born." And after Rogan had the annulment papers in his hand he'd no doubt hate the Howards more. He'd probably think that his sister had been rejected by a Howard.

"There must be something that I can do," she thought. "There has to be something that can be done to prevent more hatred."

"My lord," Margaret said softly to Tearle. He was at the well scrubbing off the sweat he had raised while training with his men.

"Yes?" Tearle turned to her. He hadn't been in the best of spirits in the last few days. Night and day his thoughts plagued him. He was falling in love with the brat who was his wife. Maybe he had been in love with her since he had first seen her struggling with his brother's men, men who didn't have sense enough to know that she was a female. But his feelings for the girl were not returned, for she still talked of returning to her brothers' house and of the annulment. He thought that someday soon he should consider sending a message asking the king to annul their marriage.

He looked at Margaret. "What is it?"

"Lady Zared has gone into the village."

He frowned. "She is not a prisoner. Did you send an escort with her?"

"Yes, but she eluded them."

Tearle was immediately alarmed. Had she run back to her brothers?

Before he could move Margaret put her hand on his arm. "She has been found. One of the men saw her going into Hebe's place."

"Why would she want to see that old woman?"

"It is said that she is a witch." Margaret's voice lowered. Like all servants, she knew much more about what was going on between the master and his mistress than they would have liked.

"Why would she go to a witch?"

Margaret hesitated. "Hebe rids women of unwanted children."

At that Tearle's face lost its color. "Tell John to saddle my horse."

An hour later it was an enraged man who burst into the old woman's dark, dirty hut. Tearle's first instinct was to kill the woman, and after that he was going to kill the woman he'd married. He had no doubt that it was Colbrand's child she was carrying. No wonder Zared had wanted to go back to her brothers'. There she could pass the child off as belonging to a Howard and perhaps use it to try to gain the Howard lands. He cursed her and himself and all women and marriage and everything else that had to do with men and women.

"My wife was here," he said to the terrified old woman. "Did you rid her of her child?"

"Nay, my lord," she said, her voice quivering. "She carried no child."

222

"Do not lie to me. I will burn you if you lie to me."

The woman was thin with age, and she cowered back against a wall covered with drying batches of herbs. "I do not lie. Please, my lord, I do not yet want to die."

Suddenly Tearle's rage left him, and he sat down on the only stool in the hut, his body deflated. It was not the old woman's fault that his wife had wanted to get rid of her child. Perhaps Tearle should be glad that Zared wanted to do away with the child rather than keep it. Considering how she felt about Colbrand, it was a wonder that she did not want to put the child on the throne of England.

"What did my wife want?" Tearle asked sadly.

"A love potion."

Tearle's head came up. "A what?"

"Your lady wife asked for a love potion. A potion to drive a man insane with lust."

"Who?" was the only word he could get out. He had thought that he had given her little time in the last weeks to form an attachment to another man. But perhaps she planned to see Colbrand later, and—

"You, my lord. She wanted the potion for her husband."

Tearle blinked a few times, not understanding.

The old woman saw the way Tearle relaxed, and she began to gain some courage. She stood up straighter, not slouching against the wall. "The Lady Zared asked me to make her a potion that she could give to her husband so that when he drank it he would be so overcome with lust that he could not resist her."

Tearle stared at the old woman for some minutes. "You are sure of this?" he asked softly. "She said it was for her husband?"

The woman managed a bit of a smile. "I did not get

this old by being a fool. I was not going to give a potion to the wife of a powerful man who planned to use it on a man other than her husband. Were she a farmer's wife I might have done so, but not her. I told her that, should she lie to me and use the potion on a man other than her husband, she would suffer ill luck all the rest of her life. She said . . ."

"Yes, out with it. What did she say?"

"She said that her husband—you, my lord— looked upon her as a child, and a boyish one at that. She wanted to give you something to drink that would make you see her as a woman."

Tearle got off the stool and took two steps so that he was standing at the far side of the hut. His head grazed the underside of the thatched roof. With his back to the woman he allowed himself a smile. She thought he did not desire her, did she? And all the while he had thought she was pining for that fool Colbrand. She had certainly changed her affections easily, hadn't she? But he wasn't going to quibble about that. If he could get her to go to bed with him willingly, that was the first step toward making her return the love he bore for her.

He looked back at the woman. "What did you give her?"

The woman could see that Tearle was amused. She had seen him since he was a boy and suspected he was not a violent man. She straightened. "My potions are a secret known only to me." When Tearle frowned she continued. "I told her to invite you to supper in her room. There was to be a fire and candles, and she was to boil water with sweet-scented herbs in it, and she was to wear her lowest-cut gown. She was to put the herbs in her husband's ale, and when he drank it he would be unable to control himself."

Tearle could no longer repress his smile. "It is to strike me as a bolt of lightning?"

The woman was offended by his tone. "I do not cheat my customers. The potion will work."

"I can guarantee that," Tearle said with good humor. "I shall be the most thunderstruck of lovers." He reached under his tunic and withdrew a small bag of coins. He started to open it and give the old woman a coin or two, but on second thought he gave her the whole bag. It was doubtless more money than she had earned in all her lifetime together.

The old woman was speechless as she held out a trembling hand and took the bag.

When Tearle left the hut he was whistling.

Zared had had some trouble getting Margaret to do what she wanted her to do. For the first time since she arrived the woman seemed to be snubbing her. She answered all Zared's questions curtly and supplied little or no information beyond what she had to.

Zared wanted a special gown, and she had to ask repeatedly where Tearle's mother's gowns were kept. Margaret evaded her as best she could until Zared was ready to take a knife to the woman's throat. At last Zared was taken to a storeroom, and there, amid bolts of fabric that were waiting to be cut and sewn, was a large wooden box. Reluctantly, with a look of great distaste on her long face, Margaret opened the box to reveal a dress that, even in the dark room, glowed. It was made of cloth of gold.

Zared had never seen such fabric. She took the gown, still in its box, to the doorway and held it to the light. "What is it?" she whispered.

Reluctantly Margaret told her that the fabric had come from Italy. Solid gold was drawn out into extremely thin wires, then wrapped about a strong fiber of silk. A loom was then warped with silk, and the gold thread was woven into it. Margaret also informed her that the fabric cost over thirty-eight pounds a yard.

Gingerly Zared lifted the gown from its box. There was much cloth in the gown. She had no idea how to add, but she knew that the gown cost almost as much as her brothers' castle was worth.

Zared took a deep breath and tried to look as though she wasn't frightened as she lifted the gown from its box. She was doing it to save her family from going to war, she told herself. Perhaps her husband had been right and they could create a child together, and that child would inherit the lands that the Howards held. It wouldn't be right, of course, because the lands should go to her oldest brother, but at least there would be Peregrine blood in the owner of the estate.

"I will wear it," Zared said. The gown was very heavy, and it was stiff. She smiled as she draped it over her arms. Men thought women were weak. Her brothers said that no woman could ever wear a suit of armor, but the stiff, heavy gown was another type of armor. Zared smiled, for she was, in a way, waging a war, a war that she meant to win, and the golden dress was the armor she needed.

She turned to Margaret. "Shall we suit me?" she asked, and she saw a hint of humor in Margaret's eyes, as though she understood what Zared meant.

An hour later Zared had her room prepared just as the old witch-woman had said it should be. It glowed with candlelight, and it was fragrant with herbs boiling in a pot. There was a table with succulent food waiting. It hadn't been easy to arrange, since Margaret had questioned everything that Zared wanted. She had also asked her young mistress repeatedly if she felt well, if she was ill in the mornings.

Zared found all the questions annoying, but she answered them as best she could, for the answers seemed to put Margaret in a better mood.

At last all was ready. "Do I . . . do I look all right?" Zared asked, smoothing down the gold of the dress. The silk that had been used in the weaving of the gown was red, and the red-gold of the gown combined with Zared's fair skin, her reddish hair, and the glow of the fire to make her a breathtaking sight.

Margaret looked at her young mistress and smiled. She didn't know why she had gone to the old witch-woman's place, but she was convinced that it was not to rid herself of another man's child. (All the castlefolk and half the villagers knew that his lordship had not slept with his young wife since their marriage.)

"You are beautiful," Margaret said.

"I do not look like a boy?"

Margaret could only laugh at that. Zared's hair was pulled back and draped in a sheer white sheath, and there were rubies along her forehead. "You could not look less like a boy." On impulse, because she was so much older and because it was easy to tell that Zared had no idea what was wrong and what was right for servants to do, Margaret kissed her young charge's cheek, then smiled at her and left the room.

A few minutes later Tearle knocked and entered her room. She could instantly see that he was in a bad mood. "What has happened?" she asked, afraid that it had to do with her brothers.

He sat down heavily on a chair before the fire. "My horse stumbled and threw me in a bog. One of my men knocked me down in sword practice, and I seem to have a rash growing on the right side of my body. And when I came in I was told that I could not have supper at a table but must go to your room. What do you want from me, Zared? To tell me that your brothers have come for me? It would be a fitting end to an ugly day."

Her first impulse was to tell him what he could do with his dinner, but instead she smiled. "I am wearing your mother's gown."

He turned as though he were glancing over his shoulder, but he didn't really look at her. He gave an enormous yawn. "Yes, so you are." He looked at the table laden with food. "Call someone and tell them to serve me. I am hungry and I am tired."

"I will serve you," Zared said quickly. "We need no one with us."

She went to the table where the food was, lifted the silver covers, and began filling a silver plate for him. When it was heaping she handed it to him, then took a seat on a stool at his feet.

He used his spoon to shovel in a large mouthful of carrots and then talked to her, his mouth full. "What is it you want?" He pointed at her with his spoon.

"I want nothing. I am not used to all the servants, and I wanted to be away from them."

"You never could lie." He narrowed his eyes at her. "Have you had some message from your brothers? Is that why you went to the witch?"

Her eyes widened.

"You will find that my people are loyal to me. They will tell me all that you do."

"I have not had a message from my brothers. I did not invite you here for talk of war."

"Ah, but what else can you talk of? What other reason would you have for visiting the witch?" He put

228

his plate in his lap, and his voice lowered. "She rids women of unwanted children."

Zared gave him a look of disgust. "It is not possible that I carry a man's child, if that is what is in your mind."

"Not even Colbrand's?"

"You are a hateful man," she said, rising from her stool.

"I am a Howard. How do I know what you have done with another man? You seemed to have found the man more than desirable. You thought him the strongest, bravest, most handsome knight in all of England."

"You downed him," she said, some exasperation in his voice. "You downed *all* the men at the Marshall tournament."

At that Tearle leaned back in his chair and smiled at her. "Are you saying that Colbrand is not the best knight in all of England?"

She realized then that he had been teasing her. "You are a dreadful man. Are you never serious?"

He held out his empty plate. "I am serious about needing my bed. I have never been so tired in my life." He stood up and gave a great stretch and another yawn. "There is nothing tonight that could keep me from my bed. Were the king himself to come to me, I would not tarry from it."

Zared did not want to have to use the witch's potion. She wanted to think that she herself had enticed her husband to her bed. "You did not say if you liked your mother's gown."

He was yawning again. "I have always liked it. She wore it in France. Even the king remarked on it."

"It is heavy. Feel the skirt."

He stretched some more. "I have felt cloth of gold often, as well as cloth of silver. I have even removed a few of those gowns from court women." He scratched at his side. "I must get to bed. I find that my clothes are beginning to itch. Perhaps it is just my great desire to get them off."

She didn't know what to do to get him to look at her. The hard corset inside the dress pushed her breasts so flat that they ached, but they swelled above the gown's neck as though they were overripe melons. As far as she could tell, he hadn't yet seen them.

"Your mother's corset hurts me," she said. "I do not think your mother had as much to fill the dress as I have." She held her breath to see what he would say to that remark.

"I do not remember looking at my mother in that way," he said stiffly, as though she had offended him.

"I did not mean—"

"Yes, yes, apology accepted. Now, are you sure that there was nothing that you had to say to me, other than telling me that my mother was an ugly creature?"

"I did not say—" She cut herself off and turned away from him. "Oh, go on, go to bed. It no longer matters what I wanted. You are tired, and you must have your rest."

She expected to hear the door open and close, but when it did not she turned to look at him. "Go on, I will keep you no longer."

He sat back down in the chair. "You are upset about something. Has the message from the king come so soon? Is that why you have dressed in my mother's best gown and planned this dinner? You want to celebrate the good news?"

"I have heard nothing from anyone. I have not heard from my brothers, or from the king, or from the Peregrine ghost, for that matter. No one has talked to me all day."

He smiled at her in a knowing way. "Ah, so that is

it. You desire company. Come, then, talk. I will try to
stay awake long enough to listen."

She turned away from him. "I had a purpose when
you came, but now I do not know what it was," she
muttered.

He was so silent from behind her that she turned to
look at him. His head was back against the chair, and
he was asleep. She felt anger when she looked at him,
then she felt a bit like crying. Why were other women
so able to entice men when she was not?

She walked to him and put her hand on his cheek.
He was better-looking than her brothers, better-
looking than Colbrand—in fact, better-looking than
any man in the world.

He awoke with a start. "I was dreaming," he said.

She smiled at him. "What were you dreaming?"

"That I was at court and Lady Catherine was
coming to my room. I think it must be the gown. She
had a blue cloth-of-gold gown."

Zared stiffened and moved away from him. "I
would like for you to leave now."

He stood and ran his hand over his eyes. "I must go
to my room and finish this dream." But before he left
he walked to the mantel and lifted a fine silver goblet.
It was filled with ale, and there were herbs floating on
top.

"I am dying of thirst," he said before he downed the
entire drink.

"Do not drink that!" Zared shouted.

Tearle finished the drink, then looked at her in
surprise. "You would deny me something to drink
when I am so thirsty? Come now, I would have
thought more of a Peregrine, not to mention a woman
who is my wife." He paused. "Or, as you shouted at
my men, one who is not my wife. Why are you looking
at me so strangely?"

"I am not looking at you at all," she said softly, but she was looking at him so intently that she didn't even blink.

He gave another little stretch. "I must go now. It's time for bed for me." He suppressed a yawn, then leaned over and chastely kissed her forehead. "My mother's gown looks good on you. I daresay that she did not look any better in it than you. Now you really must excuse me."

He turned away toward the door, Zared's eyes following him. He had drunk the potion, yet nothing had happened! Tomorrow, she thought, she would go to the witch and demand her coin back. She would not pay for a useless spell.

It was as Tearle put his hand on the door latch that he paused. For a long moment he didn't move. Then slowly, very slowly, he turned to look at her. His eyes were wide, as though he'd had some great shock. For a moment he looked at her face, his eyes dropping to her lips, then his eyes fell to the floor, and he looked from her hidden feet up to her face, his eyes lingering a long time on her exposed bosom.

Out of instinct Zared put her hand to her bosom and took a step backward. Tearle stepped toward her, his eyes hot and full of longing.

Zared looked at him, and immediately her heart began pounding. That was how she'd wanted him to look at her. That was why she had bought the potion. But she began to feel afraid. He had always been kind and gentle with her, but would the potion turn him into a monster? Would it make him into someone that he was not?

She backed away from him until she was pressed against the bed. He was stalking her slowly, like a large animal going after its prey and knowing that the prey was cornered.

232

"I . . . I think that . . ."

She couldn't finish as he reached her and put his hand on the side of her face. "I have never seen you this beautiful," he whispered. "I have never seen any woman as desirable as you. Not in all the courts of France or Italy or England have I seen another woman to rival you. I desire you above all others."

She looked up at him and blinked. Those were the words she had wanted to hear, the words that she had purchased when she bought the love potion.

Very gently he kissed her lips, and Zared felt her knees weaken. He caught her about the waist and lifted her to the bed, where he lay her gently on the coverlet. He stretched out beside her and kissed her face and neck and then moved to her breasts, exposed above the gown. Zared closed her eyes and enjoyed the sensation for a moment, then looked down at his hair. He had such thick, dark hair. She ran her fingers through it.

He leaned on his elbow and looked down at her, his hands running over the skin of her chest, playing along the swell of her breasts. "I do not seem able to help myself. It is as though some outside force has taken over my body. I must have you or I will die."

He pushed her to her stomach and began to unlace the back of her gown, his fingers slipping inside to touch her skin through her linen undergarment. Zared closed her eyes at the sensation. It was what she had wanted for so long. Too bad that she'd had to resort to using a love potion to make him desire her.

Easily and with more knowledge than Zared wanted to think that he had he unfastened her gown, then expertly slipped it off over her head. She was wearing only her undergarments, and he made quick work of relieving her of them.

It wasn't long before she was unclothed, wearing

only her stockings, fastened at her knees with pretty ribbon garters. For a long moment Tearle lay beside her and looked at her, then he sat up and looked at her some more until she began to become anxious.

"I do not please you?"

"I have never seen a woman such as you," he said softly, and he meant it. He had seen many women unclothed before, but with the exception of a few peasant girls, they had lived soft lives. Zared's life had not been soft. From the time she could walk she had carried a sword and had been taught how to use it. She had worn demi-armor. She had learned to ride before she could walk. All her training had given her a body of firm, hard muscle. There was no fat on her body except for her soft, rather large breasts.

Zared was not experienced enough with men to know that the way he was staring at her was with lust. She started to roll away from him, but he caught her and pulled her back.

He looked at her as one might look at an unknown species of animal, and as he looked his eyes grew hotter and hotter.

"Zared," he whispered, and he moved his body on top of hers and began to kiss her with an ardor she had never felt before.

She was by nature an enthusiastic person, and she began to kiss him back with passion. He didn't so much as break the contact of their mouths as he began to fling his clothes off. She knew that he was a man who cared about his clothing, and she almost laughed when she heard a seam rip. But tearing cloth didn't slow him down in his urgency to get out of his clothes.

His mouth moved down to fasten onto her breast, and Zared stiffened in surprise, then seemed to melt in desire. It was better than she had imagined, and she buried her hands in his hair as she arched her back so that he could have better access to her body.

"You are the loveliest woman I have ever seen. Had I known what was under your clothes I would have torn them from you sooner," he said as his mouth moved down to her stomach.

It was those words that made Zared open her eyes. He would not have torn her clothes from her body because he had not drunk the potion. The potion was what was making him desire her. It was not Zared he wanted. His desire was caused by the spell of the witch.

She pushed at him. "Let me up! Release me!"

She pushed and pushed at him, but he did not move. He kept kissing and nibbling at her hips, moving down to her legs. Zared lifted her leg, put her foot on his shoulder, and gave him as hard a shove as she could manage.

Dazed, befuddled, Tearle looked at her as she moved to the far corner of the bed. "I have hurt you?"

"You do not want me."

Tearle was too stupefied to understand her words. He could not take his eyes off her body: those legs, that stomach with the two muscles running down the sides of it. She looked like a woman, but she also looked like the sleekest racing animal in the world. He reached for her.

Zared eluded his hands. "It is not me you desire. You are under the spell of a witch."

"Aye, that I am," he said, leering at her. His palms were beginning to itch from wanting to touch her. In another moment of looking at her he would not be able to control himself; the man in him would flee, and he would become the animal that he felt like.

When he lunged at her again Zared left the bed and

went to stand behind the post at the corner of the bed. "You do not want me. You have never wanted me. It is a trick. Go to your Lady Catherine."

Now that her body was hidden behind the curtains of the bed his mind cleared a bit, at least enough to begin to understand her. "I do not desire you?" He reached out a hand to touch her. "I will show you how much I desire you."

"No!" She moved out of his reach and grabbed a pillow from the window seat, making an attempt to hide her nudity. But the pillow only tantalized him more, leaving her legs bare as well as the swell of her breasts at the sides.

Tearle knew enough about women to know that words were going to be needed before he could get what he wanted. "Do you wish me to tell you that I love you?" he asked. "Do you wish me to make up a poem to your beauty?" At that point he would have done *anything* to get her to come back to the bed. His voice lowered. "Do you wish me to swear to give my brother's estates to your brother?"

At that Zared sat down on the window seat, her face a study in dejection. The potion was indeed a powerful one if it would make him agree to such a thing. "I have done a dishonorable thing," she said.

Tearle sat up straight on the bed. "If it is another man, I will kill him. No man will have what is mine."

"Will you stop talking?" she half shouted. "Do you not understand that what you are saying is not what you mean? It is the witch's brew that is talking."

Tearle's concentration was on her body, so he had difficulty understanding what she was saying. "You are a witch," he murmured, and he got off the bed to go to her.

Zared jumped off the window seat and ran to the

other side of the room. On the floor in an untidy heap were his clothes, and on top was his thin-bladed, jeweled-handled knife. She picked it up and held it as though to protect herself. "Do not come closer to me," she said.

There were times when a man could cry, he thought. Her red hair was hanging down her back and falling across one shoulder. The knife somehow added to her beauty. "Zared, I will give you anything. Tell me what it is you desire. Jewels? Estates? What do you want?"

Zared looked at him. He wore not a stitch, and he looked even better without clothes than in them. She wanted him to hold her, to touch her, but she did not want him to do so only under a spell. She tossed the knife on top of his clothes. Even when he was driven by the uncontrollable lust of a witch's spell he was not a violent man. He still was not forcing her to lie with him.

Going to the witch had not been an honorable action on her part, but she would save her honor by fulfilling her part of the spell. She walked past him, not touching him, and climbed onto the bed. She lay rigid, her hands at her side, her legs held closely together. She looked up at the underside of the canopy. "I am yours to do with as you will," she said regally.

Tearle wouldn't have thought that his passion could have been killed, but it was. Some men found unwilling women desirable, but he did not. He stood by the side of the bed and glared down at her. "You are the most infuriating woman. You desire me so much that you are willing to risk poisoning me with some filthy witch's potion, yet when I touch you you draw a knife on me. How am I to understand this?" He raised his hands in a gesture of helplessness. "Would that some-one would explain women to me. Or is it just my wife I am unable to understand?"

Zared turned to look at him. "You know of the potion?"

He grimaced, then bent and fumbled among his clothes and withdrew a small bag, which he tossed on the bed. "There is your potion."

Zared turned on her side and picked up the bag. "I put the potion in the mug of ale. This cannot be it."

"I was not going to drink that filth. For all I knew it contained roasted frogs' eyes. Or worse."

Zared opened the little bag, looked inside, and sniffed. The contents smelled as awful as she remem-bered. She looked back up at Tearle. "If this is the potion I paid the witch for, then what did you drink?"

"Mint, I think. I would not recommend it. It does not go with ale, but I daresay it tastes better than that mess you would have given me."

Zared held the bag. "If you did not drink the potion, then what has inspired this . . . this newfound lust of yours?"

At that Tearle did not know whether to laugh or yell at her. He did neither. He sat down on the edge of the bed and talked very slowly. "I do not know how you came to the conclusion that I have not been eaten alive with desire for you from the moment I first saw you. Why else would I have made myself your brother's lackey? Do you think that I enjoy slogging in mud up to my knees to carry lances to him? Did I remain with him because I enjoyed his company? Or yours? At the tournament, did you so much as say a kind word to me?"

She sat up on the bed, oblivious to the way Tearle was looking at her. "But I thought you disliked me. I thought you wanted to . . . to . . ."

"Get my hands on the Peregrine wealth?" He leaned toward her, his nose almost touching hers. "I have always had one objective: to get my hands on the body of the Peregrine daughter."

Zared blinked at him. "Really? You do not think I look like a boy?"

He looked down at her bare body, then back up at her face. "I am the only man who has known from the beginning that you were *not* a boy."

Zared looked back down at the pouch. "But if you did not drink the potion, then why did you react so?" Her head came up. "And why have you not come to me on your own before now?"

He had to control himself to keep from yelling. "Do you not realize that I have been courting you?"

"Courting me?"

"Aye, courting you. I realize, after having spent some time with your brother, that the Peregrine idea of courting consists of turning a woman over one's knee, but in other households going with a girl to a fair is a much more acceptable method of courtship."

"But what of the annulment? What of the message to the king?"

He gave a bit of a smile. "What message? What annulment?"

"The one we—" She smiled back at him. "You did not send the message? I called you some awful names."

"I felt that they were temporary. I hoped that if I could get you away from your brother, you might see that I was not the monster you had been told of." He picked up her hand and kissed it. "I have wanted you since I saw you struggling against my brother's men. And I have cared for you since you came back to see if I were dead, even though I was a Howard and you had been taught to hate me."

She watched him as he began to kiss her fingertips. "I was afraid that if you bled to death, it would cause more harm to my family. I cared nothing for you."

He looked back at her with hot eyes. "Perhaps I can change that. Perhaps I can make you care." He put her small hand on his side and then moved toward her. Zared lay back on the pillows. "I do not believe that you can. No Howard could make a Peregrine squeal in delight."

He stopped kissing her ankle and looked up at her. "What do you know of squeals of delight?"

"I have heard many of them from my brothers' women, and you cannot wring such cries from me." There was challenge and daring in her eyes and a bit of a smile about her lips.

"Oh?" he said, accepting the challenge. "Let us see about that."

He began to kiss her then, and since he was not burdened by having to talk he could give himself over to his lust for her body. He kissed her and fondled her until he thought he might go mad. When he entered her he expected her to cry out in pain, but she did not.

"I liked that," she said later as Tearle was dozing in her arms. "Shall we do it again? Can it last longer this time?"

Tearle lifted one eyebrow and looked at her. "Perhaps. In a moment."

"Ah," Zared said. "I understand."

Had another woman said such a thing Tearle would have thought she did understand, but given Zared's experience in life, he doubted if she understood anything. "What do you understand?"

"That you are a weak and puny Howard, while

I have the blood of falcons running through my veins. Do you think our children will be weak like you?"

At that he caught her and pulled her down beside him. "I will see who will cry 'enough' before this night is through."

Chapter Thirteen

Z ared sat down gingerly on the chair that was pulled up to the table. Her husband looked at her smugly and with such a superior look that she grimaced. But she was happy, very, very happy.

Tearle smiled at her. "What say you we do today?"

"Teach me to read," she said before she thought, and he smiled more broadly.

What followed for Zared were two weeks of heaven on earth. She seemed to crave affection. It seemed that she wanted to make up for all the years she had been forced to act and look like a boy, and all she wanted to do were the most feminine things. Tearle, so unlike the men she had known all her life, was glad to show her all the most feminine arts.

He helped her choose gowns that he thought would look good on her. Each night he brushed her hair, both of them hoping that the brushing would make it grow faster.

They played games with each other and with the other people of his household. They rode and hunted and sometimes did nothing. He started teaching her to read, and he showed her some of the notes on a lute. Together they wrote a few poems, and Tearle told her she had a talent for poetry.

And through all of it they made love. Everything seemed to have some sexual connotation to them. The sight of a baby made them think of creating their own. Music made them retire to their chamber. Reading was lusty to them, especially since some of the poems that Zared created were quite bawdy.

Zared showed Tearle how to use a knife, and her demonstration nearly drove Tearle wild with desire. It wasn't that she was teaching him anything that he didn't know, but that she wore no clothes while demonstrating.

They played hide and seek for one whole day when it rained, and whoever found the other made love to the other on the spot, wherever they were.

Tearle, who had in the past made love to women mostly in secret, was fascinated with the freedom he had. He could have his wife any time he wanted her.

He was also fascinated by Zared. She had not been told what "ladies" should and should not do, so she was willing to try anything. Also, she was so athletic that sometimes she made him feel old and decrepit. She scampered up trees with the agility of a lizard. He followed her and then made love to her on a forked tree branch.

She had none of the fears that he had always assumed ladies were born with. She was not afraid of high places or of weapons or of charging boars or of his men.

One night as they lay together, sweaty and satiated, he asked her about her exuberance.

"Do you not see that I am free?" she said. "I have never been free before. You have had a life of such ease that you cannot understand what being a prisoner is like. You are so soft."

"Perhaps I am now, but I am not always soft," he said, some hurt in his voice.

"No, you goose, I do not mean that. I mean that you are soft inside. You are gentle and kind, and you are not driven by hatred."

"You make me sound as though I am less than a man. You can see the scars on my body. I can fight."

"You can fight in mock battles, true, but can you kill? Could you look a man in the eye and kill him?"

He held her hand in his and looked at it. "I would kill whoever touched you."

"Yes, you probably would." She sighed, for she didn't have any idea how to explain what she meant. He didn't understand hatred. He had no idea what it was like to feed off hatred—to have hatred consume the souls of those around you.

"Could you look into a man's eyes and kill him?" he asked.

"If he were a Howard," she said before she thought, then she turned to look at him, a feeling of horror growing inside her.

"I am a Howard," he said softly. "Could you look into my eyes and kill me?"

She didn't know what to say to him. She knew that she could not kill him. Or could she? If he were to threaten one of her brothers, what would she do?

She shivered, then looked at him. "I have many times looked into your eyes and killed you. You have no stamina. You are a weak and puny thing who cries 'Enough' after only a few hours of coupling. We

Peregrines are—" She didn't say any more because he started kissing her again.

It was in the middle of the third week that Zared's happiness came crashing down about her head. It was barely dawn, and since living with Tearle she had grown so lazy that they were still in bed when the door burst open.

One of Tearle's knights hurried into the room, his face red from exertion, veins pounding in his forehead. He was so out of breath that he could barely speak. "He comes."

Zared looked up, rubbing her eyes. She had been safe for so long that danger seemed a long-ago experience to her. She saw her husband nod at the man.

"How many?" Tearle asked.

"Hundreds. They come armed for war."

Again Tearle nodded. "Prepare the men. Remember they are to aim no weapon. These men are now my relatives. I will have no blood shed this day."

At the mention of blood Zared came fully awake and sat up, clutching the top sheet to her. "What has happened?"

Tearle dismissed his man, then turned to his wife. "Your brother has come with an army. I believe he means to kill me and take you to his home."

Zared didn't say a word, but felt as though the blood drained from her entire body. She started to roll to the far side of the bed, but Tearle caught her arm.

"Here, what is this you plan to do?"

"I will go to my brother. I will not allow him to kill you. You have been good to me."

His hand tightened on her forearm. "In spite of the fact that I am a Howard, I have been good to you." There was sarcasm in his voice. "And now you plan to leave me."

245

"I mean to stop a war!" she shouted.

"*You* mean to take care of this?" he asked softly.

"Aye." Her mind was working quickly. "I will tell my brother that I wanted to marry you. I will tell him that my lust overcame me. He might understand that. Although Rogan is a man of great honor. *He* would never allow his lust to make him do such a dishonorable thing as I have done. He would have died rather than marry the enemy, and *he* would have hated the enemy until the end of time. He would have not done as I have and come to . . . to care for the enemy."

Through this long speech Tearle had been silent, just looking at her.

"Do you mean to stay there all day?" she snapped at him. She didn't want to think that it was the last time she would probably ever see him again. She had no doubt that her brother would never allow her to remain with a Howard. Rogan would have the marriage annulled, saying that his sister did not have her brothers' permission to marry. "Why are you looking at me so strangely?"

"You still see me as a Howard, not as the man that I am. You still think that I am a weakling and that your brother, with his violent ways, is all-powerful. Can you not yet see that violence is not always the answer?"

She shook her head at him. "I will see if you say that when my brother's sword is moving toward your head." She went to the chest by the window, withdrew the clothes she had taken from the cook's son, and began to put them on.

"No!" Tearle said, bounding out of the bed. "You are no longer a boy. You are not a Peregrine boy, you are a Howard woman."

"I am not!" she screamed at him, throwing clothes on the floor. "I will never, never, never be a

Howard. I cannot be a Howard. Howards are my enemy."

Tearle pulled her into his arms. "Sssh, love. Be quiet. There is no reason for this fear you have. Your brother cannot take you from me."

She pushed away from him. "He will fight you. Do you understand nothing? My brothers hate the Howards. Rogan will die trying to kill you. Only if I go with him will he not declare war on you."

He smiled at her. "Then by all means you must go with him. But you will not dress as a boy. Those days are over. You will wear the cloth-of-gold dress. You will let your brother see that you have become a woman."

"I will let my brother see that the Howard money can buy dresses that cost more than the yearly rents of all the Peregrine wealth," she muttered. She was hurt, deeply hurt that he didn't seem to care that they would never be together again. She would go to her brother and her brother . . . Heavens, but she hated to think of what her brother would do to punish her for what she had done.

"What shall I wear?" Tearle asked.

"What do I care what you wear? I will not be here to see it." I will not be here to see what you wear or do not wear. Now I will never learn to read, she thought. Now I will never have children, or have a husband who holds me and makes me laugh.

"What do you think will impress your brother? Do you think riches impress him, or should I wear a suit of armor? I do not know whether to wear the cloth of silver or the armor. We will look a fine pair with you in gold and me in silver, will we not? But I fear that your brother will want me to prove myself to him, and I think that the silver is too fragile for that. And it is difficult to get blood from it."

She put her hands to the side of her head. "My brother is marching toward us with an army, and you stand there talking of clothes. You have no sense to you. Do you not realize that I will never see you again? That today I must return to my brother?" She was trying not to cry. "I knew that this soft life could not last. I knew that there could be no life such as this for me. I knew that it would end."

At that Tearle took her wrists in his hands. "Look at me and listen to what I have to say. You may think that your brother is the most powerful man in the world, but he is not. For all that you remind me every hour, you seem to forget that I am a Howard. I have men and riches at my disposal that could take your brother and his puny army at any time."

Zared's eyes widened in horror, and she stepped away, but he pulled her back to him.

"I am telling you what I *can* do, not what I plan. What I plan is to give myself to your brother."

"You cannot," she whispered. "He will kill you."

"Will he? You said that he was a man of honor. Will he kill a man who is not only a cousin by blood but is now a brother by marriage? Will he kill a man who surrenders himself?"

"You cannot give yourself to him. I will go. He wants the return of me. You do not know Rogan. His family is all to him."

He moved his face close to hers. "And you have become all to me. Do you think that I will allow you to go? Do you think that I will let you walk away from me after I have fought so long and hard to get you?"

"I . . . I do not know. I do not know what to think. My brother will kill you, that is all that I know."

"Your puny brother would have difficulty killing a Howard." He laughed at her look. "*That* is the woman

248

I know. Now get dressed, or your brother will be here and we shall be wearing nothing. I shall wear the silver. With your brother's temper he might think that a Howard in armor is an invitation to a fight, and I am tired today from a brawl in bed last night with another Peregrine."

"You could not beat my brother Rogan. He is as——"

"Yes, yes, spare me the details of the glories of your brother. Would that some day you would speak of me as other than a weakling who can barely summon the energy to get out of bed in the morning." He turned her around and smacked her bare bottom. "Now get dressed and prepare yourself to greet your brother with all the graciousness of a Howard lady."

Every time he called her a Howard her heart sank a little further. She was hardly aware when he left the room and when Margaret entered and began to help her dress.

It wasn't much later that Tearle came to get her. He was resplendent in cloth of silver that had a blue silk background. It made his dark hair seem darker, and she had never seen a more handsome man in her life.

He smiled at her look. "At last I seem to please you in something that I do." He held out his arm to her. "Shall we go to meet your brother?"

Zared found that she was trembling as they went down the stairs together, and for the first time she looked at the house not for its beauty but as a place to defend. For defense it was worthless. There were no walls to protect it, no gates to shut against intruders. And the building was not stone but wood. One flaming arrow could set the whole place ablaze. The house no longer seemed so beautiful; it seemed a useless place.

She stopped on the stairs. "Leave now and I will tell

my brother that I will go with him if he swears not to harm you."

He kissed her sweetly on the mouth. "No," he said softly. "For all that you seem convinced that I am a coward, I am not."

He put his arm tightly about her waist, and they began walking again. "And for all that you think he is, your brother is not a god on earth. He is merely a man, as we all are. Now do try to look less frightened. Your brother will think that I beat you."

Yes, she thought, she had better keep her chin up. Rogan was terrifying enough. She did not need to give him more reason for his anger than he already had.

When she realized what her husband planned to do she thought she might faint from fear. She thought he meant to meet her brother's army with his own, but instead he walked with her, alone, to the front of the house, to the little courtyard where fragrant flowers grew. They stood there, his arm about her, supporting her, the sun flashing off the brilliant fabric of their clothes.

"You cannot do this," she said frantically as she felt the ground tremble from the stamp of Rogan's men's horses. "Rogan will run you through."

"I cannot believe that your brother would be that stupid. The king would have him drawn and quartered. Now be still and smile at him. Are you not glad to see him?"

The man is crazy, Zared thought, absolutely crazy. If she had been strong enough, she would have carried him to safety, but as it was she could only stand beside him, her heart pounding in her ears, her body trembling, her hands and feet cold from fear, and watch her brother approach.

Rogan rode at the head of what must have been

three hundred men, and she wondered where they had all come from. Some of them she recognized, but most she did not. She tried to straighten her back, but it seemed to be made of gelatin.

Rogan and his men rode straight for the front of the house, their horses trampling over the pretty walkways and the flowers and the shrubbery. In spite of the seriousness of the situation she found herself frowning. Rogan would not think flowers meant anything in life.

"Good morn to you, brother," Tearle said cheerfully. "Will you come inside and eat with us?"

Rogan, atop his horse, his red hair making him look angry even when he wasn't, looked even bigger than Zared remembered. "I have come for my sister," he said in a voice that Zared had always obeyed.

She started to pull away from Tearle, but he held her fast.

"We will be ready soon," Tearle said. "Our garments and household goods are being packed now. But come and rest with us while we wait. I have ordered a half dozen cows killed, and they will be set to roasting soon. Your horses must be hungry, too."

Zared looked up at her brother and knew that Tearle must sound as insane to him as he did to her.

Rogan ignored him as he looked at his sister. "Mount and ride."

Again Zared tried to obey, but Tearle held her.

Rogan drew his sword. "Do you force her? I will kill you now."

At that Tearle released Zared, thrusting her behind him as he reached for the small knife at his side. Zared jumped between the men.

"He does not hold me," she said as loudly as her powerful lungs would allow. "No man holds me. I am

251

free. Oh, Rogan, do not kill him. I have come of my own free will. Do not harm him."

She looked from one man to the other and knew in that instant she had insulted both men. She knew that Rogan had thought that she was honorable and that the only way she would have gone with a Howard was if she had been forced, but now he knew that she was not honorable, that she had betrayed the ancient Peregrine name. And she had insulted her husband by, in essence, saying that a woman must fight his battles for him.

It was Tearle, as she knew it would be, who made the first move toward peace. He sheathed his knife. "I do not wish to fight you. We are related now, and I wish this feuding to stop. You must come and eat with me, and we will discuss the future."

Rogan sneered down at him. "How many men do you have hidden in the house, Howard? Do you plan to take us once we are inside and befuddled with drink?"

"We can eat outside and drink water if that is your wish," Tearle said.

At that there were many groans from the men behind him.

"He will not attack you," Zared said. "He believes in peace." She said this with some wonder in her voice. How could one think of peace when looking at three hundred armed men?

At that Tearle put his hands on her shoulders. "I think you should leave us. Your brother and I have matters that we must discuss."

Zared turned pale at that. "I cannot leave the two of you alone."

Tearle looked up at Rogan as he sat on his big horse. "Your brother may hate me, but he is not a fool. He knows that if he kills me and takes you, now that you are my legal wife, then my brother will wipe what is left of your family from the face of the earth. Is that not right, brother?"

"I am not your brother," Rogan muttered, but he looked at his sister. "Go. I will not kill him—not now. Ready yourself to return with me."

She nodded at her brother, then took one more look at her husband and went back into the house.

"What are they doing now?" Zared asked Margaret.

"The same as before. The men are eating, and your brother is sitting at the table in silence, but he is listening. Lord Tearle is doing all the talking."

"Yes, yes, I know that he is a talker. He could talk until a dead man would leave the room to get away from him." She remembered the way Tearle had been able to twist everything she had said to him so that it was to his advantage. "My brother is not so easily led as I was," she muttered to herself. "Rogan will not agree to what a Howard says."

"Yes, my Lady Howard," Margaret said softly, making Zared grimace.

Zared sat down on a window seat and looked out over the lovely rolling English countryside. "He will not agree to leave me here," she whispered. So I will have to return with my brother, and I will have to leave this beautiful place and my beautiful husband, she thought. I must return to a place of hatred and talk of war.

It was nearly sundown when Tearle returned to the room they shared. She jumped up at once and went to him, but she did not get close enough to touch him. "When do I leave?"

"Early tomorrow," he said, stretching. "Those men

of your brother's can eat. I do not wonder that your brother wants his title and lands back. It must cost much to feed men such as those."

"Do you jest about what is life and death to the Peregrines?"

He smiled at her. "I try to make a jest of everything. Have you not learned that yet? I am of the firm belief that laughter makes one live longer. Tell me, has that brother of yours ever so much as smiled?"

"Liana can make him smile," she said impatiently, then turned away. "So we have one last night together."

Tearle sat on the edge of the bed and began to unlace his tall boots. "Do you not plan to sleep with me when we are at your brother's house?"

It took Zared a moment to realize what he was saying, then she went to him. "You cannot go with us."

He smiled at her in a teasing way. "You can stand the place, but I cannot. Does this mean that you are more of a man than I am?"

She went on her knees in front of him. "Do not make a joke of this. My brother will kill you. If not directly, then there will be a falling stone, a blade that slips, an ax——"

"I did think of those things. I mentioned such to your brother." He paused in his undressing. "If he did not fear for the lives of those he loves, he would have killed me today. At least he would have taken great pleasure in the attempt. I have never seen such hatred in a man."

"He *will* kill you if given half a chance. You cannot think to go anywhere with him."

He put his hand under her chin. "I am not so fragile or so dumb and trusting as you seem to believe, nor is your brother as powerful as you think. Do you know that when I was a child I thought my brother Oliver was the strongest, bravest—"

"Oliver Howard is fat and weak and—" She broke off, knowing where he was heading. "You cannot think that I do not see my brother as he is. Rogan is neither fat nor weak."

He leaned toward her. "Nor am I."

She sat back on her heels. Why did each man think he was invincible? "What have you and my brother arranged?" She looked up at him with narrowed eyes. "What have you talked my brother into?"

"Ah, at last you admit that there is something that I can best your brother in."

"Tell me," she repeated.

"He has agreed to what I have always planned to do. I am going with you to your home. Your brother will not believe that I want his sister for any purpose other than as some hostage of war. I told him that I wanted you only for your body, but even that did not make him laugh."

Zared grimaced. No, that would not make Rogan laugh. "Why would you want to do this? Why would you want to leave all this finery for my brother's poor place?"

He was silent so long that she looked up at him, and the tenderness in his eyes made her look away. She knew that he was going so that he could be near her. Rogan was so stubborn, so hardheaded that he would not believe any words that she spoke if she told him that she was with a Howard because she *wanted* to be. Rogan would always think that she had been forced. And he would do what he considered necessary to get her back. Zared *had* to go with her brother.

"You do not have to go with me," she whispered. "Perhaps I can return to you . . . later."

"Ha!" Tearle said. "I think your brother is worse

than you had described him. The man does not listen to reason. Do you know that I offered to give him this place if he would stop this war of his? I offered him half of the Howard estates upon my brother's death."

"He would refuse. All of what the Howards own belongs to the Peregrines."

He smiled at her. "He wanted you more than he wanted the estates." At Zared's look of astonishment Tearle nodded. "'Tis true. He said that he had lost too many of his family, and he could bear to lose no more. He would not trade you for all the riches in the world."

Zared looked away to hide her smile. It made her feel good that her brother loved her that much. She looked back at her husband. "You see that I must go with him."

"I understand that perfectly. I also know that I will not let you go either. Who will warm my bed at night if you are gone?"

She turned away. "You will find women. Men always do."

"Not women who chase me up trees and draw swords on me. Not a woman I find as entertaining as you."

She put her face in her hands. "You cannot go with me."

"I can and I will. Your brother, who has a head of rock, will have it no other way. I will go with you and stay with your family until he is satisfied that I have married you for some reason other than a personal feud." Tearle looked thoughtful. "Although I fear for my life if he hears the way I make you cry out in the night. He might think I am torturing you."

"I do not do that."

He gave her a smug smile. "Come and give me a kiss. Tomorrow we will ride with your brother, and we will see this place of yours. It cannot be as bad as you make it seem."

"It is worse," she said as she crawled onto his lap. "You will not be able to bear it."

He ran his hand down her hip and thigh. "I am made of sterner stuff than you imagine. In fact, I think that now I am made of steel. Do you know of a sheath where I could hide my sword?"

"Oh, Tearle, you fool," she said, laughing as she put her arms around his neck and began to kiss him.

Chapter Fourteen

Rogan's wife Liana lay back against the pillows of her bed and closed her eyes against the pain. Two days before she had given birth to a large, dark-haired little boy, and the birth had almost killed her. She still could not move without pain.

"How are they?" she whispered to her maid Joice, who was straightening the room.

"There is no change," Joice said solemnly, then she looked up at her mistress. "This cannot go on."

Liana nodded in agreement with her maid. It had been a month since Zared had arrived with her Howard husband, and since then the hatred in the Peregrine castle had grown darker and deeper. Liana had not been able to reason with her husband about his hatred for the man. "He is your sister's husband now," she had said to Rogan, but Rogan refused to bend, refused to see anything in the man except what he wanted to see. And what he wanted to see was a man who was an enemy.

For the last four weeks Rogan had done everything that he could to break the Howard man. He had trained him until Liana had seen the man's shoulders drooping from exhaustion. Rogan devised dreadful tests for the man, such as having six brawny knights attack him in the hallways, and this after a long day of "training" on the field. What Rogan called training would have killed most men.

But the Howard man took it all and never complained once. Liana had seen him look at Rogan with a glare of determination in his eyes, as though he were saying that he was going to survive whatever Rogan gave him or die trying.

In the last weeks Liana had been so heavily pregnant, so uncomfortable, that she had not been able to leave the solar and so could only see and hear what was happening secondhand. But as she had sat still, her sewing in her hand, and watched, she had seen more than she wanted to see.

When they had heard that Zared had been married to a Howard Liana had at first thought that her husband was going to die of apoplexy. The violence of his rage was something that she had never seen before. Years before, when Oliver Howard had taken her prisoner, she had later been told that her husband had gone into just such a fit, a fit of such severity that the people around him feared for his sanity.

No matter that Liana had protested day and night; Rogan raised a small army to go to the Howard house and get his sister. "Perhaps she married him because she loves him," Liana had said. "Perhaps she chose the man as I chose you."

Rogan would not listen to her. Nothing she said

made any difference to him. He was bent on gathering his army and going after his sister. "It will be the end of us all," Liana had said.

She spent long hours in the chapel praying for her husband's safety, knowing that she had just a few days to see him alive. The once grand Peregrine armies were too small to take on the many Howard men.

She sat by and watched as Rogan called his brother Severn to him, forcing him to leave his new bride at Bevan Castle. Severn was as enraged as his brother, and he told how he had been tricked and lied to by the Howard man. Severn kept saying that the Howard man had assured him that Liana had sent him to help them at the tournament.

It had taken her husband and brother-in-law some days to get ready to march to the Howard house. At the last moment Rogan had insisted that his brother remain behind, for he was sure that Oliver Howard would attack the moment Moray Castle was left with only a small force to guard it.

All the time Rogan had been gone Liana had stayed on her knees in the chapel asking God for the safe return of her husband.

She had not been prepared for the manner in which Rogan did return. He had come riding home beside a handsome dark-haired man dressed in finery such as Liana had not seen for years. And beside him rode Zared, but a Zared much changed from the boyish girl who had ridden off to a tournament weeks before.

Liana had watched the little group dismount, and at the sight of her husband's face her first hope that somehow the marriage of a Peregrine to a Howard would stop the feud fled. There was no happiness or forgiveness on her husband's face; only rage lived under his dark skin.

She stood at the window and looked down at the

group, and her heart began pounding, for it was a group full of many base emotions. "Send Zared to me," she had said to her maid. Liana knew that her husband could wait, but the misery she saw on her young sister-in-law's face was something that Liana wanted to understand.

Zared came stumbling up to Liana's solar and, without preamble, threw herself at her sister-in-law, going to her knees and putting her head in Liana's lap—what lap there was left. Liana had quickly dismissed the other people in the room and run her hands over Zared's thick red hair. "Tell me all," she said softly.

Words came flooding out of Zared as she told about the tournament and about making a bargain with the Howard man that she would marry him if he could arrange for Lady Anne to marry Severn. "I never thought he could do it," Zared cried. "I thought I was in no danger."

Liana stroked her hair and listened. She listened not only with her ears but with her heart, and she heard more than just words. Zared talked of being "tricked" into marriage and of having to marry the Howard man, but there was an underlying softness to her words that told Liana a great deal.

"Tell me about your time alone with him," Liana said softly.

Zared dried her eyes on Liana's silk skirt and started telling of the few weeks they had spent alone together. "His house was a worthless place, of course," Zared said. "A dozen men could have taken it." She paused. "Oh, but it was lovely." She told about the house and described in detail the clothes she had worn there, and she told about the fair and about some of the places she had gone and what she had done.

"And what of this Howard man you are married to? Is he *your* enemy as well as Rogan's?"

Zared clenched her teeth together to fight back tears. "I do not know what he is. I do not understand him. He is so soft and so gentle. He praises me and sings to me and gives me presents and reads to me, and sometimes I feel as though I would die without him, but . . ."

"But what?" Liana urged.

"But I do not know what is in his mind. I do not know if he can be trusted. He is not like any man I have ever met before. He says only that he does not want war, but what if I trust him and he is lying? What if I allow myself to believe him and he betrays me and my family?" She put her face in her hands. "How can I let go of a hatred that I have had all my life because of a few weeks of a man being kind to me? I must be made of sterner stuff than that. I *have* to be stronger than that. I cannot allow my passion for him to blind me to the fact that he is a Howard."

At that Zared began to cry again, and Liana could hear the anguish in her voice. Zared was more than confused about what the man she had married was and how she felt about him. "I was beginning to trust him, but I do not know why he married me. Sometimes I believe what he says to me, and sometimes I am afraid of my own belief. He says that he wishes to end this feud, but I fear that I am bringing the enemy into our house. If he gains our trust, he could open the gates at night and let his brother's army in here. He could kill us as we sleep."

"But what would he gain by that?"

Zared looked at Liana as though the older woman had gone mad. "He will have clear title to the dukedom and the lands. There will be no Peregrines to claim that he does not own the lands."

At Zared's answer Liana began to be afraid, too, and she wished she had never heard of the dreadful Howard man. She began to be afraid for the lives of all of her family: her son, her unborn child, her husband, and his sister and brother. Each night she quizzed Rogan on what he was doing with the Howard man, making sure that Rogan did not let up on his vigil over the man.

Once Liana took her son to the courtyard to see some new puppies and the Howard man walked by her, then stopped and smiled down at the lovely little boy with his bright red hair who held a puppy. He was still smiling as he looked back up at Liana, but the smile faded when she snatched her son to her in a protective way and glared at the man. He gave a sigh and walked away.

Liana did not have time to concern herself with how the brother of an enemy felt. She was much more concerned with the worry she saw on the faces of Rogan and Zared and Severn. Severn felt as though everything had happened because of him, and he worked hard to try to forgive himself, but he seemed to make no progress. He never left the training field, and Liana knew that he was pining for his new wife, whom he had left in the relative safety of Bevan Castle.

With each day Rogan's eyes sank farther into his head. As Liana well knew, he slept little, for fear kept him constantly on edge. He was afraid that at any moment his family was going to be attacked. One night she did no more than turn over in bed, and Rogan jumped out of the bed, his sword in his hand, before Liana could even get her eyes open.

But it was Zared who was the most troubled. With each day she seemed to grow thinner and grayer before Liana's very eyes.

It was at the beginning of the second week that Liana looked up at her little sister-in-law, saw the haggard look on her face, and understood a great deal. "You love him, don't you?" Liana said softly.

Zared tried to act as though the words meant nothing. "What does love matter? He is the enemy."

"But he's not your enemy, is he?"

"I am one person. I must think of my family."

Liana had no answer for her except to say that sometimes one must trust in one's own judgment and not the opinions of others. She spoke from experience, for years earlier she had trusted her instinct when she had agreed to marry Rogan. People had said that she was a fool and that he was a man incapable of love, but she had proved them wrong, for she had found the heart that he had managed to hide for years.

The birth of her child took three long, hard days, and afterward she could do little but lie in bed, but she watched what was going on within her family as closely as she could.

"Zared," Tearle said, "look at me."

They were in bed together, and she was as far to one side of the bed as she could get. She didn't want to touch him, didn't know if she should touch him. Yet she wanted to.

"I am tired," she said.

"You seem to always be tired," he said, his voice heavy. He was silent for a long while, then he spoke again. "I cannot do this alone."

She knew what he meant, but she had no answer for him. Every day was hell for her. Whenever her brothers caught her alone they pointed out the horses' skulls on the walls. Years before the Howards had laid siege to a Peregrine castle, and the inhabitants, who included Zared's mother, had starved to death. Before they had died they had been reduced to eating the horses. The skulls of those horses hung on the wall as a constant reminder of the treachery of the Howards.

"It was you who wanted to come here," she said at last.

"No," he said softly. "I did not want to come to this house of hatred. What I wanted and have always wanted is for the woman I love to love me in return."

"I thought your desire was to stop the hatred," she said with some bitterness in her voice. Every day she watched what her brothers did to her husband, driving him hard enough to break a lesser man, but Tearle did not break. He did not so much as show anger.

She rolled over to face him. "What kind of man are you?" she half shouted. "Do you not know that all the men laugh at you? You take whatever Rogan gives you, and you do not fight back. The men are wagering on whether he will ask you to empty the slops next and whether you will do it."

He faced her, and his face showed some anger. "Were I to show what I felt to your brother he would strike me, and I would retaliate. Knowing your brother's anger, one of us would die. Is that what you want? A trial by combat? Shall we square off and fight each other for you like a couple of rutting bucks? Would you like to see one of us dead? Would that make you believe that I am as much a man as your brother is?"

He rose up on one elbow. "Tell me, Zared, is that what you want? Is that what I have to do to prove myself to you?"

He sat up. "It does not seem to be enough that I am willing to risk my inheritance by marrying you. My courtship of you seems to mean nothing. The fact that I, a Howard, walk into your brother's home, if one can call this den of hatred a home, alone and willing to face your two brothers, means naught to you. Whatever I do is not enough for you. You always want more from me. You said that I was not man enough to take what your brother could give to me, but I have taken it and more. I am tired and sore. And I am sick unto death of being hated. I am sick of the looks people give me."

He got out of bed and stood looking down at her. "But it would be worth it if I could change but one person's mind. If I could make you look at me with the trust I deserve, then all would be worth it."

He stopped and rubbed his eyes. "I will not fight your brothers. I will not see more bloodshed between these two families, and"—he looked up—"and you can tell your sister-in-law that I do not harm children."

He pulled on his clothes quickly and left the room.

Zared would have said something to him, but she did not know what to say. Could she tell him the truth? That every day she had to force herself to remember that he was a Howard? She saw him with Rogan or Severn, and she wanted to run to him and protect him, to keep their lances from coming at his back, to keep the men from laughing at him.

But she didn't interfere in what her brothers made him do. She was still a Peregrine, and he was still the enemy.

He did not return that night, and she did not sleep much.

It was three days later that Tearle and Rogan's three-year-old son disappeared together.

Chapter Fifteen

It was Liana who discovered that the boy was missing. For all that she had tried to raise the boy in a civilized manner, he was a Peregrine. His father had given him a wooden sword on his first birthday, and his uncle had given him a molded leather helmet. Rogan had set his son on a horse when the child was two. He was a child who had been raised amid horses' hooves and clashing swords. At two he was often out with his father on the training field, already imitating his father and uncle in the way they handled weapons.

By three years of age he was fearless. Liana had pleaded with Rogan to watch out for the boy and not allow him to run so freely about the courtyard where the men, who were usually half drunk or exhausted from Rogan's training, might easily step on the child. But Rogan had said that she was an old woman and that that was the way all the Peregrines had been raised, that he meant for his son to grow up to be a man and not a half-woman.

So when Joice had gone to see about the child and he was not in his room, she did not think anything of it. She had her weakened mistress and the new child to see to. She did not even mention to her mistress that the child was not where he usually was.

And Liana did not miss her older son because she had her husband's rage to deal with, for the Howard man had disappeared.

"Where is he?" Rogan had bellowed at his sister.

Zared had sat there in stony silence, for she had already answered her brother a hundred times. She did not know. He had spent the night with her, and he had risen very early and left the room. She had not followed him.

Zared did not tell her furious brother that they had had another fight, or actually a repeat of the same fight. Tearle had once again raged at her that she did not trust him and that he deserved her trust. But she had tried to tell him that even though she could not trust him, she was torn apart, that half of her sided with her brothers and half with him. Instead of appeasing him this had only seemed to make him more angry.

"Just as your brother will not accept only half of what belongs to the Howards, I will not accept half of what is my due." He had stormed out of the room, and she had not seen him since.

Severn said that the Howard man had not been able to take life with the Peregrines, but Rogan said that the man was probably going to his brother to tell him of the vulnerable defenses of the Peregrines.

"Stop it, all of you!" Zared had screamed. "He took whatever you gave him," she yelled at her oldest brother. "He did all that you asked of him, and he never so much as bent under the burden. He can take it all and more."

"Then where is he?"

Zared did not have an answer for them. Had he had enough of the Peregrine hatred and just ridden off? Would he have left her and not said a word? *Had* he gone back to his brother? Was war imminent? Would her family die because of what she had done?

She thought that she could bear no more agony, but it was nearly noon when Liana realized that her son was missing. Liana, already ill from the second birth, could not stand the misery of finding her son gone.

"The Howard man has taken my son," Rogan had whispered.

Zared wasn't sure that she was hearing correctly. "No," she said softly, then louder, "No! He would not do that."

Rogan gave her a look that said that he had no more use for her, that she was as much an enemy as the Howards.

Zared sat by and waited while her brothers and their men went out to search for the boy. Liana said that he might have walked into the village with one of the workers. But the village was scoured, and there was no sign of the boy or of the Howard man. Both had disappeared from the face of the earth.

By sundown Rogan was ready to wage war on the Howards, but both Liana and Zared pleaded for time. It was possible there was no connection between the disappearances of the boy and Zared's husband.

The moat was dragged with weighted nets, but there was no small body found, and Liana cried in relief.

Zared sat by a window in the solar, her eyes unblinking as she looked toward the north, hoping to see her husband come riding up. She hoped he had merely taken a day to get away from the Peregrines, a day to lie in the sun and look at the flowers. She could not tell her brothers that that was something that he might do, for they would not understand a man wanting to look at flowers.

At sundown the men took torches, went into the surrounding forest, and began to look for the child.

And it was in the forest that they found the poacher. At first the terrified man thought that Rogan and his men had come for him. His terror was so great that he could not speak coherently. When at last he realized that for once the Peregrine men were not concerned with who was stealing game from their lands he told them of having seen a large, dark man riding with a red-haired child in the saddle before him.

Rogan and Severn questioned the man for a long while until they were convinced that the child was Rogan's son and that the man who held him was Tearle Howard.

A grim Rogan and Severn went back to the castle and began to plan to go to war.

"Something is wrong," Zared said. "He did not take the child. He would not."

Rogan turned the full force of his fury on her, bellowing at her that all of this had been caused by her lust for a man, that because of her the Peregrine line was going to end. "If you carry his child now, I will kill it when it is born," he said to her.

Zared could not stand up against his rage or, she had to admit, against his logic. They had brought the poacher back to Moray Castle with them, and the man had repeated his story for the women. He had described Tearle to the color of the clothes he was wearing and the Howard emblem on his sword hilt.

And he had described Rogan's son with his bright red hair and his father's looks. There was no doubt that it was Tearle who had held the child. And with him rode three Howard men, all wearing the trappings of the Howards.

Zared wanted to believe in her husband, wanted to explain away what the poacher said he had seen, but she could find no explanation. Tearle had been seen with Rogan's son riding in the company of three Howard knights in the direction of the Howard estates.

The morning after his son disappeared Rogan rode out with Severn with nearly three hundred men behind them, all the men they could find. It wasn't enough men to wage a war on the Howards, but it was all the men the Peregrines could afford.

Zared had at one point suggested that she ride with her brothers, but Rogan had merely looked at her, his eyes blazing with rage. She knew that he considered her almost as much of an enemy as he considered her husband.

"Women wait while men go to die," Liana had said when the men rode off.

Zared was not very good at waiting, and she paced the parapets for days, paced until she wore the bottoms of her shoes out. She threw the shoes over the side of the castle into the moat, then walked barefoot, her eyes never leaving the horizon.

For two days she believed in her husband. For two days she told herself that he had not betrayed her and her family. She told herself that he could not have taken the child. She tried to remember all the sweet times they had shared and all the many times he had told her that he wanted to settle the feud between the two families.

271

In the middle of the third day Rogan sent a messenger back to his family. With the messenger came a man who told them that he had seen four Howard men who carried a red-haired boy with them, and they were heading toward the Howard estates. The man lived near enough to the Howard estates that he knew Tearle by sight.

It was then that Zared stopped believing in her husband. She was quiet, saying nothing after hearing the messenger, but she did not fool Liana.

Liana turned and saw that her sister-in-law had left the room, and she ran to find her. She found Zared putting on the armor that her brothers had had made for her.

"You are not going after him," Liana said.

"I brought him here, and I shall take him away. I shall find him and kill him. He will allow me to get close to him, and when he does I will kill him."

Liana knew better than to try to argue with a Peregrine. When it came to their hatred of the Howards, there was no reasoning with them. Liana left the room, called three men, all of them either crippled or too old to fight so they could not go with Rogan, and had the men hold Zared. She was not going to allow the young woman to leave the castle.

Zared was held under guard for two more days before the Peregrine army returned and Liana went to release her sister-in-law.

Zared's rage had not calmed under confinement, and she was so angry at Liana that she could not bear to look her in the eyes. When Liana started to touch her arm Zared moved away.

"They are returning," Liana said softly.

Zared pushed past Liana and ran up the stairs to the parapets. It was a long distance away, but she could see that her husband was with them. He rode beside

Rogan, his head down, and she could tell that his hands were tied behind his back.

She waited and watched as they rode closer, and as they neared she could see that Tearle had been beaten. For a moment, for just a tiny moment, she felt his pain, remembered his hands on her body, remembered his smile. But then she made herself remember his treachery and the way he had betrayed her family.

She went down the stairs and was waiting in the courtyard when they arrived. Liana stood behind her, and she gasped when she saw Tearle's face, his handsome face that was now black and blue and swollen.

Zared felt tears forming at the back of her eyes, but she would not shed them. She wondered why Rogan had not killed the man on sight, but then she knew that he had brought Tearle back for a public execution, an execution that Zared would have to watch.

She watched as they half pushed him from his horse and he fell, but he caught himself, having difficulty righting himself with his tied hands. When a man reached out a hand to help him up Tearle moved his shoulder away, accepting no help from the man.

Zared stood not three feet away and watched as her husband painfully struggled to stand up, and when he did, he saw her. His face was almost unrecognizable, and Zared winced, but she stood firm as she looked at him. She was not going to let her woman's softness betray her again. She straightened her shoulders and gave him a look that told him that he could expect nothing from her, that once she might have loved him but that she did not do so any longer.

He looked at her a long while, then he turned away and started up the stairs into the castle. Zared had almost gone after him then, for never had anyone looked at her as he did. Since she had met him he had looked at her in amusement, in exasperation and, lately, with love in his eyes. But never had he looked at her with hatred. She had not thought him capable of hatred. Perhaps she had thought that hatred was a prerogative of the Peregrines, an emotion that they had perfected and were especially good at.

But the look she had seen in Tearle's eyes put Rogan's hatred to shame. His hatred of her was not the impersonal hatred of one unknown family member for another, but of one person for another person. His look could only have been given by one who has loved but whose love has turned to the other side.

Zared looked away from him, could not watch him as he stumbled up the stone stairs into the lord's chamber.

"Go," Severn said from behind her. "You must hear his sentence."

Zared recovered her senses enough to look at her surroundings. Behind Tearle were several of Rogan's men, then came Liana, clasping her son to her. Behind her was Rogan, then more of his men.

"W-where was he?" Zared asked.

"We found him before he could reach the land the Howards stole from us. He was alone with the child." Severn turned from her and went up the stairs behind the others.

Glumly Zared followed him.

The sight that greeted her was worse than she had imagined. Tearle, barely able to stand, his clothes torn and bloodstained, was surrounded by Rogan's men. Liana, clutching her child, who was sleeping on her shoulder, was sitting near her husband, her eyes showing her relief at having her child back with her.

"What do you have to say for yourself, Howard?" Rogan said in a voice full of rage.

Tearle lifted his head and glared at his brother-in-law. "I have told you all," he managed to whisper through a swollen mouth. "You will hear nothing more."

"Take him and kill him," Rogan said.

It was Liana who protested, not out of any desire to protect Tearle, but out of fear of Howard retaliation. "You cannot do this. His brother is a duke." Her son woke at her outburst and immediately wanted to be put down. Liana, still too weak to hold a sturdy three-year-old against his will, set the boy on the floor. She stood up and went to her husband. "You will have to take him to London to the king."

Rogan gave Tearle a look of contempt. "The king will not see to justice. The man says that he did not take the boy. He says that he was saving him. The king will believe a Howard, for a Howard has enough money to buy even a king."

"Did not take the child? What do you mean?"

"I do not know," Rogan said. "The man is always full of words."

At the very idea that Tearle didn't take Rogan's son Zared's heart leaped, but she made it be still. She had believed in him once, but she was not going to believe in him again. She stood there rigidly, seeing that he was having difficulty in standing, but by some great force of will he was making himself remain upright. He had not looked in her direction since he had left the courtyard.

"Rogan," Liana said, "I want to hear what the man says."

"Nay," Rogan said. "I will hear no more of his lies." He turned to his men. "Take him below."

Zared would not have thought that Tearle had any fight left in him, but he struggled against Rogan's men when they put their hands on him.

275

It was at the struggle that Rogan's son let out a cry of protest and ran toward the men. The child, who was afraid of nothing, ran straight into their heavily shod feet.

Everyone else in the room was so intent on what was happening with the adults that no one but Liana saw the child. She gave a scream of fright, and when she did nearly everyone looked down and saw the boy just as one of Rogan's men's fists came toward the boy's head.

With his last bit of effort Tearle twisted and used his own body to protect the child from the blow. The fist hit Tearle's side, and everyone in the room heard the crack of Tearle's ribs.

For a moment all was still, everyone too stunned by what had happened to move. Tearle was on the floor, his body protectively over the child.

Liana went to her child, but the boy put his arms around Tearle's neck and held on.

Zared did not seem able to move as she stood to one side and watched. Tearle, with tears of pain in his eyes, rolled to a sitting position and took the child in his arms.

He looked over the boy's head to Liana, who was standing by, shaking with fear from having come, again, so close to losing her child, for had the man's fist struck the child, it would have no doubt killed him.

"We have become friends in the last days," Tearle said, his voice strained and shallow.

Rogan started toward the man and boy, but Liana put her hand out to stop him. "What happened?" she whispered.

They could all see that it was with utmost difficulty that Tearle spoke, and there was no imagining the pain the sturdy child must be causing him as he moved about on Tearle's lap, but the boy would not leave Tearle even when his mother held out her arms to him.

"I could not sleep," Tearle said, and they could hardly hear him. "I went below, and . . ." He took a breath and closed his eyes for a moment against the pain. "The child was there. We . . . we played with a ball for a while." Tearle took another breath. "I must have fallen asleep. I opened my eyes, and the gate was open, and the child was gone." Tearle winced as the active little boy kicked him in the stomach, but Tearle merely put his hand on the child's foot and gently held it.

"I went to the gate and saw the boy walking toward the forest." Tearle took a breath. "My brother's men watch this place."

"We know that," Rogan snapped. "I will not listen to this."

Liana put herself between her husband and Tearle. She was protective of the child and anyone whom the child befriended. "What did you do?"

"I saddled my horse and went after the boy," Tearle said, and he looked at the boy fondly, his big hand on the back of the child's head. "My brother's men had taken him, just as I feared."

The boy sat down in Tearle's lap and began to play with the tattered remnants of his surcoat.

Tearle looked up at Liana. "I could not kill my brother's men, and I could not risk injury to the boy. I went with them in order to protect the boy."

"I will listen to no more of these lies. He is a Howard and is as dangerous as a snake," Rogan said.

Liana turned on her husband. "Do you think your son is so stupid that he does not know an enemy when he sees one? Was the boy so at ease with the other men?"

"He was frightened of the other men," Severn said. "Remember, Rogan? The boy screamed when one of the men came too near him."

"I remember nothing," Rogan said, but he didn't move toward Tearle.

Tearle looked down at the boy in his lap. "My brother's men are barbarians. They would have killed him for the sport of it. I could not allow that." He ran his hand down the boy's leg. "He is a fine lad."

Zared had not said a word, but it was at that moment that she knew he was telling the truth. He had done just what he said he had done: He had gone after the boy and stayed with him to protect him.

"He is telling the truth," she whispered to her brother, and she could feel Tearle's eyes on her.

"A Howard does not know how to tell the truth."

"He does, and he is," Zared said, her jaw clenched. "He did not take the child." She glared at her brother. "Where did you find my husband?"

When Rogan did not immediately answer her she knew without a doubt that her husband had been telling the truth, and suddenly she felt lighter than she ever had in her life. "Where was he when you found him?" she practically shouted at her brother.

"He was returning," Severn said.

"Returning?" Zared's heart became even lighter. "You mean he was coming back here? He was bringing the child with him and coming back here? I thought you said you killed the other Howard men."

Rogan had a look on his face that said he was not going to speak, so Zared looked to Severn.

"They were chasing him," Severn said quietly.

At that both women erupted, and they attacked the

278

two brothers. "He was running *away* from his brother's men? You killed the Howard men, and then you beat the man who was *saving* your son?" This last was from Liana.

Liana went to her husband and looked up at him. "Is your hatred so strong that it colors your judgment? For weeks I have seen you punish this man, and day after day he has taken your abuse, yet I have seen no evidence that he is the devil that you claim he is." She gestured toward her son. "Look you at them. Your three-year-old son has more sense than you do. He knows a friend when he sees one."

With that she turned to Tearle and bent to him. "You may be a Howard, but you have proven that you are a friend. Thank you for saving my child." She leaned forward and kissed Tearle's cheek, then took her heavy son from his lap and stood up. "Take our friend and care for him," she said to the men. "He is to be treated with the utmost care that we can offer him."

Tearle pushed the helping hands away, hands that a moment before had tried to kill him. Slowly, with much pain, he managed to rise without aid. "I will stay here no longer. I will go home."

Liana looked at him and nodded. She felt very bad for the way she had treated him in the past few weeks, but she understood that he did not want to see any of the Peregrines ever again.

Zared moved to stand beside her husband and looked at her brother in defiance. "I am going with him."

Before Rogan could protest Tearle turned to look down at her. "No," he said.

She looked up at him. "I want to go with you. Wherever you go, I want to go with you."

His swollen face was cold and hard. "No. I do not want you."

Cold fear washed over Zared. "But I trust you. I know you did not take the child. I know now that you are not my enemy."

His face did not soften. "You did not believe in me. I saw the hatred in your eyes. You thought I was guilty, just as your brothers did." He looked away from her as though the matter were settled and looked at Liana. "May I have the return of my horse? I would leave now."

Liana's eyes widened. "You cannot think to ride a horse. You are injured, and you have no men to go with you to protect you."

"I would leave this place now," he said, gasping against the effort.

After that no one stood in his way. No one tried to persuade him to remain in the Peregrine castle. Even Zared stood to one side as he walked out of the room and out of her life. She watched him go, and she wanted to go after him, but her pride wouldn't allow her to go. If he didn't want her, then she didn't want him.

"Go after him," Liana urged Zared.

But Zared shook her head and walked up the stairs to the hallway of bedrooms. She kept her shoulders back and her eyes straight ahead, trying to will herself not to think. If she allowed herself to think, she knew that she would remember how many kind things that Tearle had done for her. From the first he had been good to her. He had put his body between her and the trampling horse at the tournament, and she had no doubt that he had saved the life of Rogan's son.

Yet she had always doubted him. Liana had told her to go with her instincts, but Zared had not. She had allowed generations of hatred to influence her, and she had based her opinions of the man not on what she saw, but on what she thought to be true. Just as she wasn't as filled with hatred as her brothers were, just as she was different from them, she was sure that Tearle was different from his brother.

As she moved down the hall she became aware that something was different. She stopped walking and rubbed her arms as though from cold. Then, slowly, she turned and looked behind her. The door to the haunted room was open.

For a moment she stood where she was. She could see sunlight streaming out of the doorway and into the hall, yet she knew that it was gray and cloudy outside. The haunted room was always kept locked, and she had never been in it in her life. Before Rogan had married the second floor over the solar had not been used because everyone was afraid of the haunted room. It was said that when the lady inside was needed the door would be unlocked.

Zared looked about her and knew that she was the only one in the hall. If the door was open, then it must be open for her.

She took a step toward the open door, and her feet felt as though they were made of stone. She could barely lift them, but she shuffled along, inching toward the door.

As she rounded the corner she held her breath, not having any idea what she would see inside the room. Monsters, perhaps? Ghouls?

She was shaking as she entered the room, and the blood had drained from her face. For a moment her terror reached a peak, and she was ready to scream or run or both, but after a moment she let out her breath. There was nothing in the room but chairs with pretty cushions on them, a tapestry frame, and carpets on the wall. For all that the room had been kept locked for years, it was clean and fresh. And there was no one in it.

Zared began to breathe easily, and she walked to the frame and looked at the half-finished tapestry. She touched the design of the lady and the unicorn on the tapestry, and as she did so a piece of paper came floating down from the ceiling.

Zared's hand froze. She stood rooted where she was, her breath held, her body beginning to tremble as she looked at the paper on the floor. She was terrified to turn around, afraid of what she would see. Would a ghost be standing behind her?

It was some minutes before she could move. There was no sound in the room, nor did she hear anything from outside the room, even though the door stood wide open.

All at once, and with all the courage she could muster, she turned on her heel and looked behind her.

Nothing. No one. There was no one in the clean room that should have been dirty. There was only sunlight in a room that should have been as dull as the day outside was.

It took Zared a few moments before she could still her shaking body enough to look back at the piece of paper on the floor. Her legs felt a little weak from her fear, but she managed to make them work long enough to get to the paper and pick it up.

She hadn't had enough lessons from Tearle to be able to read the entire message, but she didn't need to know how to read to know what the paper said. It was the correct number of words, and it was shaped the same way as the writing above the fireplace in Rogan's brooding room. She knew the words by heart, as all the Peregrines did.

THE CONQUEST

When the red and white make black
When the black and gold become one
When the one and the red unite
Then shall you know

It was a riddle that had been handed down in their family for centuries, long before the feud with the Howards and Peregrines began. No one had ever had any idea what it meant. When Zared was younger she had spent sleepless nights trying to figure out what the riddle meant. Sometimes she thought that if she could figure out the answer, then she could save her brothers from death. But she had grown up seeing her brothers and her father and her mother die. There had been times in her life when she had been frantic to solve the riddle, thinking that the responsibility of saving her family rested on her thin shoulders. She could not wield a sword with her brothers, but she could, perhaps, help in some other way.

She held the paper tightly in her hand and walked out of the room. Behind her she heard the door close itself and lock. She refused to think about such a happening. "It was the wind," she whispered, and she walked faster down the hall.

Perhaps if she could solve the riddle she could understand what was going on in her life, and perhaps she could get her husband back.

Chapter Sixteen

Tearle bit into the apple and watched his brother's men train. Or perhaps he should think of them as his men, he thought, since his brother was so ill. Tearle knew that he should feel some loss at his brother's approaching death, but he couldn't bring himself to do so. He was sure that hatred was killing his brother. Even on his deathbed Oliver Howard could speak of little else but his hatred of the Peregrines.

"They will try to take all that I have worked for," Oliver would whisper night and day. "You must be strong and keep them away from what we own. They will know that I am not here to keep them away."

Tearle didn't answer his brother. It seemed that all the world thought he was weak. His own brother thought he was not strong enough to hold the lands. The Peregrines had always thought he was made of softness. Even his own wife—

He did not pursue that line of thought. In fact, for

284

the three months that he had been back from the Peregrines' he had made a constant effort not to think of the woman he had stupidly made his wife. For weeks he had lain in bed, raging with fever, close to death as his body fought off the effects of the beating the Peregrines had given him when they had judged him without a trial.

On that day three months before, after that beating, on the long, painful ride back to the castle, he had kept the picture of his wife before him. He had thought that she would be enraged at what her brothers had done to him. He knew that at times she did not trust him and that sometimes she did not understand him, but he had been sure that she knew enough about him to know that he would never be so low as to take a child prisoner.

Yet when he had dismounted he had looked into her eyes and seen that she believed the worst of him. She thought that he had done what they accused him of. Even after having lived with him, after having spent a great deal of time with him, she thought he was capable of stealing a child. She thought that he had married her in order to perpetuate the feud between the two families. He looked into her eyes and saw that the hatred she felt was stronger than any love that she would ever feel for him.

For a while, between the pain of his body and the pain in his heart, he hadn't cared what the Peregrines did to him. It was instinct alone that had made him save the boy when he had seen the child was going to be struck by the man. That action had cost him much in pain, but in the end he guessed it had saved his life. At the time he hadn't cared much one way or the other, for his hatred of the Peregrines was equal to theirs of the Howards.

He had answered Liana's questions because for the

first time he'd seen a Peregrine with a face that was not twisted with hatred. He had watched as she had stepped between her husband and him.

It was only later, when Tearle had been proven innocent, that Zared stepped forward. She said that she was ready to go with him. She was ready to go once she had been shown that he was not the villain that she had thought him to be. But he hadn't wanted her then. She hadn't believed in him when all she knew was what she had seen of him. She hadn't believed him when he told her he loved her. She had believed only in her brothers and their hatred. Hate had meant much more to her than love.

Later he managed to get on his horse, and he'd managed to stay on it long enough to ride to where his brother's men were camped. They carried him home in a cart, Tearle only half conscious, and later Oliver's wife Jeanne had nursed him through his fever and his raging.

He was nearly fully recovered. He needed sunshine and air and some exercise and much food, for he had lost weight in his three months' recovery. Jeanne said that he would be as good as new in a few weeks, but Tearle knew that he would never recover from what had happened to him. He had been a naïve child when he had married the Peregrine brat. He had thought that love could conquer her hatred. But he had been wrong, for love had lost and hate had won.

It was while he was leaning against the wall, his body soaking up the weak sunshine, that he noticed something unusual about one of his brother's men. There was something familiar about the boy, something about the way he moved his sword. The boy didn't look very strong, but he was agile and quick on his feet and thus managed to miss most of the blows aimed at him.

Suddenly Tearle sat upright. That was no boy—that was his wife!

His first impulse was to grab her by her hair and pull her off the field, but his second impulse was to leave her where she was. But if one of his brother's men should recognize the brat as the youngest Peregrine, she would be ordered killed as fast as Oliver could speak the words.

He made himself lean back against the wall. How long had she been inside the Howard castle? How was she keeping her sex a secret from the boys? She must be living with the other men, sleeping in a bed with the boys.

Again he had an impulse to grab her, but he forced himself to stay where he was. Damn her and her whole family, he thought.

He watched her as she darted away from the boy's sword, and every time the boy came close to hitting her Tearle almost jumped up. It was when the boy knocked the sword from Zared's hand and sent it flying that he almost interfered, but he managed to make himself stay on the seat. He looked with disgust at the apple in his hand; he had crushed it.

He watched Zared dodge the boy, then run after her sword, and when she leaned over to pick it up she smiled at Tearle. She had known all along that he had been watching her, and she knew very well how it was affecting him.

He turned his head away. He wasn't going to allow her to see that he was concerned for her safety. In fact, he wasn't going to *be* concerned for her safety. He couldn't care less what happened to her or to any of her family.

At the sound of steel hitting steel he turned back quickly. The boy had Zared on the ground, his sword at her throat, and he was smiling as though he meant to skewer her.

Tearle was on his feet in seconds, and he pushed the boy away, sending him sprawling.

Zared lay still on the ground and smiled up at him. "You have recovered well, I see," she said softly.

"Not through the help of your family," he said, looking down at her, trying to remember the anger and loathing he'd felt for her on the day he'd left the Peregrine castle. What he noticed was that she was quite pretty. There was a smudge on her cheek.

"I came to be with you." She looked up at him with her heart in her eyes. "I have missed you. I . . . I do not like being without you."

He opened his mouth to tell her that he'd missed her, too. He had missed her laughter; he'd missed teaching her about the world. He'd missed her enthusiasm, her lack of artifice. He had wanted her with him even when he was ill. He had wanted her there telling him that he was weak and should have been up and about days earlier. Jeanne had been a good nurse, but Oliver had killed her spirit years before, and his convalescence had been a dreary affair.

"I have not given you a thought," he said haughtily.

She smiled up at him.

How did people not know that she was female? he wondered for the thousandth time. She was as feminine as the moon and the stars.

She started to get up, but he put his foot on her stomach. "I have but to tell anyone who you are and my brother will have you killed," he said softly.

She put her hand on his ankle. He did not put any weight on the foot that was on her. "Do you still laugh when your feet are tickled?"

"No," he said sternly, "I do not. You must leave here. I do not want you."

"But I want you. I have been miserable these months."

"You did not care on the day I left. That day you thought I had taken a child. You thought I would harm a child."

"People are staring at us," she said, and she started to get up, but he held her down. She gave a sigh, put her hand behind her head, and leaned on it. "Yes, I thought you were guilty. Can you blame me? You *had* gone with the boy. How was I to know that you would not harm him?"

"You had spent time with me. You should have known me."

"How can anyone know what is in another's heart?"

"You should have known then. You should have—"

"*You* should have taken me with you when you left. You should know what is in my heart *now,*" she yelled up at him.

At that Tearle turned and looked behind him. Every man on the field, every man, woman, and child in the courtyard had gathered behind them and was watching them with consternation on their faces. Tearle knew that it was only a matter of minutes before someone went to tell his brother that something very unusual was going on.

Tearle lifted his foot from Zared's stomach and glared down at her. "Come with me."

She stood up, dusted herself off, then gave him a hot look. "Gladly," she said in a provocative way.

He pretended to ignore her as he led the way into the main building and up two flights of stairs to his room. Since he was in front of Zared he did not see the way her eyes bugged and her mouth fell open at the sight of the riches in the Howard castle. She had seen something like it at the Marshall estate, but that was a stable compared to this rich place. Every surface gleamed with vessels of gold and silver. The walls were covered with tapestries, and there were thick rugs on the tables.

At last they arrived at his room, and he reached over her head to shut the door. "Now you will tell me what you do here. Have your brothers sent you to me to try to persuade me to give the estates to them? Have they heard that my brother is dying? Have they—"

He broke off because Zared had begun removing her clothes. She had wanted to talk to him, to tell him that it was her decision alone to come to him, that in fact she had had a raging fight with Rogan before he allowed her her freedom. But she knew that she could not out-talk Tearle. He had always been able to persuade her to do anything that he wanted, so perhaps she could keep him from talking.

Tearle stood where he was and watched her untie ties and slip cloth over her head. He hadn't had a woman since he had ridden away from the Peregrine castle. It wasn't that he hadn't wanted one. Twice he had chosen pretty kitchen maids and had wanted to take them to bed. The young women had been agreeable—so agreeable, in fact, that Tearle could practically hear the gold coins clinking in their pockets. In spite of himself he kept remembering that Zared had not come to love him for his money. She had come to love him for himself. She had come to love him when she finally realized that he wasn't her enemy.

"Do not," he whispered.

Zared removed the last of her clothes and looked at him. One minute she was standing in front of him and the next she had launched herself at him. He caught her as her legs went around his waist. He put his hands on her bare buttocks, and his lips fastened on hers, and the next minute his hose were around his ankles and he was in her.

They made love like two people dying for want of each other, as hard and as fast as their firm young bodies would allow.

When they finished Zared was half on the floor, half shoved against a wooden chest, while Tearle's back was bent in a backward curve that a spine could not manage under normal conditions.

He groaned. "You have killed me." When he could again move, he carried her to the bed, then pulled her on top of him, covering them both with the sheet.

She was still for a moment, eyes closed both in happiness and in fear. She had been in the Howard castle for four days. She had seen Tearle often during those days, but until that day he had not seen her. During those four days she had been terrified that he really did have no more feeling for her. But when she had seen him, seen the anger in his eyes when he had first recognized her, she had known then that he was still hers.

She lifted her head and kissed his chin. "Forgive me?"

"No." His lips said no, but his hand caressed her hair, and his eyes looked at her with love.

"Then I shall have to try harder to win you. When you are recovered from today I shall think of something new to do to your body."

"Oh?" Tearle said with some interest, then he pulled her hair back so that she looked up at him. "What are you doing here, brat? Is your brother waiting outside for you to open the gate for him tonight?"

"You can stay awake all night and watch me if you do not trust me," she said, wiggling her bottom against his hips.

He hugged her to him. "You are the curse of my life. I wish I had never seen you with my brother's men. Had I never laid eyes on you I would have been better off."

"You do not mean that." She raised herself up to look at him. "I have come not out of treachery or hatred, but out of love," she said softly. "I wanted to come to you long ago, but Liana begged me not to. Somehow she has managed to get messages about you. I . . ." She hesitated.

Tearle narrowed his eyes at her. "Do not think to hold back information from me."

"All right." She took a breath. "I think it was your brother's wife who sent word that you were well." Zared ran her hand down his cheek. "When you nearly died Liana and I spent long days in the chapel on our knees praying for your recovery. Anne Marshall came to Moray, and she prayed with us."

Tearle nodded. Perhaps he had felt the women's prayers. "I'll wager that your brothers did not pray for the recovery of a Howard."

"No, you are wrong." Zared paused. "Rogan has changed. I am not sure how yet, but he is different. I think it did something to him to almost lose his son and then come so close to killing the man who'd saved the child. I think that all the many words that Liana has spoken to him over the years are beginning to reach his ears. I do not think that he wants to raise sons to see them killed. I think he wants them to grow up and have children of their own."

"On whose estates?"

"I do not know. Liana says that with the money she brought and now with the dowry from Anne they could build a place or add on to Moray Castle. I think that Rogan is considering the idea."

Tearle knew that this was revolutionary thinking for

the hate-filled Peregrines. "What will your brother do without his hatred to fuel him?"

"You know only the worst of my brother. Underneath he is a kind and gentle man. He does not want to kill anyone. He was so . . . so hard on you because he thought you might harm his family. Had you thought what he did, you would have been difficult, too."

"Difficult? Is that what he was?" Tearle was trying to restrain his anger at the injustice that had been done to him, but it wasn't easy. He was cursed with being able to see both sides. "So what made you come here?"

She kissed his neck. "I have told you. I came because I did not like being without you. You make me laugh."

Tearle grunted. "Did I make you laugh on the day your brothers beat me?"

"No, I did not laugh that day. But that day I told you that I wanted to go with you, to stay with you."

"Until you believe that I have done something else to one of your precious brothers."

"No, I will believe you from now on. Now I will side with you against them."

He didn't move for a moment, then he lifted her head to look at her. He stared for a long while into her eyes, and he saw that she was telling the truth. There was more than just love in her eyes, there was commitment and loyalty and trust.

He put her head back down on his chest. "Now what do we do? You cannot stay here."

"I will stay wherever you are. Do you mean to go into battle? I will go with you."

He smiled at that. "I do not think that will be required. But if you stay here, it might be a battle. My brother will hear of what has happened this morning, and he will want an explanation."

"Tell him that you have taken a fancy to boys and—"

"Where have you heard of such?" He was genuinely horrified.

"Anne Marshall," she said simply, then she looked at him. "Oh, Tearle, she is the most interesting woman. She knows a great deal about many things. She is fascinating. Liana and I listen to her every word."

"The woman should keep her mouth shut."

"Her pretty mouth?" Zared said, looking at him. "She is beautiful, is she not?"

"Like a pretty, poisonous snake. Tell me, how does she get on with Severn?"

Zared laughed at that. "I rather think that she likes him. I do not think that he understands her any more than Liana and I do, but when he does not understand her he kisses her or takes her to their room. I sometimes think that she provokes him so that he will take her into privacy."

Tearle laughed at that. Perhaps his error had been in listening to women. Perhaps he should have behaved as Severn did; perhaps when a woman talked he should take her to bed.

"What else has Anne taught you?" he asked, hoping that her answer would be that she had been instructed in some exotic form of lovemaking.

"She has solved the riddle."

"I would think that Anne Marshall would be quite good at solving riddles." He said it in that tone that men use when they want to tell what they think of clever women. "What riddle did she solve?"

In spite of her intention of being the perfect wife

Zared gave him a look of disgust at his ignorance. "The Peregrine riddle."

"Forgive my stupidity, but I do not know as much about your family as you do."

"I will wager that your brother knows of the Peregrine riddle."

He didn't answer her but gave her a look that meant that she was to continue.

She repeated the riddle for him. "Anne said that she had little to do when she was at Moray Castle—I think that Severn was concerned that she might flee, and—"

"Wise of your brother to worry," Tearle said under his breath.

She ignored him, for she didn't like to think of what had gone on between her brother and his unwilling wife while they were away. When the subject was mentioned to some of the men who had been with them, they turned pale and shook their heads in disbelief. There were a few fresh wounds on Severn.

"Anne said it was hair color." When Tearle didn't seem to understand, she continued. "The red and the black. Hair color." She paused. "Rogan and Liana's first child has—"

"The boy whose life I saved?" he asked innocently.

"Their first child has red hair, like his father, but the second son has black hair, as Rogan's mother did."

"So this has to do with the riddle?"

"'When the red and the white make black.' See? Rogan's hair is red, Liana's hair is almost white, and they made a black-haired child."

Tearle smiled, understanding. "And the second line?"

"'When the black and the gold become one.'"

"Severn's gold hair and Anne's black."

Zared looked at him in admiration. He was indeed clever. "You and I are the last line. 'When the one and red unite.'"

He smiled at that, but then he looked at her in seriousness. "I take it that you are the red, so I must be the one. Yet I am not the one, assuming that 'one' means that I am the only Howard child. What is the last line of the riddle?"

"'Then shall you know.'"

"Know what?"

She took a while before answering. "Anne and Liana think that it means that we shall know who owns the estates." She could not look at him. If her brothers won, then it would mean that her husband lost. It wasn't that she so much wanted to own such a place, but she did not want to see her husband lose it. Nor did she want to see her brothers lose what perhaps should have been theirs.

Tearle looked at her and knew what she was thinking. "A dilemma, is it not?" He didn't tell her that he was glad that it had become a dilemma to her. A few months earlier she would not have had any doubts about who should have owned the estates. Then she had thought they should go to her brothers, and the man she married could go to hell for all she cared. But he was glad to see that she was confused about whom she should give her loyalty to.

He pulled her close to him and held her tightly. "Do not worry, my love. You will know what to do when the time comes."

"I know right from wrong," she said indignantly. "I know what must be done and who must—" She stopped when he kissed her to silence.

It was while he was kissing her that the door to his room burst open and four of his men charged inside. What they saw horrified them. It looked as though their master's brother was kissing a young boy, for all they could see was Zared's short hair above the sheet.

Tearle saw their looks and started to explain, but then he didn't know what to say. He couldn't introduce his Peregrine wife, and he couldn't very well pull the sheet down and show them that she was indeed a female.

For the first time in her life Zared saw her husband at a loss for words. She was not about to allow the opportunity to pass her by. She deepened her voice. "My lord," she said to Tearle, "you will buy me the armor you promised after I have done . . . this for you?" She motioned toward the bed.

Tearle gave her a quelling look as the men cleared their throats in embarrassment. He looked up at the men. "What do you want?" he snapped at them.

"Lady Jeanne begs you to come to her. Your brother is dying."

Zared didn't say anything as Tearle got out of the bed and began to dress. The riddle said that when the *one* and red unite then they would know. If Tearle's brother died, then Tearle would be the only Howard son left.

When Tearle was dressed he turned to her. "Remain here. Do not leave this room." He paused. "Can I trust you, or must I leave a guard on you?"

She was smart enough to know what could happen to her if word of her being in bed should get back to Oliver Howard. As long as the man was alive his hatred of the Peregrines was alive, too. "I will remain here," she said, ignoring the looks of the men at Tearle's back. There would be time in the future to show them the truth of who she was.

He started to kiss her but then straightened as he became aware of the men. "I expect you to keep your word," he said, then he was gone.

Alone in the room Zared leaned back against the pillows and looked about her. This room was what her family had fought and died for. It was what her family and Tearle's family had killed each other for.

She turned over onto her stomach and closed her eyes. Her husband no longer hated her, and that was all that mattered to her in the world. She fell asleep within seconds.

Chapter Seventeen

Zared didn't know what woke her. It wasn't a sound, for when she opened her eyes she heard nothing. It was night outside, so the room was dark, and she looked about, seeing nothing unusual or different in the room. Her eyes began to close again, but in the next moment she sat upright, clutching the sheet to her.

Standing at the foot of her bed was a woman. She was a pretty older woman dressed in a simple gown like the ones that Zared barely remembered seeing her mother wear. The woman looked at Zared with interest, then she smiled at her, a gentle smile.

Zared would have returned the smile to the woman except for one thing: She could see through the woman.

Through the woman's gown and body Zared could see the door behind her, could see the tapestry hanging to the left of the door.

Zared pulled the sheet closer about her and began to pray.

The woman's smile left her face, and she looked a bit sad that Zared should be so frightened of her. She turned away from the bed and walked to the door. At the door she paused and motioned to Zared to follow her, then she slid through the oak of the door and disappeared.

Zared sat paralyzed where she was. She had no intention of moving. In fact, she thought she might never leave the bed again in her life.

She was still shaking when the woman reappeared at the foot of the bed. Her face wore a look of urgency as she motioned to Zared to follow her.

Zared shook her head no. She was not going to go with a ghost. No doubt it was a Howard ghost who knew that she was a Peregrine.

The woman's mouth opened, and Zared put her hands up as though to protect her face. Would fire come out of the woman's mouth?

After some time Zared lowered her hands, and the woman was still there. She had a soft, patient look on her face.

"W-who are you?" Zared managed to ask. "What do you want of me?"

The woman held out both of her hands, palms up, in a pleading gesture.

Zared shook her head again. "No," she whispered. "I do not want to go with you."

The woman's face took on a look of urgency, pleading.

"No!" Zared half yelled. "I will not."

At that the woman looked about the room as though searching for something.

Zared didn't know if she was going crazy, but she was growing used to the woman. "What do you seek?"

The woman looked back at Zared, then pointed at her hair.

"Aye, it is short. I had to cut it again to be able to come to my husband. It will grow longer."

The woman pointed again and again, this time with some urgency. Zared tried to figure out what she meant, for she was beginning to realize that the ghost was not going to leave until she had something from Zared. She searched her mind to figure out what it was about her hair that intrigued the woman.

"This is as bad as the riddle," Zared muttered, and at that the woman began gesturing frantically.

"The riddle?" Zared asked, and the woman nodded her head vigorously. "You have something to do with the riddle?" Again the woman nodded.

Softly Zared repeated the riddle, and when she came to the last line she looked hard at the woman, seeing the small oak table through her. "'Then shall you know,'" she said, and her face lit up. "My husband's brother is dead, and he is now the one."

The woman nodded, and her face showed her relief at Zared's understanding.

"You are here to tell me."

The woman again nodded.

Zared leaned back against the pillows and closed her eyes. The solution to the riddle was within her grasp. The solution to who owned the rich estates was near to her, yet all she could think of was, God, why have You chosen me? If the solution was given to Rogan or Severn, they would know just what to do, but Zared didn't know. If it was found that the estates belonged to her brother, should Zared take them from her husband and give them to her brother? Or did her love as well as her loyalty belong to her husband? *Could* she take away the estates from her husband? She had told Tearle that Rogan had changed, that some of his hatred was gone, but had she been telling the truth? If Rogan had proof that the estates belonged to him, would he take them from Tearle and leave him a beggar?

She opened her eyes and saw that the woman was still there, patiently waiting for her to come to a decision.

Zared sighed. It was no use agonizing over what was. For some reason she had been chosen to be the one to settle the feud.

Slowly she got out of bed and began to dress in her boy's clothes. It was, perhaps, better to know than not to know.

At last she turned and looked at the woman, who was still waiting for her. Zared took a deep breath. "I am ready."

The woman looked Zared up and down, and at first she thought maybe she disapproved of her clothes, but then Zared realized that the woman was probably a relative of hers, of hers as well as Tearle's, since she and Tearle were cousins, so perhaps the woman was studying her descendant. Zared was glad the woman had never seen her before, because that meant she hadn't been sneaking about spying on her.

The woman slipped through the oak of the door, but Zared quietly opened it and looked into the hall. There was no one about, but there were torches in iron holders on the walls, and the corridor was brightly lit.

Zared tiptoed out of the room and into the corridor, following the ghostly shape of the woman as she floated ahead of her.

After a while Zared's fear and her pounding heart made her feel that she'd followed the woman down corridors for hours. She had some trouble when four dogs came running from a dark alcove and, teeth bared, made straight for Zared.

302

Before she could run the woman appeared and put herself between the dogs and Zared, then the dogs, with fear on their faces, turned and ran the other way. For a moment Zared's knees were too weak to allow her to walk, but the woman gave an impatient look, and Zared managed to follow.

Zared followed her down corridors past brightly lit rooms and into the oldest part of the vast castle. There the rooms were not lit at all, and from the dirt and debris it seemed they were not used very often. A rat scurried under Zared's feet, but she hardly noticed it. What were rats when one was following a ghost?

At last the woman stopped and pointed at what Zared thought was a door. It was so dark in the corridor that she could barely see her hand in front of her face. Had it not been for the glow of the woman's body she could not have followed her.

Zared looked where the woman pointed but could see nothing. Then, as Zared watched, her mouth open in horror, the woman began to turn about in a circle, moving faster and faster. As she twirled about the glow of her body became brighter and brighter. When the woman stopped her body was as light as though sunlight were shining on it.

The woman smoothed back a strand of hair, then looked at Zared, who could feel her knees giving way under her. The woman reached out as though to touch Zared, but her hand slid right through Zared's arm.

That, added to what she had just seen, was almost the finish of Zared. She felt herself sinking to the floor and would have fallen had not the woman looked so annoyed with her. She started pointing in a vigorous way to the door that could now be seen quite plainly.

Zared did the best that she could to regain control of herself and put out her shaking hand to touch the latch of the door. The old door opened rather easily, and with a trembling body Zared entered.

It was a dirty old room, one that looked as though it hadn't had a human visitor in years. Great cobwebs hung from the shattered silk of the bed hangings. There were bats hanging in one corner of the room, and wind whistled in the broken glass of the large window.

Zared looked at the woman, who, now that they were in the room, was losing her eerie glow. She wasn't sure, but she thought there were tears in the woman's eyes. Could ghosts cry? she wondered.

The woman seemed to straighten herself, then she tightened her lips. She waved her arm and, to Zared's further horror, the room instantly changed. It was no longer dirty and dim and faded but was restored to its former glory. The bed hangings were once again a brilliant crimson, and the floor had fresh rushes on it. There were murals on the walls as well tapestries.

Zared's first instinct was to climb into the bed and hide under the covers, but something told her that it was just an illusion and that the bed was still covered in spiders and rat droppings that were quite real.

She took a deep breath and turned to the woman. "What do you want to show me?"

She watched the woman float toward the tapestry and point to it, and it took Zared some time to figure out that the woman wanted her to lift the tapestry. As soon as she touched it it fell off the wall. It *looked* clean and new and strong, but in reality it had decayed in the dampness.

Zared dropped the tapestry and kicked it aside. The woman floated toward the wall and put out her hand. To Zared's eyes there was only solid wall there. "Is something under here?"

The woman nodded.

304

"I don't see anything."

At that the woman began to turn about again, and Zared somehow knew that she was again going to turn until she became a human torch. "Please don't," Zared said. "I will look."

The woman seemed to understand and stopped turning about while Zared ran her hands over the wall looking for an opening. It was some time before she found a crack, but she could not get her fingers into the narrow opening.

"I will have to go back and get a tool. I can't budge the stone."

At that the woman seemed to panic. She went to the door and put herself before it, holding out her arms to bar the way. Zared knew that the woman was right. She couldn't leave the room. It had taken too long to find the place, and soon Tearle would return and search for her. He'd be quite angry that she had left his room after telling him that she wouldn't, and he would probably put her under guard if he had to, to keep her from leaving again.

"You are right," she said. "I cannot leave. Are there tools in here?"

The woman seemed to think for a moment, then she went to a large chest against the wall and pointed. Zared opened the chest. The only things inside were yarn and knitting needles. She held up a pair of the steel needles. "You want me to remove a stone block with knitting needles?" she asked.

The only answer she got was a weak smile from the woman, a smile so human that Zared smiled back at her. "Are you my grandmother?" she asked, and the woman nodded. Zared smiled again. "I think Rogan's oldest boy is going to look like you." Again Zared thought she saw tears in the woman's eyes, but she turned away too quickly for Zared to be sure.

Zared went to the wall and began to dig with the needles. She was so intent on digging the loose mortar away from the block that she did not hear the door open or the footsteps approach her. When Tearle spoke she jumped half a foot off the floor.

"What, may I ask, are you doing?"

She turned, her hand to her heart, and stared at him. "You frightened me half to death. What do you mean sneaking about like that?"

"Sneaking? In my own house? You swore to me that you would remain in my room."

She did some quick thinking about how he had found her. "And you said you would not put a guard on me. You must have had someone watching me if you could find me here. Is your brother . . . ?"

"Aye, he is dead."

"So now you own this pile of riches."

"I own this pile of blood," he said grimly.

Zared wasn't sure what to say to that, but she looked about the room. It was once again the filthy, untouched place that she had first seen, and there was no sign of the ghost, but there were two torches on the wall that had not been there before.

"What do you here?" he asked.

"Did not the person you had follow me tell you?"

He gave her a little smile. "He said you have the eyes of a cat and that he could see nothing. He did not know how you could see where you were going."

Zared realized that the man had not seen the ghost.

"How do you know this place so well to find this room? Do you not know that this room is said to be haunted? As a boy we used to dare each other to enter here."

"And did you see no one in here?"

He gave her a strange look. "Once I thought I saw a woman in here. She looked at me with great interest."

306

Probably wanted to see what her descendant looked like, Zared thought, but she said nothing.

"Again I ask you what you do here."

Zared took a deep breath. "I do not know for sure, but I think perhaps the ledgers that tell of the legitimacy of my grandmother's marriage are behind this stone."

He opened his mouth to ask her questions about how she knew this, but he closed it. After a while of looking at her he said, "Did you come back to me so that you might get near this room? So that you might find these registers and give the estate to your brothers?"

"No," she said softly. "I returned because I wanted you. I did not know of this place. Tonight I was . . . led here."

He searched her face. He didn't ask her who had "led" her or what she meant by that statement, but he could tell that she was telling the truth. He withdrew his knife from the sheath at his side and began pulling the mortar from the stone.

It took the two of them some minutes, but they managed to remove the stone. Tearle put the stone on the floor, then took a torch from the wall holder and held it to the wall. Inside they could see two fat old books. Tearle reached out to take the top book.

"No!" Zared fairly shouted, and she put her hand over his wrist to stop him. "Put the stone back. I do not want to know."

"Do not want to know what?" he asked softly.

"I do not want to know who is the rightful owner. *You* should have the place."

"No, your brother should have it. If the registers say that his grandparents were married legally, then the title and the lands are his, not mine." He lifted one eyebrow at her. "Do not tell me that you are in truth a greedy woman. Do you want to keep it all for yourself?"

"I do not care for me," she said as she looked up at him. "What do my brothers know of running a place this size? All they know is war. You should have seen how filthy Moray Castle was before Liana came. Rogan will make this beautiful place as dirty as that."

"You would do your brother out of what is rightfully his because of a little dirt?"

She looked away from him. "No. Dirt does not matter. I am afraid of what Rogan will do to you. He might send you away. He might bar you from this place for all eternity."

Tearle put his hand under her chin and lifted her face so that she looked at him. "I have property from my mother. Will you go there to live with me?"

"Yes," she whispered. "I will go with you anywhere. But—"

"But what?"

"You will lose your title. You will not be the duke. It is a thing a man wants."

"Perhaps it is something that your brother wants. It was something that my brother wanted enough to kill for, and your other brothers were willing to die for the land and titles, but I am a different man. Do you not see that I am lazy?" He smiled down at her. "I want only to have a nice place to live in comfort and a wife to love me. It is all I have ever wanted. I should like some sons to ride and hunt with, and some daughters to play music to me when I am old and can no longer play myself. I should like to live long enough to have grandchildren. I want no more than this in life."

Zared looked at him and knew that he was telling the truth. He had never wanted any part of the feud, any part of the killing and the hatred, and, quite suddenly, neither did she. She wanted to walk away from the huge estate with all its riches, and, as Tearle said, with all its blood, and go back to his house and live there with him. The short time they had had in that house was the happiest time in her life. There the excitement was not over who had lost an arm or a foot but over which plants were blooming in the gardens and whether they could hear the baby owls at night.

She thought about him and his house and about the children they would raise, girls who did not have to dress as boys in order to stay alive and boys who would not die in battle before they reached manhood.

"That is what I want also," she said to him, then she stepped back as he pulled the first ledger from the hole in the wall.

She held her breath as he opened it and began to turn the brittle pages. She watched him as he scanned the writing on the pages, and when at last he stopped she waited until he looked at her.

"Your brother Rogan is the duke," he said softly.

Zared let out her pent-up breath and smiled at him. "Shall we go home?"

He returned her smile. Not many women loved a man enough to give up being a duchess. He put his arms around her and held her close.

Zared looked over his shoulder, saw the ghost of her grandmother behind them, and smiled at her.

The woman smiled back and nodded her head as though she was very pleased, and then she was gone.

Tearle pulled away, then took Zared's hand. "Yes, let us go home and begin those babies."

She smiled at him, and they left the room together, their fingers entwined.

THE BREATHTAKING BESTSELLERS OF

Jude Deveraux

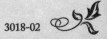

POCKET BOOKS
A VIACOM COMPANY   3018-02